MW00628180

Also by A. J. Mahler

Money — The Betty Chronicles, Volume I
Power — The Betty Chronicles, Volume II

Coming in 2018
Severence

CONTOL

The Betty Chronicles

Volume III

BY A. J. MAHLER

This book is a work of fiction. Names, characters, places, and incidents either are products of the author's imagination or are used fictitiously. Any resemblance to actual events or locales or persons, living or dead, is entirely coincidental.

For information about special discounts for bulk purchases please contact sales@whitebradford.com.

Published in Iowa City, IA
Printed in the U.S.A.

For additional information — http://www.whitebradford.com

Betty Thursten has a Facebook page — friend her at https://www.facebook.com/betty.thursten

ISBN-13: 978-0-9882628-7-4
ISBN-10: 0-9882628-7-8

For Chris Ameling

You stood forthright through strong winds and battering waves because you believed, and in believing, you made it possible for me to carry on and finish what alone seemed impossible.

One

The Lawn Goodbye

August 10, 2009 — Observatory Circle, Washington, D.C.

"GIDEON, DRIVE AROUND the bend and park—Master Howell, something is amiss." Barnes gave a pensive look over his shoulder at the Howell mansion receding from view.

Tom Howell Jr., newly elevated head of Control, glanced back to scan the same scene while he continued his phone call with David, the second-in-command at the bunker deep in the Virginia wilderness.

Betty was fidgeting with her own phone. David's call had interrupted their conversation about her new assignment in Vail, let alone her continued employment with Control. She was still in the revenge business, regardless of her status as a spy. The previous forty-eight hours had been a roller coaster of emotions. She and Karl had rescued Gil from his biological father and stopped the kidney transplant. Betty's feelings for Gil were a jumbled mess now that he was safe. They were only together for a few minutes before he jetted off with Dr. Eric Salizar to catch up with the Harpers for Linda's lung transplant using tissue from Jil's sister Ruth. Michel, the contract killer of José, was in Control custody and out of Betty's reach—for now. *I need a vacation! If only Tom were here to run off with me. Instead I have Mr. Hyde/Howell trying to corral me into another stint as a tool for Control.* She ruminated on the recent past and considered her options.

Howell raised his finger to signal to her that it would be just a moment longer. "No, David, I'm sure we are just being overly cautious since the Cabal's probe into our territory."

Yep. Tom is absent as always these days, thought Betty. Her choices were limited to unrequited love while working for Howell full time in the revenge business or return to law full time and hope for the best with Tom and seek satisfaction part time. *If I don't work for him, how will I get my revenge? If I do work for him, how do I get my revenge when he keeps putting the people responsible out of my reach? I love Tom, but I hate Howell. Will the two ever split up? That would be nice. Maybe McFluffy has something that would do the job . . .*

Gideon slowly pulled up to the curb around the bend in the road but left the car in drive with his left foot firmly on the brake, his right posed over the gas, and his shooting hand on the grip of his SIG Sauer P229. The Audi A8 sedan had been retrofitted with the latest in armored protection: laminated bulletproof glass with a transparent spider goat silk middle layer courtesy of McFluffy; a beefed-up suspension, transmission, and engine to handle the extra two tons of protection; and a wet bar to calm the nerves of any ruffled occupants.

The sight of the wet bar and the ice bucket reminded Betty of her Aunt Grace's freezer with the severed hand. *Do I want to know whose hand that is? I'm sure I could find out now. Though, curiosity did kill the cat.* Betty was tired from catching up only slightly on her sleep after being debriefed by Howell on the flight back to the United States from Denmark aboard Control's G650 jet. *A nap in the sun in a hammock would be a thing of beauty right now. Tom promised that I could get some sleep at the house. My God, what all did he inherit from his father? I'd be set if I were a gold digger!* Betty gave Howell a squinty-eyed glare and tapped her Rolex GMT-Master to remind him of the time and his promises.

Howell smiled and nodded his head.

That didn't seem to have much effect on him. Betty looked away from her former love and stared out at the expanse of expensive homes and third-world-country embassies. *What the hell do I have to do to get his attention?* Something caught her eye on the other side of the road from the Howell mansion. A rickety old 1985 Ford F-250 with *Hombre Landscaping* hand-painted on the ratty plywood siding sputtered to life. The workers tossed their equipment onto the bed loaded with lawn debris as they scrambled up the sides. Something about that beat up old truck and the men screamed at her for attention. *Is it the men? Their tools? The debris in back?* Whatever it was, something nagged at her to give it her full attention.

"Betty." Howell tapped her on the shoulder to get her attention.

"We're going to the Capital Grille for lunch, OK?" And as quickly, Howell was back to his phone conversation with David while flicking through paperwork on his touchscreen laptop. "Aha." Howell was nodding approvingly or scrunching up his face as he listened to each question or reply from David. "Yes, that will work." Betty had become an afterthought once more. "Send it anyway."

Jesus! I just can't win with this guy! Betty was about to make a scene by closing the technical umbilical cord back to David when Barnes caught her attention as he checked his M1911 pistol for a round in the chamber and a full clip.

Barnes manually unlocked his door, opened it, and stepped halfway out of the heavily armored sedan, turning back just to say, "Wait here, Master Howell, while I check things out. Mandala is either dead or incapacitated." With his free hand on Gideon's shoulder, he gave a final missive to his understudy: "Remember your mission. Always protect him—no matter what the cost."

Betty looked back at the truck and then at the enigma. "Barnes—"

Gideon spun in the driver's seat to ask how Barnes knew Mandala was so indisposed, but the bulletproof door sealed with a sound similar to a vault closing.

Howell tried to peer past his neighbor's house to his own newly inherited kingdom while maintaining his train of thought with David. "I don't know, David, what do the security cameras show?" No alarms had been tripped at the house, and Mandela was the only occupant of record for the previous two days. The motion detectors indicated he had not left his room since his morning rounds, just an hour before.

Betty screamed at the top of her lungs, "Barnes!" as she reached for the handle, but because the car was in drive, the doors were locked.

Howell looked at Betty and then back at his valet, who was about to enter the front door. The live feed of the house interior showed nothing out of the ordinary. "David—

David had been reviewing the security status of the mansion and relayed the summary to Howell. "Everything looks OK. Nothing out of the ordinary. Wait—"

An enormous explosion rocked the car despite its massive weight. Car alarms in the neighborhood began blaring all around them. Gideon quickly surveyed the area and accelerated hard, swerving from the curb to the middle of the road, continuing around Observatory Circle and as far from the explosion as he could get in the next thirty seconds. The security partition that separated him from his passengers swiftly rose up and hermetically sealed Betty and Howell into the safest-rolling seventy cubic feet on the planet.

Debris began raining down from the sky as the house returned to earth in pieces varying from the size of a fist to a section of roof, chimney still attached. Just when everything seemed to settle down, a large chunk of sod landed on the hood of the car, grass side up.

Howell yelled, "Gideon!"

Gideon rolled the partition down and asked, "Mr. Howell? Everything OK back there?"

Betty screamed, "Barnes!"

Two

Crash Course

August 14, 2009 — Somewhere in the Virginia Mountains

DAYS AFTER THE DESTRUCTION of the Howell residence and the death of Barnes, Tom Howell Jr., Betty, and Gideon had relocated to the family retreat on a remote Virginia mountaintop—reachable by helicopter or a very long hike up a steep incline. Howell was pacing behind his desk. "Enough of your false British modesty, David."

David was deep under another mountain in Virginia, the home of Control. "Thank you, sir, you can count on me. I'll do my best to keep the field operations running to your satisfaction."

"That's more like it." Tom stopped pacing, turned, and planted his palms on the desk as he leaned into the camera. "Now, what are you going to do about Gil?"

"Right. I have him in Århus watching over the Harpers to see if they can lead us to this Casper fellow."

Tom stood back up and began pacing again. "Good. He'll fight you on this assignment. But he needs some rest after what he's been through."

David shook his head and frowned. "I had some mates who survived being captured and tortured. Serious PTSD."

"He'll complain about you being a babysitter. You might have to promise him some fieldwork to keep him happy—even if it's something made up to divert his attention." Tom looked over at Gideon, who was holding an envelope for him and then back at his screen. "You know what to do—I don't know why I'm making suggestions. Carry on, David. You're in charge of field operations. Gil is *your* problem."

Howell cut the connection with a stab of his finger at the delete button. He slumped into his leather office chair and sighed before looking at Gideon and saying, "Another one? So soon?"

†

David took in a deep breath. "I could do with some field time myself." He rolled his wheelchair back and forth a few times before settling in for his next task. "Righto. On with it." He clicked a button on his screen to accept a call from a sound isolated and encrypted communications office located in the Salizar hospital. When the call connected, he verified that the person on the other end was alone and not under duress by reviewing the camera footage and checking Gil's vital-sign readout before speaking. "Your mission is to stay in Denmark and keep an eye on the Harpers."

Gil preferred working under Howell and was annoyed by David's British accent—which Betty had always thought was sexy. Perhaps he was just jealous. Gil groused, "Stiff upper lip, eh?"

"Good God, man. Seriously?" Ever since he became paralyzed, David lived vicariously through the field guys, but Gil's attitude was wearing on him like sand in a wet bathing suit. He pressed on. "When you can, follow our leads on the Cabal from Michel and Dr. Salizar. Any questions?"

"How do I get a cushy job like yours?" Gil's level of snark was reaching a solid nine and a half out of ten.

David did not hesitate. "Get your mate to shoot you in the back," he retorted dryly. "Right, we are in a bit of a hurry here, no time for slap and tickle, so sod off and do your job." David ended the encrypted video chat before his temper got the better of him.

Gil surveyed the secure room. It was brightly lit but windowless. "Shit," he sighed. He liked Betty. The sex was great, but like a Hollywood romance—on screen or maybe even off—it just was not meant to be a long-term relationship. Still, the thought of her pulled at him. He hovered the cursor over the link to securely connect with Betty. She was the drug he could not quit. He fought the urge to tap that emotional vein, but in the end, he knew he would not stop until she cut him off. "Like the bartender said," Gil professed to the soundproof walls, "if you hesitate when he asks if you want another, you're gonna have another—even if you shouldn't." He clicked the link. Twenty seconds later Betty answered, but it was audio only.

In a sleepy and quiet voice, Betty answered, "Hello?"

Gil sheepishly realized that Betty was probably at her apartment and it was five a.m. in Virginia. "Hi."

Betty was talking in a whisper. "It's early. What's up?" She stared at the clock radio on the nightstand. The red glow of the numbers hurt her tired eyes. She looked over where Tom should have been sleeping next to her. His absence goaded her out of bed. Betty slipped into the rustic living room—animal skins and rusty metal. Not her style, but well appointed just the same.

"I, uh, just wanted to say—hi. Sorry for waking you." Gil inwardly sighed. It was a bad idea to call so early.

"No, it's OK. Hey, why don't I call you back later. You're in GMT, right?" Betty checked her Rolex. Gil would be done with his day's work around six or eight hours from now, she figured.

"Yeah, GMT."

"Great. I'll call you in seven or eight hours. You'll be free then?" Betty glanced at the bedroom door and calculated what the agenda for the day would be.

"OK. I'll be available." Gil started to rethink the viability of dating Betty. Time zones and long goodbyes started piling up in his future. Maybe this was not such a good idea after all.

"OK." she paused. *He didn't say I love you. Maybe he's not completely alone.* Betty did not think he was with another woman, at least not in the biblical sense. *I want him to say, "I love you, Betty."* She needed him to say it. *Men just aren't comfortable saying it, are they.* It didn't feel right to say it to Gil anymore. Something had disappeared. The searing need to be with him. Her inner secret thoughts about their future together. The animalistic need to have sex, to make love. The passion of the chase had dissipated. Betty cleared her throat to make sure he knew she was still on the line. "Be careful." She disconnected and looked up to see Tom standing in the doorway looking sheepish.

Tom cleared his throat. "Is everything OK? I didn't mean to eavesdrop."

Betty thought about the question and the statement. Everything was not OK. But in the sense that Howell meant it, there were no crises at the moment. In the sense that Tom might ask that question, yes, everything was OK at that singular moment, but as soon as he went back to being Howell, it would be a mess again. Howell would be eavesdropping because he was a spy. Tom would be eavesdropping because he was a jealous lover. Neither looked good in the dim light of the room. "Is this really all yours?"

"Yes." Tom reflected on the enormity of his inheritance. "Everything my father owned is now mine."

Betty thought about the wealth she could see and the hidden wealth she assumed he had now. "You're well endowed, aren't you?" she teased, pleased with the double entendre—and even more pleased that it was true on both counts. *He even makes his artificial leg look sexy.* "Take me to bed or lose me forever."

Tom smiled. Pushed off the door frame and ambled over to Betty. He scooped her up into his arms, though with some minor jostling as he maintained his balance on his healthy leg. "You'll be walking bowlegged tomorrow," he boldly promised.

Betty grabbed the back of his head with her right hand and kissed him passionately while clinging to him with her left. "I hope so," she quipped, coming up for air as they passed the doorway.

Tom spied a blinking light on his phone as he threw Betty on top of the comforter. He knew that it meant the office needed him yet again. For the first time since Betty joined Control, Tom ignored duty for her. *Time for the team to earn earn their stripes without me for a bit. My father will be rolling in his grave and Gideon will have another envelope from him chiding me for neglecting my duty. Fuck'm.*

Betty saw the blinking light as well and knew what it meant. *He's ignoring it for once! It's just me and him in the room, like back in Georgetown.* Betty mentally sighed and decided to reward Tom for ignoring his awaiting message. She grabbed Tom at the waist. "Let me take care of that for you." She licked her lips, dropped his pants, and threw his artificial leg onto the reading chair. He was balanced on his one leg and holding on to a bedpost. She cupped his balls in her left hand and began sucking and licking his cock while holding it with her right. "Hmmm. I see I have your undivided attention."

"Ahhh . . . mmmm . . . that . . . ahhh . . . you do!"

†

"That went well," sighed Gil sarcastically. He shut down his laptop.

As he stowed his gear, his mind wandered to the other woman he had loved. He could not trust Sally like he could Betty, but something about her drove him crazy, both emotionally and sexually, even if she had cheated on him. Gil pulled the magazine from his pistol and checked the rounds, tapping the metal against the desk to make sure the bullets were aligned. Sally was the one girl who he would give it all up for. He drove the magazine back into the pistol grip and decided he needed to get back to work and sort out what the Harpers knew about the Cabal. After holstering his Sig Sauer P229, he quick drew it out, leaving his trigger finger parallel to the barrel, and fired two imaginary rounds into an imaginary terrorist. He wanted to finish this mission and get back to what he considered real fieldwork—something that would stoke his adrenal glands and push him physically. Maybe that was the root of his problem with David, that he was substituting emotions for adrenaline. Gil re-stowed his pistol. With a furrowed brow, he gave that thought a long mental tug, along with the whiskers growing on his jutting chin. He gathered his things, stood up straight, and gave a precise yet mocking salute in the general direction of Virginia, U.S.A. "Righto!"

August 14, 2009 — Århus, Denmark

The Harper family had converged at the Salizar clinic for Linda Harper's lung replacement surgery. Jil glared at Eric as she stepped out of his office. "This was not part of our arrangement!"

Eric had followed her to the door. "She is not stable enough for operating. Her condition upon arrival was not part of the plan either."

Jil harrumphed as she turned away and headed past Eric's secretary. She gave Claire a dirty look before pressing on. Jil only had a small window of opportunity to use the restroom before she was to meet her daddy and give him the updated schedule. As Jil approached her objective, she saw Gil enter a small office, not much bigger than a closet. She stared at the door and thought, *I need to figure out how I can turn this situation to my advantage.* A desperate feeling crept up on her. *Casper will ask me about this guy later. I better have something to give him.* Jil's hand reached into her bag and fondled her cigarette case. Inside were the typical paper wrapped tobacco kind, but hidden among those were plastic replicas that concealed what was left of her cocaine in one and a joint in another. *I better have something to give him.* Between the demands of her ethereal master, wrangling her sister Ruth and her father Larry, and keeping her administrative assistant, Parker, on task from halfway around the world, Jil was beginning to get edgy. *Better yet, maybe I can use this Neanderthal to get rid of Casper.* She had been short tempered while talking with Eric Salizar, which had awoken her need for a pick-me-up. *That little prick is fucking someone else, probably Claire!* Jil entered the restroom and checked under the stall doors to see if she was alone, which she was. *And another two girls in every other country!* A rather ironic thought, she realized, considering Jil would screw anybody to get what she wanted. *I swore I wouldn't do this anymore*, she thought as she rubbed her nose after snorting a line off the vanity counter, to prepare for the task of telling her daddy that the surgery had been delayed. *This is it.* She licked her index finger and wiped the residue off the counter, then sucked her finger clean. She looked into the mirror and did not like what she saw. *I'm not buying any more, I'm not going to do any more, I'm going to stop all of it.* She saw the whore, the young woman who had taken the extra money from her escort encounters for sex. *I'm better than this!* She wanted a smoke but looked up at the detector above her head. She gave a heavy sigh, adjusted her bra, and threw her shoulders back. "I can do this!"

Jil stepped out of the bathroom and ran directly into Gil, causing her to jump as he tried to stabilize her by catching her torso and inadvertently brushing her breasts.

Gil let go and took one step back. "I'm sorry."

Jil slapped him as she snarled, "How dare you! You need to watch where you are going?"

"What?" Gil had been so surprised by running into the woman he was trying to track down that he was not prepared for her reaction. "I—listen—"

"No, you listen! I don't know who you are, but you better not be here to harass me or my family or so help me God, I'll have security haul your sorry ass to jail for sexual assault!" Jil straightened her jacket, spun on her heels, and walked away.

Gil watched her walk away. "Shit, way to make friends and influence people."

His phone began vibrating, indicating a message from the office: *Company plane waiting for you at airport, need you here for conversation with your father.*

"I guess the Harpers can wait."

August 14, 2009 — Control Headquarters

"Who gives you your instructions?" asked the wiry, dark-complected man who looked more like a dentist than an interrogator. They were the only people in a large, concrete, windowless room with a single steel door to the outside.

Michel did not remember how he had gotten here. He could only remember coming in and out of consciousness enough to know he had been taken from the Cabal safe house he had been using in Denmark and flown to . . . somewhere else. This dentist fellow was only asking questions, unlike the previous man, who had tried to use precise measures of pain to induce Michel to talk. Some of his techniques had elicited minor divulgences—half truths and lies Michel had trained himself to believe. He had found the use of electrical current stimulating to his memory, which reminded him of Gil being tortured by Ernesto's men before he rescued his son.

Michel was chained to a metal chair with an incorporated bedpan; he appreciated the nicety, even if it lacked dignity. The new man was kind and considerate, offering him any beverage or food he might need. The room was warm, so Michel did not mind being battered, bruised, and naked—since the abuse had stopped. The IV banana bag hanging from the stand kept him hydrated. Every once in a while the fellow would come check the flow into Michel's arm and smile at him reassuringly, as if Michel were doing a good job taking fluids through his vein.

"Michel, I know all about you." The man removed his spectacles and cleaned the lenses with a cloth he kept in his lab coat pocket. "I know about your son, your brother and sister-in-law, José"—he leaned in close; the bright light shining directly at Michel reflected off his inquisitor's shaved head—"and most important, your kidneys." Inside this room was one other object besides the two men and their chairs: a dialysis machine. Michel's lifeline until he could get a new kidney. "Help me help you," the man pleaded.

"What happens if I tell you what I know? I talk and they kill me."

"You talk and you live," corrected his interrogator. "You have already told us quite a little bit, but not nearly enough about what you know. I can only guess at the right questions to ask. Now you need to tell me everything." The man smiled slightly and pointed to the discarded IV bags draped along the edge of a garbage can near the door. "We have access to donors and surgeons besides Dr. Salizar who can help you. Kidneys are pretty common these days. We can put you at the top of the list."

"You drive a hard bargain," quipped Michel. "Will I be receiving Gil's kidney or someone else's?"

"Does it really matter?" The man shrugged. "Life is life. Death seems so—permanent."

Michel raised his chin and lifted one eyebrow. "And with new kidney I get new identity?"

"Not that it would really matter. If they want to find you, they will find you. You of all people should know this."

"True." Michel furrowed his brow. "There are ways. It once took me fifteen years to find a man."

"But you did, didn't you." The man in the lab coat smiled.

Michel felt a bit of pride at having succeeded at locating that particular fugitive after so many years. "You are not doing a good job of convincing me that I will survive beyond getting my reward of a new kidney."

"No, I suppose not. But we both know that you crave life so completely that you would kill anyone to extend your time on earth for even a day."

"Yes." Michel let out a heavy sigh. He was growing weary and was overdue for dialysis. He needed to fish or cut bait. Talk or accept that this was his death chamber. It irked him that they had the dialysis machine so close, but behind his back. It increased his desire to turn around and thus his desire to earn what he needed. That desire slowly translated into obedience. Michel admired their methods, even if he did not appreciate them personally. "Very well."

"So you understand the terms?" the man asked for clarity's sake.

"Yes, I will tell you everything I know without hesitation." The man was right. Michel would kill anyone to live even just one more day. He would kill anyone to live another hour. "I will do whatever you ask." Michel resigned himself to his fate of only a day at a time for the foreseeable future. He did not believe in religion, but he did believe he was going to hell. "You will give me dialysis until I can get a kidney." Better to put off death, even for a moment, no matter the price. He had sold his soul fifty years before. He did not have much left to trade to stay on earth. This was the best deal he could hope to get.

†

David rolled his wheelchair away from the two-way mirrored console and turned to look at Gil. "Sorry, old chap, I guess we bugged you out for no good reason."

Gil tried not to scowl, but the thought of immediately returning to Denmark did not sit well with him. "No problem, David. Do you mind if I take a few days off and catch up on my sleep?"

David gave his best caring smile. "Take the whole week, I just received word that Mrs. Harper's surgery is on hold until her condition improves. No reason to rush back. In fact"—he looked at his watch—"Jil might be getting on a plane now to come back to D.C. on business due to the delay."

Gil looked sheepish, remembering their hallway encounter. "I was just making contact when you recalled me."

"No worries. Get your rest, I have a side job for you while we wait for her return to Århus." David led the way out of the observation room.

August 14, 2009 — Vail, Colorado

Karl, the six-foot-five concierge, stood his ground before the five-foot-four, stiletto-heeled, trust fund blonde vixen with her Chihuahua snarling at his ankles. No mean feat, considering she was the terror of the Ritz-Carlton. The blonde, that is.

"I want that table fixed immediately!" Hanna Lautner kept poking her right index finger into Karl's chest, which was about the limit of her reach. She was mildly surprised at how solid he was.

"Ms. Lautner. Skipper-do's pulling the table across the pool deck and into the water is not the issue." Karl raised his hand to deflect her poke and waved his index finger to stop her from interrupting him. "Nor do we expect you to pay for the repair." Hanna crossed her arms and tapped her foot as Skipper-do latched on to Karl's pant cuff. With tremendous restraint, he ignored the growling at his feet. "The tables were custom made, and we are waiting for the manufacturer to send us a replacement foot."

Hanna made a circle with her right hand, her own index finger in the air, and declared, "This isn't the end of the matter!" She left in a huff, dragging her pampered surrogate child behind her.

Karl looked down and noticed the puddle of canine urine dripping off the shine of his size-fourteen black wingtips. He had calculated the cost of drop-kicking the little pest through the front auto-sliding doors. For now, living in Vail was worth more than that particular satisfaction, but he began formulating plans for clandestinely removing either the pooch or Hanna from his daily responsibilities.

Three

The Prince of Knowledge

September 25, 2009 — Somewhere in the Virginia Mountains

"I'VE GOT IT!" BUD'S VOICE was an octave higher than normal. He was calling from his new secure location via a triple-encrypted anonymous connection, stealing his Internet bandwidth from a fiber optic cable using the same types of systems the NSA used to tap into the ocean-floor backbone cables, which was theoretically impossible.

"Great!" exclaimed Tom, who had settled in to working out of what looked like a modern, floor to ceiling glass house perched on the side of a Virginia mountain, but was in fact a ten thousand square foot retreat hewn out of the rock. "What is *it*?" Howell never questioned the value of what Bud came up with. Whether it was intelligence or his latest invention, Bud's work was always on the edge and useful.

"I hacked into the Google Street View Maps Wi-Fi database and extracted about a million data points."

Bud was willing to give excruciating details about his work, but most people were not willing to listen. McFluffy was his only ready audience, and even his attention flagged before long.

"You know how much I love watching you work," Howell said, "but I have—"

"You're swamped. I get it." Bud recognized the line and quickly got to the point. "The Cabal didn't hide their SSID from the street-view-camera cars."

"In English, please." Inwardly, Howell sighed. He never really understood Bud, but the man did produce great results. Howell had to pretend to understand. With time some of it had stuck and it had gotten easier to follow the arcane language.

"I know where the Cabal safe houses are." Bud chortled with

delight at getting to profess his prowess to one of the few people with the clearance to know just how good he was at his job. "Whoever is running their IT department must think they can hide in plain sight."

Howell thought for a moment of the possible scenarios. "Hmm. That or they have set a trap for us. How can we figure this out?"

Bud was mildly surprised at himself for not testing the network yet for signs of a honeypot. System administrators like himself sometimes set up functioning servers or networks just to see what techniques hackers might use to break into a system. His squeaky voice cracked as he tried to cover his lack of forethought on the matter. "Sure, they might be setting us up, but there is no way they would have guessed how I would find their pattern. I mean, no one has ever hacked this Google server before." Doubt crept into his mind. "I'll get back to you."

Howell smiled. He preferred extreme caution in these matters. Better to not move forward than to tip their hand.

"Director Howell?" Gideon hovered by the door of the office, waiting for Howell's attention.

Howell lost his frown and cleaned up his paperwork in preparation to leave. "I liked it better when Barnes called me Master Howell, though that would sound terrible coming from you."

"Why, because that would sound racist if you expected a mulatto to refer to you as master?" Gideon dryly remarked.

"No, it was just his upper-crust English accent. Coming from you it would sound like I'd gotten a big head. Barnes just came off as the classic butler." Howell rubbed his face with both of his palms to wipe the day's deep thoughts and problems from his consciousness. The Cabal's destruction of his father's home was disturbing. The murder of Barnes was a great loss. Thankfully, his father had seen the future need of a bodyguard/butler to replace Barnes before it was too late to transfer information or skills to an understudy. *To think I thought he was trying to kidnap me that day in D.C. Why couldn't my father do anything normal—like let me know I was being tailed for protection! He always had ulterior motives and methods that still don't always make sense to me.* "Do you have the next one?" Howell pointed at the envelope in Gideon's right hand. His brow crinkled when he realized there were two envelopes this time.

"Of course." Then, in an excellent imitation of Barnes's voice, he said, “You are to memorize the contents. In your right-hand drawer is a large bronze ashtray and a lighter. Please remember to pulverize the ashes before you walk away. Even I am not to know the contents.” Gideon gave a halfhearted smile, tossed the envelopes on the large cherrywood desk, and left the room, closing the door behind him.

The envelopes were sealed with the usual blood-red wax stamped with Senior’s personal emblem. The first letter read:

> To my son. By now you have abandoned our underground headquarters and destroyed the evidence of its existence. It saddens me to think of it as gone, considering the price Jack paid for building it, but we carry on just the same. Do not ever build another monolith like it again. There are better ways to run your administration that will make Control’s discovery even more difficult. Besides, that plane ride was awful.

The second letter was longer:

> You will have had time to get to know Gideon better as well. He is not very respectful of his elders, but you will find him just as loyal as Barnes. Barnes’s death must have come as a surprise to you, but know that in dying he saved your life. You are probably wondering how I could predict these possibilities so accurately; I assure you that I am no Nostradamus. Gideon dispenses these letters of wisdom whenever a tipping point or crisis develops for which you might need some fatherly advice. You have survived another day and must carry on with the destruction of the Cabal, or at least diminish its strength before it can gain complete dominance of the world.
>
> Oh, I should mention at this point: Gideon is your half brother; however, he does not know this fact and never should. Why tell you, then? I am glad you asked. You must trust him completely and count on him as if he is your brother even when you cannot tell him. I have arranged for the financial care of his mother until she dies. Should you meet her someday, you may understand

me a little better.

I thought she was just an affair, someone I could walk away from without loss. Instead, I learned that my love for her was all consuming. Had I stayed, I would have lost everything. Being apart hurt a little less each day that passed. Like an addict, I returned one night, but found the strength to leave again. I dared not go back ever again.

After igniting the bottom left corner of the folded papers with his solid-gold lighter, Tom Howell Jr. watched the flames race up the pages. As the heat licked his fingertips, he grimaced and dropped the embers onto the plate-size bronze ashtray "That fucking bastard." Howell snorted. "He really can tell me what to do from the grave.

Four

Loose Footings

November 5, 2009 — Århus, Denmark

LARRY FOUND DR. SALIZAR in the corridor near his office as he was heading to scrub for surgery. "Dr. Salizar, I'm glad I caught you." Larry grabbed Eric's right bicep with his left and clasped Eric's hand to shake. "Jil has been telling me a lot about you and your techniques."

Eric smiled. He enjoyed having his ego stroked, and he could back up his reputation with thousands of success stories. "Thank you, Mr. Harper. While I'm extremely confident in my techniques, we can't waste a lot of time—your wife . . ."

"Yes, Linda is in rough shape, but with Ruth's lobes and your medicines—I understand Linda will be just like new in no time." Larry could feel Eric's hand going limp in an attempt to break free, but he held on.

Eric's eyes showed a hint of concern. "Yes, the drugs are advancing nicely—no one else can do what we do—but it will be years before we can perform miracles like tissue regeneration." Eric squinted. "About Ruth's lobes, I'm still surprised Jil isn't the donor . . ."

Larry's head snapped back an inch and his brow furrowed. "I thought you had some miracle drugs already, I was going to suggest I help you get them to market before—what do you mean about Ruth and Jil—I thought Ruth was the best candidate." Larry's grip weakened.

Eric broke free of Larry's grasp and stepped back a shade. "Thank you for your offer, but check back with me in a couple years on the therapies." Eric turned his head slightly and took a quizzical look at Larry. "I thought Jil explained—Ruth is not as good of a genetic match. Was Jil from a previous marriage of Linda's?"

The suggestion—even if couched as a previous marriage—that his wife had strayed, and the realization that his daughter had manipulated the whole family, caused the craziness that occasionally gripped Larry to rage just below the surface. The rage that usually led him to beat Linda for some minor lack or disobedience. "How dare you . . "

Eric took another step back and waved an orderly over for protection. "I gave my recommendation to Jil, but she assured me it was the family's wishes that Ruth be the donor. And of course, with Jil's refusal to quit smoking, that did tip the scales further." The orderly stepped between Larry and Eric. "I must warn you that Jil's donation would have a fifty percent better chance of the best long-term outcome. In fact, I have donors lined up in Eastern Europe who might be a better match than Ruth, but not as strong as Jil."

Larry's eyes throbbed. The pounding in his head crushed his better judgment and drove him to seek out Jil.

Jil caught sight of her daddy as she came around the corner. His face was stern, with a set jaw and lips nearly white from pursing them tightly together. His expression brought her focus back to the lung transplant surgery about to begin in the surgical unit nearby. Ruth and Linda had been prepped and rolled into their respective places. Ruth was to have the lower portion of her lobes removed and Linda was to receive them. Linda's time on earth without the procedure was being counted in days, not months.

"Daddy?"

"You lying bitch!" Larry snapped his index finger to within an inch of Jil's face to punctuate his opinion.

Jil did not flinch, but she did wrinkle her nose and squint her eyes. "Now, Daddy, I have no idea what you're talking—"

His hand flew, and he did what he had promised himself he would never do to his princess. The sound of the slap echoed down the sterile hospital hall. Staff had already stopped to watch the spectacle. Some gave a slight gasp; others looked at their shoes or paperwork. The clinic was a private facility visited by the extremely wealthy and connected of the world. They knew better than to interfere.

"You lied about Ruth being the better candidate! You fucking little cunt!"

"Daddy!" Jil gasped. He had never spoken to her like this, let alone hit her.

†

She had seen her mother slapped around enough to know her father was an abuser capable of hiding most of the damage. But he had hit her in a way that was going to leave a nasty bruise and probably a black eye.

This was not the first time Jil had been slapped or abused. Never by Daddy, but several boyfriends could have learned a few pointers from him about discretion. Obviously, a man so careful in the past was trying to make a point. This was not lost on her, but she could not allow him to have this victory. Jil had manipulated everyone around her to arrange the surgery to avoid going under the knife herself. She had convinced Dr. Salizar that Ruth had pulled rank and demanded to be the donor despite Jil being the better choice. "Eric," she had purred as she cuddled next to him after sex. "Aren't you a good-enough surgeon to make her lungs work? It's what Ruth and Mother want." She played to his pride and desire to eclipse his father's tremendous advances in the organ transplant field.

Cornered, Ruth accused her of being so vain that she would rather see her mother die and her sister scarred than do what was right. Part of Jil—the small remaining bit of conscience left in her twisted soul—knew Ruth was right. *I've crossed the Rubicon*, thought Jil. *There is no going back.* Ruth had agreed out of love for their mother, but would never talk to Jil again after the surgery.

Linda Harper had been too weak to fight her daughter. Besides, Jil had always gotten her way. The two had formed a symbiotic relationship shortly after her birth, and Linda never could find the strength of will to deny Jil anything. First it was toys and clothing. Then it was travel and beauty pageants. To keep her weight down during her pageant years, Jil began smoking like her mother. The crow's-feet perched beside Linda's eyes despite Botox and expensive spa treatments were a warning sign of the ravages awaiting Jil, but the need to suppress her hunger and anxiety overcame the fear of future damage. Linda Harper was no match for her daughter.

†

Before he could inflict more pain, an orderly and Gil—who had just returned from David's side mission—rushed over and restrained him.

Jil pushed away and tongued her cheek from the inside, where it was bleeding from the intense pressure applied by Larry's unforgiving open hand. She spit a mixture of blood and saliva on the freshly mopped hospital floor.

Dr. Salizar rushed around the same corner. "Please! Jil! Larry! You must calm down." He looked over at the hovering nurse. "Fifteen milligrams of—" but she already had the needle filled and was flicking the air out of the tip as she headed to Larry to make the injection. "Jil, we must get this situation under control! I cannot have this going on in my hospital. Your mother and sister—"

"Yes, my mother and sister." Jil rubbed her swelling cheek. "I'll take care of Daddy. You go take care of them." She appreciatively accepted an ice pack from a nurse and began cooling her pride and injury.

An alarm sounded from Linda's unit. Code Blue. Dr. Salizar quickly left the hallway to attend to his patient as the nurse on duty rushed a crash cart ahead of him.

A petite nurse, who could not weigh more than one hundred ten pounds, held Jil and Larry at bay outside the pre-op room. Larry spoke like he wanted in, but blood made him squeamish. Restraining Jil was his excuse for staying put. There was nothing he could do to save Linda, and he would be in the way just like when the girls were born—he fainted the first time and just stayed out in the waiting room for Ruth's birth. And that time the Cabal goon had torn his ring finger off, when he first resisted their proposal, Larry had retched violently from the shock, pain, and fear.

It was in that moment that he knew he would do whatever they asked of him, no matter what the price, as long as his family was left alone. If Linda died, he was not sure he could carry on. The girls had been talking about this possibility when they assumed he was out of range, but he understood their concern. Without Linda to anchor him, he would do what he was told until—well, until he thought Jil and Ruth were able to protect themselves. Then he would just . . . He was too squeamish to shoot himself, and the agony of a slow death or a botched cocktail of drugs was unappealing. He liked the symbolism of walking into the ocean to die, but in the end, he would take the wet/dry vacuum hose and run the exhaust from his car into the front seat. Maybe he would do it at the beach and dream of walking into the sea. At least he would die believing he was noble. At the moment, he was attempting to appear noble in holding Jil back. His heart was racing. He felt like he did when he was twelve and about to play in his first rugby game against giants. Completely outmatched, yet he dare not let them see his fear.

Right now he feared the worst: that Linda was not going to make it into surgery, let alone out of surgery. He tried to summon the sound of the ocean in his mind, to feel the heat of the summer sun on his face, the sand between his toes with his pants rolled up and his shoes and socks in his left hand. But the image would not stay. Not with Jil barking at the nurse. The beach is where he wanted to die. Not in a hospital with family bickering over his last breath and vital signs. He would work another month for the bastards. Give Jil little hints that she had better get ready to defend herself. What more could he do? The look on Salizar's face told him his fate better than any actuarial chart. "Jil!" he said firmly while pulling her shoulders down. "Let her go."

Jil pounded her fists into his chest. She began to shrilly scream, then cry. Her plans had gone to waste. She had paid dearly for this opportunity, and the least Salizar could do was keep her mother alive long enough to at least attempt the operation and give her a chance to breathe with Ruth's fresh lungs. "Damn it! Daddy, why don't you do something?"

"I am, sweetheart. There just isn't anything we can do to save your mother." Larry closed his eyes and tried to see the beach, the one in Rochester where he and Bob used to go fishing with Rob, Bill, and sometimes Betty. Maybe he could look Bob up one last time before killing himself. Go fishing one last time. Those were good memories. The type he'd like to relive if just for a moment before he died.

Dr. Eric Salizar reached up and grasped Larry's upper arm with a firm but steady grip. "I'm sorry, but she's gone." He looked down at the floor for a moment to make sure the family knew he was saddened by the loss.

In a moment he would be off to make the arrangements for a special clinic he would perform in Vail, Colorado at the request of a man named Casper. Dr Salizar's knife-free facelift procedure, featuring his special blend of rainforest essential oils and cellular-level collagen replenishment, combined with nanoparticles and DNA repairing bacteria, was out of the lab and ready for the customers for whom price was no object. It was going to be a good winter season for skiing to boot. Life was good.

Five

Gideon's Looking

November 5, 2009 — Somewhere in the Virginia Mountains

BETTY'S CALENDAR SHOWED her departure date for Vail in two and a half weeks. Between then and now, she needed to check in with her cover—her law office—and decide what to do with Surry, Gil, and Tom. But not necessarily in that order. At least the check-in was reasonably easy to deal with, compared to the emotional toll of the other three. Life with Gil was not an option. He was fun in the moment and always had her back in the field, but home life would be a disaster. The thought of trying to raise a child with him unnerved her. Surry was content with her new home, protecting Margaret from her slob of a husband, Burt. In fact, Margaret was due for a raise at the office. What better way to reward her loyalty than to bump her pay a little extra for watching Surry, for just a little bit longer.

Betty glanced over at Tom as Gideon handed him another wax-sealed envelope. Tom had referred to them as his father's hand from the grave. A strange thought, that someone could actually influence events—if not control them—after his demise. She squinted at Tom as if seeing him in a different, brighter light. *Will there always be a Gideon following us around? Just like Senior had Barnes? The gilded cage.* Betty pondered the enormity of Tom's new wealth. *Yeah, Control can afford to pay Margaret for taking care of Surry. What else should I make them pay for?* That thought was rather nuanced in her head as she started a list of things she would need to put up with Tom's inconsistent availability.

His lighting of the letter and envelope, the fire arching up, and tilting it to ensure complete destruction reeked of ceremony. *A priest divining what the gods might say about today's crisis.* Betty sighed. Tom looked over, his face wrapped in concern and puzzlement. He dropped the last bit of cream-colored envelope not yet engulfed into the ashtray and then crushed the embers with a brass tamper to destroy any trace of the words.

Before Betty could ask about the note, Gideon announced, "Lunch is served." He waved them to the terrace. The view from the mountain ridge was stunning. The leaves of the oaks, maples, and various softwood trees were a shimmering palette from crimson to burnt orange to school-bus yellow. There was a slight chill in the air from the breeze, but the sun was warm and the stone was heated from below.

Betty grabbed her wrap and sauntered to the table. The money-conscious part of her wondered how much it cost to heat their idyllic spot.

Tom seemed relieved to have the diversion. "Karl is in place for Vail. He has your condo squared away and stocked for the beginning of the ski season."

Betty tasted the hummus spread on a rosemary-and-garlic cracker. She nodded to Gideon, who was at his own table ten feet away, positioned to watch the approach from below and the airspace above. Gideon gave a friendly smile, but returned to watching the sky and valley like a hawk searching for a morsel to feed himself, now that his nestlings were cared for. Betty noticed him squinting before he reached for a pair of binoculars as large as his head. She had used equipment like this in the field herself. *He's probably bored and just bird watching.*

Tom caressed Betty's hand. "You've been trying to get my attention all morning, and here you are fascinated with Gideon's surveillance duties." He gave a weak smile. "Nothing you wanted to talk about?"

Betty furrowed her brow and grabbed Tom's hand. "Shouldn't Gideon have a Barrett or a shoulder-fired antiaircraft rocket if he's so concerned."

Tom laughed lightly. "Oh, we have those—they're in that storage bench behind him. The radar would give him enough time for most jets, and he'd be heading for cover anyway if he needed the sniper rifle." His expression grew serious. "We can't live in fear. Father's house was a message, not an opening salvo."

Betty withdrew her hand and began rubbing the web of her thumb and index finger. "You obviously know more than you ever let on."

Tom rubbed his chin as he decided how much to tell. "I am to meet with a high-level member of the Cabal to discuss our range of operations."

"What, you mean we're surrendering?" Betty rubbed her hand harder.

Tom sniffed at the thought. "No, more like we are going to talk about what we would like to avoid, a Pyrrhic victory for either side." Tom motioned toward his desk inside the glass wall of doors separating the patio from the house. "You know I am never to speak of what is in those letters from my father."

Betty hesitated before acknowledging, "Yes."

"The last one explained how my father has, ah, *had* occasional meetings with his adversaries. For the same purpose."

"Why would he do that?" Betty tried to keep the snark from her voice, but some came through.

"There are some behaviors of the Cabal that fall out of the scope of our mission. Wouldn't it be easier to tell them 'Do not do this or that and we'll leave you alone' rather than risking assets and lives to achieve the same thing?"

"What do they get in return?" Betty paused her anxiety-induced thumb rubbing.

"We stop interfering with their—more legitimate affairs—and back off some of our operations."

"So, we stop monitoring them? That seems *foolish*." Betty looked over at Gideon. The binoculars were up, and he was scanning a particular area of a ridgeline, two or three miles across the valley. Betty tilted her head slightly and turned her right ear toward the spot. The distinct sound of a helicopter rose slightly above the birds and the wind rustling the autumn leaves.

"I'm afraid I've told you more than my father would like and more than what is prudent to keep you on the right path, but you must trust me or we need to get you out of Control." Tom pushed his seat back and stood up. "I need you to go to the spare bedroom, close the door, and lock it. Under no circumstances are you to eavesdrop or sneak out."

"What if I did? Would you kill me?" Betty snorted.

"No, *they* would." Tom pointed to the now-visible dot across valley. "Those are the terms of this meeting."

"You'd let them *kill* me?" Betty asked.

“I would not be able to stop it, but I would certainly earn my Pyrrhic victory in retribution.”

Betty got up and left the patio. “Asshole.”

†

“Mr. Gideon.” The brawny man who exited the helicopter first greeted his opposite and signaled that the area was secure with a thumbs-up.

Gideon, like a ram sizing up his opponent, gave an equally assured response to the Cabal security officer. “Mr. Max.” As Tom greeted his visitor, Gideon noticed an alarm on his smartphone indicating the bedroom door was not secured.

Betty was peeking through the narrow slit. She could just make out the friendly embrace of Tom and—*Ernesto*!

Gideon pressed a button while suppressing the desire to look in the direction of Betty. Instead he pointed to the valley with his smartphone and said to Max, “It’s just an alarm indicating a predator has crossed a checkpoint. If it were a human, the computer would have detected bipedal or even human crawling motion.”

Max nodded appreciatively. “Very nice.”

The bedroom door began closing automatically, nearly pinching Betty’s fingers as it clicked shut and the cylinder locked. The bottom of the door dropped down, sealing the room hermetically. This was the safe room of the house, stocked with supplies. The thought crossed her mind that there would be armaments in the closet to fend off an assault. She rushed over to see if there was anything usable, but that door was locked as well. Betty pulled her P229 from its concealed-carry holster and considered shooting the lock of the door, but knew that it would work only if she could splinter the wood around the deadbolt. This room, being the safe room, would not have a wood jamb. She sat down on the bed in defeat. “That *mother fucking* lying son of a *bitch*!”

Tom grabbed his guest’s elbow firmly and pulled him in for a hug. “Ernesto!”

Ernesto embraced Tom with great joy. “Brother Tom!”

Six

Devil in the Detail

November 5, 2009 — Århus, Denmark

JIL GLARED AT GIL. "Who are you really and why are you here?"

Gil furrowed his brow and bunched his lips before answering. "There was a threat to Dr. Salizar's life. I'm a special agent in charge of protecting him. I'm sorry about your mother."

Jil nodded slightly to accept Gil's condolences. "Strange that you don't just stay with Eric." The snowfall was earlier than usual for the region surrounding the hospital. The leaves still clung to the trees, making them look like sweaters covered with powdered sugar. Jil took a long drag from her cigarette. She blew the smoke upward, partially by tilting her head back, partly by jutting out her lower lip. She was tapping her foot and nervously flicking the ash more often than needed. "Special agent? For the police?"

She's pushing the right buttons. Gil felt like he was back in Ernesto's interrogation room with the goons. The memory of the burning flesh on the hot iron replaced the sweet smell of Jil's brand of cigarettes, Parliaments. He involuntarily twitched to clear the thoughts of the goons and their methods. *I gotta shake this PTSD! I don't want to admit it to David—maybe Salizar has something he can give me.* "Not a police officer, just a private contractor."

Jil flicked her cigarette into the snow-covered mound that had been flowers and shrubs when she first came to Salizar's hospital two days before. The weather had changed, just like everything else in her life. *I need to be the bright little center of my own world—the one in control of my future, not Daddy.* "Who the hell would threaten a doctor like Salizar? He's a *saint.*" By saint, she meant genius. The one who couldn't save her mother. The one who was forcing her to take charge of the family. *I never did mind the little things.*

Gil smiled, slightly. "Devil or saint, I'm paid to eliminate threats."

"So, who's the threat?"

Gil raised an eyebrow. "Right now? You and your father are the only threat."

What the fuck? thought Jil. "Surely you jest!"

"You just lost your mother under his care. Your father lost it back there and attacked you. He's obviously a loose cannon, and you—"

"Me?"

"Well, you I haven't figured out." Gil moved in close. He could smell the smoke on her lips.

"Been a long time, sailor?" Jil stepped a little closer to Gil to show she was not the type to be intimidated.

"Long enough." Gil inched closer.

Jil grabbed his crotch. She could feel Gil's tension. "My place or yours?"

†

An hour later in her hotel suite, Jil was nestled up to Gil with her leg crooked over his lower waist. "Oh my *God*," she said.

Gil put his chin into his chest to look down his body at the woman stretched across him. He had used sex many times as an agent to get closer to a target. He enjoyed the conquest and often framed it in his mind as if he was meeting someone at a bar that he wanted a one night stand with. More often than not, the targets were not as attractive as Jil, but some were washed up beauty queens. They were usually vulnerable women who were past their prime, feeling used and threatened by the circumstances of their lives. To be chased by a man like Gil gave them a spark they had been missing, even if deep down they knew they were playing a dangerous game. Gil was considering the possibility that he was about to be played. "It's not that big."

Jil giggled as she caressed his slightly hairy chest. "It's adequate."

Gil pretended to start to push her off and act offended. She snuggled harder into him. "Yes, it certainly was adequate. I could feel you pulsing and quivering."

She grabbed his balls, kneading them gently at first. "It's the shape of your cock—the way it curves toward your belly button. It hits my g-spot just right."

He was enjoying the massage, but wasn't sure about being able to perform again so quickly. "Ahh. I see. You might have to do that for a while before we go again."

Jil smiled as she moved down his body. "Oh, my skills are more than adequate."

Oh, Jesus. She is good. "*Hmmm.* Yes. Yes, they are." Gil surrendered to the pleasure.

Jil stopped suckling him but kept massaging. "Should I stop?"

"Wha . . . what?"

"Aren't you supposed to be protecting Salizar—or something?" She squeezed firmly and returned to his crotch.

"He'll be . . . uhh . . . fine." *Fuck . . . I'm in trouble.*

†

As the bellhop was pulling the door closed behind him after delivering room service, Gil came out of the bathroom, a towel wrapped around his waist and his hair tussled from drying. Jil was eating a quarter of a bagel with a tiny smear of cream cheese on a corner. Her dressing gown was loosely tied around her waist, her cleavage showing, and with one leg crossed under her bottom, exposing her Brazilian strip of pubic hair. She had a towel wrapped around her head in a turban.

"Are you refreshed?" She said with a grin spreading.

"And famished. What did they bring?"

"As requested, Denver omelet with hash browns." Jil lifted the lid off of his plate. After Gil had settled into his chair and began to eat, Jil shifted her position and extended her left foot onto his seat and firmly against his crotch. "Hungry?" she asked.

"Insatiable."

Seven

The Truth Hurts

November 5, 2009 — Somewhere in the Virginia Mountains

"UGH . . ." BETTY TRIED opening several wall panels and the door to the room, but her efforts were stymied. *I'm going to kill that son of a bitch!* She started going through the drawers she could open and searched the closet for anything of value. "Safe room my ass!" she screamed, hoping Howell could hear her.

Her cellphone was on the bed, and it started to ring the tone she had set for Tom. She sneered at the thought that he had sucked her back in, but in the end, he was always going to be Howell. She looked up at the fire alarm, assuming there was a camera watching her. "Fuck you, Howell!" She flipped the bird at the plastic detector and went back to her search. The bathroom was windowless, like the bedroom. She screamed at nothing in particular, "If this is a safe room, why is there a lock on the outside?" *I can't believe I fell for his bullshit again! How desperate am I?*

Her phone stopped ringing. Betty closed her eyes and breathed in deeply, trying to calm herself so she could think clearly about how to get out. Just then, her phone began ringing again. She hesitated for a moment, looked at the screen, thought about throwing her phone against the door, but swiped the answer button instead. "I'm a little busy right now. Go fuck yourself." She cut the connection.

The phone beeped to alert her the battery was getting low. "Shit. No charger here." She took in another deep breath and was on the verge of calming herself. "Not sure if I care if it dies."

The phone started ringing again. She immediately began tilting back to a rage, but her rational self grabbed hold with gentle reminders to her id that she needed to get her emotions in check. *Must be a weak signal in here draining the juice.* She answered it again, but this time she did not speak.

Tom cleared his throat. "Betty?"

"What do you want, asshole? My phone's almost dead. Make it quick."

"There's a charger by the bed."

"*Ernesto?* What the fuck, Howell!" She walked over to the head of the bed and found the charger plug-in. She reluctantly sat down on the comforter at the edge of the bed, put her phone on speaker, and plugged it in to charge.

"I get what you're thinking."

"How the fuck would you know what I'm thinking?" Betty considered ending the call. *No, the fucker will just call me back.*

"Ernesto has turned. He is going to help place you in with the Cabal leadership when they come to Vail."

Betty was not expecting this. "Wait a minute. This is just another one of your bullshit lines. You're setting me up to do your dirty work instead of helping me get my revenge. You need to let me out and be in that room!"

"You know how this—"

"Yeah, yeah, yeah—if you told me, you'd have to kill me. You're such a piece of shit, Howell." There was silence from the phone. *Did he just mute his phone?* "Howell?"

"I'm here."

"Why am I still in this prison?"

"It's a—you're still in there for your and my safety."

"Hah! You were going to say 'safe room.'" *I'm going to castrate him.*

"Yes. And you were supposed to lock the door and not witness the meeting."

"I don't trust you." Betty put the phone down and rolled away. *I should cut his balls off with a searing-hot bowie knife.*

There was silence again on the phone. Betty got up from the bed and began pacing the short twelve feet from one wall to the other. The room was a decent size for one or two people. With the bathroom and closet space, a small group would be comfortable for a while. *I suppose it's self-contained, its own air supply, holding tank for sewage to prevent a breech from the drain. Dehydrated food in the closet, reading material, LED lighting for efficiency. But how long could this box withstand someone trying to break in from the outside?*

The silence was broken, finally. "I trust you. I just don't trust your emotions." There was a hissing sound. "I'm sorry."

Betty knew what was coming. She did not want to collapse and crack her head, so she laid down on the bed and folded her hands over her chest. "You know I'm going to cut your balls off—" she yawned. "Right?"

Tom looked over at Gideon who had been standing next to him the whole time. "Wipe that grin off your face. You know she won't."

"I'm not so sure this time. You just gassed her." Gideon said with a chortle.

"Yeah." Tom took a deep breath and let it out slowly. "We better tie her up."

Gideon let out a laugh. "Yeah, that won't piss her off."

Tom looked at his half brother sternly. *How many half brothers do I have? Was this part of the old man's plan? Am I going to get another envelope after this?* "Is it too late to give her a roofie?"

"Hmm. I don't think you deserve to have a soft landing, but I have a trick up my sleeve." Gideon smiled at his boss. "It could have been fun the other way."

"Maybe for you." Tom rubbed his forehead. "Just do it."

†

Betty woke up, not sure how long she had been out, but the sun was setting. *Ernesto showed up at lunch.* Betty tried to work out the current time from what she knew. *We're still in the Eastern time zone. So, an hour for their meeting, one p.m., with the sun that low . . . must be about five p.m. So I've been out for about four hours.*

"She's waking up, Tom." Gideon was sitting on the bed next to Betty. He placed his fingers on her wrist and took her pulse. "She's fully out of it."

Betty considered her situation and wondered why she wasn't spitting mad at Tom. *Why was I mad at him?* She could not quite remember why she was mad at Tom, but she knew something was wrong. *He did something . . . I'm laying down and coming out of . . . what?*

"Betty?" Tom leaned into her field of vision.

"What?" She blinked several times. Her eyes struggled to focus.

"You had a bad fall." Gideon moved her hand to the back of her head.

Betty could feel a bump under her scalp behind her ear. "What . . . what happened?" She tried to sit up. Gideon moved to help her, but her head was dizzy, so she laid back down. "I kind of remember being locked up . . . or maybe I just . . . what the fuck?"

Gideon handed her an ice pack covered with a kitchen towel.

"You passed out when you fell." Tom said with a gentle, soothing voice.

"I fell?"

"Yes, when you came into the safe room before the helicopter landed, you tripped on the rug." Gideon pointed to the zebra hide at the door.

"I don't remember that being in here." *Why am I so confused?*

"Listen." Tom sat down next to Gideon. "You really bumped your head hard. Gideon gave you a sedative when you came to, to lower your blood pressure. We were concerned about the swelling of your brain."

"My brain? Swelling?" Betty licked her lips. Her mouth was cotton dry. "Then why aren't we at a hospital."

"Because it was safer to take care of you here. We just needed to monitor you and make sure your vital signs were OK. We had a teleconference with the doctor. He checked you out via the link. You're going to be fine."

"I'm really confused." Betty sat up slowly and drank some of the water Gideon offered her.

After another half hour, she was up and walking. The bump on her head was going down and she was feeling much better. They had moved to the living room to be more comfortable.

"You going to be OK for a couple of minutes?" Tom rested his hand on Betty's shoulder. She was sitting on the black leather couch, curled up in a blanket with a mug of tea cupped in her hand.

"I'm fine. I'm feeling much better. Thanks." She smiled at him, but in the back of her mind she kept thinking, *I know I'm mad at him for something. I just know it, but he's being so nice and all.* She felt the back of her head where the bump was, but much smaller now.

Gideon followed Tom into the kitchen and closed the door. The soundproof barrier dropped from the bottom of the door, sealing them from Betty's prying ears.

"Wow. I'm impressed." Tom beamed at Gideon. "I think you saved my ass."

Gideon smiled back. "The bump will go down pretty quickly now as the saline is absorbed into her bloodstream. It will be gone by morning. It will feel a little tender from the stretching of the scalp, but no long-term effects."

Tom shifted his look to a serious gaze with scrunched eyebrows. "So she really won't remember what truly happened?"

"As long as we keep gaslighting her, it'll be fine."

"Gaslighting?" Tom asked.

"We keep telling her our version of the events. We both keep telling her what we want her to believe. The sedative made her real memory foggy, so our version makes more sense than reality."

"Reality more strange than fiction." Tom nodded with his upper lip pushed out.

"Exactly." Gideon looked to the door. "We better get back out there. We need to keep reinforcing our story. Never let her get back to the beginning."

They reentered the living room and checked on her. Gideon made his excuses that there were matters needing his attention and left Tom and Betty alone.

"I was really worried about you," he said.

"I can imagine. Wow." Betty felt the back of her head. "I really don't know what happened."

"Do you want me to get the ice pack for you?" He got up and started for the kitchen.

"No, come sit back down. I think it'll be fine. Maybe a little more—later."

"OK. Doctor's orders. I need to keep you up for at least another twelve hours to monitor you."

"OK. I suppose." Betty licked her lips and reached for the glass to take another drink of water. "I'm hungry."

"No problem. Gideon will have dinner ready soon. Can I get you a snack?" Tom caressed her shoulder.

"No, I can wait." Betty tilted her head back. "I'm just so confused. I swear you had me locked in that room and wouldn't let me out."

"Hah! Like I could do that." Tom gave a little knowing smile.

Some memories were coming back to her. "I just don't know. I swear you were meeting with Ernesto Montoya and he called you brother." She scrunched her eyebrows and pursed her lips. She looked into Tom's eyes and said, "Is Ernesto your brother?"

Tom feigned a laugh. *This is dangerous. She can read me better than anyone. I cannot let her know the truth right now.* "You make it sound like everyone around me is my half brother! As far as I know, I am an only child."

"What about Timmy?" Betty thought back to her espionage work on Grace, who had mentioned Timmy on the plane ride back from Denmark, but did not make a big deal about it.

"Well, I suppose you're right, there. I just never knew he was my half brother until you mentioned it. In fact, I haven't even talked to Grace about it yet." *Better to stick to the truth. I sure as hell checked the file after you mentioned it.*

As her thinking became clearer, it dawned on Betty that she hadn't checked up on her mother recently. "Tom, what about Beth."

"Well, she and Grace had some things to work out from before you were born. To be honest, I haven't followed up." Tom considered this. He had not followed up in part because he did not want to know. *My father would remind me that my reluctance is a sign of weak leadership.*

"Can you check on her for me?" Betty was feeling slightly guilty for binding her mother to the chair, but not so much about subduing her, considering Beth had pulled a gun on her. I'm really conflicted about this.

"Sure thing. I can do it now, or wait till morning . . . ?"

"Morning. I think I've had enough excitement for one day." Betty rubbed her head again. *The welt—it's about gone. Huh.*

Eight

Date with the Devil

November 6, 2009 — Århus, Denmark

JIL TOOK A SWIG OF her scotch, thirty-year-old Lagavulin, neat. "I really have to go." She looked longingly at Gil as she brushed her hair in the mirror, which made her realize that she was coming down from her previous line of cocaine. She spied a single, thin remnant on the vanity. This was the last of her stash. She bent over and snorted the powder, then licked her finger and cleaned up the remaining film. She turned to Gil and licked her finger suggestively.

Gil chuckled. "So, you've finally had enough?" He rolled over and grabbed his phone and checked for messages—nothing critical.

"Hardly, darling." Jil turned around and faced Gil. She pouted and said, "You see, I have to make arrangements for my mother's transportation back to Rochester."

Gil face became serious. "I'm so sorry." He straightened himself and began getting dressed. "What an asshole I've been."

"No . . . no, don't be. I really would rather stay and fuck you the rest of the day." She sighed. "It's just that my daddy has become so unreliable." She bit her lip, then rested the nail of her index finger between her teeth. "I suppose I do sound like a coldhearted bitch, don't I?"

"We all deal with loss in different ways." Gil stood up and zipped his pants after tucking in his shirt.

"Yes. Yes, we all do." Jil finished putting her jewelry on and flipped her hair behind. "I guess I mourned my mother a long time ago." She pulled her dress off of the hanger on the door and shimmied into the skintight red silk dress. "You know, the cancer and all—death sentence." She placed her hands on her hips, smiled, and asked, "How do I look?"

Gil slowed his motion of cinching his belt. "My, my, my. Like you're ready for the catwalk."

Jil looked pleased with his assessment. "Why, thank you." She walked up to Gil and firmly grasped his package. "Be here when I get back in two hours?" she asked kittenishly. She kept her gaze on his eyes as she turned her body to leave. She finally let go and left.

Gil sat back down on the bed and flopped backward, his feet still on the floor. "Oh, fuck. I'm screwed."

His cellphone started to chirp. He looked at the caller ID and sighed. David. He turned on the clock radio before he took the call. "Rock and roll." Which meant he was not in a secure location, but no one was in the room with him. David would hear the music and understand.

"I'll keep this short, then. Any special requests?"

"Sex Pistols?" Gil rolled his eyes.

"Well—we've been a busy boy, haven't we." David tsked several times. "See if we can't find a faster tempo, shall we?" and he disconnected.

Gil grabbed his things, turned on the tracking software loaded in his smartphone, and searched for Jil's location. If she had her purse with her, he'd be able to tail her from a safe distance and see who she was meeting. He had bugged her phone as well with an app designed by Bud. It would record all the ambient audio, whether she was making a call or not, and convert any recognized voices to text. The text would be uploaded to Bud's server via the cell network, including the geolocation of the instance. If a call was made, the identity of the caller would be added to all the other information. Even web browser activity, texting, social media connections, and video capture were sent to Bud. If she was communicating using her phone, Bud would see it and report to Gil what to look for.

It did not take long for the first report to come in. Jil was at the local mortuary making arrangements for Linda's cremation. Which made sense to Gil—an urn would be easier to transport back to the U.S. than a casket. Bud's unique vibration identifier rattled Gil's phone and beeped in his earbud. He tapped the answer button on the earbud and said, "Yes?"

Bud's nasally voice resonated slightly higher than usual, a sign he was excited. "You need to get over to the hospital parking ramp ASAP!"

"What's going on, nerdman?"

"I'll take that as a compliment. I picked up Jil yelling about her

'Daddy' killing himself."

Gil sped up and changed course from the mortuary to the hospital. "Gun?"

"No. Carbon monoxide. Tailpipe to cabin." Bud said.

Gil rolled into the ramp two minutes later and wended his way around until he came upon Jil and Larry in the midst of a heated argument.

"You can't do this to me!" Jil was waving her arms, holding her cellphone in her left hand and keys in her right.

"Just leave me alone!" Larry looked woozy. He was leaning against his rented BMW 5 Series. Black plastic hose from a vacuum was attached to his tailpipe and looped through the passenger-side window, with duct tape sealing the window gap.

"You're going to get us all killed!" Jil said.

"That was the point, at least for me." Larry turned and dry heaved.

Gil stepped up next to Jil. "We should probably get him inside and on oxygen."

She looked at him with a mixture of pleasure and guilt. "Don't worry about him, Gil. You better get on to taking care of Dr. Salizar." Jil looked back at the crumpled form of the man she used to respect. "Daddy didn't actually do it . . . he called me to tell me . . . a cry for help." Jil threw her father's keys at him. "Don't you dare!" She pointed at him and shook her finger. "Don't you dare." She spun away and took Gil's arm into hers. "Shall we go check on the good doctor together?" A warm smile on her lips. "Maybe there'll be a spare room." Jil winked at Gil and felt his ass.

Gil smiled and wrapped his arm around her waist, giving her ass a good squeeze as well. *I'm in big fucking trouble.*

Nine

A Bump from the Night

November 6, 2009 — Somewhere in the Virginia Mountains

BETTY SLEPT IN. *What did Tom give me last night? Must have been something strong.* She stretched as she slowly got out of bed. The long, extra-thick cotton robe engulfed her. It was embroidered with Tom's initials. *Or was this his dad's?* Betty wondered. She padded down to the kitchen to see what was available for breakfast. *I don't think I've eaten since lunch yesterday!*

Tom and Gideon were deep in discussion when Betty rounded the corner. Tom smiled and said, "How did you sleep?"

"Wow. I haven't slept like that in a long time. I don't remember waking up during the night at all!" Something was nagging at her, though. A thought kept trying to surface. *Something about yesterday . . . We didn't do something right . . . but I don't remember what.*

Gideon stood up. "What can I get you for breakfast?" He smiled and held the chair for Betty.

She scratched her head and rubbed where the bump had been. "Did I eat dinner last night?"

Tom pushed his paperwork out of the way and tidied the stack, slipping several documents to the bottom of the pile. "No, you didn't. We wanted you to rest as much as possible. I gave you a sedative the doctor ordered."

"Oh. That's what was bothering me!" Betty squinted like it would help her think. "Aren't you supposed to keep concussion patients awake all night so you can tell if they're in trouble?"

Tom leaned toward Betty, "Let me see your eyes." He used his fingers to spread her eyelids. "No large or different-size pupils." He let go and leaned back. "Any symptoms, like nausea, headache, problems with your balance, irritability—"

"No, none of those." She rubbed the back of her head again. "The bump is gone already."

Gideon had started the gas range and was heating up a pan for an omelet. "Denver or mixed blessing?"

"Say what?" Betty asked.

"Mixed blessing—everything I've got whether you like it or not."

"Oh, well, by all means, the mixed blessing." She looked at Tom. "This I have to see."

Tom smiled. *I think we might be in the clear.* "We should just take it easy today. There isn't anything I have to do other than take the occasional phone call from the usual suspects. We can just hang loose."

"Well, I think I can manage that."

Gideon served her omelet on a large plate with a drizzled sauce in a zigzag pattern. "Mixed blessings are served."

"What's in the sauce?"

"Are you curious or afraid?" Gideon asked.

Betty smiled. "A little of both, probably." *I could get used to this kind of service.* She took a small bite and nodded approvingly to Gideon. "I like it."

"Well, thank you, milady." Gideon bowed and scraped as he backed away from the table.

"Tom—"

He had started reading the document on top of the stack. "Hmm?"

"You were going to check on"—Betty wasn't sure how she wanted to refer to her mother—"Beth for me." It just seemed simpler to refer to her proper name with Gideon there. Or that was her excuse for going with that option.

"Ah. Yes. I spoke with Grace late last night on another matter, so I asked. Your—Beth is under observation. She tried to commit suicide." Tom raised his hand quickly to reassure Betty. "She's fine, Grace thinks she really wasn't trying to kill herself. She took some pills, but not enough to do the job."

"Wow." Betty said.

"Are you OK?"

"I don't know." Betty twiddled with her fork for a moment, then dug back into her breakfast. "I just haven't stopped to really take it all in yet. My adoption, Beth pulling a gun on me. Hell, you recruiting me."

"I see what you mean." Tom took in a deep breath and let it out slowly before saying, "We all have family issues here. Just remember, if you need to talk about it—"

Betty sighed. "I think I just need to not think about it." She chewed her next bite a little longer to break up a chunk of ham. "I wish I could talk to Jil. The old Jil, I mean."

Tom harrumphed. "Speaking of Jil. Gil has made—contact with her."

Betty's cheeks flushed red. "By contact you mean he's been shagging her for information?"

"You know the job as well as I do." Tom cocked an eyebrow. "Is that a problem for you?"

"No. No, I . . . I guess Gil is another subject I need to do some thinking on."

"Why's that?"

Gideon cleared his throat. "Sir, I have David on the secure line in the study."

"Right." Tom tried to not show his relief at being saved from asking a stupid question. He left Betty to finish her breakfast and joined Gideon in the study.

"Mixed blessings pretty much sums up my life," Betty muttered to herself. With a heavy sigh, she picked up her dishes and took them to the sink.

Ten

One for the Road

November 6, 2009 — Århus, Denmark

GIL'S MIND RACED AS he tried to figure out how he would play the situation. There was no threat to Salizar. His only mission was to keep tabs on Jil to figure out her connection to the Cabal. He was now in the awkward position of either having to pretend there was still a threat or coming up with a solid, believable reason for ending the threat. *If the threat is over, what's my excuse for sticking around Jil?*

Jil prodded him right where he didn't want to go. "So, who's trying to kill Dr. Salizar?"

They were waiting outside his office for Gil's ten a.m. appointment, which Bud had arranged on the fly. "Oh, Mr. Richardson, I'm sorry, you know how he is, always running a little behind. Can I get your usual?" Claire pretended like the appointment was a standing daily affair, for which Gil was grateful.

Gil took the hint. "Yes, a black coffee would be great." He looked at Jil and she nodded with a smile. "Make that two, please."

"Ma'am, do you want anything in your coffee?" she asked Jil.

"Just a smidgeon of cream if you have it, but don't bother if it's powdered." Jil felt her teeth grinding. *Speaking of powder, I need to arrange for more.* She pulled out her phone—fumbling slightly as it nearly slipped out of her sweaty hands—to text a man Parker had found who dealt in the purest cocaine available in Denmark.

"Of course." Claire flashed an accommodating smile.

"Gil, will you be long?" Jil asked.

"I don't think so, not unless there are any new developments. We just need to chat about the current status." He took her gently by the elbows and forearms. "Do you need to get going . . . your mother?" he prompted.

"Oh, yes, her ashes. It can wait." She drolly added, "She isn't going anywhere." Jil checked her phone again. *Oh, thank God. He's in Århus already!*

At that moment, Eric Salizar poked his head out of his office door. "Claire, is—oh, hello, Jil, Gil."

Jil's relationship with Dr. Salizar had been registered as professional until that moment. The look on his face as Eric spied Jil in an intimate pose with Gil told him everything he needed to know. The smile of satisfaction on Jil's face told Gil that she wanted—even planned on—Salizar seeing them together to instill jealousy. *She is one crafty bitch. I seriously need to watch my six around her.*

Jil's cellphone chirped. "Oh, crap. Not again!" Jil's face changed from conniving vixen to troubled soul. She looked at Gil and said one word before leaving in a hurry. "Daddy!"

Gil thought for a moment, *Just another false attempt . . . cry for attention, I suppose.* "Eric, I only need a minute." He followed Dr. Salizar into his office and closed the door.

"How is the mission going?" Eric said.

"Fine, just fine. I'm going to declare the danger to you as passed. I don't need a reason to hang around the hospital anymore."

"Very well. Is Larry OK?"

"He tried to commit suicide—more a cry for help than a real attempt. I think Jil is on her way to intercept him again."

"Well, you better get going, then."

"You two have been together before . . ." Gil said, more a statement than a question.

"Hmm. More of a bonus for giving her what she wanted." Eric rubbed his chin. "But I think she wanted more. That one gets a bit jealous. Probably just insecure—despite her fine qualities."

"Yes. Well. I didn't want to step between an existing relationship." Gil looked at his boots and decided he needed to shine them.

"No problem here. Have I paid my debt, then—to your organization?"

"I can't speak for my boss, but yeah, you and me are good." Gil gave a two-finger modified salute from his temple. “Be good, Doc.” Gil left the office and called Jil on his way to the car.

†

Gil caught up to Jil and Larry outside a café around the corner from the parking garage. She was yelling at her daddy loud enough for everyone inside the café to get the gist of her complaint. Gil approached, but did not speak or interfere.

“You can’t do this to me anymore!” Jil exclaimed.

“I just can’t go on. I need your mother.” Larry’s face was drawn and haggard. His eyes darted down and then back up to Jil, pleading for help or mercy.

Jil gave neither. She pulled her elbow back and swung with all her will a slap across Larry’s face. “You are dead to me,” she said calmly. She poked her index finger into his chest, holding it there. “Either pull yourself together and take care of business, or so help me God, I will not stop you again.” Jil grabbed Gil’s arm and walked away. “My daddy would never do this—not the man I trusted to take care of us no matter what.”

Gil did not know what to say, so he said nothing. He kept pace with Jil until they reached her car. “Remind me never to let you down,” he said as they climbed in.

“Time to go pick up Mother. She deserved better.” Jil drove several blocks before pulling the car over and parking. She began to sob with her face pressed against her hands holding the steering wheel.

Gil gently rubbed her shoulder and said, “I’m sorry.”

Jil straightened up, looked in her visor mirror and declared, “My makeup is ruined.”

Gil leaned back into his passenger door to take in her disheveled look. “It’s OK. You’re still beautiful.”

“Oh, shut up and get in the back of the car.” Jil used her handkerchief to wipe away her tears.

“Why?” Gil asked.

“Because I want to feel good, so I’m going to fuck you. My makeup is ruined anyway.” She unbuckled and put her hand on the door. Gil didn’t move. “Well, either get in back and pull your pants down or get the hell out of my car!”

Gil moved to the back.

Eleven

About What

November 6, 2009 — Somewhere in the Virginia Mountains

"WHAT DO YOU WANT?" BUD SAID over the encrypted connection.

"Am I interrupting some program?" Betty considered the possible reasons Bud might be annoyed with her. *Shit. I never did make it to Five Guys to have dinner with him.* Tom's house blowing up put a crimp in those plans.

"Of course not, they keep running when I answer the phone. Plenty of CPU cycles for those." Bud cleared his throat. "You don't think I'm running this stuff on my phone, do you?" Actually, he *was* using his smartphone for some of his work. Now that Control was no longer centralized, he had to use whatever computers were available to him. His phone was the most secure device connected to the Internet he had, so naturally, he ran his most sensitive programs there. Most of his work was now done on computers he had hacked into via a large botnet across the world. He had tens of thousands of computers connected back to his laptop. The users had clicked on a link in an email that went to a site claiming they would get a two-hundred-dollar gift card from a major retailer in their geographical area. The amount offered was in the local currency, and the graphics of the email matched the normal correspondence of the retailer. Classic social engineering. Bud knew how to manipulate almost anyone using a computer, but he had no clue how to ask a living, breathing woman out on a date—in person or over the phone.

"Hey, Bud, I'm sorry about dinner. You know we had to move locations—after Barnes died."

Bud was taken off guard by the mention of Barnes. He had

seen the information as a statistic of Control's organizational damage and had made the final arrangements dictated by Tom Howell Sr.'s instructions for Barnes's financial disposition. A second cousin received his retirement funds and a letter explaining that there had always been a fond connection, even if distant, between the two. It finally hit home to Bud that a human had died. "Oh, right. No. No problem. I completely understand." He could not help himself. *I'm always missing the signals.* Bud's blind spot was expressing empathy. *Damn it. I need to work out a flowsheet on this.*

"A rain check, then? When I'm back in town? You are still in the area, right?" Betty poked a little into Bud's usual careful security.

"Ah, I'm actually, uhm . . . You know I can't tell you, even if this is a secure line, right?" Bud wiped his forehead. *I'm sweating! Jesus, why can't I do this without stressing out?*

"OK." Betty took in a deep breath. "Well, let me get to my point for calling."

"OK."

"I need to know what we have on drugs used for causing amnesia."

"I'm not sure what you mean." Bud knew what she meant but wanted to know why she wanted to know.

"I mean do we have any special drugs for making someone forget a period of time prior to taking the drug," Betty explained.

"You're always treating me like your private concierge for secret information." Bud's frustration came through in his accusation.

"Bud, my feelings are hurt."

He was unsure of how he could have hurt her feelings, but then again, he rarely understood normal human emotions. "You're kidding, right?"

"You know I'd kill for you, right?" Betty felt the need to push him in a new direction.

"Well, I suppose I do."

"That I would die to protect you?"

"I guess I never thought of it that way." Bud scratched his head and reset his POWN'D baseball cap.

"That the worse that would happen to you would be a scolding from our dear leader?"

"Tip of the spear. Is that what you're saying?"

"Yes, I'm the tip of the spear. I'm guided by your hand, but you can't see what I'm seeing."

"Right."

"Do you know what I see?"

"No. How could I?" Bud was puzzled and curious.

"I see someone misusing Control assets and endangering us all. I need to know if we have drugs for causing amnesia, short term— say, a few hours or less. What is it and how does it work?" Betty could hear Bud's keyboard clicking.

"Do you know what my college degree was in?"

"How would I know that, Bud? I guess I just assumed you were a computer science major who left early to spend all of your time hacking into government installations."

"Library science."

"What?"

"Library science. I have a PhD in library science, specializing in hacking government installations, of course."

"Get out of town!" Betty assumed he was kidding about the hacking part, but did not want to ask.

"A benzodiazepine–triazolam–lithium orotate combination with propranolol and an herbal element that is only noted, but not identified."

"OK, tell me about it."

"Causes amnesia during application, short half life on the triazolam, which is the depressant, and the herbal part extends the amnesia into the past a short time. In essence, the combination prevents the formation of new memories and the propranolol also has some healing effects on PTSD." Bud scrolled down the description, skipping parts that weren't immediately pertinent to Betty's query. "The triazolam disrupts the creation of new memories, from short-term storage to long term. The propranolol inhibits the preservation of strong emotional memories. Lithium orotate to reduce activity in the—hmm—I think they mean make you more empathetic." Bud made a note to do more research on lithium orotate's empathy effect.

"What about the herbal part?" Betty prodded.

"I don't get that part, really. Something about well-being and counteracting the fog of the other drugs." Bud hummed the words he was skipping over without fully pronouncing them. "Here it is."

"What did you find?"

"Sometimes roofies are added to the mix for an even stronger memory loss and/or creation of a new memory to replace the undesirable one. The subject can be shown a video or listen to an audio that creates a memory to replace the one you don't want."

"Son of a bitch."

"I can have some sent up to you on the next flight," Bud offered helpfully.

"No," Betty said firmly. "Don't tell anyone I asked about this."

"I won't, as long as you don't forget . . ." Bud prompted.

"What? Oh. Hah!" Betty caught on to his play on words. "I'm still going to meet you at the burger joint. Yes."

"OK." Bud said meekly.

"One last thing. Anything listed for counteracting this drug combination?"

"Nothing listed, but I'll check deeper for you if you want."

"No. We're good for now." Betty regretted saying that. "Well, we'll be good when I come to town, right?"

Bud sighed. "Yes. When you come to town."

"So, you are in Washing—" Bud cut the connection before Betty could finish saying the capitol city's name. "I knew it! He has to have his burger fix."

Twelve

That Thing She Done

November 6, 2009 — Århus, Denmark

JIL LOOKED AT HERSELF in the mirror on her car visor. "I look like absolute shit." She had just met up with her coke dealer and taken yet another line. "I have to get off this train." Her random nosebleeds had become more frequent. "Maybe it wouldn't be all bad to have my nose done." She turned her head slightly to the right and left.

Jil took in a deep breath and looked away from the mirror and down at the gearshift lever. Gil was waiting for her at the hotel. She had told him she needed to take care of a personal matter and that she would be right back. The sex with him had become as addictive as the cocaine, and she was starting to worry that she needed Gil more than the drug. She had gone through rehab periodically and kicked her habit. She wondered if there was a program for shaking a man like Gil.

She spotted her memento on the console—a ring of paper her father had given her. The label was for a premium brand of cigar, eighteen-year-old tobacco leaf, hand rolled in Cuba, soaked in premium cognac, and only available to the extremely wealthy. There was a three-year waiting list and a price tag of a thousand dollars apiece. The edges of the band were frayed and the image was faded from repeated handling. Jil had worn it many times like a wedding band. Her daddy placed it on her finger when she was five years old, telling her that it would take a special man to take her away from him. Someone who could afford such luxuries in an offhand way. A man capable of caring for his baby girl like Larry had.

Lately, he had not done such a great job in that role. In fact, for the past five years, it really was Jil taking care of the family. She crushed the cigar band and threw it into the ashtray of her rental car. It looked like it belonged. Jil lit another cigarette, took a long drag, blew the smoke out the cracked window, then crushed it out on the formerly cherished memento.

To no one in particular she said, "If—a big *if*—I get married, my engagement ring better be the biggest damn thing the jeweler can lift into a setting." She looked at her cellphone at the message from Daddy. It read, "Don't try to stop me this time. I mean it." Jil put the BMW in drive and carefully entered traffic using her turn signal. She was not going to rush or draw attention to herself. Eric owns the garage. She pressed the two-digit code for his speed dial.

"Jil. Is everything OK?"

"Eric, I want to make sure there isn't a working camera on the third level of your garage."

"I don't even want to know." He disconnected.

Jil pulled into the garage gate, took the ticket, and slowly drove to the third level where Larry had tried twice to commit suicide by running a hose to his car cabin from the exhaust. Jil had arrived the first time just as he started his engine after he saw her. The second time, his window was cracked open, allowing fresh air in. Now he was following through on his threat. The stall next to the driver's side was open. She drove closely alongside his matching BMW, scraping the paint of both cars until her mirror was touching his. She was facing her father and could see his disorientation. His mind was being overcome by the carbon monoxide. It would take only a few moments for him to pass out and minutes for him to die. He fumbled about his cabin, trying to open his door, but couldn't. His hand knocked the blinker on. Perhaps because he had grown up with cars with the shifter on the steering wheel column, he fumbled with the wiper control, spraying mist onto and over the windshield. His mouth formed partial words. He slumped over the steering wheel. The horn went off, stirring him slightly, and he slumped to the window, his cheek pressed against the glass. The skin spread tight against the window, his jaw slack, drool dripping from his lip. She never stopped watching him except to look at her watch to keep track of the elapsed time.

Jil waited five minutes before she backed her BMW up, parked, removed the hose from Larry's car, and placed it in her car's trunk. She calmly left the garage after paying her ticket for the one-hour minimum with cash. She called Eric again via the encrypted connection.

"Jil? What's going on?

"Please go get Daddy from his car and record it as a heart attack or something. It just wouldn't do for it to be a suicide."

"Third level?"

"Yes. I'll have someone pick the keys up from your office so we can return the car." There was no emotion in her voice. She might as well be arranging for her dry cleaning to be picked up.

"I'm so sorry. Both parents in the same week." Eric tried to sound sincere.

"Oh, get off it, Eric. It's better this way, and of all the people I know in this world, you are the one who ought to understand." *Asshole didn't have the balls to kill his own father. At least I had the will to make sure mine got the job done.*

"As you wish." Eric disconnected.

Jil started to light a cigarette but threw the pack out the window instead. She burned the image of her father dying of asphyxiation into the thought of having another smoke. She dialed Gil.

"Hey, beautiful. Where are you?" Gil said.

"I'm on my way to the bar to get very drunk, then I plan on taking you to the hotel and fucking your brains out for at least a week, and living off room service. I expect you to be in charge of orgasms and daily bouquets of flowers. Is that an issue?"

"I think I can handle that." *I am so screwed*, thought Gil.

THIRTEEN

ROGUE FEMALE

November 6, 2009 — Somewhere in the Virginia Mountains

ON THE SURFACE OF the water in the bath was a floating bar of Le Labo soap. The bubbles collected to it, yet stayed off the top. Betty poked the solid mass under the foam. "Always more under the surface." She caught the fragrant bar and took a deep breath of the perfume. Suddenly, Betty saw with clarity what she had been trying to remember for the past two days. Tom had met with Ernesto on the helipad. No dream or false memory. He had been trying to get her to forget—but why? She searched her emotions. For some reason—probably the effects of the propranolol—she was not upset by the thought of Ernesto's presence. The issue was Tom's, or rather, Howell's manipulations.

I try to live in a black-and-white world of what's right and wrong, but I would have to kill both Tom and Ernesto if I used that lens here.

She needed to learn more about what their plans were and why they were working together. Ultimately, the question came down to, did Ernesto order José's hit or not?

Betty dressed and prepared for confronting both sides of her lover, Dr. Tom and Mr. Howell. *Do I go in guns blazing, taking him off balance to get the answers, or should I do it in bed—seduce him into revealing his plans. Or, I could drug him! That would be an eye for an eye!* She tossed the possibilities around in her mind as she tried on different outfits. *If I'm seducing, I can't be obvious or he'll be on guard. If I go in on the attack, he'll become defensive and I won't get a straight answer.* Betty unbuttoned her blouse to expose her cleavage and a hint of the red bra underneath. *Too obvious!* There was a chill in the air, so she changed to a silk camisole and an angora sweater. *A softer look and no bra.*

She smiled at her reflection and then checked her holstered SIG Sauer, ejecting the magazine and inspecting the rounds. Satisfied, she reinserted it with extra force, chambering a round by snapping the rail back. The sound of the metal on metal and the round loading gave her a warm feeling of control. Betty stowed the pistol so it showed over her sweater, and headed off to confront Tom, her cowboy boots ensuring everyone would hear her coming.

Gideon looked up from the paperwork he was holding in front of Tom. "Oh, hi, Betty. Can you give me a minute with the boss?"

Betty rested her hand on her pistol and gave an overly nice smile. "Funny, I was going to say the same thing, Gideon." She spread her feet slightly as if she was in an Old West shootout and was daring him to draw.

Tom looked up from the papers, then pressed a hand on Gideon's arm to signal he should put the papers down. "Gideon, I could use a warm-up on my coffee, do you mind? Thank you."

Gideon slowly dropped the papers and leaned in close. "Annie's got a gun, maybe you should run."

Tom tried not to laugh at the joke; he managed a slight smirk. "No hurry. I'll let you know when Betty and I are done." He forced a smile and leaned back in his leather-and-wood antique chair. The cowhide murmured and the old metal spring creaked.

Gideon shook his head in resignation and disbelief. "Dead man walking," he whispered loud enough for Tom to hear.

Both Betty and Tom waited ten seconds before talking. Both were willing to wait for the other to start. Betty shifted her weight slightly. Tom took that as an opportunity to invite her to sit down. "The couch is comfortable, or—" he gestured to the office chair on the other side of his desk with an open hand.

Betty casually sat down on the couch arm to ensure her weapon showed and she had easy access to it. "Time for you to fess up."

Tom made up his mind how to handle this conflict. "Yes, it's time that you knew the truth. But I'm not sure you'll handle it in a way that is beneficial to us all."

"This isn't about what is beneficial anymore." Betty fondled the grip of her pistol menacingly. "You've owed me the whole truth for a long time. Start talking."

"All right." Tom started to move his hand to the desk drawer to remove a file, but stopped when he noticed Betty tensing. "May I pull a file for you?"

Betty nodded.

Tom removed a manila folder with about an inch of papers and placed it open on his desk. Some were stapled, others paper clipped; there was also one large binder and several loose pages. There were eight-by-ten surveillance photos and reports, phone records, and bank statements. He pulled a batch of photographs clipped together, removed the clip, and put the first one on top of the folder, then spun the pile 180 degrees to face Betty. "José worked for Ernesto. That is why I was pretty sure who arranged his murder."

"What the fuck, Howell. That's the best you could do? A doctored photo, no doubt, or from some economic confere—" She stopped when she saw the image of Ernesto and José greeting each other warmly. The next photo Tom placed on top was of the two working on many pages of accounting information. The third was of the two men with slutty women in their laps. Betty began to shake slightly from an adrenaline surge. "When and where were these taken?"

"You can see the time stamp as easily as I can. Four weeks before your wedding was scheduled." Tom leaned back into his chair. "I have many more, if you want to see them." He wiped his chin. "Some are"—Tom paused, choosing his next word carefully—"pornographic." Betty did not stop him, so he began dropping photo after photo of José transitioning from cuddling the woman to stripping her clothes off and kissing her body to all-out sex on the same work table the documents had previously been reposed. Then it started again with a different woman. Betty looked away. One too many soul-penetrating photos after another that proved once and for all what she had suspected but had not wanted to believe about her José. He was a philanderer of the first order.

"That fucking bastard." She spun back to the couch and fell backward into the leather, seeking comfort that would not be there. She embraced the embroidered pillow and began to cry. Through her tears she said, "Why didn't you tell me?"

Tom closed the folder and deposited it back into the drawer. "I thought it better that you continue to believe José was true to you than to crush you with the evidence. I believed you would hate me and think I was using the photos to get closer to you."

Betty's face was a mess. She looked around for a tissue, and Tom got up from his desk to bring her his handkerchief. He sat down next to her but did not try to physically comfort her. "Yes, Ernesto was here and we—I tried to deceive you about it."

"Asshole. You're such an asshole, Tom."

"Part of the agreement in bringing Ernesto in was that he give up this evidence. José worked for Ernesto. Ernesto entrapped José to ensure he had those photos to hold over him, to keep him in line. José fought back. Michel and Slim were brought in to convince him that was foolish. They let the situation get out of control and when you arrived at the door, they panicked at the realization of the damage they had done to José, so they killed him to keep him from talking."

Betty blew her nose and handed the handkerchief back to Tom. "Fuck." She closed her eyes, trying to block the images out of her mind. She refocused herself and stabbed a finger into Tom's chest. "So you drugged me to forget!"

Tom let her keep the finger poked into his chest despite the pain. "Yes, because it seemed the better way, to be able to talk to you later about working with Ernesto to take down all the Cabal instead of just killing him."

"You seriously thought I wouldn't kill him?" She poked him several times to add emphasis to each word.

"No, but I hoped that you would see the value in making them all pay. They are evil, that bunch." Tom tried to engage Betty's worldview of right and wrong.

"You manipulated me."

"I'm in the spy business. It's what we do."

"But to me! You manipulated me!"

"In doing so, I was protecting you."

"Nice. Exactly how are you protecting me?"

"If you had gone after Ernesto when he arrived, you'd be dead. His bodyguards would have reacted quicker to your actions than I could have likely done to protect you." Tom got up from the couch and paced slowly. "Betty, we have the opportunity to take their whole top level out."

"What do you mean?" Deep down she wanted them all to pay, just like Tom had thought, but she did not want to play into his deceptions.

"We have a plan, but we need you to make it work." Tom wheedled.

"Bullshit. You don't need me, you just need me to step out of the way."

"We need you. You know how to work your way in, you know Vail, you know the languages . . . you are the eye candy they can't resist."

Betty snorted. "That bit kills you, doesn't it." She enjoyed seeing Tom squirm.

"Hmm. Yes. That is my least favorite part and what keeps me jealous." Tom reached over to take Betty's hand. "I love you and never want to see you hurt. I'd kill someone to protect you and even put my life on the line to save you."

"I know you would. I suppose that is the one reason I keep coming back to you after you fuck up."

Tom took that as the sign that Betty was ready to move forward. "There is going to be a conference in Vail soon. Eric Salizar will be administrating his latest secret anti-aging treatments and vaccinations to the top echelon. You can be there in place with Karl to identify the leaders and help prepare the plan for taking them out."

"And if I say no?"

"I'll do it without you."

"Jesus, you're such a bastard."

"Yes. Regretfully, I sometimes remind myself of my father."

"Now there was a bastard!"

"Amen."

FOURTEEN

THE ELYSIAN

November 7, 2009 — Somewhere in the Virginia Mountains

"BETTY IS READY," TOM SAID to Karl over the encrypted line.

Betty nodded her head in agreement, but did not speak. She was out of view of the video feed. Different backgrounds, like what a studio photographer would use, were pulled down behind Tom's desk to ensure information gleaned from the images could not be used to trace their secret location. The camera even kept a tight focus on his face to prevent someone from seeing his desk or the papers that might be on it. The screen could be split to display digitized images or computer-generated documents. Because it was a computer-based system, the screen image Tom was seeing could be split to show Betty and anyone else included on the conference call, with the added ability of each member only seeing the digital content they were cleared for observing.

Karl sounded edgy. "Yeah, I'm getting tired of minding Little Miss Froo-froo and her pooch. It would be nice to see some action." His latest run-in with Hanna Lautner involved a valet and ankle biting. The dog, not Miss Lautner.

"Just remember, we don't want to kill anyone—yet." Tom was sympathetic to Karl's desire to permanently resolve the trust fund troublemaker, but discretion was more important. "We need to take away their operational capacity first. Cutting off the head might just lead to many new leadership groups with split assets."

Karl nodded in agreement, out of habit rather than a real desire to focus only on the plan. Skipper-do's time on earth was quickly coming to an end, if he had any say in the matter. "Right. OK. Everything is ready.

I've arranged the fourth-floor unit. Günter is indisposed for the winter."

Tom looked over at Betty. Deep down he had convinced himself that every manipulation he was performing on her would be justified in the end. But in that moment, his heart fluttered ever so slightly as he contemplated the possibility that Betty could end up dead if things got out of hand. She looked up from her iPad when she noticed his gaze was not at the camera but instead on her. She smiled at him. Betty really was on board with the plan. He had almost lost her over her prying into his meeting with Ernesto. Someday he would have to tell her the rest of that story . . . but for now . . . just something better left unsaid even if he implied it.

"Karl, do I have a car as well?" Betty felt the need to be part of the planning. If she did not ask, she might have to take care of it later anyway.

"Yes, I've taken the liberty of acquiring a rather nice Audi A4 for you. Red with tan leather. Stands out nicely."

"Sweet!" Betty chirped.

"OK, kids, let's focus on the task at hand. Betty will arrive at 1400 hours at the Eagle Vail Airport on the 23rd. Please have her transportation ready."

"Time to visit my old haunts, but this time with a Black Card!" Betty squealed. "Did you know there is a twenty-one-thousand minimum per month?" She grinned devilishly at Tom and pumped her arm. "Ka-ching!"

Tom's face colored slightly. "Please remember to keep the receipts so we can return what is not absolutely necessary."

"No problem. I'll be sure to focus on personal services, then." Betty looked at her nails and fluffed her hair. "I'm overdue for a decent spa treatment," she deadpanned.

"Karl?" Tom pleaded. "Never mind on keeping an eye on Betty, just keep an eye on that Black Card, OK?"

"My name is Paul and that is between ya'll." Karl quoted Quentin Tarantino's *Pulp Fiction*.

"Karl, have you ever taken lessons from Pepi?" Betty said. "You know, Jil and I stayed at Pepi's Hotel Gasthof every year over winter break when we were in college. I'd be happy to sponsor you and pay for them."

"This conference call may go down as the most expensive in Control history. Say goodnight, Karl."

Karl was grinning by now too. It wasn't often that he talked to the director, let alone in such a good-natured-ribbing way. He could not resist. "Goodnight, Karl," he said.

The connection was ended and Gideon raised the background behind Tom to return the view to the Virginia mountains. "That went spectacular," he said as he rolled his eyes and head. "Gideon, remind me to cancel that card the moment the mission is done."

"Not on your life, mister!" Betty said, and she meant it.

"OK, then I pay the bill out of your retirement," Tom sniped.

"Perfect, because I plan to marry an elderly, frail gentleman of enormous wealth." Betty got up from the couch, leaving the iPad behind. She stuck her tongue out and said, "Phhbt!"

"Go get packed. I have to put some family heirlooms on eBay to cover your first month's expenses."

"Oh, give me a break, you've got that much in change in this couch." She pointed to the full-grain leather couch she had just vacated.

"You're probably right," quipped Tom. "I haven't looked there yet."

Gideon was suppressing his enjoyment of the ongoing banter, but he needed to get them moving on or dinner would be a mess. "I'll leave you two to your negotiations. I have dinner to finish. Be at the table in twenty minutes, please." He turned back before leaving. "Rib eye steak, garlic mashed potatoes, asparagus, homemade rolls, and a beet salad."

"Who needs Vail?" Betty said.

"I certainly don't!" answered Tom.

"Party pooper," pouted Betty.

Fifteen

Wrangling for Answers

November 7, 2009 — Somewhere in the Virginia Mountains

"YOU'RE NOT LISTENING to me, McFluffy. We are not in the energy business, and I do not want you wasting time on cold fusion." Tom was particularly upset with his chief scientist today. Since the destruction of the Control bunker, staff had either found secret labs to work from, logged in from home, or, like Bud, moved from location to location—usually coffee shops with free Wi-Fi. McFluffy, on the other hand, started his own limited liability corporation to produce or sell product licensing of his best inventions. The gruff old Scot claimed he had an agreement with Tom Howell Sr. that permitted his profiting from inventions made under Control's umbrella. The suspect documents showed a split in profits of fifty-fifty, but the scientist had full say over his work *if* he was ever forced out of his Control-provided lab.

"Laddie, for the millionth time, this is my pet project and funded by my LLC." McFluffy's voice swelled as his brogue took back over, "You ken I do as I please, yet you get half the cake!"

With his face turned away and his hand over his mouth, Tom sighed under his breath, "Christ." He looked back at McFluffy and said, "Well, as long as we understand and agree that the essential bits like our body armor, gear, and specialty weapons won't suffer."

McFluffy smiled broadly—not that you could really tell from his beard and wild hair. "Aye, I have a new mannie on the job, a real sleekit, that one." He panned the camera to show his apprentice: a tall, skinny, thirty-ish man, with hair tightly cut on the sides but extra long on top, tattooed arms, and the sleeves rolled up on his plaid shirt with the company name and logo on the pocket. Tuechtar LLC's logo was a map of Scotland with the loose bits of islands in motion to form a larger land mass. “Say ’ello to Tooker.” Tooker’s name tag showed the spelling as Tucker. He waved politely but did not say anything.

“Well, we all know cold fusion’s science has been laughed at for decades. Why go there?”

“Nanoparticles, laddie, those wee nanos are the key to making cold fusion work. Tooker and I are having a right good go at it, and I like what I see. So bugger off. Tooker will make sure all of your goodies make it on time to keep your lads—and lady—safe.” McFluffy’s demeanor softened. “How is the lovely Betty doing? You better be taking good care of her or you’ll answer to me!”

Tom rolled his eyes. “She’s fine and doing great. Let’s talk again in a week.” The connection was severed, and Gideon rolled up the backdrop.

“You know, if Betty doesn’t kick your ass, there’s a line of guys ready to defend her honor.”

“Don’t tell me you’ve joined the queue!” Tom got up from his desk and began walking around to get the blood flowing in his wounded leg. “You’re the one who got me in trouble with the amnesia drug!”

“Just trying to help, boss.” Gideon folded his arms over his chest. “And you better take good care of her. I don’t want to lose my job from an inside attack.”

“But you’d defend me if she came after me in one of her moods, right?”

Gideon shook his head slowly in the negative. “Hell hath no fury like a woman scorned.”

“Great—with help like that, I might was well load and cock the gun for her.”

“You generally do, from what I’ve seen.” Gideon goaded his boss. “You’re just lucky she loves you too much to pull the trigger.”

“Yeah,” Tom retorted, “I’m one lucky guy.” He sat down and pulled off his prosthetic to adjust the sock on his nub end. “Say, did the new leg for skiing come in?”

“You bet, a Tooker special.” Gideon mimicked McFluffy’s pronunciation of his new right-hand man’s name. “A spring-loaded shock absorber and a fully articulated ankle shrouded in fake flesh so you can change the boot out for next year’s fashion statement.”

“Did it come with a warranty?” quipped Tom.

“Thirty seconds or thirty feet, whichever comes first,” answered Gideon.

Sixteen

Through the Narrow

November 7, 2009 — Near Bern, Switzerland

"MARIE, THANK YOU for hosting us in your home." Charles raised his Baccarat champagne flute, custom made and hand etched with an image of the chalet and the now-pristine vista, sans the now-removed village. Upon draining the glass, he threw the two-thousand-dollar stemware into the fireplace to christen the meeting. Gustav, Pierre, and Marie echoed, "Here, here" and threw their pieces in as well.

A servant brought a tray with fresh glassware while another gently pried open another Moët & Chandon's Charles and Diana 1961 Dom Pérignon. Marie raised her flute. "I've been saving this for you, Charles—it is from Diana's birth year and the one served at their wedding. A rare vintage, just like you!" She drank deeply of the bubbly. The others cheered their approval. The servant gently wiped the rim of her glass to remove her riverine-rabbit-red lipstick, and then topped off her flute as she held it aside.

Gustav raised his glass, turned to the large window overlooking the valley below, and with his lisp said, "To the beautiful view, Marie."

"Yes, Marie, it is beautiful," assured Pierre with a wave of his left hand, followed by a kiss of his bunched fingers, like a chef might do to signify a delicious preparation.

She held back a tear. "I wish my sister were here to see it." Marie glared at Charles.

"Yes, she would have loved the view had she lived to see it." Charles looked far off into the distance, straining to see something that wasn't there.

Pierre placed his hand on Charles's shoulder, "Let's not speak of unpleasantries. We are celebrating our successes." He let the opposite hang unspoken, the family failures.

Marie continued to glare at Charles. "It was a tragic blow to the family, the way she died." She spit at Charles's feet; a servant immediately wiped his shoes and the floor.

Gustav, lisp in full force, jumped in and split the two. "We have all erred at one time or another. The four of us are all that are left, and we must keep looking forward—just as you are moving forward with the valley, eh, Marie?"

She had loved the village that had once been the main focal point of the valley, but her recently late husband had it torn down after she had complained one too many times about how it bothered her that it wasn't being kept up to her standards. It was rebuilt out of view, but not exactly as it had been. One of her favorite shops, a florist, did not make the transition and she now had to have her floral arrangements brought in instead of handpicking the flowers herself, one of her great pleasures. "I've found a new florist. See that bare spot in the middle." Marie pointed to a glade surrounded by young pine trees about four hundred meters away. She grew happier, thinking of the coming year. "There will be a greenhouse, cutting room, and for form's sake, a small sales area for the peasants." She stood on her toes as if that would give her a better view. The stilettos clicked on the cherrywood floor as she turned around. "I think Herbert would have been pleased"—she took a sip of her champagne and held the glass to the side for the servant to wipe the unavoidable lipstick stain off—"had he lived to see it," she drolly finished.

"Yes, to poor old Herbert." Charles raised his glass in another toast. "May he hear more clearly in the afterlife than he did on earth." The others affirmed their delight at his little joust at her husband's sudden death not long after his unilateral decision to raze Marie's village. "Well, this is your home, Marie, and your show, but may we get to dinner?"

"Why the hurry, Charles? We're here for a month."

"I do love your man's cooking."

She smiled and waved everyone to the table. "Shall we get started, then?" The flute was removed from her outstretched hand and a small gong replaced it. She struck it three times and the servants scurried to make it so.

†

A week later, Marie confronted Charles. "I'm dying here. Why won't you let me go?" Marie said.

Charles held her passport in his hand. "My dear, sweet sister-in-law," he said in his blithesome English accent. "Always the melodramatic one of the family."

Marie harrumphed. "You know I always get my hair done the first week of the month!" She stomped her foot. "This is cruel and unusual punishment!" It was a week later than her usual appointment and a streak of gray and white was appearing down the middle of her head.

"Marie, Marie, Marie. Do you really think I would somehow impede your ritual. I've arranged for your treatment here." Charles waved her passport in the general direction of the southern end of the chalet and the rebuilt village.

"Well, such a kind gesture, but you also know that I have a personal relationship with my stylist and her staff." Marie flipped her hair in defiance. "It isn't so simple as bringing someone in to do the job."

Charles chuckled. "But of course. I understand. Do you think I planned a monthlong meeting for my convenience?" He pointed to his makeshift office, complete with the rugs, paintings, and bric-a-brac artwork that regularly belonged on his island in the Indian Ocean. "This room is much too small, and as lovely as the view of your former village is, it is not the vista I am used to."

"I don't care about your damn office! Ciara is expecting me. The entire spa is mine for the day that I come. She depends on me and I on her."

"Yes, of course, your dye job, Brazilian for Pierre, mani-pedi, and facial are all important. That is—"

Marie did not let him finish. "Fuck you!" She picked up a bronze dog from his desk and threw it at his head. He ducked slightly to the right as the missile sailed within millimeters of his left ear.

Charles winced at the sound of the impact behind his chair, a rare Louis XIV. "Now, Marie, that was not necessary." The thrown Egyptian relic had been specially procured from King Tut's tomb by the famous Howard Carter in 1922 and never documented, though its diminutive, three-quarter-inch cousin was held by the Met. The deep scratch to the long table matching his prized chair would be repairable, but it gravely hurt him, much worse than any physical injury. He was certain Marie had intended to hit his head and not the table, but the damage was done. His eyes grew fierce. "As I was just saying, Ciara is here with her entire staff. I took the liberty of buying her a new shop, and all of the items you are so fond of from the old are here, including that special chair for your . . . perverse pleasure in having your body hair ripped from the follicles. It is no wonder you and Pierre have such a special bond, since he loves to give pain as much as you enjoy receiving it."

"Oh. Charles." Marie's Bavarian accent grew stronger but her sincerity did not. "I am so sorry about the table." Marie had been aiming for his skull. This had been the first opportunity she had to strike back at him for the murder of her sister—Charles's wife—five years before.

"It was the only perfect one left." A slight tear was forming in his eye. He fought to maintain his calm exterior demeanor, to not expose the raw volcano that was raging underneath. He began planning how to extract his revenge for her temerity.

"It amazes me that you show more emotion for the loss of a perfect table than the loss of your son—or your wife. Someday, you are going to explode again—like Vesuvius." Marie got up, intending to go straight to Ciara. She felt a strong need for a cleansing that only pain could provide her. "When it happens, you will bring us all down with you, I'm afraid."

"Tut, tut. Off with you to your dear Ciara." As Marie vanished through some large tapestries, Charles muttered under his breath, "While she still lives."

He turned to his vintage L. M. Ericsson Eiffel Tower hand-cranked telephone and called his butler, Christian. "The bitch threw the dog and has damaged the table. We'll need an expert to repair it. Spare no expense. And send in Pierre."

Seventeen

A Thorny Issue

November 14, 2009 — Near Bern, Switzerland

AFTER THEY HAD EXCHANGED pleasantries, Pierre asked Charles about early arrangements for a trip to Vail for special anti-aging treatments. "What do you think about Dr. Salizar's advances—shall we partake?"

"Why not? We'll look young forever, preserved like the kings intended." Charles looked back at his beloved but damaged table. "Listen, Pierre. I know how you and Marie love it when you inflict pain. I need you to punish her in a different way."

"How do you mean?" Pierre asked.

"Tonight, do not touch her. Make her beg for pain, but do not give it to her."

"That is not a normal request from you."

"Feel free to bind her so she cannot move, but not so tight as to give her pleasure," Charles said.

"You usually give me playthings and encourage my interests."

"She was naughty today and needs to be punished, but not in a way she enjoys." Charles ran his thumb over the scar on his prized bronze Egyptian dog. "I know you will be pleased with the present I'll make to you in Vail to make up for this minor inconvenience."

"Yes, as I am to pain, you are to pleasure." Pierre nodded knowingly. "As you wish."

"Excellent. Let's move on to proper business, then, shall we?" Charles opened his folder.

Pierre paused, unable to resisting turning the blade. "I'm surprised at the way you treat women. You were such a momma's boy in the day."

Charles smiled and held his tongue rather than bring up the

whippings he received as a young man at the direction of his late stepmother. Instead, he straightened his posture and cleared his thoughts of anything not of importance. "We must be very careful with our American cousin. If we stray from the path even the slightest, I fear he will target us instead of aiding our cause."

"What are you seeing that I am not?" Pierre said.

"There is something afoot in his organization. Without the easy access we had before, I do not know for sure, but there is one person there I think he would sacrifice it all for."

"Yes. I understand, but how is that possible?" Pierre thought about Charles's wife, but would not dare bring up the subject of her death. She had been caught in bed with the man who was replaced by Casper. It was one of the few times Charles's temper could not be contained. He had used the very bronze dog he fondled now to beat his wife Charity and her consort to death. Neither could be identified by their faces afterward. Not that it was necessary.

"I blame his father for not killing her with José."

"Yes, Ernesto warned us that José wasn't as stable as first imagined," Pierre reminded Charles.

"I accept responsibility for keeping him until the end. I still believe his brilliance could be managed, but obviously not his lust for flesh." Charles looked keenly at Pierre. "Perhaps an important reminder for us all."

Pierre's cheeks grew red and his brow furrowed. "You tarnish the memory of your wife and my stepsister."

Charles stood up but kept his hand on the bronze dog. "Let me remind you that our dynasty has been fed time and again on marriages of convenience. Many of your late father's wives—Gustave's mother included—came from my family tree and were the source of his wealth."

Pierre interjected, "But he built on that wealth!"

"True, we both stand on the shoulders of giants." Charles clasped his hands behind his back and began to pace back and forth behind his desk, like a professor instructing a class that was almost good enough to learn from him. "However, the marriage to Marie's"—Charles paused to fondle the bronze dog and take in a deep, soothing breath—"and Charity's mother doubled your father's wealth."

"Well, yes," Pierre agreed.

"And we are all in this together because we own the controlling interest to the House of Saud. We guided them—or rather, our fathers did—to the nationalization of the oil fields and their immense wealth." Charles began ticking off items on his fingers. "The current value of the Saudi oil conglomerate is ten trillion dollars, one of our nicer investments. If they were to issue an IPO—"

Pierre burst in, "Never happen!"

"Of course not. But if they issued an IPO for the subsidiary companies, we would finally be able to cash out some of our investment in them. All told, with our control of the Iranian oil fields, less the loss of the Iraqi inventory—Goddamn war did not go as planned, which is why we are here!"

Pierre cleared his throat.

"Yes, I digress. All of our holdings in the Middle East, as Ernesto has summarized nicely, are currently valued at twelve trillion dollars. With the oil we own through intermediaries or 'undiscovered deposits' in various regions we control—just in oil—our holdings are valued at twenty trillion. If you add in the value of the land, minerals, diamonds, platinum, and the raw timber, we approach thirty trillion."

Pierre cleared his throat again. "What about the derivatives?"

Charles shuffled some paperwork to find the actual number. "We currently have two hundred seventy trillion U.S. dollars in derivative stock bets. Half bull and half bear."

"Can we make a move and cash out some of our bets?"

"If we do, we show our hand or take a loss. I find neither attractive." Charles used his pen to flip the paper back to the first page.

"We've moved the market before—Casper has used his people to push it to do our bidding." Pierre pointed out.

"Be as that may be, our past operations are not our current operations. Our current plans require patience and a timed exit. If we rush the process, our other derivative bets lose their value and we have gained nothing. Or worse, we have a net loss," Charles said.

"Your lectures are most divine, Charles. It is like being back at Oxford listening to my venerable professors of economics. Do pray tell. What do we do when we run out of cash?"

"We just tell the banks to increase our capital accounts," Charles said with a wave of his hand.

"We have already been doing that. That is my point. It is going to become obvious to someone that we are manipulating the cash balances, we need to do something different. Our bankers are going to break soon if we *do not stop* our cash outflows," Pierre said, stabbing his finger into his palm.

"But our liquidity has always been an issue," Charles sat down and forced a smile, then nodded his head and squinted his eyes as he said, "Yet, we have always been able to tell the banks how many zeros we need in our accounts."

"You know my position—that while Gustav has done well choosing our long-term assets, his liquidity management, well, leaves me sodden."

"Yes, liquid assets, my point exactly." Charles jammed his finger at the pile of papers in front of him. "We tell the banks how liquid our assets are; they do not tell us."

"I'm selling artwork to make things work as it is!" Pierre said.

"And at two million per painting, you're barely getting by." Charles quipped, but he was correct. Pierre had inherited a vast fortune from his father and mother, but very little in cash or easily sold assets. The cost of maintaining his households—let alone pliable governments that would honor the Cabal holdings in contested regions—was a vast drain on his cash reserves. Usually he was able to bribe officials via business transactions, skimming from the top of the deal, but sometimes cash had to come from untraceable accounts.

"We just don't have enough in the slush fund to make the next payment to the Sudanese, Nigerians, Georgians, Mongolians, and Indonesians to keep our positions without sacrificing something else. Now, if Gustav had listened and bought a few gold mines, I could use bullion instead of cash." Pierre made a small dig with his reference to gold, Charles's pet savings plan. "Ever since the whole Sierra Leone diamond fiasco . . . what did they call it?"

"Blood diamonds." Charles rolled his eyes. Pierre had tried to use the assets Charles controlled for bribes, but he had been steadfast in his refusal. Charles did not have as large of a piece of the Cabal pie, but he controlled the group's gold, silver, bonds, and stocks. All much more liquid assets than the ones Pierre and Gustav had at their disposal, but also easily traced to the group if they were used for nefarious purposes.

Part of the reason they all stuck together to get through the ups and downs of the global economy. Each had a role to play and strings to pull, just as he used Casper to manipulate others downline, such as Larry Harper to short stocks for massive gains.

"Yes, ever since they put a stop to the blood diamonds—damn De Beers!" Pierre said.

"OK. It's time you had your shot at managing the black portfolio. Of course, you will have to meet with Ernesto and Gustav to work out the details and make the changes per your desires."

"I will get Ernesto here next week to make the transition," Pierre agreed. "Do I tell Gustav, or are you going to do it?"

Charles preened slightly. As the titular leader, it always fell on him to convey the bad news and let the others reap the good. He did not mind as long as the size of the pie kept increasing for his trouble. "Just do be careful that after I announce the change you don't over leverage us—again." Charles rubbed his temples.

Pierre attempted to defend himself. "You know as well as I do that there was no way to predict the crash of 2008!"

"But it was you who caused it!" Charles pointed his bony index finger at Pierre. "You cornered the market in those toxic assets, and when you tried to dump them too fast to meet our cash-flow needs"—Charles slammed his fist into the desk—"everything crashed." He tried to calm himself, aware of the dark energy he was awakening with his anger.

Charles pushed his chair away from the desk and Pierre. Standing up, he put the bronze Egyptian dog statue back on his Louis XIV table. He ran his finger across the scarred surface, back and forth several times as he tried to let go of his darkest thoughts, as if rubbing the wound would cause them to leave via his fingertip. Returning to his chair, he settled himself back into the role of family patriarch. "But that is the past. I know you won't make the same mistake again." Charles smiled broadly, touched his hands together, then spread them wide. "I have complete faith in you."

Pierre considered his past error of judgment and decided to give Charles a sign that he had learned. "Give Gustav the shipping cartel to manage. I don't want to be too stretched, nor to leave him with nothing to occupy his time. Idle time and the devil's playground, you know."

"Yes, as your father used to say, better the devils you know."

Charles stood up to dismiss Pierre. "Right. See you at tea, then." Once he was alone, he rang his butler using the antique phone. There were easier ways to connect, but he did enjoy his toys. "Get Gustav in here. No, I—that is fine. He can come in a robe, for all I care." He replaced the handset in its spring-loaded cradle. Charles was willing to use any advantage to make the transition easier. "Between his lisp and the emasculation of being summoned in his robe after—" He shook his head to clear the image of the type of sex Gustav preferred. Charles had his own peccadilloes, but he kept them private. He made a point of indulging the needs of the others, but would abstain, himself, until he was home, out of view. "Self-control—always self-control."

Eighteen

Bark, Attack!

November 14, 2009 — Old Town Virginia

"YOU SHOULD JUST PUT it all in storage, like everyone else in the world does," Margaret said. She was walking around Betty's apartment in D.C., putting items into a box as directed by Betty as they talked via cellphone.

"I won't be coming back for a long time. I know that now." *I can't even think of possibly living above Grace at this point, family or not!*

"Oh, Betty, the view! It's to die for." Margaret stood staring out at the city in the distance. Betty's window was just a little higher than the surrounding buildings, allowing a view to the north and east. "I just can't believe you're giving it up."

Betty looked over at Tom. She bit her lip. "You know, you're right. Hang on." Betty muted her cellphone and threw a wad of paper at her boss and lover to get his attention. "Hey, stingy boss man. What if I want to keep my apartment, just in case down the road you really piss me off."

Tom grinned mischievously. "We own the building. I don't care, either way."

Betty furrowed her brow, "You mean Control owns the building, *you* do, or *we* own the building?"

"Well, you have to sign this document—" Tom strafed through some manilla folders until he found the right one and pulled out a legal document with a "Sign Here" sticker attached to several places. "Then it becomes 'we.'" He looked over the legalize of the writing. "The survivor retains one hundred percent ownership, so if you kill me, it's yours." He raised his left eyebrow and half grinned to match. "Not that I'm encouraging you," he said.

"Hmm. Interesting."

"Remind me not to tell you about any life insurance policies I might buy in the future."

"What about the ones you already have?" Betty asked.

"I don't think I should answer that question."

"Well, I think Margaret should live in the apartment with Surry until I make up my mind. Do you have a problem with that, partner? It'll save me the monthly storage rental fee and get her away from that asshole husband of hers."

"Wow. I just see land mines here. Do whatever you think is best." Tom retreated to his paperwork.

Betty took her phone off mute. "Margaret, why don't you stay there until I make up my mind. Turns out I can't break my contract and it's already paid up for the next two years."

"Oh, wow. I don't know what to say." Margaret said.

"Hey, Surry will be more comfortable, your soon-to-be ex can keep the house, and you get a great view of the city. You work from home and go in to collect the mail on Mondays and Thursdays."

"Betty, it's too generous!"

"You're keeping my practice alive while I deal with family issues, let alone taking care of Surry. Plus I don't have to put anything in storage."

"What about your personal items?"

"Just put them in the closet of the spare bedroom. They should all fit."

"I can't thank you enough. I'll pay you for subletting," Margaret added.

"No, you won't! I insist, and I can afford it." Betty was not going to take no for an answer. "That two years of rent was paid for by contract work I did." She decided to stretch the truth, further than she normally would. "I can't get it back and there are strict sublet rules. You're doing me a favor."

"You're my hero, Betty," Margaret said.

Betty disconnected and stared at Tom, who was trying to ignore her. "Sometimes you do just the right thing and it makes up for all the bullshit you do."

Tom hesitated before looking up. "Thanks, I think."

Gideon rushed in from the kitchen. "Sir, Grace is on line three, something about being attacked by a dog."

Tom grabbed the handset and selected the secure line Grace was calling on. "Hello, Grace."

Grace's voice sounded edgy and out of control, unusual for her. "That damn dog is back!"

Tom held the receiver away from his ear. Betty could hear Surry barking and could not resist a smile.

The sound of a door closing diminished the volume of the barking and Tom was able to place the ear piece against his head. "Grace, Betty won't be back for some time. That is Margaret, Betty's administrative assistant."

"That damn dog tried to attack me!" Grace said.

"Well, I guess you'll have to figure out some form of detente. Surry will be there with Margaret for the indefinite future." Tom rolled his eyes and made the head of a dog barking with his free hand. He missed Surry and was enjoying Grace being on the defensive. "Grace, I need to know if you can talk about Beth. I have Betty here—and she would like an update."

"Am I on speakerphone?" Grace asked.

"No, should we be?"

"That would be unwise, I think." Grace resumed her normal, controlled demeanor. "Beth isn't well and needs extensive watching for now. Additional shock treatments are in order for improved psychological balance. I'm afraid she is suffering from severe PTSD. I've started her on propranolol."

"How much longer will she be under your care?" Tom asked.

"As long as it takes for my sister to recover. She has some emotional problems from our youth that need to be resolved before she can move on with her life."

"How long, Grace, and what condition?" He hated to ask that question with Betty present, but there was no easy way to ask if Grace would let Beth live.

"I expect another couple of weeks before she'll have healed what was broken." With that, Grace was finally admitting she had been torturing her sister. An admission that penetrated her cool, controlled presentation of her emotions. It finally dawned on her that she did not want Beth dead, just to have suffered like she had. "Maybe sooner, actually." Grace's voice sounded softer, less frigid.

"Just keep me posted, please." Tom disconnected.

"Well?" Betty queried.

"I think Beth and Grace are rebuilding their relationship. Unfortunately, it's Beth doing most of the rebuilding and paying for the past." Tom closed his eyes and tried to not think of what he was allowing to happen. "Do you really want to know what is going on?"

Betty searched her soul and her bond with her adoptive mother. "I guess I'd rather not know what those two are working out."

"Probably for the best."

"Will she be OK, though?"

"I hope so. Beth never gave me cause to wish her harm or difficulty in her life. Lord knows she has done the bidding of my father." Tom considered her future role and what decisions he would have to make about Bob and Beth someday. *I suppose this would be a bad time for a mother-in-law joke.* Instead, he hypothesized, "Perhaps this is an opportunity for Beth to reinvent herself and have a new role."

"I'd like her and Grace to get along, bury the hatchet." Betty said.

Tom nodded. *At least, not in Beth's head.*

Nineteen

The Price of Knowledge

November 6, 2009 — Old Town Alexandria

GRACE PLACED HER PHONE on the counter and turned to look at her sister Beth, then at the state of her home. For the first time in her adult life, Grace had not kept her kitchen spotless; her obsessiveness about cleanliness would not have been classified as OCD per any psychological evaluation, but a casual observer might use the term to describe the complete control she maintained in her household to ease the torment in her brain. It calmed her to have everything in its proper place. Her career as a cleaner for Control also brought her peace, believing that she had made a significant contribution to the stability of the world by removing inconvenient evidence to the contrary. It was at this moment that the madness cleared from her mind. The look of her sister, eyes barely opened, body prostrate on the couch with her mouth drooling on the leather, and the tray of needles and drugs close by gave Grace pause. "What have I done?"

August 6, 2009 — Old Town Alexandria

Grace twisted the knife as she pushed it slowly in, all while looking intently at her half sister's eyes. She cradled the back of Beth's head and whispered into her ear, "Do you remember how it felt to be loved by him? Do you still take joy in that thought?" The wound began leaking blood down Beth's arm and dripped rapidly onto the plastic tarp covering the kitchen floor. The curtains were drawn and the lights were dim to ensure no one would see Grace's work. Beth tried to scream, but the ball gag in her mouth muffled the sound almost completely. Grace wiped the blade off on a white towel. The sheer terror in Beth's eyes and the ragged wrinkles in her face spoke of the anguish and raw punishment she was feeling. Grace's mind began purring with delight at the pain she was inflicting. She believed that every ounce of Beth's pain came from the deep well inside Grace's own belly. The pain put there by Beth's boyfriend all those years before.

Grace hissed into Beth's ear, "Karma's a bitch, ain't she, sis?"

Grace pulled away and removed the knife. She filled the wound with a blood-clotting agent, bandaged it, and placed a compression wrap over that. "It will be tender for a while. Hmm? What's that, Bethany?" Grace started her hand toward Beth's mouth as if she were going to remove the ballgag, but instead pulled her hand back and slapped Beth hard. "That arm doesn't hurt so bad now, does it? Maybe I should slap you again so you don't feel the wound at all." Grace picked up the knife and showed it to Beth again, the razor-sharp edge glinting in the dim light like the headlight of an oncoming car.

Beth violently shook her head no. Tears piled upon tears as she tried to seek forgiveness without voice to express her remorse. She wanted to say again that she did not know about the abuse. But in reality, she had suspected, and eventually Beth had known it was happening and did nothing to stop the repeated raping of her younger half sister. Part of her psyche knew she deserved anything Grace wanted to do to her, but that did not stop her terror at Grace's vindictive torture to extract revenge. She wept in her heart and prayed for forgiveness that might only be granted with her death. And she prayed for the end to come quickly.

Grace hovered around the chair, whispering to Beth, "The first time, he used my jealousy of you to get me into bed. He told me how it would be OK because you did it too." The whisper became a hiss. "But you never gave yourself to him, did you?"

Beth's eyes winced with the pain of remembrance and the pain of the moment. She tried to hide what she knew in her heart, the guilt that she had been denying. She shook her head ever so slightly, knowing that there was nothing to placate Grace. Nothing she could say or do that could possibly make up for her decisions four decades before.

"Then he used the first time as the cudgel to make me submit every time thereafter. He threatened to reveal me to Mother, to tell her what a whore I was." Grace pulled back and slapped Beth's left check just below her eye. "I eventually tried to resist. I was growing stronger, so he had to hit me to submit. He was smart—he didn't touch my face."

Beth shook violently from the agony of the torture and her own self-loathing for what she had allowed Ralph to do to Grace.

"Then, when that wasn't enough, he said he would kill you if I told anyone." Grace threw her head back letting a laugh burst out. "Now I've told you, so I suppose he will have to kill you." Her eyes were wide with animal rage. "But"—she clicked her tongue with a tsk— "he isn't around to follow through, is he?" She suddenly moved in close to her sister. The knife slowly pierced Beth's other arm. "This is going to take a while," Grace said with a venom ripe with age.

Beth's pupils were blown wide from the shock of the pain and terror of not knowing what would come next. Snot was dripping from her nose, down the gag. It was getting hard to breath. Her face was beet red from the effort of crying with her mouth secured and the pressure she generated from squeezing all of her neck and shoulder muscles tight in her vain effort to deal with the rising pain. She was moments from blacking out.

"Come to think of it, this is the knife I killed Ralph with." Grace quickly removed the blade and patched up the new wound. "Would you like to hear some music?" she asked as if she were soothing a sick daughter staying home from school. "I've downloaded some of your old favorites. You do remember turning the music up on the phonograph while Ralph and I played. I suppose you didn't want to hear my headboard banging against the wall. You poor thing!" She wiped her hand on the towel to make sure it was blood free before tapping her iPod to start the sound. The song was "This Girl Is a Woman Now" by Gary Puckett and the Union Gap.

While not loud enough to disturb her neighbors, the blaring sound was like another tool on Beth's shattered nerves. She could remember her boyfriend needing to use the bathroom. The first few times she assumed he was masturbating, but then, she did not really want to know. That was why she turned the record player up. Beth would have begged to die if her mouth was not gagged.

"You do remember the B side, don't you? 'His Other Woman.'" Grace smiled pointedly. She twisted her body to make the force of the next slap as hard as it could be. Her hand stung from the impact. It felt good. “At first he wanted me to enjoy the sex. Then it was just about him. I faked it as best I could.” A thousand-yard stare came to Grace’s eyes as she thought about Ralph’s abuse. “Sometimes I just tried to be still and look at the wall.” Beth passed out. Grace waved smelling salts under her nose. “There we are,” cooed Grace. “Are you ready to beg my forgiveness?” she said in a little-girl voice.

Beth nodded her head as solemnly as she could. She begged with her eyes.

“You knew, didn’t you?” Grace prodded.

Beth nodded her head almost imperceptibly. She had known. The torture had forced her to admit it to herself. Her guilt forced her to admit it to Grace.

“Yet you let him do it over and over and over again, didn’t you?”

Beth hung her head and nodded again.

Grace pinched Beth’s chin hard and brought their eyes together. “Do you want to know how I killed him? How I started my career as a cleaner? Maybe I should be thanking you. Just think, if you had had sex with Ralph, maybe I would have just been a homemaker,” she said wistfully.

Beth did not try to respond.

“He wanted sex, and instead of resisting, I encouraged it. He must have thought I’d finally come around to his way of thinking. You were at the store with Mother. It was just him and me. I brought him into the bedroom and sat on the edge of the bed and took off my blouse off.” Grace turned her head slightly and gave a wan smile. “I unbuckled his belt and slid his pants down. I kept rubbing him, sucking him for a bit. I had him in my complete control. I got him to lie down on the bed. I told him I what I wanted to do, and he let me. I tied his hands to the headboard. He was very excited. I think I actually enjoyed sex that time”—Grace paused for a moment—“knowing that I was about to kill him.” The thousand-yard stare returned. She refocused and continued. “I climbed on top of him and used his dick to stimulate myself. He was going mad with desire. I eventually inserted him and took my pleasure.” Grace’s eyes were wide in remembrance. “I reached under the pillow and pulled out this knife while he came and had his eyes closed. I slit his throat before he understood the danger.”

A knock at the door startled Beth. Hope grew in her that her punishment was near its end, that she might be rescued. That her sister would at least have to stop for a while to deal with the visitor.

Grace smiled, and the mirth in her face grew when she looked back from the front door. "Oh, Beth, I forgive you. But with forgiveness, there must also be punishment for the crime committed." Then, she asked in that same little-girl voice as before, "Are you ready for your punishment?" Grace moved to the door, looking back at Beth to see the hope in her eyes. Grace smiled devilishly and opened the door to reveal the visitor.

Beth's expression faded quickly at the sight of the burly, heavily tattooed man with a wicked grin of anticipation.

"Beth, meet Ralph. Ralph, meet Beth." Grace laughed at the absurdity of such a formal introduction. "You're finally going to get to fuck Ralph—well, not your Ralph. He's dead and buried in the neighbor's cistern."

TWENTY

A THOR POINT

November 22, 2009 — Somewhere in the Virginia Mountains

"BETTY, I NEED TO KNOW if you can refrain from killing someone," Tom said.

"Well, I haven't killed you yet. Does that count?" Betty smirked.

"Well, that does vouch for your restraint, but to cut to the chase, I need to have another meeting with Ernesto to go over how we are going to ensnare the Cabal in Vail." Tom waited for a visceral reaction. Betty's face flushed, but no objects flew at him.

Betty cleared her throat. "Is this a test?"

"No, I really need to have a strategy meeting with him. We can have no written or electronic communications. In fact, this meeting can only be called off, not set up." Tom leaned back in his leather office chair, which reminded him of his father and the blood connection he held with Ernesto.

You're such an asshat, thought Betty. "So, if I object, you'll call it off?"

Tom cleared his throat. "No, actually, I would just have you go to Vail now instead of waiting for the morning."

"You're such an asshat!" Betty considered throwing something at him. Maybe it was the propranolol or lithium. *Or maybe it was learning that José fucked around right up until his death*, thought Betty. Either way, she was trying harder to make it sound like she was more upset than she really was. *Maybe I can use Ernesto to squeeze more information out of Tom.* "OK, I promise I won't kill him if you promise to let me kill the next asshole who screws me over."

"Seems like a fair trade." Tom said, realizing that he would not likely have a choice in the next round.

"When?"

"Lunch."

Betty pursed her lips. "Well, I guess I better go put on my big-girl panties, then." She bumped into Gideon as she passed through the kitchen on her way to the bedroom. The steam rising from several pots on the stove smelled of garlic and citrus. "What's for lunch?"

Gideon grinned broadly and said, "Chimichurri-covered steaks, large-cut fries, sweetbread, and dulce de leche for dessert."

Betty smiled. "Make sure you put a side of arsenic in for Tom. He asked for it specifically."

Gideon started to agree, "Sur—hey, now!" He shook his head at her disapprovingly and said, "Tsk tsk."

Betty stuck her tongue out at Gideon and scrunched her nose. "You're no fun!" she said as she passed into the dining room and spied three place settings. Obviously for Tom, Ernesto, and herself. *I wonder, if I left my knife in here hidden, would the bodyguards find it or could I get across the table before they could stop me?* The thought lingered as she stood there. She no longer hated Ernesto enough to sacrifice herself to kill him. Or rather, her longing for revenge had waned, and what she had thought was love for José did not warrant losing her life over. But that did not mean she would pass up giving pain to someone who had wronged her, even if it was a small reminder instead of a blade in the heart. She went to the study and retrieved the sewing kit and removed a small needle. Returning to the dining room, she placed the shaft point out . . . It was angled toward the middle of the chair and would poke through the embroidered material from the pressure of being sat on. A lovely little surprise. Betty smiled and went to get ready for lunch.

†

The usual entourage accompanied Ernesto off the helicopter. Betty spotted the same big brutes as the last time. *Predictable. Same crew.*

Max moved to Gideon's side and two began comparing notes. The meeting was carefully orchestrated to ensure the safety of Tom and Ernesto. The helicopter left the helipad as soon as its passengers were clear and Max gave a thumbs-up. It would be on standby five minutes away under a camouflage canopy.

Tom walked up and embraced Ernesto like before. Betty cringed inside.

I was looking to kill this man for so many years. It was difficult for her to keep her hand away from her waistband. The agreement between the two teams was that they would be armed, just in case an external intruder appeared. And each had the right to fire on the other if any aggression was shown. Only through the most extreme restraint she had ever felt was Betty able to keep her hand by her side. "Showtime." Betty walked over to the protective agent teamed with Max. She extended her empty hand, arm stretched out with almost no bend in her elbow. "Betty."

"Thor," said the six-foot-four, two-hundred-twenty pounds of muscle.

"You're kidding, right?" Betty said.

"I was named after Thor Heyerdahl, the explorer, not the Norse god."

"Oh. Sorry."

"I'm Norwegian."

"I get it now." Betty wanted to let go of the handshake, but Thor was hanging on, testing her and her grip. "The Kon-Tiki voyage. Easter Island."

"Close. French Polynesia." Thor had his eyes locked on Betty's. Most men would have looked her up and down by now.

Betty gave her hand a quick squeeze and an up-and-down motion to signal it was time to let go. "You can let go now." He didn't.

"You are a beautiful soul. Dangerous as hell, I understand." Thor tried to pull her slightly closer. Testing her balance and determination.

"I'm going to count to three. If you don't let go, I am going to put my knee on your throat." Betty said. "One."

"I am much taller and stronger than you."

"Two."

"I don't bel—"

Betty gave Thor a slight push back so he would set his stance, then pulled him forward, using his resistance to pivot her body around him, pulling his arm down and back as she knocked his right leg out from under him. Thor buckled and landed on his chest. Betty pulled his arm and twisted his wrist until his fingers were by the nape of his neck.

Ligaments creaked. Thor grunted in pain. Betty put her knee into his back and pressed hard. "You got me. I didn't put my knee on your throat. That was a diversion."

Tom left Ernesto's side at the first sign of trouble and bent down to whisper into Betty's ear, "You know how I love to watch you work, but my half brother is wondering if you wouldn't mind letting his second-best bodyguard up off the ground. He doesn't want him broken."

Betty gave Thor an extra little tug before letting go, just to make sure he knew what she was capable of. When she stood over him, she offered her hand to help him up.

He hesitated, but took the proffered hand. After getting back on his feet, he brushed off his clothes and smiled to acknowledged he had been bested—this time. "You have a strong grip."

"I'm lucky, it was an uneven surface, or who knows what would have happened."

"Yes, of course." Thor welcomed a return of his dignity. "Two out of three?" he asked with a raised eyebrow.

Ernesto scowled. "On your own time, Thor, not mine," he scolded.

Twenty-One

Operation!

November 22, 2009 — Salizar Clinic, Århus, Denmark

"ERIC, IT'S YOU, NOT ME." Jil said.

"Probably for the best," Dr. Salizar said with his best bedside manner. "With this new procedure, I will be quite busy for the next year."

"What new procedure?" Jil had not been in the loop.

"We can turn back the clock on aging. Using DNA, nanoparticles, herbs, and secret ingredients, wrinkles go away and your skin becomes baby smooth again." Eric moved closer to Jil and looked at her smoke-damaged face. The puckering was starting to show, her crow's-feet becoming resistant to her cosmetics. "I thought you knew. Casper knows."

Jil turned away from Eric, knowing what he saw around the corners of her mouth and tired eyes. "Fuck Casper. If he hadn't kept me busy arranging things instead of attending to my mom, you would have gotten to her weeks ago."

Eric considered that for a moment, then reached his left hand out to Jil, almost touching the skin of her face. "I could do your face for you, no charge. It's the least I could do."

Jil felt the emotional twitch of her ego. The corners of her mouth involuntarily started to go wide at the thought of the procedure, which only reminded her of the damage to her skin and the short shelf life left of her beauty. Her chin quavered as she fought back tears. *I can't let him see me be weak about my looks.* Jil fought her chin and changed the subject back to her mother. "That would be lovely, Eric, but that won't bring back my mom."

"Jil, you know I love you and care deeply about you, so please—I would have done anything to save her, but she needed surgery long before you came to me." He looked down at his feet. "Even with my techniques and drugs, it's obvious to me now that it would have been a miracle for her to survive the table, let alone more than a few months."

"That is cold comfort, Eric."

"Think of Ruth—she has been spared." Eric wistfully thought of how Jil had seduced him, the sex and breakfast in bed. Her easy ways of pleasing him, the way she made his life comfortable and pleasurable, and yet, how her quicksilver temper could end those luxuries. "I wish there had been more I could have done—for you."

Jil lost it. She could not contain her egocentric self any longer. "Fuck you! Fuck Ruth! Fuck my mother! *Both* my parents are dead, and my sister will never speak to me again." She scowled at him. "If someone—Casper—had lifted a finger a year ago, I wouldn't be in this spot." Jil turned to leave Eric's office, stepping sideways and pushing a lamp over before slamming the office door. As she passed Claire's desk, she could not resist one last insult. "Cunt!"

Gil caught her as she rounded the corner. "Whoa, there." He had just come out of the secure communications room, having just briefed David on the death of Linda and Larry. He, in turn, had been updated on the convergence in Vail of all the actors and instructed to make sure Jil would be there. He turned to face the same direction as her and took her arm in his. "Let's go get a cup of coffee, laced with Baileys, OK?"

Jil snuggled into his shoulder and took a deep breath. "My knight in shining armor."

Gil's phone vibrated along with "The Imperial March," better known as Darth Vader's theme, which meant he had a message from Bud. *Jesus, he's been fucking with my ringtones again.*

Jil noticed the buzzing and said, "That isn't—"

Gil blushed slightly. "Yes, it is. My tech guru is the world's biggest nerd." Gil glanced at the message: *Find out who Casper is.* He deleted it with a swipe of his finger. "Yep, some software update he wants me to load. It can wait."

"Wow, your own personal nerd?" Jil pursed her lips and raised an eyebrow to signal faux respect. "Where do I get one?"

"Comes with the job. Total desk jockey who's never worked in the field. Always making suggestions that don't make any sense, at least to me." Gil chided himself for his lack of control. He felt like he had diarrhea of the mouth, sentences rolling out long after he should have stopped. *What is it about her that makes me forget my priorities, and feel the need to explain everything?*

Twenty-Two

Thor Loser

November 22, 2009 — Somewhere in the Virginia Mountains

ERNESTO'S TOUR OF THE HOUSE ended at the living room bar, where he and Tom leaned against the walnut slab with a live edge while Gideon expertly prepared Manhattans. Max watched over his preparations while Thor stood guard outside. With a pinch, Gideon extracted the essential oil of the orange rind while simultaneously igniting it with a Zippo, the burst of flame popping over each of the drinks. With a final snap of the lighter's cap, he announced the completion of his concoctions and served up their drinks.

Ernesto looked around at the others. He controlled fifty trillion dollars' worth of investments, Tom headed Control—arguably the most secretive and powerful spy organization in the world—and Betty just controlled her temper. "A toast to Betty," he began. He raised his glass and continued. "To the spy who could have killed me, the woman I wish I was young enough to pursue, and a soul as complicated and beautiful as this drink."

Tom and Betty clinked glasses with Ernesto, the trio took sips, and all nodded their approval to Gideon standing to the side. Tom saw something in Betty's look that told him there was going to be trouble.

"Betty, I'm sorry, but Ernesto and I have some catching up to do—about our mutual father." Tom said.

"You're fucking kidding, right?" Betty replied. "Did I say that out loud?" she added, rolling her eyes.

Max stepped forward, prepared to do his best to protect Ernesto. Gideon moved slowly around the bar to protect . . . Betty if Max moved against her, or Tom . . . for the first time since taking the job as Tom's protector, he was not one hundred percent sure what he would do.

Tom stepped between Betty and the rest and whispered into her ear, "This is exactly why I wanted you in that room last time. You need to check your emotions and decide why you are here."

Betty reached down and grabbed Tom's balls. "Maybe you should be wondering when I'm going to cut them off, not if. Stop being a little prick to me." She let go and walked to the patio to get some air. She approached Thor, who was scanning the sky with Gideon's binoculars. Thor handed them to her.

"Kicked out of the meeting, I see," Thor said.

"You seriously don't want to piss me off, Thor."

Thor rubbed his shoulder involuntarily. "It wasn't a fair fight."

"How do you figure, tiger?"

"I was assuming you were a girl."

"Yeah, and I was assuming you were a man." Betty handed Thor back the binoculars and walked away, toward the far end of the patio. The moon was rising. The sun had passed behind the mountain range thirty minutes before, which made for a strange marriage of light and shadow. The valley was still bright, yet fading fast; the far range was lit spectacularly, yet on the patio the lights had come on to compensate for the darkness of the mountain's shadow.

Betty scanned the valley with her unaided vision and spotted a vague movement down below. "Yo, God of Thunder, give me the binoculars."

Thor walked over and handed her the set. "I was named after the adventurer, not the god."

"Obviously, 'cause if you had any god in you, you would have spotted the climbers in the valley." She handed the lenses back to Thor and pointed where he should look.

"*For fanden!*" Thor swore.

"Yeah, those aren't walking sticks they're holding." Betty walked over to the patio door and rapped to get Gideon's attention. She pointed at him and Max and waved them out.

"What?" Gideon asked as he came through the sliding-glass door.

"Three scouts below, about a half mile down, coming for us."

Gideon and Max walked to where Thor was keeping track of the approaching men. Each took a turn assessing the situation.

"I don't see any SAMs—do you want to call in your bird?" Gideon asked Max while checking his phone for the radar images that might show other threats.

Max used his phone to call down to the pilot and ordered him up immediately as he walked back into the living room. He leaned into Ernesto and whispered that the helicopter was coming to take them away.

Tom and Ernesto came to the door but stayed inside while Max rejoined the others.

"Jesus, you guys are a bunch of pussies," Betty said as she walked over to the chest Gideon kept stocked with defensive weapons. For a moment she paused over the rocket launcher before picking up the sniper rifle. "Windage?" she asked.

Gideon looked below at several known areas. "Maybe five knots, pretty calm. Remember—"

"I've done a mountain rotation. I know what I'm doing," Betty said as she set up the rifle over the edge of the patio in a spot designed for shooting downhill. "Max, tell the bird to hover high—I want my targets deaf and dumb."

Max passed the request to the pilot and took the binoculars from Thor. As the helicopter approached, the men looked up, raised their weapons, but did not fire.

Betty took a deep breath, let it out slow, took another, and began firing. The first shot was long. Firing downhill and with a slight swirling wind made it a difficult shot. Betty saw the bullet hit ten feet behind her mark; she adjusted her scope for her next shot. She dropped the farthest intruder first so the others would not notice, then the second man. Perhaps the leader sensed something—or maybe he was just concerned by the helicopter sitting above him without moving. He looked over his shoulder at his comrades, but it was too late to hide. A pink mist told Betty everything she needed to know. She took no pleasure from killing, but eliminating bad guys by doing her job well did give her satisfaction. Her dreams were still haunted by the death of Slim, even if he deserved such a grisly end.

"Very impressive," Max said. He ordered the pilot to take the helicopter back to the holding area.

"Shouldn't we use the helicopter to sweep the area?" Gideon asked.

"Helmut was scanning while he hovered. We are clear for many kilometers. I am confident your agent"—Max gestured at Betty as if both his hands were holding a rifle—"has eliminated the threat."

Ernesto and Tom came up to their protectors to get their reports. Tom pulled Gideon aside and asked, "What was that all about?"

"Good question. I'll fly the drone down and see what these guys had on them."

"Good. I don't want you or anyone else going down there until we know there isn't going to be any other attempt. We only need an hour, maybe two to finish what has to be done."

"I think we're good for that much time." Gideon nodded, then headed to a closet to retrieve his drone. The controller had a screen built in for viewing the camera footage, though it could be viewed on any computing device connected via wireless.

Betty grabbed a tablet to watch the feed and sat down in one of the patio chairs. "This should be interesting." She usually confirmed her sniper kills with a scope. This was the first time she would see up close the damage she had wrought.

Tom and Ernesto retreated to the bar area and continued planning the Vail operation in private. Max moved to the doorway to stay close to Ernesto while Thor scanned the valley with the binoculars. Thor really wanted to watch the drone footage instead, but his pride forced him to keep on the lookout instead of admiring Betty's work.

As Gideon guided the craft to the kill zone, he called out to Thor, "You should check this out—impressive."

"Leave him alone, Gideon, me kicking his ass is a Thor point."

"You saying he's a *Thor* loser?"

"I can hear you," Thor said. "Maybe you and I should dance, Gideon."

"You'd have to go through me first," Betty said.

Thor returned to looking through the binoculars.

"Geez, Betty, try not to pour salt on an open *Thor*," Gideon said.

The drone's video feed showed the carnage wrought by the .50 caliber Barrett sniper rifle combined with Betty's accuracy. Her face showed a mixture of pride and disgust. She had been raised by her adopted parents to be a weapon for Control; seeing how well they succeeded and knowing who they really were—and their motives—diminished her warm fuzzy feeling about her triumph. The remaining features of the men's faces showed jawlines and noses reminiscent of . . . holy shit, Gil and Michel's cousins. "Gideon, see if they have any visible tattoos. On their forearms."

Gideon complied. "Nope, can't see anything, they are all covered up. I'll have to go down and check it out after our guests leave." Gideon brought the drone back to the patio. "What makes you ask about tattoos?"

"Those guys could be cousins of Michel or Gil by their looks, probably Belarusians. We've seen a common tattoo marking them as members of the Cabal. A dragon on the forearm."

Max tapped her shoulder with his right index finger while rolling up his sleeve with his left hand. "You mean like this?"

Twenty-Three

Russian Rule-ette, Anyone?

November 20, 2009 — Near Bern, Switzerland

"MS. HASPBERGER—" PIERRE'S SON attended a prestigious boarding school in Switzerland. He had not seen any of his children in several years. He had to think for a moment how old the ones from his second marriage were. "Peppin is a mature boy."

Ms. Haspberger was not pleased. "Yes, your son is quite mature for his age; in fact, I do not know of any other twelve-year-olds attempting to have sex at this institution."

Pierre wished the boy's mother were around to manage this problem, but seeing as how she died during one of his more severe episodes of sadism following his disgrace brought on by the crash of 2008, Pierre was left with managing the occasional parental detail himself. Her death was ruled a suicide and he sent the children, Peppin and Sophia, off to Switzerland for year-round schooling. "Ms. Haspberger, please have the poor child's parents contact me directly. In the meantime, might I suggest a sexual education curriculum be added—a donation will be forwarded to cover the cost. And be assured that Peppin will be disciplined appropriately."

Ms. Haspberger sputtered and began to complain but Pierre ended the call as Gustav barged into his study.

"You—you have-ve ne . . . nerve!" Gustav strained to get his words out. He usually had better control of his stuttering by using acting techniques like exaggerated enunciation and slowing down his cadence. Unfortunately, he was awash in an emotional fit of anger over being shunted from his financial duties.

Pierre stood up and puffed out his chest, preparing to go on the offensive to keep Gustav stuttering, but he stopped moving and slowly let out his breath when he saw the old-fashioned revolver aimed at his chest.

Gustav took a deep breath himself and tried to calm his mind. He focused on his animal spirit, the sloth, and deepened his voice. The words came out eloquently, without a stutter. "As Chekhov said, once a gun is shown on the wall, it must be used." He waved the Colt 1851 Navy like a professor admonishing his student with a piece of chalk.

Pierre twisted his face slightly. "I have no idea what the hell you are talking about—Chekhov? Gustav! Put that damn thing away. You'll probably just blow your damn hand off." Pierre stretched out his hand, half offering, half demanding the pistol from his younger half brother.

Gustav narrowed his eyes. "I'll see you in hell first." He pulled the hammer back, aimed the revolver first at Pierre's heart, then his groin, and finally at his feet. "Dance!" he demanded as he fired a round through his brother's foot.

Pierre fell to the floor. "You fucking idiot!" He pulled off his loafer and writhed in pain as he inspected the wound. "You shot me!"

With great control and paced speech, Gustav declared, "No shit, Sherlock. Go fuck yourself." He spun around and left the study, a newfound confidence in his stride. He had never in all his years allowed himself to seek such gratifying revenge from Pierre. He no longer cared that he would be managing the shipping business. For once, he had told the son of a bitch what was what—and had inflicted the pain instead of receiving it. Gustav smiled and began to whistle as he headed to the armory to put the pistol back. It was an original, unfired-until-that-moment, vintage pistol. It hadn't even occurred to him that it might not fire. After placing the revolver back into its velvet-lined home, he snatched the wooden case and took it back to his quarters. He decided to have it mounted on a wood plaque to hang in his home office. A token of his right of passage long delayed.

†

Pierre pushed his index finger into the hole leading to the shattered bone in his foot, the third metatarsal, and blacked out. When he came to, he did it again, and passed out again. He found it odd that no one came to check on him or to investigate the sound of the cartridge exploding. Almost as odd as his sudden desire to inflict pain on himself. The third time he poked his finger into the wound, the pain was excruciating, but he did not pass out. A wave of desire and sadness overcame him. He wanted the pain to be severe enough to lose consciousness. He wanted to know the boundary he had just crossed in an exquisitely twisted way. Pierre had frequently caused others—such as Peppin's mother—to pass out from the pain, but he had never experienced it himself. He wondered if the third time was from lack of will to induce enough pain or if he was becoming used to that repeated exposure. He poked his finger through the bottom of his foot instead. When he awoke the third time, Pierre wiped his bloody hand off on his trousers and called his butler for aid. The man took him to the bedroom, Pierre hopping on one foot with his arm over the smaller man's shoulder. Once prostrate on the bedding, he insisted his man tie him down and prod the wound multiple times to induce blackout. Pierre eventually just writhed in pain and screamed for the butler to stop, which he didn't immediately, later claiming he was following orders, else why would he have been instructed to tie Pierre's hands and ankles to the bed.

With the experiment in masochism completed and the wound cleaned and bound, Pierre sought out his brother Gustav.

Time had diminished Gustav's bravado, but he attempted to restore it with thoughts of the plaque he had designed in his mind. "What can I do for you, Pierre?"

Pierre, using a single crutch and his left foot in a plastic boot, hobbled forward another step. "This will sound strange, Gustav, but I came to thank you for shooting me. For the first time, I've experienced a level of pain I—well, the type of pain I usually mete out. It was enlightening."

"Shall I shoot you again?"

"Hah!" Pierre expelled his entire breath, half giddy with the thought of experiencing the exquisite pain and half desiring to shoot his brother so Gustav would know it himself. "That won't be necessary." He considered his next words carefully. "I want you to tell me about what you were doing with the rare earth metal investments in China."

Gustav worked to control his excitement; he did not want to start stuttering. "Ah. So, you recognize the importance of controlling a commodity through multiple entities."

"Yes, I see the genius of what you were doing. I want to build on that and use it to leverage our portfolio—I want to inflict precise pain on manufacturers. I want to cause predictable, to me, spikes in pricing so that I can reap the reward of a cornered market without anyone knowing it is cornered." Pierre placed a folder with economic data, company analysis, and several government official biographies on Gustav's desk.

Gustav briefly looked at several pages. "I think I see what you are after. Yes, we could make a few billion on this."

Pierre snorted, "Billions? We'll make a trillion. But I need you to look over it completely. I don't want Charles to blame me for the next global financial implosion."

Gustav cocked his head. "What do I get out of this?"

Pierre swallowed and squinted his eyes. He did not want to give away too much. "Besides a tidy profit?"

"Yes, besides the possibility that you are correct and we don't cause another meltdown—or at least in causing it, we scrape all the wealth off to ourselves this time—what are you suggesting? What if you're wrong?"

Pierre swallowed again. "I'll let you shoot my other foot."

He looked away for a moment, not believing he was wrong, but a part of him wanted Gustav to shoot his other foot, to experience the blackout pain again. He wondered if this is what drove Marie to his chambers. If this is what kept Peppin's mother from leaving him. He wondered if giving up control to receive pain was better than having control to exert pain.

Gustav leaned back in his chair. "Interesting."

Twenty-Four

Tats the Point

November 22, 2009 — Somewhere in the Virginia Mountains

THE TATTOO ON MAX'S ARM was identical to the ones Betty had seen, and Tom confirmed with a his nod. He had seen the tattoo in person when he double-tapped his tail, Boris from the Belarusian embassy, in the shoulders on the trail to the Omni Shoreham Hotel through Rock Creek Park in Washington, D.C.

"Gideon, I need you and Thor to stay on guard. Betty, Ernesto, Max, I need you to come with me to the dining room," Tom said.

Shit. The last thing I need right now. "Tom, I need to tell—" Betty tried to warn him about the needle, but he interrupted her by holding up his index finger, signaling it needed to wait. "Fine, you'll find out soon enough," she said with a scowl on her face.

The group entered the dining room, which had security provisions for private conversations. Seals lowered on the doors, and an interference system was engaged to prevent various forms of eavesdropping. A device created a humming sound on the exterior wall, which was not physically attached to the inner wall. There were no windows for lasers to bounce off of to "hear" a conversation; an electronic jamming system prevented any possible bugging from working, be it a lapel pin or other device. During the Cold War, the CIA had mistakenly allowed an ornate wood carving of the great seal of the United States to be installed in the ambassador's office in Moscow, not knowing that a passive transmitter was smuggled inside. Tom Sr. had been aware of such devices and made every effort to make his hideaway a place where any kind of conversation could be had, be it a state secret or the tender words of his latest paramour. Tom Jr. now waved everyone to their seats, and just before he sat down, Betty tried one more time to warn him.

“Tom,” she said while rolling her eyes.

“Son of a bitch!” Tom jumped from his chair and looked down. Betty gave him an impish grin and a tilt of her head.

“I tried to warn you.” She looked at Max and Ernesto, who were hovering over their seats, about to sit but hesitating. “What? He pissed me off. Your seats are safe—at least from me.”

Tom’s face was pinched and his lips pursed as he pointed his index finger at Betty with a slight downward motion to emphasis his next sound, “Nnnhhn.” His lips parted slightly to reveal gritted teeth. Ernesto and Max sat down slowly, trying to show more faith than they had that the seats were not booby-trapped.

“As I was about to say, we are now in a secure room. No one can hear what we are saying, nor can any recording device pick up an intelligible signal. What I am about to tell you cannot be spoken about in any other venue for the safety of all in this room.” Tom almost made a signal to cut off Betty, who wanted to interrupt, but considered the pin incident and allowed her to interject. “Yes, Betty.”

“I’m sorry about the pin.”

“Anything else before I reveal why we are sequestered in here while murderous goons are trying to stealthily attack our perimeter?” Tom asked.

“No, I just wanted you to know you deserved it, but that I’m sorry I sunk to the temptation,” she answered.

“Well. Thank you.” Tom took the napkin at his place setting and wiped his brow. “OK. Max, please show us your tattoo again.” Max obliged. “Max is a Control agent who went undercover immediately after joining. He has infiltrated the Cabal as a protector. It has taken ten years for him to work his way to being head of Ernesto’s protection detail.”

Ernesto interjected, “I did not know this.” He looked at Max with one eyebrow raised. “You have served me without fail.” He looked at Tom. “I am surprised you did not kill me before the lovely Betty interrogated me.”

“We are at the beginning of the apex of a plan that was put in place sixty years ago to counteract the Cabal’s plans. Sometimes things that appear to be our main thrust are merely feints to distract you.”

“Such as . . ” It was Betty’s turn to look at Tom with one eyebrow raised.

"If everyone would just sit on their hands and let me tell the story—" Tom's voice had risen in volume. "I'm sorry. Please just let me tell the tall tale about how my father planned for this very day before you, Max, and I were born. Please?"

Betty, Ernesto, and Max all nodded briefly.

"He planned several scenarios. First was to get control of the accounting of the Cabal; second was to disrupt their operations whenever appropriate; third was to train operatives to be placed into the Cabal structure. Max, you know your role." Tom nodded at Max. "Max's family was placed into Belarus during the Cold War. He was trained and guided to become a special forces member and purposely trained in many languages, and not to expose his knowledge of those he did not learn in his formal education."

Tom slid a small box covered in felt to Max. "This is your only reward for having faithfully upheld your part of the bargain."

Max opened the box and revealed an intricate jewel-encrusted egg. "Is it . . . ?"

"Yes, from the czar's personal collection. It is a Fabergé worth one point four million dollars at auction. A lot less if you take it to the pawnshop."

Max looked bewildered. "I don't know what to say."

Tom nodded his head and looked earnestly at him. "This is also your parents' reward, but I understand they passed several years ago," Tom said for the benefit of the others.

"Yes, they died not knowing what I was doing, but I did make their funerals."

Tom raised his water glass and was about to take a sip when he looked at Betty and asked, "This isn't poisoned, is it?"

Betty tilted her head and raised an eyebrow. "No, should it be?"

Tom sipped his water and continued. "Ernesto is my father's son. He told me, in one of his many beyond the grave missives Gideon gives me—"

Betty interrupted, "Sealed with red wax."

Tom nodded his head slowly and tried to grin. "Sealed with red wax, yes." Tom looked directly at his half brother. "Ernesto, Father said that he could not return to Buenos Aires to be with you and your mother personally. He loved her too much, so much that he would have given up

Control for her, so it was for the best that he never see her again."

Ernesto sniffed slightly. "I still have the letters he sent to her. They are the one possession I have kept all these years and carried with me everywhere. But they ended when she died and I entered the Jesuit school." He drew out of his sport coat a packet of letters bound with a rubber band. They were tattered and worn from constant reading. One in particular showed what was left of a red wax seal on an envelope. Ernesto wiped his eyes. "Why did he stop writing?"

Tom leaned back. "He didn't. The Jesuits withheld his letters, and he lost track of you when you moved on. They kept their part of the bargain, to train you to be the best possible accountant and financial manager the world would ever not know about." Tom took an envelope from his stack of papers, one that matched those in Ernesto's collection. "This is his last letter to you, written before he died." He slid it to Ernesto who, with shaking hands, opened the long-delayed message.

After reading the letter several times while everyone either watched or tried to avert their eyes, Ernesto said, "I understand." He removed a handkerchief from his breast pocket and blew his nose, took a sip of water, and said, "Please continue."

Tom cleared his throat. "Betty and I were never supposed to become lovers or significant others. That is where I strayed from the plan. I was supposed to just do a checkup by meeting you, using Surry as a tool to get to know you and ascertain if your training was complete. You were to fall in love with José and marry him, and be activated later as an agent after he had taken over Ernesto's role as head Cabal accountant."

Betty kicked Tom under the table. "What the fuck, Tom!"

Tom flinched and winced. "Betty, in front of Max and my brother Ernesto, I am here to tell you that I did not obey my father because I love you. Please let me tell the damn story without killing me—you might enjoy the ironic twist."

Betty sat back with her arms folded. "Go on."

"Because my father lost contact and control of Ernesto, he engaged a backup plan to replace Ernesto, but he was not ready to retire. And besides, José had a serious character flaw."

Ernesto nodded. "This is true. Both parts." He let Tom continue.

"José was Ernesto's equal as an accountant and financial planner, well versed in world economics and definitely under our father's thumb, but we needed an insurance plan regarding him." Tom pointed at Betty. "You were to be José's wife to manage and correct him as needed. Unfortunately, well, you know what happened."

Betty leaned in and squinted her eyes. "Tell me anyway."

Tom continued, "You interrupted Michel and Slim's attempt to persuade José to find different work. They went too far, Slim was a sadist, so they killed José to cover their tracks and fled out the window." Tom looked down at his glass and paused to let that seep into Betty. "As I have already explained to you in a previous conversation—and showed you the evidence—José was not faithful. Ernesto entrapped him, and Michel was trying to use the evidence to convince him he needed to let go of replacing Ernesto."

"So, what was your father's new plan for me, then?" Betty asked.

"He encouraged me to terminate you, especially after you went rogue to rescue Gil." Tom pursed his lips. "He did not have any further ideas on how to use you and just wanted you and your parents to go away. Their usefulness had ended as well, which is another subject entirely."

"What a peach, your old man," Betty said.

"Yes. Everyone was expendable." Tom moved his pen and straightened the stack of papers in front of him. "Except perhaps me." Tom looked up." But I wouldn't bet on it—I was the only option left for his replacement, so that is why I wasn't sacrificed . . . somehow."

"Nice to have insurance," said Betty.

"I was *your* insurance, which is why he considered other options besides me. I wasn't as dependable as he wanted." Tom leaned back in his chair.

After a long pause, Max asked, "What next?"

Twenty-Five

Quick, Follow Me!

November 22, 2009 —Århus, Denmark

JIL PUSHED THE LAST OF her coffee laced with Baileys Irish cream away from her and backed the chair from the table. She excused herself by placing her left hand on Gil's shoulder while leaning over, exposing the better part of her breasts, and placing her right hand on his crotch. "Give me a minute, then join me for a quickie in the lady's room?" she whispered into Gil's ear before tonguing it.

Gil had become used to Jil's proclivity for public sex acts; it seemed to be her way of controlling the men in her life while showing disdain for the normal decorum average people provided to those around them. He watched her saunter away, exaggerating the swing of her hips and flipping her hair back over her shoulder as she leered one last time at him before taking command of the women's restroom. Gil leaned back in his chair and sipped his coffee. The drink had cooled somewhat, but the creamy texture of the Bailey's lingered in his mouth. The taste reminded him of Sally. He had not spoken to or seen her in over a year. "Why now?" he quietly asked himself. When he was captured by Ernesto's men and held prisoner by Michel, Sally had never entered his mind—only Betty and the hope of her coming to rescue him, as desperate and implausible as that seemed. It dawned on Gil that the connection was the use of sex. He had no illusions about Jil's or Sally's willingness to fuck any man or woman who stood between them and their goal. Unlike Betty—who as a Control agent, did it out of duty—Jil and Sally took pleasure from manipulating others. He shrugged his shoulders in resignation and put the cup down on a twenty-euro note for the staff. *I'm sure they'll earn it cleaning the bathroom*, he thought.

Twenty-Six

I'll Be Back in a Flashbang

November 22, 2009 — Somewhere in the Virginia Mountains

BETTY PUSHED HER CHAIR BACK from the table and said, "I don't know about you guys, but hearing I was to be killed—just because my existence was a threat to your dad"—she pointed her finger at Tom and then looked at Ernesto—"kind of just makes me hungry."

Tom checked his phone to see if there were any status updates he might have missed. Nothing new; Gideon and Thor were still on guard. "Can you wait just a little longer? Thirty more minutes?"

Betty harrumphed. "Feed me or I kill someone."

Tom rolled his eyes but relented and unlocked the sealed door to the kitchen. "OK. Is fifteen minutes long enough for you to get a plate of food and go to the restroom?"

Betty narrowed her eyes and pursed her lips. "I'll make do." Betty looked back at the door as it sealed the three men inside the soundproof isolation room. She entered the kitchen and spied Gideon and Thor through the window They were peering over the edge of the patio at the valley below. She grabbed an apple off the counter and took a large bite out of it. As she turned back to face the rattling window, she spit the apple out and dropped the rest while reaching for her SIG Sauer P229. A shock wave had knocked both men back from the edge and laid them on their backs, unconscious. "Shit," Betty whispered through clenched teeth. She started running at full speed through the house to the safe room and weapons cache. Betty pressed the hidden button under the bed frame so that a large drawer opened from underneath, exposing a rocket launcher, MP5 submachine guns, hand grenades, flashbangs, and canisters of ammunition. She strapped on what she could and used a pillowcase to gather the loose items. Within a minute she was fully armed and moving out the hidden entrance at the back of the house, built into the mountainside, and up a shaft to a sealed manhole. The exit was shielded from view by a circle of evergreen shrubbery and the terrain beyond could be surveyed with a remote camera system. Using the image feed displayed on a monitor by the exit, Betty determined the area was empty of any immediate threat. She opened the hatch and exited, stopping long enough at the protective hedge to see her path was clear to the lip. Moving to the edge of the roof on her belly, she could see Gideon and Thor, now trussed up with their backs to each other, with duct tape over their mouths, and their captors communicating with someone else. A third man was moving toward the patio door with his noise-suppressed CTAR-21 at the ready. Looking in the distance, she could now hear a helicopter and then spotted the Sikorsky S-70, the civilian version of a Black Hawk military helicopter. This one had .50 caliber machine guns mounted on the belly and was painted to blend in with the mountain terrain. Betty tossed two flashbang grenades down onto the patio, then—without mercy—she aimed her MP5 at the man directly below her by the patio door, who got a burst in the head. She quickly stepped back, covered her ears, and turned away from the patio. After the flashbangs detonated, she set up the PZR Grom anti-aircraft launcher and returned to the roof edge. The helicopter was approaching. She armed and launched the guided missile and then returned to the protection of the manhole shielding as the impact resonated in the valley below. She had only a few seconds to get down to the patio to deal with the intruders before they could recover. To give herself more time, she threw down two more flashbangs. Their eyes would be stunned for only five seconds, but the hundred-seventy-decibel noise would cause them to lose their balance. *Poor Gideon. I'll blame the bangs on Thor—god of thunder*, mused Betty. Peering over the edge, she could see two remaining intruders moaning on the ground, doing their best to recover. She could not get down quickly enough to subdue them without risking injury to herself. *I suppose Tom will want to ask a few questions.* The one closest to the edge was treated with several bursts to the back and legs. Then she decided, *Only need one to question*, and she carefully aimed and shot the closer one, who seemed subordinate, in the head.

Betty looked to the valley and saw the S-70's debris strewn on the side of the mountain. A scar of burning aluminum with occasional flashing of rounds from the belt feeding into the .50 caliber machine guns as the heat ignited the powder. "Fucking assholes."

Betty returned down the manhole, grabbed a fresh apple from the kitchen, and returned to the dining room. As she re-entered through the sealed door, the men leapt up at the site of a massively armed Betty, casually biting her apple.

"Betty, what the fuck?" Tom asked.

Max stepped between Betty and Ernesto and drew his pistol, which seemed unremarkable and inadequate compared with Betty's arsenal.

"We have some visitors. You seriously couldn't hear the flashbangs?" she asked. She shrugged her shoulders, took another bite of her apple, and walked out. Over her shoulder she threw out an aside to Tom. "Oh, I kept one alive, for now, so be careful."

Twenty-Seven

That Would Be To Go, Not for Here

November 22, 2009 — Århus, Denmark

GIL IGNORED THE POUNDING on the door and finished climaxing inside Jil, who was clawing at his back and moaning loudly. The voice on the other side of the door was speaking first in High German but then repeated the question in English.

"What the fuck are you doing in there! This is not a hotel."

Jil laughed and replied, "Just freshening up. Out in a jiffy." She pulled her panties back on and smoothed her skirt before sliding her feet back into her Jimmy Choos.

Gil tucked his shirt back in and looked in the mirror to smooth his hair, which was too short to comb, really. He reached out a hand to steady Jil as she settled into her shoes. "Ready?"

"Yes. I'm famished, aren't you?" Jil licked her lips.

"I could use some lunch, sure." Gil agreed. He pointed to her nose and the white residue clinging to her nostrils.

Jil looked in the mirror and wiped her nose while sniffing. "Where should we dine?" she asked.

"I know just the place, but we'll have to suffer with lunch on the plane to get a great meal tonight."

They pushed through the restroom door and past the manager of the coffee shop, whose face was beet red and sweaty from the pounding and yelling. The duo smiled broadly as they swept past the embarrassed patrons, who averted their eyes for the most part.

"I just have the most awful hankering for Italian."

"And pray tell, where is dinner going to be?" Jil asked.

"Does it really matter? Just a place I know in Vail. We can be settled and squared away in time for opening day of skiing Friday—they just got twenty-five inches of fresh powder."

Jil stopped on the sidewalk with her left hand on her hip as she adjusted her bag. "And whose jet are we taking?"

Gil tilted his head slightly and raised an eyebrow "Air Canada coach OK?" He could not maintain the ruse at the sight of Jil's mouth puckered as if she had just sucked on a lemon. "I'll have a G6 ready in an hour. It'll take us longer to go collect our things and get to the airport. Lobster for lunch, or filet mignon?"

Jil smiled and said, "Only if there is Dom Pérignon and fresh asparagus to go along with the lobster."

Gil mirrored her smile. "Done." He took out his phone and connected to Bud. "I need the G6 fueled for cross-Atlantic travel."

Bud started typing commands and notes into his keyboard. The crew was alerted via their smartphones before he finished the sentence, "Welcome to Air Contraire. Any special requests for this flight?"

"Two meals, lobster with fresh asparagus, and a bottle of Dom Pérignon." Gil looked at Jil and considered their drinking habits. "Make that two bottles of Pérignon."

"Any particular vintage, since we're living large and you're ahead of schedule?"

Gil smiled and replied, "Oh, any in their prime will do." He hit the remote control to unlock the car and walked slightly ahead of Jil to open the passenger side. Jil flashed a sweet smile.

Bud tapped away, sending the food order to the caterer along with the liquor request. The caterer would also prepare meals for the flight crew, each pilot getting a different meal in case of accidental food poisoning. "Anything else? A magic pony, maybe?"

"I think we're set." Gil held the car door open for Jil with his free hand. "See you shortly."

Bud finished typing the orders and in an officious tone said, "Thanks for flying Air Contraire."

"All set?" Jil asked after Gil settled into the driver's seat.

Gil checked for traffic before putting the BMW into drive. "All set." He pulled out and into the light traffic. "Anywhere special you want to spend the first night?"

"Hmm. I happen to have a place we can use at the Ritz-Carlton." Jil smiled a satisfied grin. "Maybe even the penthouse, if it's available."

"Living large." Gil replied "Living large."

Twenty-Eight

Don't Take This Personally

November 22, 2009 — Somewhere in the Virginia Mountains

HOWELL HURRIED TO THE PATIO and knelt beside Gideon and Thor. Betty advanced to the still-living attacker, who was moaning in pain, he had opened his shirt to inspect his wounds only to cause his intestines to spill out of his open gut. The burst of three hollow-point 9mm rounds Betty had put through the man's back had opened a grave wound in his abdomen. A large pool of blood was growing underneath him. If he received immediate medical attention he would survive, though it would take a skilled surgeon to stitch his innards back together. Without proper care within twenty-four hours, he would die a painful death, even with a blood transfusion.

"Gil, get him an IV," Betty said before she realized she was talking to Max. "Never mind, cover him. I'll go get one." She returned to the kitchen and removed two saline bags, an O positive blood IV, and a small handful of morphine syrettes from the refrigerator. She returned to Max looking over the wounded man, who was doing his best to stuff his guts back into his abdomen. Howell had used Gideon's own knife to cut the plastic cuffs from him and Thor; they were removing their gags and sorting themselves out.

Howell gave Gideon back his knife and walked over to Max, Betty, and the dying commando. He stood back a bit and asked, "What's your plan?" He kept operational protocol by not using her name. Something Betty had forgotten when referring to Max as Gil. Something he would have to remind her of—later.

"I don't suppose one of you is a medic?" Betty asked as she held out the IV bags.

Gideon walked over. "I'll do in a pinch." He reached out to Betty and took a saline bag.

Betty knelt down near the man. He posed little threat in his current condition, but she stayed just far enough away that he could not lunge at her and gain control. "Do you speak English?" she asked.

The man nodded his head slightly.

"My man is going to give you a liter of saline IV. You're dying." She held up the blood bag before placing it out of his reach but in sight. "You can have this when you spill your guts. Oops," she said, as if she had made an innocent mistake. Betty showed the man a small plastic tube with a needle sticking out. "See this syrette? It's morphine. I'm going to stick you with it. Don't move." Betty thought about the times Gil had given her lectures about field medicine. He had trained her for his own safety and well-being, but for once she was glad he had insisted on teaching her. *With the gut wound, I don't want to stick him in the gluteus maximus—so, let's do the arm.* "I'm going to stick your arm." Gideon held the man while Betty stuck him with the syrette. He did not flinch, but kept moaning. "That will take about fifteen minutes, but you'll feel better."

Gideon pulled the man's shirt sleeve up, took note of the dragon tattoo, started the IV in the man's arm, and used the same duct tape that had been used on him to hold the needle in place. "Don't move around or you'll rip that out," he said.

Howell circled around and checked over the side of the patio edge; Max looked back at Ernesto while trying to keep an eye roving for new intruders, especially from the roof of the house. Everything seemed calm—other than the writhing man, two dead commandos on the patio, and a smoking wreck below their position. Max looked at Betty with admiration and newfound respect. Howell nodded his head and moved back, sure that there were no other survivors.

"Who do you work for?" Betty asked as she put on latex gloves.

Nothing from the wounded man other than a light moan.

"Hold him down," she said to the others. They complied, Max taking one arm, Gideon the one he had stuck with the IV, Thor sitting on the man's legs. None questioned her actions. Howell kept looking around their position for any other source of trouble. Ernesto sat down at the table.

Betty looked the man in the eyes. "This is going to hurt like a motherfucker." Without waiting for his answer or even acknowledgement, she reached into his gut with her left hand and pulled on the man's intestines, squeezing, twisting, distending. She wanted to hurt this man. He screamed.

"Jesus," Thor said under his breath.

"Are you going to talk?" Betty asked as she let go of his guts.

The man panted and moaned and gasped, but he made no effort to answer her question or give up any information.

"Fuck," Betty said as she stood up and snapped the latex gloves off her hands. "I hate to see animals suffer." She stood up and drew her SIG Sauer before the others realized what she was doing, too busy holding appendages to see her line of thought. "Last chance." The man did not give her satisfaction. She aimed at his forehead and pulled the trigger.

"Seriously?" asked Howell. "That's your interrogation method?"

Betty aimed the gun at Howell. Gideon let go of the man's arm but did not move to stop her. "OK. Let me try again. This time with Ernesto. Just him and me." She looked at Max, Gideon, and Thor. One by one and with her eyes, she asked if they were going to object. All moved away from the dead man, but none moved to interfere. Thor was taking his cues from Max—who, being a Control double agent, was looking to Tom for *his* cues.

Howell looked to his half brother. "Ernesto. You don't have to do this."

Ernesto stepped forward. "Why not? She could have killed me in my bed." He pulled a handkerchief from his pocket and wiped his brow. Ernesto looked at Betty and said, "You should clean up before we start—don't you think?" He moved to hold the door for her.

Betty straightened her shoulders and moved past the men toward Ernesto and the open door. He waited by the kitchen table as she scrubbed the commando's blood off her. When she had dried her hands, she looked at Ernesto. "The dining room? Or do you want some food first?"

He shrugged and made a face to emphasize his indifference. "I am in no hurry."

Betty looked at the refrigerator and shook her head. She thought about the times she had stalked quarry in Colombia and Venezuela. Her trip to Denmark to rescue Gil. All the times she had denied herself food until her mission was completed. Ernesto was the man she had been hunting for years. Food could wait. "I'm good. Shall we? Or do you want to go to the bedroom and recreate our last interrogation?"

Ernesto smiled slightly. "The dining room will be fine." He got up and moved to the door, holding it for her.

"No, I insist, after you," she said. She looked over her shoulder to see the men cleaning up the patio, removing the bodies and hosing the blood off the edge. She squinted at Howell. You're next.

Twenty-Nine

Your Haberdasher or Mine?

November 22, 2009 — Århus, Denmark

JIL WAS WATCHING GIL put his meager collection of clothes into his carry-on, a miniature suitcase, and a folding garment bag. For the past week, she had been more interested in seeing him out of his clothes than in them, but the totality of his wardrobe in one bag made her shudder. "We really need to take you clothes shopping," she said with a look of disgust as she used a wire hanger from the cleaners to hold up one of his well-worn dress shirts.

"Well, I need to get some ski clothes, that's for sure." Gil looked at his wardrobe in a new light. He had not bought any new clothes in—"Hell, I don't even know when I last went shopping."

"Darling, I know just the places to take you in Vail. I'll even make Casper pay for everything since you're my official bodyguard"—Jil winked—"now."

"Sounds like a demanding job."

"You have no idea!" Jil smiled and looked at his crotch. "I can attest to your ability to give me cover."

"Well, all righty then. Should I have my office bill Casper as well?"

Jil tossed the shirt and hanger on the floor. "Why not. As your first duty, I will need you to make me orgasm. Are you up for it?"

Gil smiled. "It might be better if I was down for it—to make sure you orgasm, that is."

Thirty

Trust Me, I'm a PhD

November 22, 2009 — Somewhere in the Virginia Mountains

A LONG SILENCE PERMEATED THE dining room after Betty and Ernesto settled back into their seats so recently vacated. Betty was trying to decide what she wanted to know. Ernesto was trying to figure out how to stay alive.

"Before you begin your interrogation, may I ask you a few questions?" Ernesto prodded her.

Betty rubbed her chin. "Why not." She waved him to begin, like a queen telling her prime minister it was OK to question her decision.

"You could have killed me—back at my compound. Why didn't you?" he began.

"Hmm. Tom had given me strict instructions. I would only be allowed to kill you if I could prove you had ordered José's death." She furrowed her brow. "I never got a good answer from you."

Before she could re-ask that particular question, Ernesto pressed forward. "Do you trust Tom?"

"That depends."

Ernesto waved his hands, "Please, expound on that. He may be my brother, but I hardly know him."

Betty bit her lip. "There are two sides to him. One I call Howell—the spymaster; and the other one—the one I know loves me and would kill to protect me—is the one I call Tom."

"Sort of a Jekyll and Hyde character?" Ernesto asked.

"Yes." Betty looked down at her hands, uncomfortable with the telling a stranger, and probably the man responsible for the death of her fiancé, her most intimate thoughts of her boss and lover.

"He has saved your life in the past, no?"

Betty cleared her throat. "Yes, if you mean from your father."

"Yes. My father." Ernesto replied. "Tom loves you, that I know. Father—the one I knew—abandoned me and my mother, though he sent us more than enough money to live on, quite comfortably. He saved my mother from Nazi Germany, but, I am told, he loved her too much. Think about that for a moment, if you don't mind, that he loved her so much that he abandoned us in Argentina. My mother died when I was twelve, so I ended up with the Jesuits. Likely where he wanted me anyway. For all I know, he had her killed, though I doubt that. Can you imagine not knowing what your parents' true intentions are?"

"I can, actually. Turns out I was adopted. By Control agents, no less."

"Ah. So, it is very difficult to trust anyone, don't you think? Even the ones you love?"

Betty nodded her head, a sad look in her eye.

"I have spent my life trusting only that the Jesuits wanted to save my soul and that the Cabal would not kill me as long as I did not steal from them."

"I can believe that," Betty said.

"But then the Cabal decided to replace me." Ernesto paused.

"José?" Betty's face flushed. Her hand ached to reach for her pistol, but she had resolved not to kill Ernesto, not until she knew everything about Tom, Tom Sr., and the Cabal. Everything that Ernesto would tell her without force before she resorted to force.

"Yes, your José." Ernesto took a drink from his water glass, the same one he had drunk from before the assault by the Cabal men. Holding up the glass for her to witness, he said, "You realize that I have lived in a prison of my own making for the past forty years. Only by doing my job well and without significant error could I have no trepidation about drinking a glass of water I did not pull from the faucet myself. Even then, I would have had to ask myself, is the glass safe? If they wanted me dead, I was surrounded by armed guards. The only security was that each of the guards came from a different family with an equal interest in my survival."

"That would be a stressful lifestyle, I would think." Betty said.

"Yes. Which is one reason they thought it was time to replace me, I suppose. Or maybe it was because I did not do their exact bidding during the last financial crisis."

This piqued Betty's interest. "What do you mean?"

"I could have destroyed many governments and all of the multinational companies by simply withholding liquidity from them. Some people think that the Federal Reserve in America is in charge. Some think it is the Bank for International Settlements. Others might think something else. Each provides liquidity to those below them."

"OK, but how could you possibly keep them from doing their job?"

"I had stockpiled massive amounts of physical and digital currency from every nation, not just the G8 or G20. By buying or selling the right ones at the right time, I could cause massive losses for them and incredible gains for the Cabal. They did not ask for it, but they wanted me to take more from everyone than I did. Had I been greedy, the Cabal could have literally owned every government by insuring that their fiat currency would not be destroyed by me. We left trillions of dollars on the trading floor in those first few hours."

"I see where they might not have appreciated your conservative touch," Betty said.

"The game would have been over." Ernesto took another sip of his water. "Please understand that I made them wealthy beyond anyone's imagination. They are worth fifty trillion dollars, but only think they are worth thirty trillion dollars."

Betty was confused by this. "I thought you said you only stayed alive by not making mistakes or stealing from the Cabal."

"I did not steal from them. They can see every transaction I make and know that I have no wealth of my own. Like a Jesuit, I have vowed poverty." Ernesto smiled broadly. "I merely crave complete control over the financial markets. Had I destroyed the currencies and governments of the world, I would have lost control of them."

"How?" Betty asked.

"Because there would have been total chaos. Revolutions. At least a billion people would have died from war, famine, and disease." Ernesto looked at her seriously. "The Cabal earned ten trillion that they know of that day. I buried the rest, so to speak, digitally."

"Buried treasure," Betty drolly noted. "And you're a pirate."

Ernesto smiled again. "Yes, yes I am. But I think one of them suspected—a man named Charles—which is why they started to arrange for José to replace me." Ernesto's grin vanished. "José was willing to destroy those I saved. He wanted both control and power. You may choose only one."

"That isn't the man I knew and loved." Betty's face flushed again as she thought of the man who was jealous, the man who would have taken her letters away from her. The man who was so South American in his ways, believing he was better than Betty. Her words belied her true understanding of him. Back then, she was willing to ignore his lesser qualities and focus on just the positives. *Why did I love him? Was it because I had found someone who I thought loved me as much as Tom?*

"He was cheating on you, did you know that?" Ernesto quietly asked.

Betty started rubbing the web between her thumb and finger. "I didn't then, but Tom told me about it. He showed me pictures of you and him at a conference."

"Yes. He had an appetite."

"What do you mean?" Betty asked.

"He liked to bind them up and torture them."

"No," she said weakly.

"Tom did not show you the one he killed?" Ernesto leaned in slightly.

Betty suddenly realized she was not in control of the interrogation, that Ernesto had her in the palm of his hand. He controlled her by slowly revealing the José she suspected but never saw. "He never—"

"He never tried the kinky stuff with you? Did he ever tie you up?"

"Well, yes." Betty shook her head. "I don't like where this is going!" She put both her hands on the table and prepared to push back her chair. "OK, so we liked to role-play sometimes. That was just one time! It doesn't mean—"

†

"Did Tom tell you that Father arranged for you to marry José? That José was manipulated into proposing to you?"

Betty closed her eyes and tried to envision the days leading up to her dating José. "I asked him out, after we were done getting his residency squared away. No one arranged that."

"No one asked you to ask him out, that is true. But he made you want to ask him out, didn't he." Ernesto was not asking, he was stating.

Betty's voice quieted as she realized how much of her life had been manipulated, her parents, José, Tom—or rather, Howell . . . both of them. Everyone she had worked with led back to Control. Everyone she had loved, back to Control. Everywhere she turned was Control. She was feeling dizzy and lost. *I need to eat something. When did I last eat? What is going on?* "Stop!" she shouted. "Wait here. I need to get something to eat." Betty got up and left Ernesto alone in the dining room.

Thirty-One

Doctor, Vail—Stat

November 22, 2009 — Århus, Denmark

"GOING WELL?" BUD ASKED GIL over the usual encrypted connection as he shuffled papers marked "Top Secret" on his desk.

"Extremely. I just sent you the contact information for Casper."

Bud reread the message Gil had sent. "Excellent! We'll get someone on the scene to check it out."

"We need to start billing him for my time as a bodyguard for Jil Harper." Gil looked to the bathroom door from across the bedroom—the sound of water running and Jil singing would drown out his words to Bud. He had poured a lot of olive oil on her back for a massage so she would want a shower afterward and Gil would be able to talk candidly. "We'll be staying in the penthouse of the Ritz-Carlton, Vail."

"Living large, aren't we. I'll get the usual kit in place before you arrive."

"Great. We'll be going shopping after we arrive, so if you need more time . . ."

"Did you get clearance on these expenses? It's one thing to show off with the jet, but shopping and the penthouse?" Bud could not imagine Tom going for such extravagance unless it was really needed. But then, Bud had never had a girlfriend and wore the same three sets of clothes in a cycle for months on end. A new piece of technical equipment or computer hardware—that he could justify.

"No worries—she's having Casper pay to ensure that my clothing blends into the crowd. And they own the penthouse." Gil said.

Bud whistled. "How sweet it is to be a kept man."

The shower stopped. After a moment of silence, Jil started to blow-dry her hair.

"Gotta go. Oh, please have some flowers and Dom waiting for us, will you," requested Gil.

"I'll get Karl on it. He's the concierge and your contact at the Ritz."

"Karl, huh. He's a legend," Gil said.

"Semi-retired, but fresh from the field."

Gil opened the bathroom door to reveal Jil bent over at the waist, her hair dangling down and her breasts sumptuously rocking back and forth as she worked the dryer.

"OK. I'll install the update. Jeez." Gil disconnected from Bud and held his phone up for Jil to see what he was talking about. "These geeks. Always have to have the latest software."

She turned off the dryer to hear him better. "For what?"

"I sent my guy the address for billing, and he insisted I install the latest billing software . . ." Gil stared at Jil's body with fondness and longing. "Damn shame the plane is waiting on us."

Thirty-Two

OK. Shoot.

November 22, 2009 — Somewhere in the Virginia Mountains

"GOING WELL?" TOM ASKED. He was lingering in the kitchen waiting for Betty.

"I haven't killed him, if that is what you're asking," Betty replied.

Tom grabbed a bottle of water from the refrigerator and held the door open for Betty. "Leaving Ernesto all by himself—or is he tied up?"

"He stayed there of his own volition. I have to get something to eat." Betty selected two bottles of water, one for her and one for Ernesto, and placed them on the counter. The bowl of chicken legs caught her eye, so she grabbed one and began eating it. With her mouth full of meat, she turned to Tom and poked the leg bone at his chest, nearly touching his shirt. "I have some questions for you before I go back in there." She glared at him and took another bite.

"OK. Shoot." Tom regretted that particular word choice, but grinned to pretend he did it on purpose.

"Don't tempt me, mister." The bone was mostly cleaned off, leaving just some gristle, cartilage, and tendon, so she threw it away. She finished chewing the meat and followed it with a swig of her water.

Tom waited, leaning against the island counter, bent at the waist, his elbows resting on the brown-speckled marble.

"How did you find out about José's death?" Betty removed her pistol from the holster tucked in small of her back and placed it on the counter, out of Tom's reach but easily within hers.

"Bud was monitoring the police scanners as always when your 911 call came across. He had a pattern-recognition program watching for specific addresses and more generally for any information about people we watch."

"People you watch?"

"Our agents, staff, major political leaders, businessmen —and -women. All the usual suspects." Tom glanced at the pistol and mentally noted that it was not cocked. He automatically calculated how long it would take to move within reach of the gun, without the intention of doing anything—just old habits distilled from fieldwork and military training. "José's address popped up, so we arranged for friendly personnel to be the first on the scene."

"Sure. OK. What else?"

"José was a person of interest to my father, since he was lined up to be the next Ernesto. I was against it, but he had tried to manipulate the both of you to ensure your marriage." Tom inwardly sighed, knowing that revealing this could trigger Betty in a negative sense.

"Were you actively involved in this arrangement?" Betty placed her hand on the P229, caressing the handle gently.

"No, I had told my father I was flat out against it, so he had other operatives assigned."

Betty found this hard to believe, but plausible. She pulled her hand away slightly, to give him encouragement for telling only the truth. "What did you do about José's death?"

Tom fidgeted for a moment with his fingers. "Well, we never like having our plans destroyed—"

"Or people murdered who are supposed to stay alive?" interjected Betty.

"We had spent ten years getting him to that position. There were others who had been primed, but he was the one who had been vetted by the Cabal and selected," Tom said.

Betty itched to pick up her weapon but resisted, lest Tom get the wrong idea. *Was José an agent? How could I not know that?* "So you're saying that José was a Control agent?"

"No, nothing like that. He had no idea of our involvement. We just made sure the right doors opened for him without knowing who was opening them." Tom considered his words carefully. "He didn't even know he was an asset. We just had some control over his growth and direction."

"So when the time was right, you would be able to manipulate him as needed?"

"Yes—we had knowledge of his proclivities . . . his weaknesses."

"I know what the word means. I also know—now, thanks to Ernesto—that his proclivities were far greater than I imagined when we were together." Betty picked up her pistol and cocked the hammer for dramatic effect. "You would let me be with someone who killed call girls." She saw his muscles twitch and already knew where his mind was going. "Even if it were accidental."

"I think you know me better. Like I said, I was against the idea of using you, let alone with José." Tom slowly pushed up from his elbows and gripped the counter with his hands. Gideon started to move toward the patio door to check on the situation, but Tom shook his head no to warn him off.

Betty turned her head slightly while holding the SIG Sauer on the counter, to see who and what had gotten Tom's attention. She saw Gideon back away from the door and head back to Max and Thor, who were on lookout. "Just when I think I know you, I find out I don't, so never assume I believe a word you say. Me not shooting you is your only sure way of knowing I sort of believe your bullshit."

"Well, since you haven't shot me, I am assuming what you learned from Ernesto at least somewhat lines up with what I've told you." Tom slowly slid back down to his elbows and put his right hand under his chin. "You should probably get back to Ernesto. He's just getting back from the bathroom."

"Why—what haven't you told me?"

"He has high blood pressure. It makes you go to the bathroom more often. It's been awhile." Tom said.

"Oh. I suppose you're right." Betty uncocked her pistol and holstered it before gathering an apple and Ernesto's water bottle. She cracked the dining room door and leaned against its frame, peering in, she smiled at Ernesto. "Do you need a bathroom break?"

Ernesto smiled back. "Thank you, but I just went."

She turned back to Tom and said, "It's really obnoxious when you're right about these things."

"I don't mean to be." Tom got up from the counter and headed for the patio. "Try as best you can to not kill him. We really do need him in Vail."

"I'll do my best."

"I really need you in Vail too." Tom said as he left the kitchen.

"No shit." Betty retorted to the closing door.

"Shall we?" Ernesto asked.

"Yes, we shall," Betty replied.

Thirty-Three

Better Than Dead

November 22, 2009 — Near Bern, Switzerland

PIERRE REMOVED THE LARGE PLASTIC boot the doctor had ordered him to wear as his wound healed and propped his foot on his desk to ease the throbbing. The bullet had caused enough damage to require him to stay off it as much as possible, but he had been walking on the boot all morning without his crutches because he was too stubborn and proud to use the motorized wheelchair the foundation had thoughtfully provided for the dedication of the new aviation museum he had funded. The building was named after his deceased mother and was designed to hold his vast collection of vintage planes. He was particularly proud of his nearly complete line of World War I biplanes from around the world. He had chosen Arras, France, because of the notorious Bloody April battle of 1917. The British Royal Flying Corps lost four times as many planes as the German Luftstreitkräfte, which included the Jasta 11 led by the renowned Baron Manfred von Richtofen. The centerpiece of the museum was the only existing Fokker Dr.I Dreidecker triplane, serial number 425/17, which had been faithfully restored from thousands of parts scavenged across the world. Cost had been no barrier. Parts that could not be purchased were stolen, fakes left in their stead. It was the plane Richtofen had been flying when a shot from the ground struck him in the right armpit and exited near his left nipple; the cavity caused by the .303 round destroyed his heart and lungs. He lived long enough to land the plane and supposedly to tell the first man on the scene his final word, "*Kaputt*."

The plane was destroyed by scavengers desiring a trophy from the death of such a significant warrior. A vast diorama around the reconstructed plane depicted the life and heroics of Richtofen and gave tribute to his death, including a portrayal of his funeral replete with uniformed mannequins and a historically accurate audio interpretive presentation that ended with the three volleys of shots and the roar of the formation flying over the assemblage. During peak visitor season, an actor dressed like the mannequins would step out of his stiff posture and expound on the story while answering question from the visitors.

Pierre's only regret of the event was that his foot precluded him from flying the restored plane himself, as planned, before it was permanently parked in the museum. He had trained for hours in similar planes and with a full-size simulator. The museum director and major recipient of his largess assured Pierre that when he was ready, the plane would be rolled out for his opportunity to fly it personally. For the unveiling, a pilot dressed as Baron von Richtofen swooped in from the sun, blanks firing from his twin machine guns, as the crowd ducked for cover—except Pierre who was privy to the stunt.

The phone rang. Pierre winced and reluctantly put his foot back down on the floor to reach the handset. "Yes." The voice at the other end informed him that a certain director of a national bank was not following orders. "Cut him off." Which meant that the director would not receive his weekly shot of an antidote that kept him alive. Unbeknownst to the director, a semipermeable capsule of poison had been planted in his body during an elective surgery two years prior. He became suicidal a week later, and his doctor gave him the first injection. Upon recovering, the truth was told to him—or rather, as much of the truth that was required to control him—that he would return to his suicidal ideation and kill himself without the shots and that no one would be able to identify the poison, its source, or an alternate antidote. For two years the man had done their bidding and kept his weekly appointment for a massage that masked his receiving orders and the shot. He had finally found a doctor who thought he understood the issue and was giving him an alternative treatment of lithium. Pierre knew that the director would either die trying or quickly come back around. It was only a matter of time to find out which the man would chose.

The call ended and Pierre waited for a prompt reply before putting his foot back up. The Cabal owned stock in all of the banks controlling the reserve bank; Pierre could order the director fired immediately, but that was not enough. He needed the man to fear for his life and his family's well-being. He needed absolute control over what the man would and could do. Pierre was not disappointed. The phone rang again and the voice confirmed that the director had chosen to rejoin the fold rather than kill himself. "The coward. Remind him of his lack of loyalty. Add his wife to the cycle. Inform him that if he fails again, his children will be added and he will be removed from the list of approved antidote recipients." The call ended.

Twenty minutes later Pierre dialed the cellphone number of the director, who answered it on the first ring. "Ah, Director. How are you this fine day?" he asked.

"I am feeling much better now, thank you," answered the director.

Pierre smirked at the phone. He thought he heard absolute terror in the man's voice. The terror of a man staring at a devil who held his very soul in his hand. "I hate to trouble you, but my brother and I agree that there seems to be one too few zeros in the balance of our main account at your bank."

The director's voice shook as he tried to reassure Pierre. "I—I am sure it is just an error on our end. I will make sure it is corrected immediately. Will one zero be enough, or should I make it two?"

Pierre smiled. "Yes, I think you are correct, now that I look at it again. Thank you, Director. Stay well! Goodbye." Pierre ended the connection. He put his foot back up on his desk and sighed. "They are so easily controlled."

Thirty-Four

Control Equals Power Equals Money — Part One

November 22, 2009 — Somewhere in the Virginia Mountains

BETTY WASTED NO TIME SETTLING IN. "You said that you haven't stolen from the Cabal, yet you somehow have earned them more money than what shows on the books. How is this possible? Two sets of books?" Betty asked.

"Yes and no—there is a set of books which conservatively accounts for all of the groups assets and liabilities. There are tens of thousands of entities—some shadow companies, some shell companies—but mostly they are partnerships three layers deep via proxy. Some property is owned via trust, but the income is transferred through exorbitant management fees or directorships. We even have charities set up that do actual, real good for the world—but, they also lower the taxes of the group." Ernesto smiled with pride at the deviousness of the last confession.

"Back that up. You said there is only one set of books—yet you imply there is another." Betty looked at him with a cocked head and pursed lips, trying to envision what the trick was.

"Yes, there is another set of books that accurately accounts for wealth owned by one individual, who must stay anonymous for now." Ernesto conceded. "Those books currently account for one-tenth of the world's wealth. The Cabal's books represent over a quarter. If we succeed in Vail, their percentage will drop to merely obscenely rich."

"So, Mr. Anonymous, *your* books?" Betty waved her hand to signal him to elucidate.

"No. I am actually quite poor and intend to never own more than what I can carry to my grave."

Betty pulled her gun from its holster and placed it on the table.

"So whose money?"

"You might as well kill me now if you must know that one fact." Ernesto folded his hands and leaned back in his chair. Then he suddenly leaned in. "I'll even tempt fate and tell you that that one person—a good and decent man, who does not even know the extent of his wealth—is ultimately responsible for José's death."

"Well, that narrows it down." Betty checked her pistol to see if a round was chambered. "You really aren't going to tell me, the guy doesn't even know it's him, and you're pinning the death of a man I thought I loved and now really don't give a shit about on one of the richest men in the world." Betty stood up and aimed at Ernesto's forehead. "Give me one good reason not to ruin your day."

Ernesto did not seem a bit bothered by her threat. He smiled and said, "If you kill me, the Cabal wins and owns ninety percent of the world."

Betty cocked her P229.

"Everyone will be their slave, governments will fall, wars will erupt on every continent, including Antarctica. You will be responsible for the destruction of the world as we know it today."

Betty uncocked her pistol, put it on the dining table gently, and put her face into her palms, elbows on the table. "Why am I always being put into these impossible situations?" she asked no one in particular.

After a long silence, Ernesto asked, "Do you know what the Federal Reserve does?"

Betty looked up from rubbing her eyes with the palms of her hands. "I think so. Why the hell does it matter? They manage the U.S. dollar, so what? The president appoints the Fed chair."

"So you know what they want you to know. Shall I tell you what they really are?"

Betty smirked. "Why not."

"The Federal Reserve is a private corporation owned by the banks. Not all banks, just the largest ones. The banks are owned by the wealthy, like the Cabal."

"But the president appoints the chairman."

Ernesto leaned back in his chair. "They would like you to believe it is so simple as an entity owned by the banks but controlled by the government. There is the usual fanfare appointment by the president of the next Fed chair, but the President is given a short list of candidates to choose from. There really is no choice." He noted that the seal broke as he opened his water and smiled slightly. "Just as this cap assures purity, and the seal leads you to believe there could be no tampering of this water between the factory and my drinking it, the Federal Reserve chairman is the cap that assures corruption of the management of the money supply." Ernesto sipped, then returned the cap precisely to the threaded neck of the bottle. "It has been opened, but because I believe I have controlled the security of this vessel—a bank for water, if you will—and I have complete faith in the manufacturer. Everything seems safe and normal. There is nothing to fear. My water will stay the same whether I drink it now or in an hour."

"OK, I kind of get what you're saying," Betty said. She picked up and stowed her pistol in its holster.

"Now, suppose I, as the Federal Reserve, was able to bottle as much water as I wanted without you noticing it—a poor analogy, perhaps, but it will do." Ernesto lifted the bottle.

"How does that compare to the Fed?"

Ernesto smiled and put the bottle down. "By increasing the money supply, sometimes called helicopter money, the Federal Reserve decreases the value of your money. The law of supply and demand." He paused for a moment to see if Betty had a question. "Now, you must understand that there is a central bank for every country—well, the little ones don't count—and all of those central banks are controlled by the same people who control the Federal Reserve. The head of that country's government seals the bottle with a chairman titularly under his or her control, but the reality is that the chairman is only one vote of many on what is to be done with the monetary supply."

"Why even have the central banks, then?" Betty said.

"Because, if you let the elected officials control the money supply, you have out-of-control inflation shortly after they start spending more than they take in to retain control of their jobs. Zimbabwe, Weimar Germany, Venezuela, and so on."

Betty nodded at the mention of Venezuela. She thought of Ernesto's compound and the raid where Gil sacrificed his safety to get her out of danger on the hang glider. A memory she'd rather forget. He had rescued her after her interrogation of Ernesto and killed at least a dozen guards even before they got to the pool deck. She did want to remember the sex on the cabana couch, though. That was pretty sweet. The harrowing firefight after was not so grand. Ernesto had escaped in his Bell helicopter with Max and two other guards. Later, as Betty and Gil were making their way up Monte Ávila to escape via the tandem hang glider, the remaining guards closed in. His sacrifice gave Betty enough airspeed to make it to the pass and out to sea. Miller rescued her and patched her wound on the way back to Colombia.

Only after going rogue and defying Tom Howell Sr. did she and Karl find Gil in Denmark and prevent Michel from taking Gil's kidney. *I swore I'd never work for Tom again, yet here I am, doing his job for him—trying to convince myself not to kill Ernesto and to turn my vengeance on the Cabal instead. Jesus. The things I do for that man*, Betty thought.

Betty shook her head slightly to clear the thoughts of the past and to focus on the future. Ernesto waited for a moment to make sure she was still with him. She parted her lips slightly as if she were going to ask a question but instead grabbed her apple and offered it to him. "Are you sure you don't need something to eat?" she asked.

"No. I'm fine. Please." Ernesto waved her to eat the fruit. As she started to take a bite, he said, "Wait. I'll give you a dollar for it."

Betty looked confused. "You can just have it, I can go get another."

"But what if that was the last apple? Ten dollars!" Ernesto pulled his wallet out and removed several bills.

"What are you getting at? OK, it's the last one. Ten dollars would be a good deal for me."

Ernesto laid the money out in front of him. All dollars in various denominations. "What if I am many people, several of whom have just gotten government bonuses, money created from thin air, fiat currency with no backing, no gold or silver. How much is your apple worth?" He spaced several hundred-dollar bills out across the table. "Imagine these are three different people bidding for your apple. Is it worth ten dollars or is it what the market will pay?"

Betty looked at the money. "Well, if there are three people offering one hundred dollars, I guess it's worth at least one hundred."

"Exactly. Now the price goes up until only one bidder remains." Ernesto placed a fourth hundred dollar bill on top of the middle of the three. "Now you have an offer for two hundred. If the apple used to be worth one dollar, but now two hundred, what does that do to that bottle of water?" Ernesto grinned broadly.

"I suppose everything becomes more expensive, or rather, the relative price goes up . . . " she started speaking slowly as she thought it out. "All commodity prices would increase—bread, milk, vegetables, and the most scarce items would become really expensive."

"So, if the government keeps printing money, with nothing to back it, you see how your paper money becomes worthless." Ernesto pulled out a foreign piece of money, an einhundert billionen mark note from 1924 Weimar Republic Germany. "This is a one-hundred-trillion bill. Would you take it for your apple?"

"I don't know what it's worth." Betty slumped her chin into her hand and put the apple down, it being too valuable to eat now. "Where did you get that?"

Thirty-Five

Cold Comfort

November 22, 2009 — Somewhere over the Atlantic

JIL SUDDENLY REALIZED HOW tired she was. The pace since both of her parents had died remained at a steady frenetic speed that prevented her from even starting the grieving process for either of them. While Gil slept across from her, she finally took the time to read both of their final messages to her. Linda Harper had spent her last day writing her daughters letters, in case the surgeries went poorly. Jil pensively slit the gilded envelope and pulled out a fragrant folded piece of paper with a lilac watermark, which matched the fragrance of the linen rag stock. The cursive writing with extra loops and accents was distinctly her mother's. Jil had tried to copy Linda's style, but settled on a simpler script for her own personal letters.

My dear, sweet Jil,

If you are reading this, the surgery was a failure. If he hasn't already done it, your father will kill himself, so please keep a close eye on him and get him help. But, knowing you, it is already too late because you did not read this letter right away.

I know you lied to Ruth and your father about the surgery. I know you've been lying about a lot of things since your father's business was taken over by those bastards in Denmark. We have always done what needed to be done, but you crossed the line. You are a bitch.

I gave you all of my attention when you were young—the beauty pageants, the shopping, the lessons. Ruth got so little, and yet she was the one who stepped up to save my life. She deserved better. You will find that the will stipulates that Ruth gets whatever wealth we have left, but I am leaving you my clothes. We are still the same size, even after all these years.

I hate what money has done to you and your father. The things both of you are willing to do turns my stomach. If you learn anything from my letter, learn that it is not too late to change your destiny. Wealth is not evil, but to pursue wealth at any cost—well, that is what you two have done.

Do something to help a friend in need. Get a dog from the shelter and love it like your own child. Work in a soup kitchen but don't tell anyone. Make a sacrifice, time or money, for someone else's benefit. Save someone's life and you might just save your own.

I love you and always will, but I do not like you anymore.

Mother

There was a small heart drawn with *xoxo* next to it, Linda's way of saying hugs and kisses. Jil began to cry, just tears, no sobs. She had lied and she had cheated and she had used herself in so many ways to please Casper, Eric, and any man who stood between her and the wealth she sought. The acidic truth etched her heart with the words her mother had written. Jil clutched the paper to her chest. She wanted to throw the letter away, burn it, destroy the words so they would not sting, but she knew they still would. The smell of the lilac scent etched the words deep. There had been long rows of lilac bushes along the quarter-mile driveway to their house in Rochester, New York. Her youth was distilled from the essence of lilac, the smell ubiquitous with her mother. Jil started to lose control of her emotions, and the wracking sobs finally came. For her mother, her father, and the little girl who had been their pride, the little girl that Jil had left behind when she chose to do Casper's bidding, when she had decided to be an escort to earn money back in Georgetown where she and Betty had shared the ivy-covered house. She had succeeded beyond a doubt at sleeping her way to her current spot, on a plane with a man she really did not know going to a penthouse she did not own to keep her way of life just one more day.

Gil woke to the sound of her pain and knelt down before her, his hands on her thighs, but reaching for her, trying to pull her to him to comfort her. She fell into him and sobbed louder. Her humiliation would be complete soon. Casper would learn that she had no intention of securing the information he desired. She knew nothing about what Betty had been doing the past few years and had hardly spoken to her childhood friend other than for business, which was all her life had been since she took that first escort call.

After five minutes of bawling, Jil finally had no more tears to give. Gil had held his handkerchief to her nose for Jil to blow like a small child. She clutched it in her hand now: it did not smell of lilac, but of Gil. She willed herself to focus on his smell, to forget the lilac, or at least to replace it in her mind if not her soul. Gil moved her to the couch that ran along the starboard side of the Gulfstream G650. He brought the champagne bucket over and poured Jil a fresh glass of Dom Pérignon. She wiped her eyes one more time before accepting the proffered drink with a truly sweet smile. She willed her brain to remember the smell of Gil as she sipped the effervescent wine. "Thank you." Gil sidled up to her and Jil leaned into him, holding his hand in hers. "Don't leave me."

Gil looked at her eyes. The sapphire blue irises with the deep purple rims. She was an asset, it was his job to be with her, but at this moment, seeing her vulnerable for the first time and feeling the naked emotion of her pain, he could not imagine being anywhere else.

Thirty-Six

Control Equals Power Equals Money — Part Two

November 22, 2009 — Somewhere in the Virginia Mountains

ERNESTO PUSHED THE 1924 WEIMAR Republic one-hundred-trillion-mark bill closer to Betty. "It is the highest-denomination German mark note printed before the Depression. Not many were printed, so it is actually valuable as a collectable. Hmm. I could sell it for about five or ten thousand U.S. dollars. More, actually." He flipped it over and showed her a signature that was not preprinted on the paper. "Horace Greeley Hjalmar Schacht. He was a mentor to me and taught me a great deal about the value of money—by that I mean the perception of the value of money. He had just become the president of the Reichsbank the year before this was printed. Inflation was out of control, and he came up with the plan that worked to reign it in."

"A Nazi?"

"Oh, no, only as an honorary member because they needed him. He left the government at the start of the war." Ernesto picked up the rest of his money and placed it back into his wallet, leaving the pecuniary artifact prominently between them. "When governments make money from nothing, it becomes worth nothing. That is, if the people find out that they are running the presses at breakneck speed. When the denominations skyrocket like they did in the Weimar Republic, it is impossible for the people not to notice. When it was issued, it was worth about two U.S. dollars. Can you imagine the pile of money you would need to buy a house?" Ernesto leaned back in his chair, tipping the front feet off the ground.

"A wheelbarrow full, I suppose. I seem to remember a photo in my high school history book."

"Ah, yes, someone off to buy a loaf of bread near the end. People burned the worthless notes for heat, used them as wallpaper—children would use bundles of notes as building blocks. It was a horrible time."

Betty eyed her apple and then the German mark. "Do you want the apple?"

"No." Ernesto laughed. "You eat it. This note means more to me than its market value. It is my reminder to never allow the Cabal to cause hyperinflation."

"Why not?" Betty asked just before she took a bite of her apple.

"Because, while hyperinflation can be a huge inconvenience for the people, they can pay off their debts quite fast and bankrupt the lenders who loaned expensive money and got back worthless notes that technically paid the debt. You could agree to buy a house on Monday and by the closing on Friday the seller would be getting half as much as they bargained for."

"So, what does this have to do with the money you made but the Cabal doesn't know about?"

Ernesto grinned broadly. "You are most wise and insightful." He rubbed his chin and considered the value of what he was about to reveal. "But, before I answer that question, we need to define what money is, especially in relation to power and control."

"Control? As in Tom and his bunch?" Betty asked.

"No, as in you have the power over whether I live or die at the moment, and I sincerely doubt all my hidden money would be enough to pay you off. Tom has the control of us both. He has chosen to allow you to use your power."

"I didn't really think he had a choice." Betty pulled her pistol from the holster to display it and then put it back.

Ernesto placed his palms on the edge of the table to show he was not resisting. "Oh, he made that choice before you and I were in the same room. I am quite certain he made sure you would sequester me to ask me these questions."

"School is in session," Betty remarked.

"Yes, and this is the abbreviated master's program." Ernesto raised his hands in welcome.

"So, what is the correlation between money, power, and control—little c."

"Money is the Wall Street banker buying laws from the powerful lawmakers by funding their reelection. The Cabal, through me, controls the bankers by manipulating the value of their holdings. Because I control such a large part of the world's assets—land, stocks, bonds, minerals, and such— I can easily destroy a wealthy investor as easily as I can take down a bank."

"How's that possible?"

"Suppose you own an orchard and you agree to sell the local grocery store apples at ten dollars a bushel, but because you need money to buy a new tractor, you sell the apples to a broker for twelve when the price is higher before the picking season, thinking that you can make a few extra dollars. But the store has a contract for your apples, and now both are calling for your produce. You had planned to buy apples on the market at harvest to supply either one—more likely the broker, as the store wrote a provision into the contract that the apples would be locally produced, per their marketing. But I tell my Wall Street broker to start buying up apples left and right. Now the price is twenty dollars a bushel. You have to pay because of the contracts. But now you must mortgage your farm. Then we dump the apples on the market before the price goes down. You lose your farm, my banker makes money, and I have control of your farm."

"But why wouldn't I just wait until you dumped them?" Betty asked.

"I am the only one who knows that I am going to dump them." Ernesto nodded to acknowledge her insight. "I know when your contracts are due and sell right after you are committed." Ernesto sighed. "But this is just a whimsical example."

"What is the real one?"

"Say you are the programmer who created the software for managing the money supply of the United States, for the Federal Reserve, really."

"They would be watching me pretty closely," Betty said.

"Yes, they would. But what if you wanted to trade your power over the software for something else?" Ernesto asked.

"Like what?" Betty was perplexed. "If I took money, they would see my accounts increase, even if it was an offshore or Swiss bank account, right?"

"Exactly. But you are an ardent supporter of the environment. You think the rainforests should be protected, so you agree to create forged digital money in exchange for that money being used to buy up huge swaths of land that go into a trust."

"OK." Betty frowned slightly. "How does that help me ultimately? The land is locked up in a trust."

"But then I sell the mineral rights—oil, coal, precious metals—and selectively cultivate plants for medicines or ancient trees that needed to be culled for the wood, selective pruning. No one is checking a charity's management of the forest, and the profits are needed to 'maintain' the property. I take a large fee as the director of the board," Ernesto explained. "Of course, this is a small example and would be more likely to happen in Brazil than with someone in the Federal Reserve."

"What would happen if someone at the Federal Reserve helped you?" Betty asked.

"Ah, the trillion-dollar question." Ernesto looked pleased. Partially because he would get to boast and gloat, but also because his student was learning fast. "It is important to understand that when someone from within agrees to such a transaction—and dare I digress to talk about the government, in general as well, whenever these deals are made—only roughly one to ten percent of the funds are diverted to their cause. Someone like me takes the rest and the helper is ecstatic to have gotten that much for their cause, be it rainforests or reelection."

Betty paused Ernesto by raising her hand slightly. "Wait, what do the politicians have to do with counterfeit money?"

"Nothing, actually. I was referring to things like military contracts or changes in laws that favor the Cabal." Ernesto frowned slightly. Though he liked her questions, he thought Betty would be better versed in these types of transactions by Tom. "It is more difficult to arrange for counterfeit digital money, but the reward is significantly higher and the risk of losing the money afterward is quite small."

"Why?" Betty asked.

"The reserve banks will do anything to keep the markets from getting spooked. If it became known that trillions of dollars were forged, the markets would crash and gold would soar."

"Can't they just claw it back?"

"No. By the time they might discover the duplication, I have already traded the funds for other reserve currencies. Clawing it back would be even worse than admitting to the original incident."

"But you can't be the only one trying to do this," Betty observed.

"Hardly, unfortunately, but the others are using brute-force counterfeiting of bonds and such. The Chinese government has a vast operation printing forged American dollars and euros." Ernesto paused and considered the recent news of failed forgeries. "There have been several attempts in recent years to use euro-denominated bonds worth billions or trillions of dollars to secure credit from banks, such as the Istituto per le Opere di Religione—or rather, the Institute for the Works of Religion, commonly known as the Vatican Bank."

"They used faked documents to get real documents," Betty said.

"Yes. But these attempts were stopped in time. No transaction was allowed to happen."

"Was this one of your attempts?"

"Oh, no." Ernesto chuckled at the thought of getting caught. "I have a one hundred percent success rate. There is no indication any of my manipulations have been detected."

"So—what have you done at the Federal Reserve?" Betty asked.

"Two trillion dollars." Ernesto said with a wry grin.

"How could you pull off getting two trillion dollars without getting caught?"

Ernesto raised his left eyebrow. "You use a very tiny armored car."

"Hah. No, really, how do you pull that off without them figuring it out? Isn't accounting supposed to notice something like that?"

"Yes, they are, but we really did use a tiny armored car—at least, that is the way it was explained to me. I do not know the real method, nor do I really care." Ernesto took a sip of his water. "Actually, it is better that I not know the how."

"I suppose, but I want to know." Betty pulled her phone out of her pocket. The lodge was not in range of normal cellular service. Bud had established a microwave link back to the nearest city, which had the added benefit of providing unbreakable encryption.

"Who are you calling?" Ernesto asked, not believing Betty would compromise him, but curiosity was pulling at him.

"My IT guy." Betty hit the speed dial for Bud.

"He may be a very fine IT guy, but I doubt . . ." Ernesto trailed off.

Bud answered the call after one ring. "Hey, Betty. When are we meeting for burgers?"

"You'll have to talk to the boss. I'm stuck here until he says otherwise."

"I kinda figured. Don't forget me!"

"How could I? Listen, I'm going to put you on speakerphone. There is one other person here and I trust him."

Bud sounded wary. "OK."

"If you wanted to forge digital money and you worked at the Federal Reserve as the programmer managing the software that controlled the value and location of all U.S. digital dollars, how would you do it?"

"Hmm. Well, first of all, they would have two guys working on it simultaneously, so you would have to collude. Not very likely, especially with the management watching over your shoulder." Bud paused for a moment. "I would actually set up my coworker to do it so that if it was exposed, he would get the blowback. Second, I would use a virus-like piece of software to have his computer insert the code."

"But—how would you keep the accounting nerds from seeing the fake money?"

"Well, I once wrote software for managing apartments, back in my early teens, so I had to learn double-entry accounting. There would have to be two independent procedures. One that monitors database calls for reconciling the digital money for reports and another one that handles authentication requests from foreign banks."

"So, you would make a digital middle manager?"

"That's part of it, but the database would have to have both the authentic version of the money and the fake version. The fake version is not supposed to be there and the normal accounting system would be told to ignore it. The part that tells others—wait. I think I've got it. It gets really technical."

"That's OK, nerdman. I know you know how to do it. Now, can you figure out how to detect it in the wild?"

"You mean, can I detect a forgery in the real world? Sort of the colored pen for hundred-dollar bills?"

"Exactly."

"Well, I'd have to have access to the database of authenticated digital currency."

"So—"

Ernesto tried to wave Betty off. He did not want to draw scrutiny to his work.

"I'd hack a foreign bank to start, then use that platform to hack SWIFT or CHIPS—the Clearing House Interbank Payments System. That would allow me to watch all the biggest banks in the world at will. Then I would be able to—"

Ernesto lifted his hands, pleading to Betty to stop her IT guy.

"I don't actually need you to do that right now, but keep it simmering on the back burner." Betty winked at Ernesto. "OK. That's all I need for now. *Ciao!*"

"Yeah, right. Don't forget our—" Bud's last words were cut off as Betty ended the connection.

THIRTY-SEVEN

SMOKE SIGNALS

November 23, 2009 — Eagle-Vail Airport

GIL HELD THE DOOR OPEN for Jil as she climbed into the blacked-out airport SUV limo while the driver, a man with a name tag that read "Miller," loaded their luggage. The drive from Eagle to the Ritz-Carlton would take a half hour, and Gil did not expect her to be talkative after the long cry she had on the flight over, especially since she seemed so sullen upon exiting the jet. There was an eight-hour time difference between Århus and Vail—to their advantage—and the flight time was just over ten hours. They had taken melatonin shortly into the flight, which reset their biological clocks and allowed them to sleep for five hours during the trip. Gil felt rested and ready to go. Jil snuggled into his arm and pressed her cheek into his shoulder. After five minutes of silence, she broke the slight humming sound of the tires and the blowing air of the heater with a slight clearing of her throat.

"My mother is right, of course, but I can't change who I am," she said softly as she raised her head and settled back into the headrest, releasing Gil's arm and halfheartedly searching her purse for her lipstick. More to have something to do with her hands than to improve her makeup; it had not changed since she touched up her lips before leaving the plane. Instead, she fondled the hard, smooth surface of her cigarette case, which had survived her purge after Larry's death. She pulled a cigarette out and tamped it on the flat surface before fiddling with it in her right hand.

Gil reached his arm over her shoulders and gently rubbed her right shoulder. He had not read the letter, but from what little he gleaned from her reaction and the tears on the plane, it was not a touchy feely note of encouragement from Linda. He leaned close and kissed her forehead. "I like you just the way you are," he lied. He was enjoying the sex and the excitement of the frenetic lifestyle she kept, so different from his own, always on the go and always seeking the hormonal rush of conflict and crisis. While he would not want to be on her bad side, he certainly had no problem going along for the ride as an agent monitoring her. It made him think about the what-ifs of a relationship with her—not that it would even be possible after this assignment. Gil allowed himself the luxury of thinking about it, just so his words and actions would be authentic. "Well, there is one thing I'd ask you to moderate."

Jil slapped his right shoulder and tsked. "You said I was perfect!" she said mockingly.

Gil smiled. "Your smoking." *And your coke habit.*

Jil puckered her lips, stuck the cigarette between them and reached for her lighter.

Gil removed his arm from her shoulder and leaned against the window.

"You're serious?" Jil asked.

"They're going to kill you like they did your mother, God rest her soul, and I don't want that to happen."

The front partition rolled down and the driver's hand pointed to the "No Smoking" sign in front of Jil. "No smoking, please," he said, and the partition rolled back up.

"Jesus!" Jil exclaimed. "I can't make anyone happy."

She pouted, then threw the lighter back in her purse. The gold glittered next to the mirror-smooth cigarette case. "OK. I'll stop for now, but I get to choose all of your clothes. And I'm getting you a new cologne as well."

Gil tilted his head. "I'm not wearing a cologne."

"Exactly." Jil reached over Gil and pressed the button to roll down the window, then she threw the single cigarette out the window.

The partition separating the driver rolled down. "I appreciate you not smoking, but please don't litter." The partition rolled back up.

"Fuck. I can't win!"

"No, you just did." Gil pulled her close and whispered into her ear. "I love you for doing that." And he meant it.

Thirty-Eight

Splitting Woulds

November 23, 2009 — Near Bern, Switzerland

MARIE STARED AT PIERRE INCREDULOUSLY. "I don't believe you." She waved him off and turned her back to dismiss him.

"I can understand why you hesitate to believe me, but for the first time I understand why you enjoy pain." Marie turned back to look at Pierre and he pointed to his foot. "Gustav shot me and it shattered a bone. The pain was excruciating when I probed it. I blacked out." He looked down, away from her stare, ashamed to admit the last part. "I was aroused."

Marie crossed her arms and took on the air of a schoolmarm lecturing. "You want me to tie you up, probe the wound, and then deny you release until after you've begged my forgiveness?"

"Yes, it does sound like a trick coming from me, doesn't it," Pierre acknowledged.

"And I can finish you off any way I want to?" Marie asked.

"Sexually, yes," Pierre clarified.

"My, my. You never cease to amaze me, Pierre." A large grin crept onto her face. "I might just wait to tell you my answer." She looked down at his crotch. "You're getting aroused just by me withholding my answer!" she exclaimed. "Tsk." Marie shook her head in amazement. "I never imagined myself a dominatrix, but I think I could get used to this."

Gustav stopped pacing and put his hands on the back of the chair in front of Charles's desk. "I am growing concerned with the new Pierre."

"I have no idea what you are talking about." Charles said.

"He is no longer the one giving out pain, but the one receiving it."

"Gustav, you are speaking in riddles."

"I shot Pierre in the foot. He has offered to let me shoot the other one if his plan doesn't work out." Gustav pointed to the pile of financial documents he had placed in front of Charles. "He had his butler probe the wound, hoping to pass out again from the pain."

"I see," Charles said.

"He is no longer rational, I tell you!" Gustav exclaimed.

"Gustav, you seem to have lost your stutter. Pierre is not the only one to have changed in this scenario."

Gustav reached his hand up to his mouth. Memories flooded back of his youth and the beatings he got from Pierre after their father had beaten the older boy. Every time Gustav would try to say something to stop his brother, Pierre would hit him again. Gustav couldn't finish a sentence before the belt would land. The source of his stutter suddenly became clear to him. The cure seemed to be having the upper hand on Pierre. "You might be right." He could feel the start of a stutter in his throat, but by thinking about shooting Pierre and the pain he had inflicted, he was able to control the welling.

"If you think Pierre's plan is sound, act on it. If you need to shoot his other foot, by all means, fire away. Just don't cause another financial crash." Charles slid the papers to Gustav. "Am I clear?" He raised his left eyebrow for emphasis.

"Crystal." Gustav picked up the papers and left. The thought of shooting Pierre again was exhilarating, but he doubted he would either get the chance or be angry enough to follow through. Pierre's condition made him feel sorry for his brother. Gustav tested his voice to see if the stutter was coming back. It wasn't. He smiled. "The rain in Spain stays mainly in the plain. By George, I think I've got it!"

November 23, 2009 — Ritz-Carlton, Vail, Colorado

Karl reread the message from Bud one last time before using the special delete button on his phone. Pressing it initiated a cleaning process that involved repeated cycles of overwriting the memory location of the original message with an innocuous piece of junk mail from a Nigerian prince claiming to have millions of dollars sitting in a bank that just required someone with the surname of Middelburg to get them released. It was an old scam. No matter how improbable the story, that rare bird came along often enough to make the process worthwhile to the man or woman toiling away in an Internet café somewhere in the world.

Karl, let alone Bud, had never fallen prey to one of these frequent scams, but Bud loved to play with the senders on occasion. He would turn the tables on them and drain their bank accounts instead. It was his dream to someday show up in one of the cafés and confront the kingpin—of course, with someone like Karl backing him up in case the situation got violent. Bud had asked Karl if he would go along on such a personal mission. Thinking of that scenario—the nerd standing up to a gangly bunch of con men and their rat king—amused Karl, but did not entice him. He had promised to back Bud up if he ever grew large enough balls to follow through. Using the scammer's message was Bud's way of reminding Karl of his promise. Karl smiled and laughed to himself. "The boy still hasn't grown a pair."

The information Karl had committed to memory concerned Gil and Jil's arrival to stay in the penthouse. Having met Gil in person during the rescue mission, there was no need to use a call sign or any sort of stealth measure to establish credentials. Gil would spot the six-foot-five-inch bald-headed man in a crowd, and Bud had sent a recent photo of Gil in the message to refresh Karl's memory. This was going to be a cakewalk, or so Karl thought to himself.

A half hour later, Gil and Jil walked into the foyer of the Ritz-Carlton.

"Miss Harper, we've been expecting you," Karl stood up from behind the concierge desk. It had a large screen for the computer and a second one for the surveillance camera system. The split screen showed sixteen images simultaneously and would swap out every few seconds. Some cameras panned from side to side to cover odd angles or large areas. Karl had seen the blacked-out Excursion arrive and had the envelope with the penthouse credentials in his hand. "I am Karl Middelburg, your concierge."

Jil took the envelope from Karl and gave him a slight smile. She waved her hand at Gil and said, "This is my security chief, Gil Richardson. He will need complete access to the facility since he will be supervising when our guests arrive."

"I understood that as happening next week, but of course, he will have complete access now, as you wish, Miss Harper." Karl mused at how easy Gil had it on this mission. He could not remember ever having authentic security credentials handed to him with such ease in all his years working for Control. Karl opened a drawer in his desk and removed a key card. He programmed it by swiping it through the reader after setting the protocol on his computer. He handed it to Gil and said, "This will get you in anywhere in the building. I trust there will be no unnecessary intrusions upon our other guests."

Gil smiled back. "Of course. Complete discretion is always called for."

The bellhop rolled the baggage cart onto the elevator and inserted a key to hold the doors open while he waited for Jil Harper and her companion. Half of the building was condos, the other half time-shares. The service was first rate. Jil and Gil joined the bellhop just as Hanna Lautner and her Chihuahua, Skipper-do, entered from the great-room area, heading straight for the elevator. Jil's eyes narrowed as she willed the doors to close on the intruder.

"Miss Lautner," Karl called out. "I have a package for you here."

Hanna turned and smiled, inadvertently jerking the collar of Skipper-do hard enough to spin the tiny dog around as he tried to make a break for Jil's ankles. "I wasn't expecting anything."

The bellhop released his hold on the elevator by turning the security key to gain access to the penthouse level. This area of the Ritz-Carlton was designed to provide high enough security for heads of state or visiting dignitaries. No expense was spared.

As the doors closed and the VIPs departed, Karl handed Hanna a box of chocolates that he had stashed under the desk for just such an occasion. They were See's candies imported from California, but doctored by a specialist with an odorless and tasteless laxative, then shrink-wrapped and packaged for shipping. The return address was a generic post office box in San Francisco.

Hanna Lautner squealed with pleasure after tearing the paper open. "Oh, these must be from Hank!" —who had been trying to get Hanna to invite him to her condo for ski season.

Karl smiled. "I hope you have a splendid rest of your day, Miss

Lautner."

Skipper-do made a charge for Karl's ankles. He did not move or flinch, but when the dog stepped onto the clear plastic mat Karl was standing on, Skipper-do let out a high-pitched whelp. The mat was electrically charged, but Karl's rubber-soled shoes protected him.

Hanna watched her dog make the move and did nothing to stop him. She was aghast at the cry and was sure Karl had done something to cause her pooch's pain. She scooped up her Chihuahua and stormed off to the elevator, chocolates clutched under her arm. She scowled at Karl until the doors closed. Later, Hanna spent the rest of the afternoon in her bathroom, switching between the toilet and a bubble bath to sooth her nerves. Sadly, Skipper-do also got into the chocolates.

Karl removed the thumb drive from the security computer and smiled to himself. He had copied the footage before, during, and after the encounter with Hanna Lautner to prove he had done nothing wrong. The package could not be traced back to him. He removed the electrical box that provided the charge to the mat and put it in a drawer of the desk, just in case he might need it again, but he doubted it.

Thirty-Nine

Splitting the Diffidence

November 22, 2009 — Somewhere in the Virginia Mountains

BETTY AND ERNESTO'S MEETING ran for three hours while Tom, Gideon, Max, and Thor stood guard and cleaned up the property. Tom had Bud tap into NSA security satellites to watch over the area to see if there was any other inbound air traffic. Mostly, he just paced in his office. When the dining room door opened and Betty released Ernesto from her control, she thanked him for teaching her about world finance and assured him that the time had passed for wanting to kill him.

"You understand now, that José was a bad man and would have made you very sad?" Ernesto asked as Tom approached.

"I suppose it is all relative. Tom can be a very bad man sometimes," Betty said.

Ernesto looked at his half brother. "Does he make you sad?"

"Sometimes. Very sad," Betty answered.

"You want I should kill him for you?" Ernesto winked at Betty. She shook her head no. "Very well. He is your problem, then."

Tom's face turned red from embarrassment. "I am sure, if the day comes, she will not hesitate to kill me, should the need arise. I'm more worried about her than I am of the Cabal killing me."

"That's just because you have me guarding you," Betty said.

"Well, you and Gideon," Tom corrected her.

"Do you see what I have to put up with?" she asked Ernesto.

"No—do not put me in the middle of this. He may be my half brother, but he is your problem, not mine."

Tom held up two envelopes and handed one to Betty and Ernesto. "Read these, then use this lighter and ashtray to destroy the envelope and letter, please." He pointed to the bronze ashtray he had brought from his office and placed on the kitchen counter. Tom Sr.'s lighter lay beside the oversize art deco piece. The envelopes were sealed with wax, just like the ones Tom received from Gideon. They had been inside an unusually large envelope handed to him just an hour before with a message for him that gave simple instructions: Tom was to distribute them and make sure they were destroyed. His curiosity burned crisply as he watched the two digest their messages from the grave. Betty finished first. Lit the paper on fire and used it to start the envelope. The wax smelled of frankincense, which is known to relieve depression and anxiety. Betty breathed the fragrance in deep, not knowing the therapeutic qualities, but knowing she liked the smell, which reminded her of childhood and the Catholic Church.

Betty,

I will not apologize for the missions I selected for you or the times I thought you were a threat to the organization. Any such words from me now would ring hollow. I think more highly of you than that.

Sometimes threats can be used to manage the actions of others. Just maybe, by putting you in the positions I did, you became a better agent and Tom became a better man. You would not be reading this letter if he had not stood up to me and done what was necessary to preserve not only your life, but your position in this organization. I assume he did it out of love. If I were still alive, now would be the time for you to decide to either put a bullet in my head or accept me as your father-in-law. I do not regret much of my life. Every choice has been the natural consequence of my first choice in 1943. You may think that I am evil, but I spent my life fighting evil. Perhaps it takes one to know one.

You and Tom have my blessing. I know he wants to spend the rest of his life with you, but just has not figured out how to make it work. It will if you want it to.

Warmest regards,

Tom Sr.

Ernesto read his letter several times and looked to Tom. "Must I burn it?" A tear was forming in the corner of his eye. He blinked several times and it ran down his cheek.

Ernesto,

Your mother was my greatest weakness and my greatest love. If I had not pledged my life to the mission of Control, I would have given up everything to be with her. That was not possible, so, after my last visit, it became clear to me that I could never return, even for an hour or two. We all made a great sacrifice. You most of all, losing both parents and being raised by the Jesuits to be what you are today. I am so proud of you and what you have become. You have done well, my son.

Love,

Your Father

"I'm sorry, Ernesto, but you must." He contemplated what the letter could possibly say to touch Ernesto so deeply. Tom Sr. had never been demonstrative to Tom Jr.; he was a brusque father who used emotion to manipulate, not to convey feelings.

Betty's fire had burned out. Ernesto reluctantly reached for the lighter and, after hesitating, lit the pieces of paper and watched the words invert, the paper charcoal and the ink a dusky gray. He took the offered wooden utensil and smashed the carbon into a fine dust. The words would only live on in his mind, which would fade someday soon as he came closer to death. He too breathed in the aroma of the frankincense. It reminded him of the many hours spent with the Jesuits in Argentina.

The long hours of study and prayer. His education stuck. The Catholic religion, not so much.

"Now," Gideon said, "who's hungry?" He waved them into the kitchen, where he had set up a buffet of food to feed the troops. "The patio is safe, now, and the evening air will be glorious. I have a cooler of drinks out by the table."

"You first, Betty." Tom prodded Betty and Ernesto ahead of him. Max and Thor stayed outside and would not come in until the others had gotten their food.

"I think you've outdone yourself, Gideon," Betty said.

"I'll let the carcass of this buffet be the judge of that." He smiled and fiddled with spoons and forks, stirring this and that to improve the presentation as they worked through the line.

†

"Got everything?" Tom spoke quietly into Betty's ear as he hugged her close. He could feel her SIG Sauer P229 in the hidden holster tucked into the back of her jeans, something a casual observer would not be able to spot with her jacket covering her waist. He imagined her using it, on someone besides himself, and the pride he felt made him pull her closer, as if he could manage her independence—the most dangerous aspect of Betty, and the one thing he wished he could control. Only if he knew which way she would lean, could he influence which way she would go.

"Everything but you in my bag." Betty said. She had avoided sleeping with Tom since the Ernesto incident. Smelling him now, along with the thought of being separated again—for the first time since Denmark and Gil's rescue—created a deep need to feel his bare skin on hers. The need to feel secure in his arms as they lay under the covers with nowhere to go and no agenda but mutual pleasure. Betty grabbed Tom's ass and massaged his haunches, pulling his crotch closer to her pelvis. She did not trust him fully, but she longed for what he had always promised her in their relationship. Security. In reality, the security was elusive and fleeting. They were chess pieces in a game with the Cabal, and sometimes she felt like he was playing the game and using her instead of standing with her. The letter from Tom Sr. reminded Betty that Tom and Howell were the same star: one rising as the promise of a beautiful day; the other, the regret of a setting sun.

"You can leave now or you can leave in the morning," Tom said.

Betty heard the faint sound of the helicopter arriving. Ernesto, Max, and Thor were waiting on the patio to keep the layover as short as possible. She thought about all the times she had allowed her decisions to be influenced by his words and actions. *Which way does he want me to go this time? Does he just want sex? He's a man, so . . .* "Which do you want? One last night of sex or one last night of being together?"

"You wouldn't believe me if I said I didn't want sex. But I do want to spend one more night with you without our guests." Tom stepped back from her. "But it's your decision this time. Your flight won't leave till morning, so that won't change. I am who I am. You need to accept that I am not going to change because you want me to."

Betty bit her lip and looked down. "Yes. You're right. And I won't change because you want me to." Betty picked up her bag and looked Tom in the eye. He looked like a sad puppy. "Are you going to make a lady carry her own bag to the bedroom?"

Forty

On the Balance

November 23, 2009 — Ritz-Carlton, Vail, Colorado

JIL HANDED GIL AN ENVELOPE with cash. It was a mix of bills about an inch thick. "This is your folding money."

Gil held up his hand. "Wait a minute, I have money."

"Remember, Casper is paying, so I don't want any lip. Sometimes I won't want to carry my purse. Then you'll be the one to get our coffee or do the tipping." She smiled sweetly, stood on her toes, and gave him a peck on the lips. "You really need to learn to do as I tell you, since you are my chief security officer now." Jil patted the bulge caused by the holstered firearm just under his armpit.

Gil squinted his eyes and pursed his lips. "I should have known there was a catch." He snatched the envelope and stuffed it in his inside jacket pocket on the right side. He did not want the extra bulk getting in the way of his holster on the left.

Gil moved over to the couch and plopped down, spreading his arms out on the back.

"Don't get too comfortable, big boy, we have shopping to do."

"We just got here!" Gil wanted to lounge around until dinner, but he knew she would win the argument. "Amazing view of the mountain from here."

Jil straddled Gil's hips and put her arms around his neck, pressing her breasts suggestively into his face. "Yes, the view from here,"—Jil rolled her shoulders and expanded her chest by breathing in deeply—"is the biggest attraction, don't you think?"

Gil smiled and looked up at her. "It's beautiful."

Jil rolled off his lap and sat beside him. "Can you believe the broker tried to get me to take the fourth floor instead?"

Gil put his arm around her and pulled Jil close. He liked the way she snuggled up to him, now and in general. It distracted him from thinking of her as an asset. Instead, she was his girlfriend. On one level, it was the best kind of cover. If he thought of her on such a personal level, it would be impossible for anyone to uncover the dissemblance of his true intentions, Jil most of all. Then again, he had to remind himself that she was trying to use him just as much as he was using her. Her disguise—of liking him and wanting to be close—fooled him regularly until he remembered his own machinations to fool her. *Oh, the tangled webs we weave when we first attempt to deceive*, he thought. "I can't imagine him even standing in your way."

"Hardly, darling." Jil smiled and thought of Dick's feebleness at Casper's threat at pulling the financing of his valley project. "He folded like a card table—do people even use card tables anymore?"

"Just the poor folk," Gil said.

Jil lightly hit him on the arm and pulled away. "Come see the view from the balcony. You could jump into the pool from here." She did not really mean that she would do it. Jil's idea of jumping into a pool started at the deck and did not go higher.

"I can totally see you doing that." Gil considered the prospects of surviving a leap from the sixth story. The pool was really at the level of the second floor, so the distance was about fifty feet. He had jumped from much higher points both during his training and in high school at the local quarry. The most important part was landing with your arms crossed and legs together.

"You'd be surprised at my athleticism. I'll have you know I won the loving cup at Pepi's ski school, when I was younger." Jil leaned over the railing and balanced herself, leaving most of her weight on the safe side.

Gil reached out and placed his hand on her ass to make sure she didn't accidentally flip over, but mostly just to feel the smooth, taut muscle and think of having sex. "Maybe I should stand behind you, to make sure you don't go over," he suggested as he moved to place both hands on her hips and grind himself between her legs. He had her in a position she could not squirm from without taking a chance on going over.

"Not now." Jil would normally have enjoyed the unusual setting for sex—the danger of the balcony, doing it in public, and making Gil happy—but the thought of falling made her think of death which led to thoughts of her parents and the letter from her mother. For once, her enthusiasm for sex had waned.

Gil kept pushing it. "You're always ready for sex."

Jil clung tightly to the railing and used her buttocks to push Gil away. She turned and slapped him across the face. "I said not now, damn it!"

Gil backed up and sat down on a patio chair. "Sorry. I thought you'd like the thrill."

"You men!" Jil stormed off the balcony and into the master bedroom, sniffling as she went. She threw herself on the bed, her face in the pillow, and began to cry.

Gil entered the room slowly, sat on the bed, and began rubbing her back gently. "I'm sorry."

"It's just not right," she said, her voice muffled.

Gil thought she meant his attempt to have sex on the balcony. He started to apologize again, but she started talking before he could figure out how to say it.

"I was supposed to have grandchildren and a husband. Daddy was to walk me down the aisle. My mother will never hold her grandchildren."

Gil was thankful that he hadn't apologized again, but still did not know what to say . . . "I'm so sorry." He got up from the bed, unsure of what to do. If this was a battlefield, he would do something, even something foolish, to kill the enemy. Here, the enemy was an absence, a displacement in Jil's future caused by cancer and her father's lack of will to win. He had no weapon or strategy for defeating an enemy like this. He sat down on the loveseat opposite the bed. "What can I do?"

Jil sat up and wiped her tears. "For starters, you can go find some scotch. The bar should be stocked."

Gil knew how to do that, so he ambled out of the bedroom and over to the bar, poured a couple of stiff drinks and splashed them with water. He grabbed the fresh bar towel and brought it to Jil, handing her the drink with the towel held underneath. She took both.

"Did you give it a splash of water?" she asked.

"Of course." Gil smiled.

Jil took a swig of the drink and took a deep breath. “Give me a few minutes so I can clean up. Then we’ll go shopping before dinner.” She looked at Gil, his tender eyes pleading like a puppy who didn’t know what it did wrong. “OK?”

“Got it. Should I move the reservation to later so we can shop longer?” he asked.

“That would be nice.” Jil took another sip of the scotch and then waved him off. “Now, scootch.”

Forty-One

I'm Only Going to Say This Once

2300 Hours, November 22, 2009 — Somewhere in the Virginia Mountains

BEFORE TOM COULD CLOSE THE DOOR to the master bedroom, Gideon called to him. "I'm sorry, but I have another letter for you."

Tom looked to Betty and rolled his eyes before she could do it to him. "I'll only be a moment."

"Take your time." Betty tossed her things onto the couch to the side of the king-size bed. "Like usual," she said softly.

Tom heard her last comment but pretended he did not. He accepted the letter and walked over to his office desk to read and then destroy the missive. Gideon stood near the door and waited for any instructions. "You have great timing, Gideon."

Gideon smirked, then smiled. "We all have our jobs to do."

Tom slit open the wax-sealed envelope with a pen knife from his father's desk drawer. This note was different from all the others. The handwriting neater, as if his father had taken his time and carefully pondered the words. The shakiness of his old-age handwriting was not evident.

> Tom,
>
> My letters will become fewer and fewer as time goes on. It is becoming difficult to predict future events accurately. There are letters you will never see because I prepared for multiple outcomes. Perhaps now I should explain why I started this chain of events seventy years ago.

During World War II, while working with the OSS and Allen Dulles, the horrors I witnessed tempered me for the moments of weakness all human beings find themselves in. Sometimes I removed myself from the temptation, such as never seeing Ernesto's mother again or even writing to her. I sent funds to pay for their needs and then some, but because I was not there to protect her, the love of my life died of a curable disease.

You surely think of your mother as my true love. I loved her; of that there is no doubt. But Ernesto's mother came from Germany and the darkest crevices of the war. She saw things that I saw. Horrible, unspeakable human suffering that no one should suffer, let alone live through, or worse, visit upon their victims. We were with each other at our worst moments and in our grandest hours. She knew what I was capable of and did not judge me for my decisions.

Your mother came from the horrors. Your grandfather Fritz caused a few in his pursuit of a cure for her blindness, but she never lived amongst them, in part because she could not see with her eyes what the rest of us endured. I will never regret marrying her—I have you from that commitment. But I will never apologize for the others. The ones who made my life whole, who helped burn away the memories and visions of what we had to do to win the war. The people we fought then are the same ones we fight now. The difference is timing. Now we are ahead of them and able to slow down their advance to power. It is up to you to stop the Cabal from amassing the wealth necessary to control the key weapons and militaries of the world. With that power, they will start the third world war. In their minds it will just be a skirmish meant to drive earnings; in reality it will mean the death of a billion people or more. The worst-case scenario is that more people will die from this looming battle than had ever lived on this earth before World War II. They will not have global annihilation on their minds, for they must have enough of the proletariat left to grow the crops and tend the herds. There must be servants and roads and airports to sustain the lifestyles they are accustomed to. But, just like our best-laid plans, theirs will go asunder and the world may go with them. Releasing the four horsemen is the ultimate result of their machinations, whether they believe it or not.

It is up to you to find them and bend them to your will. Then kill the ones who are strongest. You will think for a short while that they can be managed, that your heart is pure enough to withstand their evil. It is, until they find something you love and dangle it in front of you as the flames of hell burn the flesh of your true and only love before your eyes. I wish there were another way. You are not ruthless enough to do what must be done, so I can only hope that you are cunning enough to make those evil bastards do it to themselves. Turn them against each other and you will not have to sacrifice your morals for a Pyrrhic victory.

Protect the one you love. Send her far away on any mission that removes her from the dangers before you. Otherwise, turn her loose with the knowledge that she alone has the power to destroy the ones who would use her to destroy you.

You are about to lose some very good soldiers in this fight. Some will die. Some will leave. Some will turn on you. You will have pity for them—of that I am sure, because that is your way. I might as well ask the moon to leave the ocean alone. Use your enemies against themselves and you will not have to visit your love's grave prematurely.

You are as ready as you will ever be. There is nothing more I can teach you even if I were still there. I groomed

> others, but you alone have what it takes and the will to do what is necessary to keep the world from revisiting that smoldering pit of hell on earth. Do not let us down.
>
> By writing the words I cheapen the emotion, but know that I love you to the core of my bones.
>
> Your Father

Tom reread the letter again. The second time he read it without the jaundiced, practiced eye of someone perpetually manipulated. This time he read the letter with his heart. Just this once, he allowed himself to believe that his father was capable of exposing, let alone feeling, love for his child. Tom had seen Ernesto's response to reading his letter, and Betty's to hers. He shook his head. *It's just another one of his games, pulling on the heartstrings this time instead of loyalty to the cause—to maintain loyalty to the cause.* Tom looked to Gideon. "So, do you get your own letters?"

Gideon clenched his jaw and screwed up his face. "I'm not supposed to tell you." He relaxed his face and smiled. "Sometimes. Mostly just letters of encouragement with instructions mixed in."

"He was a piece of work, you know, our father." Tom had not meant to tell Gideon that bit of information and hoped this half brother assumed he meant Ernesto, but he no longer thought it really mattered.

Gideon paused before replying. "What do you mean, our father?"

Tom pursed his lips. "I suppose I could just say that I have several half brothers, one dead."

"Who died?" Gideon asked, his head tilted slightly and eyes slit.

Tom considered his next words carefully as he paused before touching the flame of the lighter to the paper. "Grace's son, Timmy, died on a mission. We were about the same age. I suppose, if he hadn't died, Father might have replaced me with him as the head of Control." He withheld the information that Timmy had died saving Tom's life. Considering Gideon's role, the information would not be very helpful at the moment.

Gideon was surprised by this admission. "Why do you say that?"

"I was always at odds with him. Timmy always did what he was told to do." Tom smashed the ashes of the letter with the wood utensil.

"What makes you think he wanted someone at top who would do what he was told?" Gideon asked.

"I guess I just always assumed he was disappointed with my combativeness. We didn't get along very well since—just after I turned sixteen." Tom thought about the incident that led to the estrangement from his father. He had broken curfew, yet again, to be with his girlfriend and high school sweetheart. To stop the romance, Tom Sr. arranged for her father to be transferred from Virginia to California. Tom Jr. overheard his parents arguing over what had been done. Heartbroken and incensed, he moved out and bounced from one friend's house to another while he finished high school. A year later he was attending Virginia Military Institute, against his father's wishes, and he was told not to come home. It took two years for his mother to convince Tom Sr. to allow a visit. It was only after Tom graduated that he was brought back into his father's orbit and into Control.

"Did you ever think that you got the slot because you never gave up on your positions and stuck to your guns, even when it cost you dearly?" Gideon asked.

"I suppose I never thought of it that way, but I—you're probably right."

"Don't you have something better to do than jaw with me?" Gideon pointed to the bedroom and the waiting Betty.

"You know, as much as I like you, I think you are absolutely right." Tom looked one last time at the ashes and the only time his father had ever told him he was loved. Tom understood now why Ernesto had asked to save his letter, a weakness evidenced by the bundle of well worn mementos he kept in his coat pocket. Tom turned to look at his brother Gideon before leaving. "I guess I was the lucky one."

"More like the prodigal son, but go with what makes you happy," Gideon said with a sly grin.

Forty-Two

Just Let Go!

0200 Hours, November 23, 2009 — Old Town Alexandria

"DAVID, I NEED TO SPEAK WITH HIM immediately," Grace said.

"You sound under pressure," replied David.

"I have something he needs to know about. Now. Not tomorrow. Not in a week." Grace was drumming her fingers on a wood table.

The thumping resonated through to David. "I don't mean to sound like I do not believe you, but maybe you should just tell me—that way I can tell him when he surfaces."

Grace drew the same knife she had tortured Beth with out of it's metal sheath, the sound cut through the line. "I have my blade out." Grace stabbed the point of the blade into her cutting board. The handle danced back and forth, the blade flexing. When it slowed down, she pulled it back and released. "Either he gives me a few moments of time or I just take care of business as needed without guidance." Grace walked over to the chairs where two prisoners were tied up. "Oh, and Bob showed up. It would be a twofer at this point."

"I'd hate to be related to you. Give me a few minutes to reach out to him."

"That's a good boy." Grace flicked the knife again; it twanged this time.

David put Grace on hold and picked up the other line, the one he had already made contact with Gideon on. "She is threatening to clean Bob and Beth if she doesn't talk to him—now."

Gideon looked over his shoulder toward the bedroom. "Fuck. Now isn't a good time, but I see where this is going. He's with Betty and they have been trying to get time alone for hours."

David glanced at his display of agent statuses. "Right, she leaves in the morning for Vail. If it weren't her parents, I'd say leave them be."

"Good point." Gideon started walking to the door.

"I'd hate to be you 'bout now, mate." David switched back to Grace. "Working on it. Give me another minute or so." He didn't wait for her to respond before switching back to Gideon. He could hear knocking on a door.

Gideon rapped once softly, then louder until the door opened just a crack.

Betty stuck her face out, but hid the rest of her body. "He's sleeping. For God's sake, can't it wait till morning?"

Gideon frowned. "No, it can't. You should know it's Grace and it involves your parents."

Betty was confused by his words. "Wait, what—how is my dad involved?"

"I can't say, I'm not privy to all of the details. David needs to connect the director directly to Grace."

"Oh." Betty looked back over her shoulder at the slumbering man who seemed to float between being her true love and greatest nemesis, depending on who else was involved. "I guess I better wake him."

Tom was rousing from his sleep, the sound of Betty and Gideon talking enough to draw him out of his dream. "What's up? What's going on?"

"Give us a minute, OK?" Betty closed the door on Gideon.

"She's getting him. He was asleep," Gideon relayed to David, who then relayed the information to Grace.

Tom turned the bedside light on and swung his legs out of bed. He stretched and yawned before he rose out of bed and began getting dressed.

Betty slipped her robe on and sat down on the bed. "It's Grace. Something about my parents and it's an emergency." She looked up at Tom. "I guess I want to know what's going on, but I don't want to be the one to make a decision."

"Got it." Tom rubbed his face and eyelids while yawning again. "I'll take care of it. Don't worry." He headed to the door and Betty hugged her knees.

Gideon handed him the phone as he walked to his office. "OK, David, fill me in."

"Not much to tell you, boss. Grace said she'd clean Bob and Beth if I didn't get you on the horn double time."

"OK. Connect me. I'm ready." Tom sank slowly into the leather of his father's office chair. The mantel of responsibility it represented seemed heavier than he remembered.

"Tom?" Grace asked.

"Yes, I'm here, Grace. Sorry it took so long for them to rouse me." He looked at his watch. It was two a.m. both in his part of Virginia and in Old Town Alexandria.

"I have Bob and Beth here. You know the story on Beth."

Tom nodded, "Yes."

"Bob crashed the party and threatened to release information to WikiLeaks about something called Line X if I didn't let Beth go." Grace took a deep breath. "I don't know what that is and I don't want to. What I do know is that he made a threat and it needs to be dealt with." She stared at her brother-in-law, a man she had never had a cross word with, nor had she ever really known him. Her life had been split from her sister's before the marriage, and there had been little contact since Grace had turned eighteen.

"Ah. Those two always were tight." Tom scratched his head. "Grace, are you done with Beth yet?"

"Well, I was mostly done before he showed up and caused the ruckus," she admitted.

"Do you want Beth to live?" he asked.

"I don't want her to die, if that's what you mean."

"Has Bob ever done anything to deserve your ire?" he asked.

"No, we really haven't had anything to do with each other. Compartmentalization, you know." Grace cast her eyes to her shoes. She felt like the little girl who had been trained to believe she was overreacting, except back then, she wasn't.

"Then, can you do me a favor and put Bob on the phone?" Tom asked.

"Well, OK."

There was a ripping sound and Tom could her Bob say, "Son of a bitch!" Then the sound of the phone being pressed to Bob's cheek.

"Yeah."

"Hey, Bob, Tom."

"Oh, hi, Tom. How's my Betty?"

"She's doing fine, Bob." Tom cleared his throat. "You know my father is dead, right?"

"Oh, no, I hadn't heard. I'm real sorry to hear that. He always treated me right. I wondered why I couldn't get a hold of him the old way." Bob and Tom Sr. had a special protocol for communicating that predated the larger Control. Tom Sr. had continued using it only for nostalgic reasons and his long relationship with Bob, one of the first Control agents. "I suppose that's why I overreacted."

"How is Beth?" Tom hated to ask that question, but he needed to de-escalate the crisis.

Grace was holding the phone for Bob, so when he turned his head from the phone to look at his wife, his words became distant for a moment. "I don't know all the particulars, but she needs to get the hell out of here, that much I can tell you."

"Bob, there was a bad time, before you, between Grace and Beth. You could say Beth had it coming, even if she didn't deserve it. Can you understand that and let it go?"

There was a long silence. Tom could hear Bob take in several short, deep breaths as he assessed how badly his wife had been damaged by his sister-in-law, someone he hardly knew. "I just want her home. Can we just go home and back to the way it was?" Bob started to blubber and cry. "I just want my Beth back."

Tom waited a moment to let Bob catch himself, which he did after about ten seconds. "Bob, I like that idea, but instead of going back, can we move ahead? Can you help Beth do that?"

"Yeah, I can do that." Bob sighed harshly.

"OK. I'll make it right with Grace. Can you hang on for a bit while I talk to her?"

"Yes." Bob cleared his throat and his voice became faint. "He wants to talk to you."

"Yes,"

"Grace."

"Yes."

"I need you to back away from all of this and let it go. Can you do that for me?" Tom asked.

"But—"

"Grace, it is a yes-or-no question, no ifs or buts." Tom said.

"Yes. I can let go." Grace had already extracted her revenge, and if Bob hadn't shown up, Beth would have been released in the next twenty-four hours.

"Good, because we are all family and that is what I want," Tom said.

"I hurt her pretty bad, Tom. I don't know if she'll forgive me."

"She will, Grace. You'll have to trust me." Tom nodded his head to Gideon, who knew he was to contact David and get things moving. Gideon signaled that Miller, who had flown back to Washington D.C. the previous evening, would be nearby and sent in to help Bob and Beth home. Miller had been the agent who rescued Betty from the Caribbean Sea off the coast of Venezuela. "You trust me, don't you Grace?"

"I trust you, Tom." Grace turned back to look at her sister and brother-in-law, making eye contact with each before continuing, "We're all family, right?"

"Pretty much." Tom shook his head as he thought about all the unbelievable connections his family had, and here he was, just one step away from being the son-in-law of Bob and Beth, and the nephew-in-law of Grace. "Thank you, Grace. Miller will be there shortly. He will get Bob and Beth home. OK?"

"OK," Grace agreed.

The connection ended and Tom tossed the phone onto his desk. Betty entered the office with Gideon.

"Do I want to know?" she asked.

"Bob and Beth are going home with Miller. It's going to be OK, after everyone has some time to step back and take a breath." Tom stood up and walked over to hug Betty. "If you only knew how much and why I want Bob and Beth to live—" he whispered into her ear.

"Why don't you tell me, then?" Betty asked.

"Ask me again after Vail," Tom said.

"I can do that," Betty said.

Forty-Three

Hash Browns, Stat!

November 24, 2009 — Ritz-Carlton, Vail, Colorado

"GIL, BE A DEAR AND TURN OFF THE SUN." The master bedroom had a stunning view of the ski runs and lodge pole pines. The snow was starting to accumulate. The combination of the sun peeking over the mountains and the glare of the reflected light off of the snow—and more precisely, the window of a new home being built on Forest Road—was acting as a mirror focused on Jil's face. If she just covered her head with a pillow for a few minutes, the sun would move on and the focused light would disperse. She felt like the ant below the magnifying glass held by a prepubescent boy bent on finding out if spontaneous combustion was viable.

Gil rose and pulled the curtain. He ambled to the medicine cabinet in the bathroom and got them both aspirin and glasses of water. Like a hotel room, the bathroom was stocked with all the necessities and luxuries, such as cut-crystal glasses that were washed and replaced daily by the cleaning staff. He sat down next to her and nudged her with his elbow. "Hey, open your eyes for a moment—I swear it's worth it."

Jil doubted him, but opened one eye just the slightest bit and saw the drink and aspirin in his hands. "I love you." She raised herself on one elbow and gulped both down before plopping back into bed, Gil holding the empty glass. "What happened last night?" came Jil's muffled question.

"Hmm. I think we finished the bottle of scotch, had dinner and drinks, then I poured you into bed."

"Is that your best guess, or did I do most of the drinking?" Jil asked.

"I think I held my own shot for shot, but then, I weigh almost twice as much as you."

Jil moaned, "Ohhhh. Why did you let me do that?"

"Since when have I been able to tell you what to do?"

"There's always a first time." Jil rolled back over to look at him. "What's for breakfast? I think I need something greasy to sop up what's left of the alcohol."

"There's a fruit basket in the foyer, but I can get something brought up in short order."

"Is there watermelon?" Jil asked.

"Why?"

"It's the best hangover cure in the world."

Gil chuckled. "Well, I can do one better than that." He went to the closet and pulled out an IV bag from his kit and grabbed a hanger. "You probably didn't know I'm a trained medic." Gil hooked the hanger on the wall sconce and set up the IV bag. "Roll over."

"What are you doing?" Jil asked.

"This is the best hangover cure in the world. Saline and glucose. And you can sleep while it drips, if you want to. I'll keep an eye on it." Gil smiled and swiped an alcohol pad on her forearm. "This will only hurt a tiny bit if you hold still." He quickly inserted the needle into her vein and taped it in place. "Just sit back and relax. You'll feel like a million dollars in no time." Gil grabbed the phone and called Karl, who suggested takeout breakfast from the Little Diner and promised to rush it.

Jil licked her lips and said, "You're my hero." She looked over at the couch and spotted her handbag. "Be a good boy and grab my bag on the couch."

"Yes, ma'am." He retrieved the bag and checked on her drip. Everything looked good.

Jil found her lip gloss and treated her tender skin to a mixture of vitamin E, lanolin, special herbs that caused her lips to puff slightly, and a secret ingredient that Eric Salizar refused to reveal. "Ahhh. Between my gloss and your IV, I'm in heaven. Now, where's that breakfast?"

"I'm sure it is about to arrive. I'll go see." Gil patted her IV arm at the shoulder, checked the drip one more time, and went to the foyer of the penthouse. He grabbed an apple from the fruit basket and had just started to bite it when there was a knock at the door. He opened the door to find Karl there holding a takeout bag. "Just what the doctor ordered!"

With a wince on his face as if the size of the tip pained him, Karl took Gil's proffered five-dollar bill with his middle finger and thumb. "I'll charge it to your room."

At the sound of the door closing, Jil called out to Gil, "Is breakfast here at last?"

"Daddy's here with breakfast!" he said.

"Thank God." Jil looked up at the IV bag and noted how much had drained into her veins. "I'm feeling much better already."

Gil handed her the clamshell Styrofoam container with her Denver omelet, hash browns, and a wedge of watermelon.

"No plate and silverware?" she remarked.

"Oh, my mistake, madam." He snatched the breakfast from her hands. "I thought you wanted it stat. You know you can only have two sides of an iron triangle."

"What on earth do you mean?" Jill asked.

"You can have quality, speed, and price, but only two at the same time."

"I'll take quality and speed, please, so hop to it and go get me a place setting. There should be a breakfast tray in the pantry."

"Yes ma'am. Will you be wanting ketchup for the hash browns?" he asked.

"Now that's the kind of service I expect." Jil smiled at him and settled in, content from the IV to wait just a little longer for her breakfast.

Forty-Four

Dead Relations

November 24, 2009 — Somewhere over America

BETTY HAD FOUR HOURS TO MENTALLY prepare before landing at Eagle Vail under her trust fund cover story. *The best lie is the truth with the unfortunate parts left out*, she thought while sipping her freshly brewed espresso aboard Control's G650. The recent family turmoil had to be forgotten, so she let it go with a deep breath and a sigh. She needed to make the details of her cover her own, but Control provided the bank accounts and credit card in her name.

The inheritance came from a distant relative, a fact that would be difficult to verify or even refute. She felt the Rolex on her wrist, the one Uncle Buck had given her at graduation from Georgetown Law. He claimed to have worn it in Korea as an aviator—a story she liked, but had never thought to check out. *No time like the present!* The airplane had wireless Internet and something about his story had always seemed off, but now that he was "dead," she wanted to know for sure. *Hell, I don't even know his last name.*

Searching for the history of the Rolex GMT-Master revealed that the watch was introduced in 1954, Pan American Airlines pilots were the first to wear and test the watch. *I've been taught to not trust Wikipedia, but damn! They're more reliable than Uncle Buck!* The Korean War technically has never ended, but an armistice treaty was signed in July of 1953. *Nothing about my family seems surprising any more. Hell, he was probably Beth and Bob's handler and a member of Control.* She looked at the watch again and began to wonder, *If this watch came from Control, it has to have a transmitter or something.* Betty took a pocketknife out of her bag and worked the back cover off of her watch. She didn't know what she was looking for. Some sort of device hidden in it to keep track of her? It took diligence, a few scratches to the watch and her fingers, but in fifteen minutes she was able to expose the movement. *I don't know why I thought I'd find something, there's no room for them to hide much more than a piece of thread, let alone the workings of a transponder.* The story of how the KGB hid a passive amplifying microphone in a hand-carved wooden seal of the United States of America crossed her mind. The building across the street had had twenty-four-hour surveillance and a laser pointed at the seal to energize the diaphragm and bounce the vibrations to a receiver. Moscow knew everything discussed in the ambassador's office for several years until the Secret Service finally caught on to the ruse.

She looked the watch over more closely, envisioning the possibilities. She wasn't keeping her watch stationary long enough for anyone to bounce a laser against it. *I guess sometimes a gift is just a gift and a watch is just a watch.* She put the watch back together and refocused on her cover story. *Sometimes an inheritance is just that. I guess I'm trying to make too big of a deal about this. Uncle Buck gave me a watch and when he died he gave me some money. A lot of money. It was a surprise, my parents never knew about it and he never told me. I got a letter and then a call to come in for the reading of the will.* Betty imagined a white-shoe law firm with walnut paneling. *I was the only beneficiary. He had no children and I was the one he chose to pass everything down to. There's nothing to it. I don't have to work anymore.* She thought about her immigration law practice—the one that introduced her to José, the one she had barely tried to maintain the past year. *I decided to spend a couple of months in Vail. I bought a condo as an investment and for year-round visits. I'm worth twenty million, earn a million dollars a year that I can spend as I wish and I can afford the finer things in life, as long as I don't go crazy. I can make that work. Wait a minute—how come only twenty million? Tom, you're such a cheapskate!*

"Miss Thursten?" The steward had drifted over to her seat with a tray of snacks, shrimp cocktail, edamame, and chips made from kale and beets.

"Oh, yes, thank you." She put her tray table down and let the steward situate the food.

"Would you like a beverage?"

"What are my options?" Betty asked.

"We like to say the sky is the limit. If we don't have it, we can go down and get it." He winked at her. His tag said "Barrington."

"Well, Barrington, I would like a brut champagne."

"Easy-peasy." The steward went back to his station and returned with an ice bucket and a bottle of Dom Pérignon 2008. He showed her the bottle and Betty nodded.

The bubbles fizzed and the effervescence tickled her nose. "It's perfect." She smiled at Barrington. It crossed her mind that she should tip the crew when they landed. All the years of hanging with Jil and flying on Larry's jet was paying off. She knew what to do. *Piece of cake, being a trust fund kid. I just need to ask myself,* "What would Jil do?"

Forty-Five

Slumming at a Five Star

November 24, 2009 — Bern, Switzerland

"I THINK, CHARLES, THAT LEAVING for Vail early would be for the best," conceded Marie.

The unbelievable had happened: a major plumbing disaster that required the sudden evacuation of Marie's beloved mansion. A corroded waste pipe had failed, causing all of the effluent from the household to accumulate in a pit that had then overflowed into the well. The smell had been building for several days. Incense and candles masked the odor while plumbers crawled through the property looking for the cause. They were too late. The water was contaminated. The thought of bathing in or ingesting raw sewage, boiled or not, was enough to drive them to a five-star hotel. The scullery staff were left behind to contend with the cleanup and sterilization. A skeletal crew of key personal, the butlers, maids, chefs, dietitians, personal assistants, and massage therapists took up residence in the floor below. The daily cost of the catastrophe was nearly a million dollars.

Charles clicked his tongue. "Yes, of course, either that or we better send Gustav down to buy the hotel." He looked at his calendar and pointed to the day they were supposed to leave.

"You love to turn the screw, Charles," Marie said.

"Yes, speaking of sadists, Pierre isn't in any condition to ski, is he?" Charles lifted his foot high enough for Marie to see him point his finger at it and pretend to shoot.

"Sometimes you are such an ass." Marie turned away and looked to the door that separated them from Pierre. She lowered her voice to a whisper. "I'm worried about him. He is absolutely obsessed with that wound. It isn't healing—he keeps prodding it and poking it open. The doctor is threatening to put on a plaster cast to slow him down."

"I'll talk to him. It is getting rather annoying to listen to him whine these days. It's become a downright nuisance, to be truthful."

"He's on antibiotics for the infection. I overheard the nurse mentioning MRSA."

"Really?" Charles looked puzzled. "What on earth is that?"

Marie smirked as if her knowledge of such things showed her superiority to him. "A staph infection, Charles, a staph infection!"

"Dear Lord. Thank God we have separate accommodations. Will you be burning your house down? Did he get it from your water?"

"Charles!" Marie was sure he was just giving her a hard time, but her pride took a hit from his criticism. "He might lose his foot."

"Well, to be frightfully honest, I'd rather they cut it off now than have to listen to the bore for another week if it's going to come down to that." Charles closed his calendar, a leather-bound affair handcrafted by artisans in Rome who normally restored ancient manuscripts. Each page had been hand drawn with ink infused with gold specks. It was a work of art that he desecrated every day with his scribbling. He noted Marie's horror and abjured, "Now, I don't really mean that, Marie. I hate to say it, but I truly did prefer the sadist Pierre to this sniveling wimp we have now. I wouldn't have said it a month ago, mind you, but seeing the difference is enough to convince me . . ." He let the thought trail off when he remembered that Marie had been the frequent recipient of Pierre's sadism. He had been about to say how weak he thought masochists were, but even if she was one, he had offended her enough for one day.

"Convince you of what, Charles?" She said.

"That a change of scenery would be for the best. Yes, let's alert the pilots and get the staff packing. If we get moving now"—he looked at his Patek Philippe Platinum World Time watch with twenty-four time zones noted around the face—"we can be in Vail in time for cocktails."

"You are such a wit, Charles. It's always five o'clock somewhere."

November 24, 2009 — Århus, Denmark

Eric Salizar finished packing his messenger bag and walked out to the reception area of his office. "I'll let you know when I've landed. Is the team ready to head to the airport?"

Claire, his secretary and sometimes-lover, pouted. "You said I would get to go this time."

"I did, didn't I." He scrunched is chin and nodded. "I also said that if you didn't get to go we would do those surgeries you wanted, which you agreed was worth waiting a little longer to travel with me."

She straightened her back and puffed out her chest. "You want them bigger, don't you?"

"I want what you want, when it comes to working with your natural beauty." Eric believed what he said. The most successful outcomes he had ever seen from plastic surgery were when the patient chose changes that pleased them, not their admirers. "You need to believe any change is enhancing, not replacing your beauty."

"Humph."

"Besides, I truly need you to watch over the hospital while I am gone. I am not fully confident in Dr. Smildjik's ability to keep everything running smoothly, without a little help from you."

"Flatterer."

"If the truth flatters you, then so be it." Eric shifted his grip on his bags. "Claire, I need you here more than I need you in my bed in Vail."

"That's because you'll have someone else in your bed there."

"Tsk tsk. How can you say such a thing. Surely it will be some ultra-wealthy trust fund child and it will be her bed," he teased.

"You're such a tomcat—I totally hate you!"

Eric smiled. Put his bags down and went over and kissed her, pushing into her lips while holding the back of her head. "May God forgive you for thinking like a jealous woman."

Forty-Six

Causa Belli

November 24, 2009 — Eagle-Vail Airport, Colorado

ERNESTO SWORE IN LATIN, "*Nam fuit ante Helenam cunnus taeterrima belli causa* . . ." He reached back with his right hand and violently threw his cellphone against the wall, shattering the electronic device. The indignation of being denied use of the corporate jet to fly here had just been topped.

Max turned quickly, the sound of his boss's anger taking his attention away from the sparse group of people waiting for their flights. The airport staff had abandoned the gates to load the luggage onto a commercial flight. "Boss?"

Ernesto closed his eyes, drew in a deep breath, and held it for a moment. With his lips shaped like an O, he blew the air out of his lungs slowly. He turned to Max and said, "We are truly on the other side."

Max looked perplexed. He had started learning Latin to complement his other languages and knew Italian well enough to think Ernesto had just blamed Helen of Troy's anatomy for the war. "How's that, boss?"

"Charles is being a dick. His desire for control, my job, has caused this war. First he tries to replace me, then he starts trying to set up investments without going through me, and now, we are to find our own lodging." Ernesto sighed. "Please arrange for a new cellphone, a different number, and get that information to Howell." Ernesto took another deep breath, held it, and slowly released it before saying, "Charles and company are arriving earlier than planned. They've lost a facility to flood and we are being bumped from the Ritz-Carlton to make room for their cosmetic procedures."

"I know someone there. Let me call him," Max said.

"What can he do? This is Charles we are talking about."

Though he could not hear what was being said, the conversation had garnered Thor's attention as he approached with the luggage on a cart. "Is there a problem?" he asked.

"No problem," Max said to Thor. He turned back to Ernesto and said, "Just let me call him. Let's see what he can do."

"What the hell, why not." Ernesto waved him on.

Max used his cellphone and dialed Karl, who had already been updated on the situation thanks to Bud's eavesdropping system.

"Ritz-Carlton, Karl speaking."

"Max here. Are there any units available? Two bedrooms would be adequate. I tip well."

"Of course not, but by the time you arrive I will have performed a miracle and you will be all set. It better be an excellent tip."

Max gave Ernesto a thumbs-up. "Don't bet on the ponies."

"Hah."

Ernesto had a perplexed look on his face. "What was that about ponies?"

Max gave a slight chuckle. "He said I better tip him well, but he would perform a miracle and find us a unit to use."

"You continue to amaze me, Max."

The group trundled off to the waiting ubiquitous black SUV with heavily tinted windows. The exhausted looking man waiting to load their luggage wore a name tag that read "MILLER".

November 24, 2009 — Eagle-Vail Airport, Colorado

Betty had not been told who would be her driver from the airport. She was pleasantly surprised when she saw a man dressed in a dapper black suit and thin black tie who looked exactly like Miller, but with longer hair. He was pretending to not know her. Betty focused on his longer hair and tried to hide her familiarity with the man who had saved her from drowning in the Caribbean Sea. It was after the escape from Ernesto's compound and Gil's sacrifice to make sure she was airborne in the glider for the flight over the Ávila mountain pass. At the time, she did not know that Gil had survived, been rescued by his biological father, Michel, only to be held hostage to donate his kidney to the dying man. *If Miller hadn't saved me, who would have saved Gil?* she thought.

Once they had pulled out of the airport and were cruising down I-70, Miller rolled the partition down and handed Betty a packet.

"What's this?" Betty asked as she turned the items around in her hands.

"Some sales literature for housing that you might be interested in." Miller said. "Be sure to give them my name as a referral if you buy. I could use the spiff."

"I doubt the boss would like me spending that kind of money."

"Just don't forget me."

"Are you planning on retiring here too?"

"That is a long ways away. Use it, toss it, hide it, I don't care." Miller focused on the road as he passed a slow moving semi truck that had just entered the highway. After a quiet moment, he said, "How ya been?"

"All right, I suppose. It's been a crazy time since I last saw you," she said.

"That's an understatement." Miller looked back at Betty in the mirror. "That was some crazy shit, the kill order being rescinded and all. Never seen anything like it."

Betty thought about the mountain retreat and the attacks she fought off. "Wait around awhile. You haven't seen anything yet."

Forty-Seven

How Do You Say "Cheeseburger" in a Romance Language?

November 24, 2009 — Washington D.C.

"BUD, I DON'T CARE HOW YOU get these things done, it makes no difference if you explain it three different ways—I will never understand the mechanics of what you do," David said to the Control technology genius. They were connected via a secure encrypted link. David had moved his operations to a warehouse in Washington, D.C., along with several other members of his staff. The mostly empty outer shell had an office suspended in air by opposing magnets built inside yet another rectangular box. No radio or sound waves could be detected outside the envelope. The network connection was a special laser that connected the floating cube to the outside world for telecommunications and Internet. Electricity was provided via a principle first demonstrated by the inventor and technological genius, Tesla. The method was called resonant magnetic inductive coupling and could transmit AC power over short distances wirelessly. No one outside of the cube could hear or detect the communications of the new heart of Control. The trickiest part was the air-handling unit, which resembled the type of system used on the International Space Station. The poisonous waste was scrubbed out and the air purified, leaving no direct path for sound waves to exit the structure.

"Well, the money is in the account now. Try not to spend it all in one place," Bud said, his voice slightly distorted from the multiple security measures combined with his low-quality Wi-Fi connection he was stealing from a coffee shop.

"Hah! Like I could spend ten billion dollars in one place," David said as he checked again, blinking his eyes to make sure it was not a dream that Control's balance sheet just had a cash infusion that was desperately needed.

"I bet you could if you put your mind to it." Bud had considered ordering himself a grid of satellites with the money, but decided he would wait until the next time he siphoned money from a bank. Besides, he still had access to the NSA's complete arsenal of spy equipment, so why recreate the wheel. He didn't care if the bank noticed what he had done. The bad publicity from admitting they were robbed by a cyber criminal would do more damage than finding a way to plug the hole caused by Bud lifting billions of dollars from their digital vaults.

"So, about your request to schedule a time to meet Betty—what is this about?" David was looking at Bud's vacation request that matched one from Betty exactly. Betty had never bothered with such mundane bureaucracy paperwork, nor would she have to. Her time was coordinated directly with Director Howell. This was obviously an attempt by Bud to arrange a meeting.

Bud cut the video but maintained the audio portion of their connection. "She promised me."

"Promised you what, exactly?" David asked. He tried to reconnect the video signal, but Bud had blocked it.

"She owes me a lunch date at Five Guys." The nasal tone of Bud's voice went up an octave. "Cheeseburgers."

"Seriously, Bud. Thank God your skills are better at stealing money than trying to get a date."

"I'll remember that remark next time you ask for an increase in funding," Bud said in his full-on nasal tone.

"You're just going about it the wrong way."

"Well, how would you do it, then, Mr. Smarty Pants."

"Tell you what, mate, I'll set you up."

"With Betty?"

"Seriously, mate? You are bonkers." David shook his head side to side. "Tomorrow night, five p.m., a very nice redhead will be waiting for you at Five Guys."

"Seriously?"

"Yes. I will make it happen for you. Code word 'cheeseburger' and counter sign 'the works,'" David explained.

Bud did not know what to say. The line was silent for several beats.

"Bud?"

"I don't know what to say," he admitted.

"Start with 'cheeseburger' and go from there," David suggested.

"I can do that," Bud said.

"Good. Now, please unhack our system and remove Betty's request for time off before Director Howell catches wind?"

"Sure, sure." There was the clicking of keys and a computer mouse. "Done." Bud reconnected the video portion of the feed but wouldn't make eye contact. "Thanks, David."

"You're most welcome, Bud. Do you remember the protocol?" David prodded.

"'Cheeseburger' with the countersign of 'the works.'"

"And then?"

"We talk."

"Exactly."

"About what?" Bud asked.

"Oh, for the love of God—you're hopeless."

Forty-Eight

What Did You Just Say?

November 24, 2009 — Ritz-Carlton, Vail, Colorado

THE VOICE ON THE LINE WITH JIL had always given her shivers of intimidation. But for the first time since crossing paths with Casper, she was more angry than afraid. She was looking forward to shaking free of Casper's grasp once and for all, after the task of managing the Vail gathering. Losing her family was the ticket to her freedom. Cancer, suicide, and . . . Ruth. *Ruth isn't going to ever speak to me again—she might as well be dead.*

"What do you mean, they're arriving earlier than expected?" she asked.

"Charles et al. will be arriving later today. They will be staying in separate accommodations around the area, but will be using the penthouse as their gathering point each day. The bedrooms will be set up for spa and medical procedures."

"I thought we were using the new clinic that was being built." Jil's disappointment oozed from her voice.

"There was a fire. The location is useless to us now, and no amount of money will correct its deficiencies in time." Casper said.

"Exactly where I am supposed to stay?" Jil asked.

"The second-floor unit. I have informed Ernesto that it is no longer available. You should be thankful. I—"

"Oh, yes, of course I am." The second-floor unit, in Jil's mind, was purchased for staff such as guards and masseuses, not for someone like herself. To be lumped in with the proletariat offended her deeply. It was a narrow unit with mostly a view of the building itself, twenty feet away. The master bedroom, if you could call it that, had the only decent view of the mountain and in her opinion should have been designed as the living room instead. "I was expecting a week to prepare for their arrival," Jil insisted.

"Jil—"

He had never called her Jil before, always "Ms. Harper." Something had changed. She wanted to believe that the work she had done in the past for the mysterious voice had earned her a position of equality, but in her gut she knew better. Casper had no equals. "I'm sorry, Casper, I am still distraught over my parents death. Please forgive me." She did not really mean the last part, nor any of what she had just said. It was just part of the game of appeasement.

"I am most distraught at the death of your parents as well. Ruth has said you are not on speaking terms, so I suppose it is up to me to tell you that we are engaged."

Jil turned to Gil—who had been eavesdropping—her mouth slightly ajar. "What?" Ruth had been Casper's hostage the past year in Denmark. Jil could not fathom how this was anything but an arranged marriage. She started to say that it was not possible since Ruth had not told her, but then the gravity of their estrangement became clear. "Well, I'm happy—for the both of you." She slanted her eyes sideways at Gil and flipped her hair. "Have you picked a date?"

"Not yet, but I do look forward to meeting you in person. We should plan something in Europe after the Vail gathering, perhaps. I am sure I can get your sister to relent. Paris?" Casper suggested.

Jil was aghast at the idea of having lunch with the man who drove her daddy to take his own life, let alone the one who ordered the removal of his left ring finger. She felt a little bile come up her throat, which she quickly washed back down with a sip of champagne. Her eyes were wide, and Gil offered nothing but an inquisitive look. "Paris! Of course, what a spectacular idea."

"Wonderful. Now, please do take care of the particulars that I have forwarded to you. The staff will be arriving this evening to start setting up the penthouse. And Jil, have you found out anything more on what your friend Betty is up to?"

"No specifics yet, but I have someone near who has knowledge and I am working on it."

"Please work harder on that. I do want Paris to be a vacation for us all, hmm?"

"Yes, of course, Casper."

"Excellent. That is all." Casper ended the conversation and left Jil holding her phone to her ear ready to say goodbye to her soon to be brother-in-law.

"Oh, Mother of Mercy!" Jil exclaimed.

"What?" Gil asked. It was unlike Jil to use religious exclamations. Her normal cuss words were mild in public, but she could swear a blue streak in private.

"Ruth is engaged and she didn't tell me!"

"Well, you two aren't on the best of terms right now," Gil said.

"How can you defend her not telling me?"

Gil realized he had stepped into a trap, one that the military had never trained him for; nor did he know how to disarm it. "No, no, I'm not defending her." He felt like a flashbang grenade had just gone off in the room. His senses seared from the unfamiliar terrain of the conversation.

"My sister! Not telling me about getting engaged to the man responsible for my parents' deaths?" The thought of being on the bad side of her future brother-in-law put a fire in her belly. She wanted to tie up Gil and interrogate him about Betty. She knew they had to be connected, but there was no way to directly ask Gil without exposing her purpose. She needed to get a grip on her emotions and figure out something from her past that would give her an excuse to pry some information from him. He was obviously a spy and playing her. She was no fool, even if she was falling for him.

"More champagne?" Gil asked.

Forty-Nine

What I Wouldn't Do for You

November 24, 2009 — Ritz-Carlton, Vail, Colorado

"DAMN TRUST FUND KIDS!" growled Karl under his breath.

Hanna Lautner had just passed through the lobby of the Ritz-Carlton and had threatened to report Karl to the authorities for poisoning her baby, Skipper-do the Chihuahua. She knew it wasn't the candy itself—Skipper-do had been fed chocolates his whole life, and never suffered canine toxicity. The emergency veterinarian bill for pumping the dog's stomach and several days of observation would break most household budgets, but it was a drop in the bucket for Hanna. It was the principle of the thing. She could not prove it, but she was sure Karl had been the one responsible.

It surprised him that she was more concerned with the pooch than she was with having had diarrhea for twenty-four hours after eating the tainted See's chocolates. He knew his tracks were covered—he had been trained well in the art of espionage—but since it was an emotional decision to make Hanna pay for all the trouble she caused him, he retraced his virtual steps in his mind to be sure. The bigger problem would be the hassle of any inquiry. He was not supposed to attract attention to himself, but just like his temper getting the better of him at the shipyard in Belarus, he let a rich pain-in-the-ass civilian draw him into a conflict he might technically win, but would lose when it spilled over into his real work for Control. Karl's mission was to use his retirement from active fieldwork as a way to keep tabs on the activities of the rich and powerful. Hanna might be wealthy by most standards, but she certainly was not powerful. Her kind of wealth allowed her to lounge about comfortably, flitting from one social event to another while dressing in the latest fashions, but it was not the kind of wealth that could be translated into power. She was the gnat circling his head at the moment. In his younger days, he would have just ignored her.

"I need some better repellent." Karl looked at his list of arrivals and top concerns for the day, vis-à-vis the Ritz-Carlton. Betty would be arriving and staying in the fourth-floor condo. He needed to have Bud tweak the system to make a reservation for Ernesto and company. The usual contingent of wealthy South Americans, trading the heat of home for the cool of Vail, were due for the beginning of the ski season, but he had no idea which one he could bump. "First things first." Karl typed up a message on his phone giving Bud the particulars, two- or three-bedroom condo, charge it to Control, and make sure it was as far from Hanna Lautner as possible.

Just as he hit the send button, Betty arrived with her luggage. He suppressed the urge to give her a bear hug. The short time they had spent together in Denmark had been intense and the basis of a lifelong friendship. When you save someone's life and they save yours, how could it not?

"Hello, welcome to the Ritz-Carlton," he said. He checked his clipboard and pretended to find her name on a list of expected arrivals. "Ms. Thursten?" It would not have been much of a guess in any case. The list had an image of the incoming patron to facilitate the staff's ability to keep riffraff out and personalize the experience for the expected guests. There was a blank page on top for notes to prevent anyone knowing they used this particular cheat. The clientele liked to think they were important enough to be identified by the staff on sight.

Betty herself had a rush of emotion as she thought of the rescue mission to get Gil back from the clutches of Michel. The raw danger of being shot at, the plane ride in a cargo container ending with Karl waiting for her. Knowing that if it were not for Bud's intercession, Karl would have likely acted on the terminate order sent out by Tom Howell Sr. Betty extended her hand and said, "Yes, and you are . . . ?"

"I am Karl, your concierge. Please don't hesitate to call me if you need anything." He handed her his card, which had his cellphone number printed on it, and the envelope with her card keys and information about the Vail area. "May I have your ski equipment moved to the guest equipment room at the Arrabelle for you?"

"That would be lovely." She turned to look at the bellhop pushing the luggage cart with her bags and equipment. He paused in front of Karl, who removed the soft-side bags holding the boots, poles, and skis.

"Philipe, why don't I help Ms. Thursten to her room and you can bring up her locker key."

The junior man nodded his head and trundled Betty's gear off to the guest locker space across from the gondola at the Arrabelle.

When they were in the elevator and alone, Betty moved over to Karl and gave him a big hug. "It's really good to see you again! You settling in?"

"Doing great! Glad to see you, too. Hey, watch out for Hanna Lautner—huge pain in the ass, carries her Chihuahua with her everywhere." The doors opened to the fourth floor and he guided her to Günter's place. "This is a loaner. There shouldn't be any surprises, but yell if someone comes looking for Günter."

The space was enormous for one person, but the right image for a newly minted trust funder with too much money to spend. The view from the floor to ceiling patio windows was stunning. The snow was falling gently, and the forecast called for twelve to twenty more inches. The skiing was going to be amazing. "I've got you on speed dial. You'll be the first one I call." Betty spun around the like a dancer in the huge living room. This condo was basically the same layout as the penthouse, just not as prestigious. "A girl could get used to this," she said.

"It's yours for the next month, longer if you need it."

"Hmm. I think I *will* buy it. I'm quite wealthy, you know."

"Do tell! Single?" he asked with a crooked eyebrow.

"For now and maybe forever, but if I ever weaken and decide to take on a houseboy, you'll be the first one I call." She pulled his bald head down to hers and kissed his forehead.

Fifty

Don't Forget Me

November 27, 2009 — Ritz-Carlton, Vail, Colorado

THE COMMOTION IN THE LOBBY was spilling into the great room, a large airy space with compliant leather furniture, ample natural lighting, and a collection of kitsch that said old money purchased by the nouveau riche. It was five p.m., the official start to drinking for those tenaciously holding on to the fiction that they did not have a drinking problem and those too introverted to mingle without social lubrication. The pool had been covered with a translucent, kaleidoscope-backlit dance floor and a band that once headlined stadiums—and still had enough mojo left to fill amphitheaters—was setting up on the stage built at one end. The sort of group that could command fifty thousand dollars to show up for a private concert. This was FAC, Ritz-Carlton style, to celebrate the start of the ski season. Just as with everything else at the Ritz, the bar stock was a notch or two higher quality than the average Vail establishment. The well booze was premium, and the back-bar inventory was not available where Joe Sixpack caroused.

Betty was mingling with the other trust funders, making small talk about which runs they were going to start on, with some boasting about chartering to Telluride for heli-skiing. She found herself channeling Jil, pretending that she had her old friend on her arm to fill the void in the conversation when Betty did not know what to say. Before long, she was latched on to a slightly younger new friend named Hanna—the one Karl had warned her about, but who seemed to know everyone at the event. Betty passed muster when she asked to hold Skipper-do, recently recovered and back to his old self, and the little Chihuahua snuggled contently into her arms and actually nipped at Hanna when she reached to take him back.

"I've really missed my Surry!" Betty exclaimed as she held Skipper-do up to her face and let the pooch lick her cheek.

"Why didn't you bring her?" Hanna asked.

"Life, I suppose—I was on a European adventure and decided to leave her with a friend."

"Do tell, where'd you go?"

"France and Denmark, mostly."

"I just love France!" Hanna started speaking in French until Betty waived her off.

"Sorry, I only know Portuguese and Spanish," Betty admitted. "Here, you better take Skipper-do back before I become attached to the little devil."

He resettled into Hanna's arm, his chest riding on her wrist and hind legs dangling from her elbow.

Betty turned to pick up her drink and out of the corner of her eye spotted Jil and Gil. She had been told of the development, but it still startled her to see her former best friend, arm locked with her former lover and partner.

When Jil's gaze caught sight of her one time wingman, she put her hands into the air and shrilly called out her name, "Betty!" and scurried over as fast as she could to hug. "What a surprise to see you here!"

Gil floated toward them, but stood back a bit to keep from seeming familiar with Betty.

"And you too!" Betty pulled Hanna over to the conversation. "Now, this is the girl who can speak French," she said.

Hanna and Jil started a rapid-fire conversation discussing the hot spots of Paris and Provence.

Betty turned to Gil and stretched out her arm in an exaggerated movement. "Betty Thursten."

He took her hand and shook it. "Gil Richardson."

Betty picked up her drink to give herself something to hold, and tried to start the sort of conversation a woman would have with the boyfriend of her former best friend. "How long you two been together?" *Damn it, it sounds like I'm interrogating him.*

"Not too long, but long enough," he said.

Betty read too deeply into Gil's words and imagined he was saying that not only had he moved on from their relationship, but he was implying that it was Betty's fault. "Jil and I are old friends. We grew up together."

"Ah, I see," Gil looked back and forth at the two women. One he had hoped to have a long term relationship with but failed; the other—well, he didn't really know what he had. "That explains a lot."

Betty looked askance at him. "Explains what?"

"Why she was so excited to see you."

"But you're wondering why she's so absorbed with Hanna?" Betty asked.

"Yeah, something like that," Gil admitted.

"She's trying to make me jealous or to punish me for not keeping her in my life more. Take your pick."

"I'd vote for the jealousy angle," Gil said.

"Of course you would. You're a man."

"I think I'll go get us some drinks. You need anything?" he asked, pointing to her half-filled drink.

"Nope—wait, yes, please. A vodka tonic with a slice of lime would be nice. This one is getting warm."

"And Hanna?" he asked.

Betty looked over at Hanna's glass. "She's drinking a cosmo. Just point her out to the bartender, I'm sure he'll know what she's having."

Gil worked his way through the crowd and waved a bartender over. He looked up at Gil and nodded, too busy to come right away. Gil reached for his folding money, produced a hundred-dollar bill, and dropped it on the bar as a tip.

The guy quickly finished the server's order and scooped up the bill and placed it in the tip jar with a broad smile. "What can I do for you?" he asked.

"Two vodka tonics, a brut champagne, and whatever that woman with the dog is having, a cosmo?"

The bartender gave a thumbs-up and got to work. He grabbed the premium vodka and poured the cosmopolitan first. He added cranberry juice, Cointreau, and a generous squeeze of a lime. He poured the vodka tonics from the same bottle and popped a fresh bottle of champagne, Dom Pérignon 2008, for Jil. "What room number?"

Gil leaned in, the bar was noisy. "What?"

"What is your room number to charge it to, or did you want to start a tab?"

"Two-fifteen." He put another hundred dollar bill on the bar. "Don't forget me."

The bartender smiled and placed the drinks on a tray and came around the bar to carry them for Gil. "I wouldn't dream of it!"

Fifty-One

Wall of Noise

November 27, 2009 — Somewhere in the Virginia Mountains

TOM WOULD LEAVE THE MOUNTAIN retreat after the last of the personal effects and Control materials had been loaded into a civilian version of the Black Hawk helicopter. The property was now staged and would be sold at a discount to ensure a quick sale. Back in Washington, D. C., Bud and an army of medical consultants were busy scanning, then destroying the last of Control's paper documents. Items too sensitive to be handled by just anyone came to Bud for processing, who was bored out of his mind.

"My work is falling behind—this scanning is driving me crazy!" he said to Tom over a double-encrypted connection.

"You're nearly through it all. You can do it, Bud."Tom scanned the horizon. There hadn't been another assault since Betty took on the four commandos and "mercy" killed the remaining wounded man whose guts had spilled out of his wound. They would be leaving for good in a few minutes, yet he feared an imminent attack. "Besides, I'll be there in a few hours to relieve you."

A second office in the warehouse had been set up just for this project. To speed the construction, shipping containers were used instead of building the elaborate structure David was in. Electronic white noise was being flooded into the warehouse space from special emitters designed by Bud and McFluffy. They resembled massive photocopiers, because that is what they were in a prior life. By stripping away the foil insulation covering wiring and circuit boards required by the FCC, the electronic emissions were amplified. An LCD screen scrolled images of the Warren Commission's report on the assassination of JFK for the scanner to pick up and the electronic brain to process, thus creating a white noise similar to the signature of the equipment being used by the staff. Brilliant in its simplicity. Organizations like the NSA and other countries' versions of the NSA would be listening around the Washington, D.C., Metro area for this type of digital signature. The sensitive equipment would pick up the signal and decode it with a black-box device that magically produced an image that matched the document being photocopied or scanned for an analyst to look at. Bud knew about this type of surveillance because he had helped design it for the NSA, as a consultant. By the time their broadcast would be identified and scrutinized, the conversion project would be complete or the analyst would move on, looking for more promising material.

"Good. I'm going stir-crazy here," Bud said.

"OK. OK. You'll get a medal for bravery," Tom deadpanned.

Gideon was aware of Bud's disdain for the project. He had been fielding a constant barrage of requests to be released or talk to Tom from Control's director of technology for several days. "For what, surviving multiple paper cuts and poking himself with staples?"

Tom looked at Gideon and shushed him with one finger to his lips. "Go see what's taking so long. We're sitting ducks here."

Gideon gave him a disbelieving nod and said, "Right," slowly and sarcastically.

"Anything else on your radar while we're talking?" Tom asked Bud.

"I did that infusion from the Bank of Madrid like we discussed. Are we good for now?"

"We're solid. Thank you, Bud. That *will* earn you a medal."

"I'd rather have my own satellite network," Bud said.

"But then you'd have to monitor it, and people would start asking questions about who owned them, let alone the time to get them into orbit—"

"I have prototypes built, they're just one foot square, and we can deploy them like throwing marbles on the ground."

"But in space."

"Yes. In space. They are so small everyone will think they are just space junk from the explosion of the rocket right after deploying them," Bud explained.

"You've put some thought into this, haven't you."

"I've been a little bored the past few days with this project. Lots of time to think."

"Well, give me a dog and pony show when I get there." He disconnected the link as he watched the helicopter with the last of the cargo lift off and head east after gracefully turning on a vertical axis for the pilot to view the airspace in all directions. Gideon was waving him to the last helicopter. Tom visualized the Saigon CIA station evacuation at the end of the Vietnam War. He was going to be the last man out. He locked the door to the mountain retreat—a place he had visited many times as a boy—and took one last look around. There was a seat cushion sticking slightly out of the storage bin, which he pushed inside, and he latched the lid. A small weed was making progress along the stone stairway to the helipad. He paused and pulled it from the crack it had wedged itself in and tossed it under a shrub. He took in a deep breath as he looked around one last time. He gave the pilot a nod and a smile as he jumped on board for the flight to Washington, D.C. Two minutes later they were several hundred feet above the compound, doing the same vertical-axis spin to view the valley and mountain ridges for any potential threat, when a large object—perhaps a Tomahawk cruise missile—streaked over a ridge opposite the house and slammed in through the doors Tom had just locked. The pilot peeled away and dropped altitude quickly to get below and past the blast of debris that was sure to follow, and it did. The shock wave of the explosion swept above them, but the reverberation against the valley walls shook the aircraft. The pilot returned to an altitude above the leveled boyhood retreat to reveal nothing recognizable left.

"I guess we better tell the realtor to lower the asking price," Tom observed dryly.

Fifty-Two

Shop Till It Hurts

November 28, 2009 — Vail, Colorado

THE DOOR TO THE AXEL clothing store swung open as Betty and Hanna reached for the handles just as Jil and Gil were pushing the doors open. Shades of emotion swirled through Betty's mind, a rainbow of feelings that blurred into muddy brown ruts.

Jil recovered first, being the consummate beauty queen. "Oh, Betty—Hanna! What a treat."

Hanna was facing Jil and grabbed hold of her arm. "Jil, so good to see you again."

Gil and Betty just stared at each other until Gil raised one of the bags and said, "Doing a little shopping."

Betty drolly replied, "I never would have guessed."

The meeting dance would have continued until the first surrender, but another couple wanted to leave Axel, their purchases in hand, so the group parted, Jil calling out, "Join us at Gorsuch when you're done!" more to warn them than to encourage.

Hanna missed the clue. "We'll be there before too long!" Skipper-do gave a sharp bark to remind everyone that he was part of the group.

Betty smiled and waved, her version of pageant friendliness, the type Jil might give in a parade from the back of a convertible.

Once inside, Hanna immediately pulled Betty to the first blouse on display. "You'd look fantastic in this," she said. Hanna grabbed the hanger and held it in front of Betty, measuring her beauty against her own. "Jil always makes you feel in second place, doesn't she."

The cutting remark brought back the feelings Betty had at the entrance to Axel. Jil had always used Betty as a measuring stick, for her wealth, beauty, and standing in society. There had only been a few times when Betty felt superior to Jil, one of which was the time she caught Jil working as an escort to pay the rent. Larry had fallen prey to an investor in Denmark and nearly went bankrupt. This was just before Jil started working for Senator Bolden. "She hasn't always been on top."

Hanna pushed the blouse at Betty. "You know, now that you're set, the best revenge is to spend like mad."

Betty had the American Express Centurion card—the Black Card— and her mission was to be an über-wealthy girl, ripe for the picking by the likes of the Cabal . . . *I would never buy this stuff on my own.* She looked at the price tag: three hundred thirty-eight dollars. *Holy crap!* Her first reaction was to put it back as quick as she could. As a lawyer who needed to dress sensibly but be able to fit in with the highest reaches of public life, she had always carefully picked clothing from the discounted rack. Being a season or two behind was OK. Spending four hundred dollars on an outfit was reasonable, but on just the shirt—*no way!* But then her mission refocused her thoughts. The desire to make Tom pay for past troubles aligned with her trust fund cover and pushed her hand as the saleswoman came over. "I'd like to try this on," Betty caught the woman's name tag and added, "Mandy."

Before long, Hanna and Betty had picked out half a dozen complete outfits, fully accessorized—some she would never wear outside of Vail, and let Mandy ring up the sale. With a certain amount of nervousness and trepidation, Betty handed over the company credit card.

Hanna gave a smile of recognition. The Black Card was an exclusive card that required the holder to spend money to keep the privilege. Her spending in a typical week overqualified her.

Betty watched the readout of the cash register, not believing that she could really pay for twenty-five thousand dollars of cashmere, down, and leather. The display said "Approved," and she pretended that it was never in doubt.

Before she could reach for the bags, Mandy asked "Where are you staying? I'll have the bags delivered."

"The Ritz, room 405," she said with a smile. *I could get used to this.* Then the thought of tipping came to her mind. She had never had this kind of experience, even with Jil. She walked Hanna away from the clerk and said quietly, "Am I supposed to tip for the delivery now?"

"You really are green, and I love it," she said to Betty. "We'll tip when they deliver the bags, and you can send Mandy a nice gift basket if you want to keep working with her." Hanna held out her arm for Betty to link her arm into. "Gorsuch?"

"Gorsuch!" She thrust her arm into the crook of Hanna's and they set off for the next adventure in shopping.

Fifty-Three

I Have a Bone to Pick with You

November 28, 2009 — Bern, Switzerland

"PIERRE, YOU ARE THE ONE who loves to ski, not me," Marie said as she reapplied her riverine-rabbit-red lipstick in the master bedroom vanity.

"And here I am, foot in a cast, bedridden until further notice." Pierre tapped his plastered foot with the cane once used by Voltaire. He was taller than the long-dead writer, so a bronze extension was added to the foot to make up the difference. It was the bronze end that made the thunking sound against the cast.

"If you had left it alone, you would be on the slopes this week." Marie grabbed his free hand and quickly placed a noose around his wrist and attached the other end to the bed frame with a Velcro strap.

"What do you think you're doing?" Pierre asked. He waved his cane at his stepsister.

"Oh, poor Pierre. In such pain and suffering." She lashed his good foot to the bed.

He tried to resist, but only halfheartedly. His constant exploration of pain via prodding his wounded foot had weakened him. He was on a strong antibiotic to combat the resulting infection and on morphine for the pain.

Marie dodged the cane as it swept past her head. As he swung it back at her, Marie clasped his wrist and tied it down too. "You are weak, Pierre," she tsked at him. "A shell of the man you once were." Marie moved around to the foot of the bed, a massive sculpture of elk horns and wood. "Don't you want something for the pain?" she asked as she pulled the noose around his free leg.

Pierre was too weak to resist her lashing his cast to the bed. He pleaded with his eyes as his mouth opened and closed slowly, like a fish out of water. The desire for another shot of morphine or for Marie to poke a stick into the cast to scratch the scab ate at him. He managed, "Please . . ."

"I know, my poor, poor Pierre. How many times you have taken care of my needs." Marie had always been the passive of the pair, only becoming actively sadistic when Pierre had finished with their latest sex slave, but now that Pierre had become dependent on the pain of his foot to feel alive, she was the one in control of their appetites. Marie walked over to the bedroom door and ushered in a young woman in a nurse's outfit, reminiscent of a porn movie or Halloween costume. "Duchess, Pierre needs someone to scratch his itch."

Duchess really was a noblewoman, one whose family gladly sold daughters to men seeking peerage. Hard times in this case meant falling prey to Casper and becoming the latest plaything for Pierre and Marie. Her predecessors would have been bound and sexually abused. For once the tables were turned and she would be the one abusing. Duchess smiled at Pierre. She had been violated many times as a child in many ways. The price a family might pay for appearance's sake and an income to maintain a family home. She approached the foot of the bed and caressed his cast. "Is this what you want?" Duchess pulled a knitting needle made of bone from her bag and held it aloft.

"Oh, please, yes!" Pierre gasped.

Marie approached his side with a small leather pouch. She removed a stainless steel syringe and a vial of morphine. She showed him the needle and the drug. "Do you want it?" she asked.

Pierre nodded and looked to his arm. He knew how pathetic he must look. He had been the one in control of their sexual adventures, often binding Marie along with whatever succulent Casper had arranged for them. Eventually, during the course of their debasement, Marie would be released and put in charge of the poor thing sold off by her parents. Marie was bisexual and had always gone along with his sadistic ways, not because she enjoyed masochism, but because she would get her turn to be a sadist. Pierre could see where this was going. He would not have the pleasure of being in charge ever again if he could not kick his new habit of morphine and pain. It would take fifteen minutes for the morphine to take effect. Duchess would elicit great pain in that brief time. He no longer blacked out and needed the opiate to give the same effect. He was an addict of both pain and release. He was a masochist. He started to laugh in short, halting bursts, anticipating the pain as Duchess drew the bone needle back and forth across the cast as if she were playing a stringed instrument, taunting him. Marie drove the syringe into his flesh and injected the drug. Pierre began counting down the minutes to his release. He both hated Marie and loved her simultaneously. He would kill her for letting the torture begin and bless her name when release took it away.

Marie watched Duchess. They made eye contact. Marie smiled.

Duchess drove the bone knitting needle into the opening of the cast, pushing and prodding to find the greatest pain. She imagined all the men who had hurt her; Pierre's screams were music to her ears.

†

Charles waved Gustav off before he could say what was on his mind. The technician closed his laptop and left the room. "I knew Pierre was troubled, but this—this is something else entirely." Gustav tapped the conference table with his index finger. The presentation had been of video showing Pierre's spiral into masochism and drug use, as well as spreadsheets and reports of his financial decisions, the latter provided by Ernesto.

Gustav leaned forward in his chair and slapped the massive wood surface with his hand. "We need to remove him from decision-making before it is too late. The risk he has put us in with those derivatives could wipe us out in a single day!"

Charles removed a handkerchief from his pocket and wiped his brow. "Ernesto says he can unwind the positions in time. We do not need to panic."

"Yet," Gustav said. He pulled a file from his satchel and slid it to Charles. "If we make these adjustments after unwinding the positions and use our influence to manipulate the market, we will make more without any risk." The document showed opposing positions that canceled each other out. "We can get the material for another dirty bomb from Russia or Pakistan—"

"Worst case, we deal with that idiot in Korea," Charles said.

"But the best would be to use the Iranian's own material." Gustav was referring to the terrorist group that Betty and Slim had been tasked with defeating in Venezuela. Betty had retrieved the canister of low-grade uranium and escaped down the river while Slim was to blow up the terrorist camp. Slim had skipped his part of the mission and hidden himself at the coffee plantation, lying in wait for Betty to arrive. Slim's cigar ember alerted Betty to his presence and if not for the noise of a cistern cover, she might have subdued him before he could poison himself with cyanide. Betty stripped Slim of identifying materials and burned his body underneath a diesel tank, both to destroy the evidence and to create a diversion to escape to the pickup point for extraction. Slim was Charles's son, and the means for the Cabal to know what Control was up to. With Slim's death and Tom Jr.'s uncovering of General Getner as the source of the leaks via Babs McGillicutty to Casper, Charles's ability to outmaneuver Control had markedly diminished. Gustav did not want to bring up Slim's failure by talking about resurrecting the dirty bomb plan, but it was the only way to make his investment idea work. "We win if the bomb is used on the Iranian oil fields and we win if it is stopped."

Charles glared at Gustav. The implication of his son's failure was there, even if not said. "How do we win either way?"

Gustav pointed to his report. "If the fields are unusable and radioactive, our investments in Norway, Brazil, Venezuela, and Russia become immensely valuable. If the bomb is discovered and stopped, we make sure the news gets out this time. The fear of a success will drive up oil prices until we can succeed in destroying capacity."

"How long will the area be unusable?" Charles asked.

"It will be too radioactive to send humans in for at least a hundred years. Eventually, we will use robots to get the oil, which we'll need to replace the North Sea oil with or perhaps the Brazilian offshore fields. It all depends on which experts you want to believe."

"So, in essence, we are protecting the Iranian fields until the others run out," Charles said.

"Exactly," Gustav said.

"And we blame the Israelis?"

Gustav gestured with his hand and gave a look of innocent shock. "Of course. Who else would attack the Iranians?"

"And our Saudi plan is still viable?" Charles asked.

"I am working on that. We win without the Saudi ownership, but we double our profits with it."

"OK." Charles slid the report back to Gustav. "I will deal with Pierre when the time is right. In the meantime, Ernesto will unwind his positions."

Gustav smiled. He had not stuttered once during the meeting. He was looking forward to watching Pierre squirm.

Fifty-Four

One of Everything, Please

November 28, 2009 — Vail, Colorado

THE ENTRANCE TO GORSUCH was propped open despite the cold air of November. The heat rolled out to the cobblestone street—a waste of energy that screamed luxury. If you cannot afford to run up your utility bill, why would you have a shop in Vail? An obscenity to an environmentalist, but they were not the target customer anyway. Betty and Hanna let go of each other's arms as they entered the bastion of capitalism and drifted to the ski gear and clothing floor.

"I usually buy my stuff at Pepi's," Betty said.

"Good enough to ski in, but darling, it just won't do for après." Hanna shook her head no. "I mean, really, buying your clothes in the same building where you're having drinks on the patio?" Hanna tsked. "So gauche." Hanna looked out toward the street. "Besides, anyone can afford to shop at Pepi's."

Betty was taken aback. The prices at Pepi's were not much lighter than Gorsuch, unless you shopped the sale rack. *Does Hanna really know what gauche means or is she just parroting someone else?* "I suppose you're right. Old habits." She picked up a neck warmer and checked the tag—two hundred dollars— and put it back.

Hanna noticed Betty's expression as she put the item away, but had missed the surreptitious price check. "Those are so last year. What you need is a scarf." She pulled one off a display mannequin and wrapped it around Betty. "This is so you."

The men's floor salesclerk had Jil and Gil's attention as they rounded a corner and came into view, so they did not spot the duo one floor down.

The scarf was absolutely something Jil would purchase, wear a few times, and then hand down to Betty. "It's perfect!" she said loud enough for Jil to hear her.

Jil glanced down the stairs and spotted the pair. Her lip started to curl in disdain at the usurper, Hanna. Betty had always followed Jil's lead and enjoyed the privilege of mooching off her during their college years—free rides on the company plane and sharing a room at Pepi's Hotel Gasthof Gramshammer for ski lessons with the man himself. All Betty had to pay for was the occasional meal, and Jil usually picked up the expensive ones or the occasional bottle of champagne. It still ate at Jil that Betty discovered her work as a D.C. escort. Venomous thoughts dripped in her mind. How she would crush the upstart Hanna. Perhaps she could feed the poor thing's trust fund to the Cabal as an appetizer.

"We'll take it all," Jil said as she pulled out her own Black Card. The leather chukka boots, Brunello Cucinelli periwinkle cashmere sweater, Fioroni denim shirt, Eleventy chinos, and charcoal jacket with zip-out down liner totaled over six thousand dollars, and that did not include socks or underwear. "In fact, we'll take the other set as well."

"Wait." Gil tried to complain, but Jil showed him her hand.

"We made a deal at Axel. You agreed to take my next two choices no matter what," she said.

"But there's five items in each outfit," Gil protested.

"But only two choices. Hell, I *could* say it was only one choice."

"How's that?" Gil asked.

Jil smirked."Whether or not we buy all of it."

Gil chuckled. "Well, I actually do like this better than Axel."

Jil snorted at him. "That's only because you're too conservative in your taste."

There was a commotion several floors down when Hanna felt Betty was not getting the level of attention she deserved. Several clerks were scurrying about the women's section grabbing one of everything and all in Betty's size. Hanna stormed over to the manager and demanded to know what was going on.

"Why are you pulling everything? Isn't there stock in back for you to rifle through?"

The manager was ringing up each item and handing it off to a clerk to fold and place in a bag. "I'm so sorry. We have a rush order to fill. A client has asked for one of everything."

"Can't she come to the store like the rest of us?" Betty asked. "I was going to try that on."

The manager pulled a lime-green cashmere sweater away from Betty. "Please—I'm sorry, but the client isn't trying these on, she is buying one of everything."

This was a staggering statement to Betty and even took Hanna aback for moment. The stack of clothing was growing by the moment. The bags were starting to take up all the available floor space around the register. A staff member came out, dressed down for backroom work, and whisked the bags outside to an idling blacked out SUV that had pulled up on the pedestrian mall outside the store.

"Holy shit," Hanna said.

Holy shit, thought Betty. *That has to be someone I need to track down. Probably a Cabal member.* Betty considered the meager pile of clothes she had collected to purchase compared to the mountain. She quickly looked at the paperwork not covered by the clothes being processed for any names or phone numbers. Underneath a blouse with a massive ruffle and a twelve-hundred-dollar price tag—something Betty would never even consider trying on, let alone buying—she spied the slip of paper with the name Marie Ch—, with the remainder of the last name covered up. There was a phone number also covered, but the address gave enough information, 397 Beaver D—.

Hanna gasped when she realized the enormity of the bill—the manager was not even halfway done with her task and the cash register display already was in the mid-six figures and growing. Some of Hanna's friends hired professional shoppers, women who had better fashion sense and loved the process, but even they would never buy one of everything to bring back to the client to try on. For Hanna, most of the fun of shopping was the conspicuous consumption and the freedom to try on exquisite outfits that she would never buy. Then it occurred to her, the downside to Gorsuch allowing this to go on. "You love her now, but you'll hate her for returning most of this," she sneered.

The manager did not even pause to look up at Hanna. "She never returns anything. Please—Ashley," she said to the clerk who had just brought another huge pile of clothes, "please help our clients." She stopped long enough to look up at Betty and Hanna. "Can we get you some champagne? I'm so sorry for not giving you the attention you deserve."

Ashley had disappeared for a moment as soon as the manager engaged her. She quickly returned with a bottle of Dom Pérignon, two crystal flutes, and an ingratiating smile. Hanna smiled back. She was not going to spend a million dollars at Gorsuch, even in her lifetime, but being treated with complimentary beverages sure smoothed her feathers. Besides, she now had quite the story to share with her friends.

Betty mentally repeated the information gleaned from the paperwork on the counter to make sure she would remember. She would have to make Beaver Dam Road part of her next running route.

Fifty-Five

Bazinga-Blanket Bingo

November 28, 2009 — Washington D.C.

"YOU DON'T UNDERSTAND," Bud said. "I have access to over two hundred million cameras worldwide, but without more information, I have no way to know which camera I should be looking at, much less who I should be following."

The conference call was being listened into by Tom and David. Betty had initiated the secure communications from her condo kitchen counter at the Ritz-Carlton. Bud was in one of the scanning rooms housed within the same warehouse, but at the other end of the quarter-mile-long cavern. "I gave you an address, isn't that good enough?" Betty asked.

"Well, sure, you gave me an address of a house. What I need is the IP address of their router or modem. Of course I can infer that information by cross-checking several databases, if I knew an email address or maybe some banking information, but none of the usual stuff correlates to the house. An offshore account pays for the utilities and property taxes with no direct tie to anyone who lives there, never mind someone who doesn't have any tie to the property at all." Bud was droning on while simultaneously running more documents through the scanning process. He had been working the piles for a week and was on autopilot. He had his usual office setup— a bank of eight computer screens two rows high, and a dorm fridge filled with high-octane energy drinks mixed with holistic additives.

Betty was getting frustrated with his barrage of words and what-ifs. "If you can't come up with something with what I've given you, then I guess I'll just have to break into the place. Of course, if I do that, they know we are on to them and—"

"Fine. Give me a minute to try something." The line went silent except for a steady stream of keyboard tapping accompanied by the mixed stream of sound from CNN and Fox News. Bud also had CSPAN and MSNBC with the sound muted, and a comedy channel streaming on his top tier of computer screens. "Bingo."

"What?"

"I got it."

"I thought you said you needed more information to get it," Betty said.

"Well, you said you would break in if I couldn't figure it out."

"Yeah, so?"

"There's a website that lets you watch any security camera in the world that hasn't had the password change from the default one."

"And this house has one of those?" Tom interjected.

"No, no. Of course not. But their neighbors do. So from that I got an IP address in the same range and then used that device to run a custom app I uploaded to the Unix server of the security camera box, which let me access the back door of the router, which then allowed me to scan devices in the neighborhood. So—"

"Wait. I don't want to know," Betty said. "What I want to know is do I need to check this place out on my run tonight."

"Holy shit," Bud said.

"What?" said Betty, Tom, and David simultaneously.

"This is the same hardware as the Cabal stuff I cracked before. Hang on." There was a similar stream of sound from Bud's connection as before. Keyboard clacks, commentators arguing over the Middle East conflict, and the occasional burst of laughter from the crowd being entertained by a comedian. "Yeah! Bazinga!"

"What?" said Betty, Tom, and David simultaneously.

"I cross-referenced the Google Wi-Fi database to this address and the Cabal locations we know about. I ran the passwords through a black-box program that guesstimates similar possible passwords and then—"

Tom cleared his throat. "We don't want to know your methods, actually. Can you get to the point?"

"I have access to their security cameras and can monitor all of their data traffic in real time."

Betty slapped the counter with her hand. "Yes!"

FIFTY-SIX

DON'T CALL ME SURELY

November 28, 2009 — Ritz-Carlton, Vail, Colorado

BETTY STRETCHED HER LEGS in the elevator, using the mirrored walls to observe her form. The new Lycra running outfit from McFluffy's lab looked like high-end gear and even had its own logo, copyrighted and trademarked. She had the only complete set of the prototypes and was impressed with the fit. Then again, she had undergone the laser scanning of her bare body. *So it better be form fitting*, she thought. Interwoven with the Lycra was the spider-goat-silk anti-ballistic material that had been modified to incorporate nanoparticle technology. The goats had been fed a mixture of Purina goat feed laced with minute particles of carbon fine enough to be absorbed into the udders and dispensed along with the silk. The theory, which Betty was supposed to test in the real world, was that the nanoparticles would provide superior flexibility, strength, and extended durability, while the interwoven fabrics would still give the same protection as a garment made of pure spider-goat-silk. Tooker/Tucker had spearheaded the addition of the nanoparticles while McFluffy worked on the cold-fusion project. There had been press releases from Tuechtar LLC, hinting at the possibility that the unlimited energy potential of cold fusion was near at hand, but as usual, pundits eviscerated anyone who claimed it was viable.

The doors of the elevator opened and Karl was there to greet Betty. "Damn!" he said, then looked around to make sure no one had heard his unprofessional assessment of her new clothing. "Money looks good on you."

"Thanks, I guess, but this isn't store bought. It's a McFluffy special." Betty said.

"Prototype, huh?"

"Yeah, I think I'm supposed to get shot while wearing . . ." Betty did not finish her sentence because Hanna and Skipper-do had entered the foyer from the street.

Hanna rushed over and pulled her aside to whisper into her ear, "Betty, stay away from him! I think he tried to poison Skipper-do and I."

Betty bit her lip. The desire to correct Hanna's English nearly got the better of her. "You can't be serious," she said instead.

Hanna pulled her farther from Karl. "Dead serious. I got this mystery box of See's chocolates, I thought they were from an old flame trying to rekindle, but there wasn't a note or anything. Skipper-do got in the chocolates and spent forever at the emergency vet." Hanna glared over her shoulder at Karl. "I spent twenty-four hours on the toilet with diarrhea!"

"That's horrible! You're right. I better be careful." Betty suppressed a desire to giggle. The thought of Karl extracting revenge on the trust funder Hanna by giving her chocolates laced with a diarrhetic was just too rich.

Hanna changed the subject by admiring Betty's running clothes. "Damn, girl, you look amazing! What brand is that?"

Betty had not been told to keep it a secret, but she knew she could not talk about McFluffy, so she decided to stretch the truth on her new Lycra. "Oh, this? Just a prototype for a clothing line I'm helping with."

"Did you design it?" Hanna asked as she pulled her hand up to her mouth in excitement.

"Oh, no." It was Betty's turn to lean in and whisper. "But I did go into their lab to be scanned with lasers." She looked over at Karl, who was pretending not to listen. "Buck naked."

"Wait, a laser?" Hanna touched Betty's arm in a comforting way. "Did it hurt?" Hanna asked.

Betty blinked several times as she tried to sync her memories up to Hanna's questions. "The room was a little cold, but no, and I was wearing goggles to protect my eyes."

"The laser thing sounds like something a villain from a James Bond movie would use."

"Naw, more like Q than a villain, I'd say," Betty answered.

Hanna squealed. "You could be a spy, Betty, like in a movie." She reached for Betty's hand and twirled her around. "You kill in that outfit!"

Skipper-do barked in agreement.

I need to get away from her—even if it is all in fun, it's too close to the truth! thought Betty. "All right, Hanna, you let me know when the audition is. I need to go for my run." She broke free and headed out through the great-room area to the pool deck. She planned on running the trail along Gore Creek to Vail Village, up Vail Road, and onto Beaver Dam Road. *Jesus, what have I gotten myself into again?* With a nervous bounce in her step, she headed down the back stairs and passed through the security gate to the trail. The sound of Gore Creek was soothing. *Settle down. Just checking things out.* She sighed as she passed under the bridge at the gondola. *Hell, if I were on the slopes, I'd be fighting all the idiots showing up for opening weekend.* Watching her footing, Betty kept moving forward.

Hanna eyed Karl as she got on the elevator and used her first two fingers of her right hand to signal she was keeping her eyes on Karl as the doors closed.

Karl stood there with his arms folded, leaning against the desk, just daring Hanna to engage him. "Yeah, you better keep your eyes open. Twenty-four-seven."

Fifty-Seven

Get the Flock Out of Here

November 29, 2009 — Vail, Colorado

BETTY APPROACHED BEAVER DAM Road at a trot. She had been running hard along the trail, past the Vail Valley Medical Center and through the village, but wanted to lower her heart rate and breathing before getting near her destination. The length of the run so far had been just right to warm her up—a light sweat had broken out on her skin despite the chilly temperature. Betty pulled off her new two-hundred-dollar beanie cap from Gorsuch that had been protecting her ears and tucked it in her waistband. *Tooker needs to add a pocket or something*, she thought. There was no place to put her card key for accessing the Ritz-Carlton and her condo, so she had laced a Velcro pocket onto her shoe. There was also enough room for a bit of cash in case she stopped for a cup of coffee along the way. *Well, at least I'll have some feedback for the nerds.*

As she rounded the bend and entered the stub road, a man wearing a fedora was standing on the pavement holding a smartphone with his left hand extended away from his body. *Must need bifocals*, Betty thought. It made her curious why he was using his left hand alone until she came close enough to see that his right arm was missing at the elbow, his leather coat pinned up.

"This is private drive," the man warned her.

Hmm, Slavic accent—I must be in the right neighborhood, thought Betty. "I didn't see any signs saying that," she replied. She looked around and noticed that there were an unusual number of domed cameras dangling from light poles and jutting from the houses. She had noticed more cameras on this run than any walk in the village before, probably because of Bud's description of the ubiquitousness of surveillance gear around the world.

"You'd be surprised what isn't posted in this town." He grinned at her and turned slightly, as if to let her pass. "You're just on run, right—you're not some kind of spy prodding around?" he asked, half joking.

He knows more than he should or is an amazing guesser. Is he baiting me or giving me a chance to walk away? "The homes are just so beautiful along here, especially with all the flocking." There had been another snowfall overnight, six inches of fresh powder for the slopes. The road had been meticulously plowed, and the warmth of the sun was already melting the thin layer of remaining snow on the black asphalt. Some of the driveways were entirely bare. *Geothermal heating? A minor cost, I suppose, when your home is valued at ten to twenty million dollars.*

"Yes, flocking. You really should go back down to trail, safer run, less likely get hurt," the one-armed man said as he removed his hat to look up at the fir trees covered in snow.

Betty tilted her head slightly. His words hinted at the danger the Cabal represented. They had proven themselves to be ruthless and willing to lose the lives of minions at will. *He is warning me off*, Betty thought. "I'm pretty steady on my feet," she assured him.

"I not lose this arm"—the man held out his severed limb—"playing patty-cake." He put his phone away in a jacket pocket and stepped closer to her. "They know who you be. They expecting you. Don't do it."

"Don't do what," Betty asked. She was even more sure she needed to get inside 397 Beaver Dam Circle than before.

"They make you pay for failure and they make you pay for orders not followed. First a finger."

Betty thought of Jil and Larry, how he had lost his left ring finger, supposedly in a boating accident when his wedding band got caught in the rigging.

"That because I failed," the man said.

"I suppose they got that idea from the Yakuza," Betty said.

The man ignored her observation. "Then I disobey. I to kill a small child as a warning to international banker."

"Couldn't pull his finger?" Betty asked.

The man ignored her rejoinder again. "I not kill girl, so they send someone else—rape her and dump her body parts on dinner table."

Betty tasted bile in the back of her throat, but did not allow herself to show any visible sign of intimidation. "Seems like they might have overreacted."

"Then same man come cut arm off at elbow. Prosthetic arm no good—cut above elbow." He said.

"Won't they punish you for telling me this?"

"Depends—spy, yes. Rich kid sticking nose other people's lives, no." He put a cigarette in his mouth. "Maybe rest of arm, no big deal. Or"—he cocked his head slightly—"kill me." He pulled a Zippo lighter from his pocket. Emblazoned on the side of the metal was a dragon, just like the tattoo Max had on his arm. When he opened it and lit the flame, it appeared to come from the dragon's mouth. He snapped the lighter closed and put it away. "Of course, you rich kid, right?"

"Of course. I was thinking of buying this house, is it for sale?" she asked.

"No," he said.

"Everything is for sale, if you can name the right price," she said.

He stepped aside and waved his hand with the cigarette between two fingers. "Be my guest. Knock yourself out."

"You aren't afraid of losing your arm?"

"If you what I think, I lose more than arm trying to stop you."

"And if I'm that kind of girl, they want me to come in anyway, right?"

"Correct."

"How could I not go ask if the house is for sale, then?"

The man took a long drag on his cigarette and let the smoke out slowly, the lack of wind combined with the moisture of his exhalation, creating a large cloud between them. "Worse say is no."

"Right." Betty started toward the front door of the house. It was built into the slope of the mountain. The third story faced Beaver Dam Road, while the first floor faced the Circle. Each section of the house appeared to be square and seventy feet per side, or about five thousand square feet per level. Attached to the lower portion was a four-door garage that could probably fit eight vehicles. Doing some quick math in her head, Betty tried to guess the value of the home. Between the visible part of the building and what might be hidden underground, Betty estimated the value of the house at forty million dollars. *It could be higher depending on the finish*, though, she thought. She visually inspected the exterior for exits and threats. *Nothing out of the ordinary, except . . .* The door had a massive bronze knocker shaped like a female hand holding a brass ball. There was no doorbell. As she reached for the lifelike appendage, she paused midair, on the hand was a diamond ring set in white gold. The gem appeared to be at least eight carats. *My God, if that's real, it's worth millions!* thought Betty. Even the fingernails were encrusted with diamonds. She looked closer at the ball held by the hand and realized it was not brass, but gold, as was the striker plate the ball rested on. The thought that the gold was the least-expensive part of the knocker struck her as ludicrous but true.

She started moving her hand forward again, but as she was touching the knocker, the door swung in revealing a woman in a period maid's uniform. *Perhaps the eighteen hundreds?* thought Betty. As the woman was about to speak, the lady of the house approached and called her off.

"No, no, Nanette! I'll handle this," she said with a Bavarian accent. Despite her small frame, the lady brushed the stout woman easily behind her.

Betty was awestruck by the interior of the home, just by what she could see. The spiral staircase that swept counterclockwise kept going up to the third floor. The rail was being polished by several servants, all dressed in period costume as well. There were paintings on the walls that would have easily hung in any national museum, including a Cézanne, Gauguin, Monet, and Seurat lining the stairwell. In the center of the foyer was a full-scale bronze statue in the style of Rodin, a woman hiding her face and covering her breasts as she backed away from something she has discovered.

"May I help you," the lady of the house stated, rather than asked, with one eyebrow raised, her own arms crossed as if she were concerned Betty might somehow diminish the value of her home by standing on the intricate welcome mat, a wool piece that resembled Seurat's *A Sunday Afternoon on the Island of La Grande Jatte*.

Betty had not thought of what to say, so she just went with what was on her mind. "I'm considering building a home in the neighborhood, and I was just wondering who your architect is. Your house is beautiful."

The woman's demeanor lightened, her pride in what she had built was evident. "How nice." She quickly assessed Betty's net worth with a glance head to toe and back up again. "I *sincerely* doubt you could afford it."

"You might think that from window-shopping me, and, to be honest, before my uncle died, I would not have been in the market. But now, anything on the mountain is in my price range." Betty fibbed a little. She was not sure even Tom's inherited wealth could afford the grand luxuries this foyer boasted.

Marie smiled warmly. "Well, my lamb, in that case, come inside. I have a few spare moments and I would be pleased to show you the foyer." She waved for Nanette and said, "My name is Marie."

"A pleasure to meet you, Marie, I'm Betty. Betty Thursten." *If I use my full name, maybe she'll tell me hers.* Betty thought it was odd that she was being offered a viewing of just the foyer, but she was not going to wait to be asked twice.

Marie did not give a last name. "Please put your booties on." Nanette handed Betty a pair of cloth pullover covers.

Betty complied and slipped the booties on before crossing the threshold. The view, once she had stepped inside and moved to the statue, was even more breathtaking. She had never been in a museum so stunningly appointed, but then, most museums tried to be understated and spaced their art out to allow each piece to breathe on its own. This house was like a dense garden filled with majestic plants, all fighting for space and air. Sort of like the staff, who were so plentiful they were practically on top of one another as they worked to clean the already spotless home. "Is this a Rodin?" Betty asked. "I don't think I've ever seen one like this."

"You have an art history background, I take it." A servant appeared bearing a tray with two flutes of champagne. "Ah, here we are. Dom Pérignon?" she offered Betty.

Betty smiled and took the glass, then shook her head. "No, but I have been to many museums and fine homes over the years." She did have several art history credits at Syracuse, but not enough to claim a minor. *Better to make my knowledge seem eclectically gathered*, she thought.

After Marie took a drink from her flute, a servant wiped her riverine-rabbit-red lipstick mark off the rim as she took the stance of a docent, waving her free hand as if revealing the true identity of the artwork and saying, "This piece is in fact by Rodin, produced in 1891, cast in 1897, it is his statue Eve. My great grandfather was a prominent collector and liked the rougher feel of this version over the smoother, smaller one he had exhibited in 1882. I do believe Rodin took the criticism well and modified his technique and became comfortable with showing his work incomplete or in fragments."

"So this is an original and not a copy?" Betty asked.

"Yes. It is the first casting." Marie considered her specimen. "To be honest," she added in an offhand way, "the piece is getting rather old to me. Jeremy! Nanette, where is Jeremy? Get the fool here immediately, I want to change out this statue. In fact, I think it is time to move on from the nineteenth century and remodel to the early twentieth." Marie grabbed Betty's gloved hand. "Oh, this is so exciting! You've inspired me!"

The staff began removing paintings from the walls, and a Jeremy appeared with two other men and moving equipment. They began loading the twenty-million-dollar statue, with padding for protection, on to a low-slung cart to wheel it from the foyer. Jeremy prompted Marie for his orders. "Madam, what shall I bring out from storage?" he asked nervously.

Marie put her hand under her chin and looked at Betty and then where the Rodin was being wrangled onto the cart. She sipped her Dom Pérignon. "What do you think, Betty?"

Betty nearly spit her champagne back into the flute. "About what?"

"My dear young thing, we need to pick a period and style."

"Art deco?" Betty asked.

"Such a lovely period. Elegant lines, but good Lord, no, child, simply too close to what was here." She turned to her art director and gave her command. "Picasso. Jeremy, just pick out one of the Picassos—something from the Roaring Twenties, I can't make up my mind right now." Marie whisked Betty over to the double French doors that opened automatically. "You must see this piece I have in here. This is my modern art room."

Inside the six-hundred-square-foot space was a splattering of art with no apparent theme. The most recognizable pieces were Warhol's, but Betty had no idea of their provenance. Marie took her around and introduced her to the artist of each piece, be it a painting or sculpture, and in fifteen minutes, the whirlwind tour was complete. They left the modern art room and returned to the foyer. To Betty's surprise, the staff had not only redecorated the walls with examples of 1920s classicism, but they themselves had transformed their clothing into the stylish form of the Gilded Age servant. They were in the final stages of making sure the pieces were properly dusted and straight as Jeremy and his helpers were adjusting the Picasso sculpture. They had used a hand truck to move this piece in and no padding was required.

"Isn't it lovely?" Marie asked, as the servant, who was following her, wiped the rim again after she had sipped her champagne

Betty nodded her head, though the artwork was not of her taste. *Though this champagne is to die for*, she thought.

"You don't like it, do you?" Marie looked crestfallen. "Take it back, Jeremy—no, send it to Christie's. I never want to see it again."

Betty was aghast. She had not meant to convey that kind of opinion unto Marie, but obviously, the woman not only had vast resources to play with if she could pull art at will from her storage that had a combined worth greater than the value of her house—*and that's just what I've seen so far!* thought Betty.

Jeremy looked like he had been caught stealing and regretted his error with horror in his face. "Yes, madam, I am so sorry, madam, right away, perhaps the art deco period, *Atlas*?"

Marie thought for a moment, considering what it was that would please her. She waved her hand dismissively. "Yes, that would do, and get the Tiffany stained glass out as well."

Betty started to say the art deco period was her idea, but thought better of it. "*Atlas*, as in the statue at Rockefeller Center?"

Marie turned to Betty as the staff scrambled to make their mistress happy. "Yes—"

Betty looked up to the peak of the foyer and thought it was nearly tall enough to fit the massive piece. *But how would you get it through the door?*

Marie continued in a quiet voice, "But this is the half-scale model—a much more valuable piece from Lawrie." Marie looked around at her scrambling staff with a pleased look. "No one knows I have this piece." Marie turned back to Betty, her face grave. "If you ever speak of it, I shall have to kill you."

Betty smiled and thought it a joke until enough time had passed and Marie's countenance hadn't changed. The smile left her lips.

Marie waved her to the front door. "Now, my dear, I am so sorry, but I must ask you to leave." "I have to get ready for skiing, an appointment this afternoon, and then there is the group dinner at Game Creek. Thank you for stopping by, please come again when you finish your house, hmm?" She turned and walked away, leaving Nanette to see Betty out. "For the love of God, no!" Marie yelled at her staff.

Betty slipped the booties off as quickly as she could and handed them back to Nanette. The door quickly closed behind Betty as she stepped into the falling snow. The one-armed man was not in his position; the fresh powder showed no footprints. She started her run back to the Ritz-Carton, now with more questions than she had before arriving. *Who is Marie?* she thought.

Fifty-Eight

A Rare Opportunity

November 29, 2009 — Ritz-Carlton, Vail, Colorado

JIL THREW THE PILLOW at Gil's head. "Some help you are!"

He had been napping on the oversize cowhide couch while Jil reorganized their possessions in the smaller condo after moving from the penthouse. He snagged the pillow, rolled to his side, and put it over his ear to muffle her complaints. "I'll make it up to you—I'll buy dinner at Mountain Standard."

"Seriously? That's the best you can do?" she chided him. Jil moved to the kitchen and picked a knife from the knife block on the counter and pointed it at him. "Mister, I expect breakfast in bed in the morning." She took an apple from the fruit basket and whacked it in half on the cutting board, cut out the core from each half, and sliced it evenly into eight pieces. Jil took some seven year aged white cheddar cheese from the refrigerator, sliced it, and placed it along with the apple slices on a serving board and brought it to the sofa. "I cannot believe they put this living room here." She pointed to the view of the western wing of the building across from their couch. "Seriously."

Gil rolled to a sitting position and took a slice of cheese and apple, stuffed it into his mouth, and chewed it before saying, "Breakfast in bed, huh."

"Yes."

"Is that before or after I make you orgasm?" He licked his lips and raised his eyebrows.

"Depends."

"On what?" he asked.

"Do I have to satisfy you?"

"Not necessarily, but it would be appreciated, of course." Gil said.

"Plan on not and maybe you'll get lucky. And before breakfast. Two eggs, hash browns, and orange juice," she said as she moved a slice of cheese and apple to her mouth, taking a small bite.

"Anything else?" Gil grabbed another slice of each and stuffed his mouth.

"Make the reservation for seven tonight."

"You drive a hard bargain," he said while chewing.

"Damn straight." Jil looked at him, wiped off a bit of apple from his mouth, and said, "You're like having my own child."

†

As they entered the restaurant, Jil noticed a couple at a table next to the west windows of Sweet Basil, the sister establishment above Mountain Standard. The woman—who was significantly younger than the man—was unknown to her, but Jil knew immediately she was the man's mistress. She whispered to Gil, "Senator Bolden."

Gil had never met the man, though he had seen his picture in the news from time to time. He was the chairman of the Finance Committee and a party bigwig. His name had been floated as a possible presidential candidate in the past, most likely as a trial balloon from his own office, and on several short lists for vice president. "Why would he be here?" Gil asked.

The hostess showed them to their booth near the kitchen.

Jil turned her nose up at the location. "Seriously? Next to the kitchen?" she asked the hostess.

The restaurant was packed and there were no other tables open. The hostess tried to sound as soothing as possible, yet firm. "If you would like to wait, I can get a different table in about a half hour."

"Forget it. Thank you." Jil took her seat.

"Kayla will be with you shortly," the hostess said as she left.

Jil glared at Gil. "You need to specify a table location when you make a reservation."

He smiled and acknowledged her suggestion. "I had never considered it before, but you are so right." Gil looked around at the other guests and evaluated any potential threats. The only viable ones involved poor color choices and an awful comb-over. "You were telling me about Senator—"

Jil held her finger up and said, "Shh!"

Kayla appeared. "Can I get you some drinks?"

Gil ordered the oyster shooter and a Laphroaig ten-year-old single malt. Jil ordered a bottle of Veuve Clicquot.

He noted that it was the most expensive champagne on the wine list and smiled, knowing it was not his paycheck footing the bill, but Control's. As Kayla left, he held his hands up in surrender. "As you were saying."

She considered kicking him under the table, but decided to wait until after dinner. "His wife is getting a complimentary treatment from Salizar while he cavorts with his latest plaything," she explained.

"How do you know she's his mistress?"

"I used to sit in that chair. She probably is listed on his staff as a media liaison—in fact, now that I think about it, I'm pretty sure she used to be a reporter for one of the cable news channels. Jesus, even with their ski gear on, I'd recognize him in a minute. I cannot believe he's being so brazen—but his next election cycle is a long ways off, I suppose."

Kayla delivered the drinks and asked if they were ready to order.

Jil read off the menu: "We'll have the bruschetta and steak tartare for starters, and I'll have the scallops à la Plancha." She looked at Gil, who was still trying to figure out what he wanted. "And the gorilla will have the hanger steak, medium rare."

Gil gave her a sad puppy dog face as Kayla walked away with their order. "You ordered for me."

"Do you like what I ordered?" she asked.

"Well, yeah, but that isn't the point."

"Then next time, get your ass off the couch and help."

"Point taken," he said.

Jil checked her bag for her cigarettes and remembered that she had given them up. "Oh, what I wouldn't do for a cigarette right now." She began fidgeting with her phone to compensate for the urge.

"But you can't smoke in here."

"It would give me an excuse to check on our friend upstairs," Jil explained. She closed her eyes and breathed in deeply. *I need some coke.* She had run out the day before but had been too distracted by Gil to make a call. *Why didn't I have Parker arrange something?* She opened her eyes and focused on Gil, giving him a pleasant smile as she blinked her eyes to clear the thought.

"Ah." Gil thought to himself that Jil would have made a good spy. *I'll regret this, but*—"You could always bum a smoke."

A small thrill went through Jil as the thought of a smoke triggered her brain. She looked down at her hands and rubbed her fingertips, feeling the skin that usually held the cigarette in her right hand. Jil quickly visualized her father dying, and the thrill passed. "No, I'm good. Thanks." She saw Kayla coming with the champagne and blurted, "Thank God!"

Fifty-Nine

The Cloth Pulled Back

November 29, 2009 — Washington D.C.

BUD REMOVED THE THUMB DRIVE from his laptop and leaned back in his Eames chair. He had found the chair weeks before in a resale shop not far from Betty's place in Old Town Alexandria. He had been snooping around the area, trying to get a feel for a way that he could approach her for a date, besides the one she owed him at Five Guys. Bud knew everything about Betty that could be known without talking to her. He had her credit report, employment history, driving record, social media accounts, and—via Control's complete record of her life—even her library borrowing information back to when she was six and living in Rochester, New York. Bud was a stalker with vast resources and an itch he could not scratch.

October 15, 2009 — Old Town Alexandria

Before entering the building, Bud logged into the alarm system by connecting his laptop via Betty's own Wi-Fi. He knew all of the access codes since he installed the system himself. Breaking into the apartment undetected excited him. In the kitchen, he found the furniture still in disarray from the fight with Beth, containers of takeout still littering the floor, the food dried hard. Grace would normally have come up and cleared the remains and returned the apartment to a proper state in case anyone else entered, but she had been preoccupied with her sister, Beth. His unrelenting desire to see Betty had been dimmed by her relationship with Tom, Bud's boss, but that just meant he had to keep his intentions to himself. He moved to the living room and spied the closet with her equipment bag half in and out of the closet. He unzipped it and found a mixture of weapons and ammunition worthy of any field agent, all cleaned meticulously, shiny with gun oil. He removed a SIG Sauer P229 and a spare clip. He had been trained in small arms fire in the army, but had not carried a weapon in years. He tucked the pistol into the back of his pants, his checkered flannel shirt hiding the weapon.

Moving to the bedroom, he found nothing out of place. Betty had not taken anything from her drawers when she dashed out of the apartment after miscarrying her baby, taking only her emergency bag and the dime with the microdot on her way to rescue Gil from Michel. There were many things that Bud knew about Control and its members, things that only he knew in that totality because of his access to the computer records, his actions as dispatcher, and the video feeds he watched. He sat down on the bed, a queen-size mattress with a navy-striped comforter.

"Shit." The hopelessness of his position tore at his heart. He would never be able to compete with Tom, even if he could give himself a vast fortune by stealing from the reserve banks of the world. He was just too much of an introvert. He pulled the pistol from the back of his jeans. It had begun pressing into his spine, which only emphasized that he was not nor would ever be cut out for fieldwork. He was a desk jockey, and computers were his true love. He got up and returned the gun to the bag, after wiping his prints from the metal and the magazine. After wiping any other surface he could remember touching, he retreated out the door. He took the stairs instead of the elevator and returned to where he had parked his moped, which had a ticket inserted into the seat. He looked at it and scoffed. He knew how to void tickets. The digital world was his domain.

"Maybe I need to lower my standards," he said to himself as he wound the throttle back and zoomed off to his lair.

November 29, 2009 — Washington D.C.

Bud sat up straight in his Eames chair and picked up his phone to flip through potential dates on a social media site, none of whom seemed right. They were out of his league physically or inadequate intellectually. He gave up and switched to an app he had developed—one designed for members of the intellectual societies, graded by which groups the members belonged to. An applicant had to at least be a member of Mensa or be able to prove a relative IQ above 135 to join Bud's clique. The test, designed by Bud, increased in difficulty as more questions were answered correctly. No female had risen to the level he searched for yet, but that could be because he was marketing his site poorly rather than the available pool of intelligent women. He considered that his questions could be skewed to score males higher, possibly a subliminal failure. Then it dawned on him. The last bar he had gone to was having a ladies' night. Was he using the right bait? Did his site actually even appeal to women of intelligence? The comment section was rife with complaints that there were not enough female members. He decided to act on a hunch and posted a request for input on a forum where a certain programmer whose handle was Ophelia hung out. She responded quickly and agreed to look over his app with him, after she took the test to prove her intelligence. She finished the test in record time and only missed one question.

Bud smiled. Maybe there was hope after all.

Sixty

Fisher King

November 29, 2009 — Ritz-Carlton, Vail, Colorado

"I FIGURE THE NEXT GROUP will be here in ten minutes. We'll position ourselves over there." Karl was pointing at a pile of hard-case luggage stacked next to where a van had been moments before. The staff of Dr. Eric Salizar's clinic were handling their own luggage and equipment, an anomaly for the Ritz-Carlton, which prided itself on being full service. The chief clinician charged Karl with watching over the pile in the circular drive while the team moved load after load to the elevator and on up to the penthouse. Another van with equipment and personnel was due shortly. Karl had radioed his maintenance supervisor to meet him in the covered area used by the guests for unloading skis and gear most of the winter. Today, it looked more like a pop star diva was moving in for the duration. The super was there so Karl could attend to other guests if necessary, but the nature of the equipment and the high level of the guests involved required his personal touch. The building was split into two halves. The west wing was divided into condominiums owned by elite clients who might live in the unit or just visit once a year for skiing. The eastern half of the building consisted of the time-share units owned by the Ritz-Carlton itself, and the entire fourth floor had been reserved for Dr. Salizar and the staff of the clinic. The equipment was being loaded into the penthouse where Jil and Gil had been staying. It was her job to make sure everything ran smoothly. Karl was thankful he was dealing with the head clinician at this point instead of Jil. He was less demanding. The job of concierge had seemed romantic and an ideal way for Karl to spend lots of time skiing; the reality was, he skied very little and hated most of the guests. Hanna and Skipper-do most of all.

A man who walked in from the street drew his suspicions immediately. He was missing one arm at the elbow, his jacket sleeve was pinned up, and he was finishing a cigarette. There was a dusting of snow on his clothes and fedora, which meant he had been walking for some time in the soft flakes that had been dropping for the past hour. He was not one of the guests or a resident, and his demeanor was that of a bodyguard. When he flicked the cigarette at the vicinity of a trash can, Karl spoke up. "Excuse me, may I help you?"

The man took off his hat and shook it off, then barely looked Karl's way before continuing toward the sliding doors that led to the foyer and Karl's desk.

Karl looked back at his super to make sure the man would stay with the equipment and began pursuing the one-armed man. More forcefully this time, Karl called to the man, "Sir, where are you going?"

The man spun around and showed Karl a hidden pistol in a holster under his jacket. "I'm security. I know where I am going."

Karl's first instinct was to take the man down, to yank his remaining arm behind his back and force his submission for questioning. The one-armed man's accent was Slavic, something Karl knew about because of his own heritage—he was half Danish and half Belarusian, and had grown up listening to his grandparents speak in their native tongues, one of the reasons he was a polyglot. His hand itched to reach for his own pistol hidden under his jacket, but it would be better if the man did not know he was armed. It might just cause an escalation, and Karl's primary job at the moment was to monitor the Cabal, not attack it. "Then you should come to my desk. I'll give you a special badge so the staff can recognize who you are." Karl walked the one-armed man to his desk, where he had a clipboard with a list of all the authorized personal involved with Dr. Salizar's clinic.

The one-armed man stood away from the desk and fidgeted. He kept glancing around the room like he was expecting an attack at any moment and kept adjusting his coat to ensure easy access to his weapon. He was much shorter than the six-foot-five Karl.

"What's your name?" Karl asked.

"Boris."

"Who are you working for? I don't see your name on the list."

"I am officially with the Hungarian consulate in Denver." Boris removed a leather wallet with a badge and an ID card that he quickly flipped open and closed.

"Hungarian Consulate in Denver? Why would Hungary have a consulate in Denver?" Karl asked.

"Many citizens emigrate. Hungarian Catholic church, businesses, trade with mother country, we very busy representing interests of Hungary."

"That's nice, but if that is your official cover"—Karl had not meant to use an espionage term, but it slipped out—"what is your real purpose here today?"

"I am here to protect the clients of Dr. Salizar's clinic." Boris rubbed his chin; the stubble was already starting to form a five o'clock shadow. His day had started early, and he was already tired. "On sheet you notice pass code, fisher king."

Karl looked at the bottom of the clipboard papers and sure enough, there was the passcode for personnel not on the list. "Yes, fisher king. Right." Karl took a badge from a draw in his desk and held it close. "Your accent is more Belarusian than Hungarian."

"Interesting that you noticed. Many years at consulate in Belarusia." Boris shrugged his shoulders. "Girlfriend there was bad influence on me."

Karl grinned. It did not really matter to him why Boris was here. He would keep a close eye on him. As long as he had the passphrase, protocol dictated that Karl the concierge would give him the credentials. He handed it to Boris, who reluctantly clipped it to his leather jacket.

The elevator doors opened, and the head clinician along with two helpers rolled the luggage cart out and toward the waiting pile. He smiled at Karl. Karl smiled back but did not bother to ask about Boris or make an introduction. Security details were supposed to be in the background, and they either knew him or knew he would be around them.

After the cart had moved out of the foyer with Dr. Salizar's staff, Boris asked, "Penthouse?"

Karl wondered why he asked now when he claimed in the drive to know where he was going, but decided not to question the man further at this time. "Swipe your badge in the elevator and you will be able to get to the sixth floor. Unit 615."

"Which way stairs?" Boris asked.

"Go down that hall about fifty meters and you'll see the sign."

For the first time, Boris smiled at Karl and tipped his hat. "Thank you much." Boris left the foyer and headed for the stairs.

Karl thought it was rather odd that the man would want to climb six floors. Most people visiting the mountains gladly take the break from exercise and use the elevator. He shrugged his shoulders and checked the video monitors. He could see Boris laboriously ascending a flight of stairs then stopping at each landing to get his breath. The view switched to guests coming and going from their rooms. Then residents chatting in the great room, only a few meters from his desk, so he could hear the actual faint conversation out of sync with the video. Then, to his horror, the second van had unloaded their equipment next to the first pile of luggage and the combined mass had slid into the driveway. The super was doing his best to help sort things out, but the clinician was yelling at everyone about delicate equipment. Karl grabbed his radio and called for all available hands to the driveway. "That isn't the Ritz way!" he muttered.

Sixty-One

Dead Pool Rising

November 29, 2009 — Ritz-Carlton, Vail, Colorado

THE SALIZAR CLINIC WAS SET UP without any further incident. Karl had mustered enough staff to get the rest of the luggage wrangled and sent up the elevator, and he was looking forward to the end of his shift as concierge. The assistant concierge was due any moment for a nine-to-four shift minding the minor royalty, trust fund kids, and personages—who all thought they were VIPs—giving Karl plenty of time for carving the snow moguls. He and Betty had planned on running into each other on the mountain to ski a few runs together. It would be an opportunity to update each other on the comings and goings of the Ritz-Carlton.

Hanna had implored Betty to hang out with her at Pepi's to watch all the other trust funders pose in their finest outfits. She had agreed to meet Hanna for a mimosa in the great room of the Ritz at ten a.m., but she insisted on hitting the slopes with or without her. It was now five minutes to nine as she came through the rear entrance off the deck area, and she saw Karl standing at the bar drinking a bottle of water and reading some notes.

In a low voice, Betty excitedly said, "There was a guy there, outside the mansion. He had one arm—"

"And wore a fedora." Karl finished.

"How did you know?" Betty asked.

"He showed up here about fifteen minutes ahead of you. He claimed to be with the Hungarian Consulate in Denver but is providing security for the Salizar clinic."

There was a commotion at Karl's desk. It was Hanna and Skipper-do ringing his bell.

"Oh, for the love of God," whispered Karl as he viewed the camera footage from his phone of the pair at his desk.

"What?" Betty asked.

"The ankle biter."

"Skipper-do?"

"Yeah, him too." Karl dryly noted.

"Oh, come on, she isn't that bad, I've spent time with her."

"True . . . and you haven't killed yourself yet," Karl said.

"You are so mean."

Hanna rang the bell again and cleared her throat loudly as she spotted the two at the bar.

"Meet at noon—Game Creek Bowl?" Karl asked.

Betty nodded, then added, "Oh, shit. We need a reason for being in here together since it's her."

"The one-armed man as an intruder?" Karl asked.

They nodded at each other and separated. Karl let Betty go first as he organized his notes, knowing that she would distract Hanna with the news of the one-armed man.

"Betty, what's going on?" She darted her eyes and curled her lip in disdain as she pointed her head at the man who she was sure had tried to poison her and Skipper-do, even if she could not prove it. The Chihuahua jumped from her arms, raced within several feet of Karl, and barked ferociously at his ankles before backing away closer to his momma.

"Oh, Hanna, we have to be careful," Betty said.

"Exactly—you need to watch out for that man." Skipper-do gave a short yap of agreement and hopped into Hanna's outstretched arms.

"No, there's a one-armed man in the building," Betty said.

"Why would that be dangerous?" Hanna asked.

Betty moved closer to her friend and gave Skipper-do a scritch under the chin. "He has a gun. We need to stay away from him." Then in a low whisper, she said, "He might be here to kill someone." *I mean, he will kill someone who gets in his way or attacks someone he is protecting, so I'm not lying*, Betty thought.

"Shouldn't we call the police?" Hanna exclaimed before looking around to see if she had drawn unwanted attention to herself.

"Karl has it handled." Betty smiled. *Karl can take Boris, I'm sure of that.* "Go get ready for Pepi's. We'll go there for mimosas and breakfast. I'll meet you in the great room—he wouldn't possibly try anything in such a public place." Betty mostly just wanted to give Hanna a reason to stay away from her condo while she made the call to Tom to update him and ask a few questions.

Karl steered clear of the pair as they had their discussion, but he caught Hanna looking suspiciously his way from time to time. He checked the monitor again for any visual of Boris, but he was nowhere to be seen on the sixth floor. Karl had begun to believe he might just be inside the 615 penthouse when he spotted Boris entering the fourth floor of the timeshare side that was reserved for Salizar's staff. Karl could disable the key card at will from his computer, if he felt Boris was compromising either the Ritz's security or Control's mission, but for now, there was nothing to trigger such a decision. Boris stopped to talk to one of the clinicians, but there was no audio, so Karl had no idea the nature of the conversation. The clinician pointed toward the mountain, but that gesture held no special meaning to him. Boris tipped his hat to the man and moved on to the other end of the building and took the stairs down.

Hanna and Betty were chatting away, Betty trying to disengage and head upstairs, Hanna clinging and going on.

Karl spotted Boris leaving the building through the garage and out the east entrance toward the Marriott. He quickly lost sight of the one-armed man in the fedora.

Betty finally got Hanna to let go. "I'll be there in an hour, I promise." Then, in a low whisper, as if she did not want Karl to hear: "I need to go pee!"

Hanna let her go and Skipper-do said goodbye with a short yap. Betty headed for the elevator and tried to not look at Karl while Hanna headed to the bar off the great room to grab a mimosa while she waited for Betty.

Sixty-Two

Powder-Room Fresh

November 29, 2009 — Ritz-Carlton, Vail, Colorado

BETTY PRESSED THE CONNECT and speaker buttons and propped her phone sideways on the kitchen table so she could see the tiny images split into four quadrants on her screen. She could see herself and David on the top, with Bud and Tom below. Though the Ritz-Carlton prided itself on the quality of its soundproofing, Bud had provided her with a white-noise generator connected to a subwoofer aimed at the floor, four wireless speakers on tall stands, and four at floor level facing outward around the perimeter of the condo to create an impenetrable envelope of soundproofing. The windows vibrated from this system instead of her voice and the speaker of the phone. An eavesdropper could use a laser from miles away to bounce the beam off a window, which mimics the cone of the speakers, and the rebounded laser would only repeat the unintelligible noise. If they used sophisticated computer filtering, they might hear the Beatles' "Let It Be" played in reverse at subsonic levels, which was Bud's private joke. On a very basic level, the device planted by the KGB in the ambassador's office in 1945, hidden in the carved great seal, worked on the same principle as the laser listening devices used by modern spies today.

"Betty, David here—can you describe the woman to me, physically?"

"She might as well be my twin in height and weight. She seemed very fit, but she's older by about twenty years."

"How could you tell?" Tom asked.

"She's had some work done and it's starting to show, around her ears."

"I don't understand," David said.

Tom knew a bit about facial reconstruction, partly because of his time at Landstuhl Regional Medical Center recovering from the IED that took his leg and shredded Babs's face, but also from the agents who had had their looks changed over time to be inserted into hostile environments and evade detection. Sometimes, intricate surgeries were performed to make an agent look just like the person they were to replace and altered again when and if they returned. These agents showed marked degradation of their features as time took its toll on sagging flesh. "I can answer that for you, David," Tom said. "Altered flesh doesn't age the same way natural flesh does. The scarring, the tightening—all those areas change at a different rate from the parts of the face that are original."

Betty jumped in with her own explanation. "David, you would know what I mean if you look up pictures—Bud can pull them from the security cameras—of the women sitting around Pepi's instead of skiing. Their lips, eyelids, and sometimes cheeks just look unnatural. Sometimes it's too much filler or injected fat, sometimes it's skin pulled instead of lifted. Look for the scars and you'll understand."

"I'll take your word for it. So, any other distinguishing marks?"

"She's a bitch?" Betty said.

David and Tom suppressed their desire to giggle. "Call it like it is," Bud's nasally voice cracked through the screen.

"Well, what I really mean is, she's probably a psychopath," Betty answered.

Bud pushed data as an overlay to their images. It showed information on the clinical description of psychopaths. "Only one percent of males and even fewer females fit that category," he said.

Tom chimed in, "What makes you think she's a psychopath?"

Betty scrunched her face in thought. "She has no empathy for those around her. I know that seems like a quick read, but just trust me on this one. The staff jumped at her commands. Those people were scared for their lives."

"You saying she might be the type to kill someone in cold blood?" Tom asked.

"I'm saying she enjoys it," Betty said.

Bud read off some more statistics, even though they were scrolling on the screen. "Twenty-five percent of prison inmates are estimated to be psychos. They get caught because they can't fake societal norms. I've dealt with a lot of them online. Real bastards. Behind their handles they think they can talk and act in ways they wouldn't get away with outside of the dark web."

"So, do we think she's Cabal?" Tom asked.

"Based on just the art she swapped out while I was there and what I'm assuming she has in storage, the value of the house itself, and the amount of staff cleaning the foyer, I'd say she has more money than the typical billionaire."

"I've traced the ownership of the house to an offshore entity." Bud was scrolling more data on the screen. "I got this from a friend who hacked a Panama law office."

Tom looked a little surprised. "We aren't in that file, are we?" he asked.

"I checked it out—no. You must be doing everything through U.S. corporations and legal entities. A lot easier to hide here than in the offshore ones." Bud actually knew more than he was letting on, but then, he had access to all the digital information Control had.

Tom cleared his throat. "Well, we are owning less by the day. The mountain retreat sold yesterday—got a decent price for the land and what was left of the debris."

"What?" Betty asked. "What happened to the house?"

"Oh, you didn't hear, did you?" David asked. "A cruise missile—probably the Cabal—completely leveled."

Tom cleared his throat again. "Yes, we had just gotten airborne when it came in, got away by dropping below the edge of the plateau to miss the sonic blast wave. Total loss, I'm afraid."

"Tomahawk?" Betty asked.

"No, a Russian one, from what we could tell," answered David. "I guess they got tired of sending men to be killed by you, Betty."

"I liked that place," she said wistfully.

"Getting back to focus, I want you and Karl to see about tracking some of the Cabal members on the slopes today. Figure out what their plans are for the week. We know they are going to be coming and going from the penthouse suite for treatments."

"Who all am I looking for?" Betty asked.

Tom looked at a printout. "There will be some politicians—

Senator Bolden, Governor Gansen of New York, and possibly other politicians, but we don't know for sure. There is Marie, and we think there are three other core Cabal members coming or already in place from what Miller has seen."

"Male or female?" Betty asked.

Tom looked up from his notes. "It looks like we have three males about the same age as Marie. I don't have confirmation of this yet, but they are probably Gustav, Pierre, and Charles."

Bud chimed in with his latest offering. "I have some addresses related to the corporation that owns Marie's house, I've sent those over to you in an encrypted message."

"Check these people out and see if you can put tracking devices on their vehicles or ideally on something they keep with them at all times," Tom advised.

Bud's nasally voice jumped in again. "Look in the bag marked '3' and you'll find the miniature tracking devices. The larger ones have longer battery life, but the small ones auto-recharge based on movement. Don't put them on something that's just going to sit, 'cause they'll die within a day."

"Gotcha," Betty said. "OK, I'm off to the slopes as soon as I clean up. *Ciao!*" She disconnected the encrypted feed as Bud's message showed up in her inbox.

The subject was "Don't forget about Five Guys," a subtle reminder that he was holding her toes to the fire about her promise to meet up with him. The message had three addresses on Forest Drive for her to check out, and the address, phone number, hours of operation, GPS coordinates, and website for the Five Guys near the White House.

That little shit just isn't going to let it go. I should make Gil go instead of me—he's the one whose ass I saved with that information. Which got her thinking about her onetime best friend, Jil, who was now with her onetime partner and temporary lover, Gil. She allowed herself to be sad for just a moment, but decided that taking advantage of the luxury suite's Jacuzzi tub and some bath salts would sooth her skin, if not her soul.

Sixty-Three

Fresh Powder

November 29, 2009 — Ritz-Carlton, Vail, Colorado

BETTY LOOKED CLOSELY at her face after soaking in the tub. The little wrinkles around her eyes had gotten slightly deeper in the past year. Not as pronounced as the prune wrinkles on her fingers from soaking in the tub for an hour, but still more noticeable than before. *Maybe a new wrinkle cream? Or maybe I could force my way into Salizar's clinic.* Betty envisioned holding a gun to Eric Salizar's head, demanding to receive equal treatment as the Cabal members, then shook her head and smiled ruefully at herself.. "They're not that bad," she told herself as she pulled her skin back to make the wrinkles go away. She looked down at her waist and felt her belly. It had not been very long since her miscarriage. It seemed like months, between rescuing Gil and repelling the assaults of the Cabal forces. *I haven't had a real break forever.* That thought triggered an urge to stop the roller coaster she was riding with Tom. The brief times they were alone together were rich and wonderful, but she paid dearly in between. And the physical toll of fighting the Cabal was starting to wear on her. *Karl got out, sort of*, she thought. They would be skiing together in a few hours, which made Betty glad. They had made a good team in Denmark, saving each other's lives. *Just like me and Gil, but he's with Jil now. Even if it is just his mission, I see more in his eyes, the way he looks at her—it isn't an act.*

Betty looked at her crow's feet and then her belly again. She wanted to go see a dermatologist, but her biggest concern was getting another Depo-Provera shot before her next ovulation. *I want a baby, but I want to be in control of when I have a baby*, she thought. Her hands drifted to her lower abdomen. She didn't have a six pack like some fitness instructors, but she could feel the muscles just underneath a thin layer of fatty tissue.

Each muscle defined by her daily workouts, running, calisthenics, yoga, jujitsu, and occasional weight lifting. Cupping her breasts, Betty gauged how much they sagged compared to when she was in her early twenties. *Not much*, she thought, *but I need to do more bench presses to tighten my pecs.* She knew what a pregnancy would do to her fitness level. *But I can keep working out. We've moved on from the bad old days when we were told not to exercise while pregnant.* She thought of the pioneer women who had to work right up until they gave birth and were back in the fields not long after. *I'm from that kind of stock*, she told herself. *But I definitely don't want to be doing fieldwork while pregnant.* Which made her think about the mission in Venezuela to recover the nuclear material from the Al-Qaeda cell. Strapping a container of radioactive particles to her back, no matter how good the shielding, made her nervous. *It's the things you don't see that get you*, she thought.

Betty looked at her phone to see what time it was. There was a new message from Hanna and an email from Tom, encrypted, of course.

> Hanna: "Hurry up, girlfriend, ur missing out. In the Great Room having a mimosa with Jil and Gil."

"Nope. Not gonna take that bait." Betty said out loud.

> Tom: "Just read the status reports from you and Karl. The man with the fedora is the one I encountered in D.C. He was working for the Belarusian embassy, then. I shot him twice, once in each shoulder and interrogated him. He wouldn't talk much. Be very careful with him. I am probably on his naughty list for getting him sent back."

Betty considered who was on her naughty list. Sometimes Tom was there. Sometimes he wasn't. She had tried to get him to commit to a relationship that was more important than his work, but he had never been able to keep that kind of promise. He had tried, more than once, but the siren call of Control always pulled their relationship to the rocks.

Betty had learned to be careful about what she said out loud when she became a Control agent, but it suddenly dawned on her that if Bud could listen in on Jil's conversations, he could listen in on hers, and probably was. "Bud, if you're listening, stop it. You'll never get me to Five Guys if you keep listening in on what I'm saying to myself." She hoped either that he was not listening or that if he was, he would take that message to heart and not eavesdrop when she was alone.

She was getting a little chilled from standing naked in the bathroom when it dawned on her that Bud could probably also see anything her phone camera could. "Bud, if you're still listening—or watching," Betty stared directly into the camera of her phone, "I'm going to cut your nuts off!" *I'm going to put a towel over my phone from now on!*

Thirty minutes later, she was applying lipstick that she hoped did not say Whore Red, but rather, See What You Are Missing. *Time to get dressed and go skiing!* She took a deep breath and threw her shoulders back and headed down to meet up with Hanna, Jil, and Gil.

Hanna got up from the table as she saw Betty approach, spotted the lipstick and whispered to Betty, "Interesting shade of lipstick. You know, you'd do better to visit the esthetician and get some filler for those wrinkles. Maybe some Botox."

Betty pouted and scowled. "Seriously?"

"Don't knock it, I've started using it." Hanna said.

"But you're only twenty-nine!"

"That's just what I tell everyone." Hanna confided. "February 20th will be my sixth twenty-ninth birthday."

Betty wanted to laugh and maybe cry a little. She had been comparing herself to the false advertising of Hanna's face. She turned to Jil and took a closer look at her longtime friend. The little wrinkles around her eyes and mouth still showed despite her use of Botox and fillers. *All those years of smoking.* Betty thought back to what Linda, Jil's mother, looked like when they were teens and when she last saw her. Smoking had roughened her voice and put deep creases in her flesh where the smoke had curled up around her face. Beth had similar, but less obvious damage to hers. Betty's parents had stopped smoking in the nineties, after several attempts. Though, she had caught her dad sneaking a smoke from time to time since then. Thinking of her parents and Linda triggered a thought in Betty. She took Jil's hands in hers and sincerely asked, "I'm such a lousy friend, how are your parents doing? Your mom's—". Gil was shaking his head no, Jil's eyes were misting up and quickly turned to dripping tears.

Jil needed her old friend at that moment. The one who would have dropped everything and been at the hospital with her, had she called. The friend she counted on even when she hid her problems, like being an escort to earn the rent money after Larry had been bankrupted by Casper. Jil needed a shoulder to cry on besides Gil's, and there had not been one in a very long time. She pulled Betty to her and buried her face into Betty's shoulder. "They're dead," she forced out between sobs.

"Oh my God!" Betty blurted. They moved over to the great room and sat down on the oversize leather couch. "I'm so sorry, I didn't know."

Hanna wanted to join her new friends and be supportive, but knew better. She looked to Gil who stepped closer to her. "What happened?" she asked.

Gil considered what to tell Hanna, what she needed to know versus what was appropriate to tell. "Jil's mom died as she was about to get a lung transplant and her father died in a car accident not long after."

Hanna gasped. "That's horrible! I can't imagine." Both of Hanna's parents were still alive—divorced and hating each other, but still alive. Her trust fund would grow significantly when they passed, assuming the funds were not raided for other uses. She never wished her parents dead, or at least not truly, and she had more than enough money to live grandly as it was, but she certainly had drifted away from them, calling her mother only a few times a month to keep track of old friends and cousins. "Are your parents still living?" Hanna asked tenderly.

"Mine?" Gil was surprised by the question. "Yes, they're still kicking. They moved to Florida awhile back, so I don't see them as often." Truth was, he had not seen his parents in four years. His work in Control had been all consuming. He rarely had taken any time off to travel outside of work, and he had made excuses the past few years to avoid going to his parents for the holidays, especially after kicking Sally out, who he had told his mother about and how he was considering marrying her. After the fallout and Sally's betrayal, the last thing he wanted to do was be interrogated by his own mother about his personal life failures. "What about you?" he asked.

Hanna gave a weak smile. It seemed wrong to be happy that others' parents lived while someone was still grieving for their loss. "Yes, still kicking, mostly at each other. Divorced and fighting as if I was still five years old and a bargaining chip. I switch holidays with them, still. Can you imagine?"

"Wow. Hey, your drink is a little low—may I go fill it for you?" he asked.

Hanna spotted an opening to sit down with Betty and Jil, so she handed him her glass and glided over to the couch. She noticed that both women had amazing posture. The perfection of their poses juxtaposed with the perfection of the full-grain leather couch—designed to look ancient, yet still new— stood out from the slouching crowd she usually hung with. As she approached, she changed her face to a sympathetic pout and thrust her arms out to grab Jil's hands. She gently sat down on the coffee table across from her and gave her deepest sympathies. "I'm so sorry."

Betty watched Hanna usurp her moment with Jil and let it happen. She knew too much about her old friend to provide too much sympathy. It bothered her more, though, that Tom and Gil had not updated her on the deaths of Larry and Linda. *What the fuck—how did that slip their minds?* she wondered.

Sixty-Four

Powder On

November 29, 2009 — Ritz-Carlton, Vail, Colorado

BETTY EXCUSED HERSELF from the group with a toast using the last of her mimosa. "Time for me to hit the slopes." She had deftly handed off the sympathy duties to Hanna, who was trading rich, neglectful parent stories with Jil. *Those two are made for each other*, Betty thought. She had brought her jacket, gloves, and miscellaneous gear down with her and picked them up from the table where she had left them. Betty chided herself for being careless: *Thieves live even amongst the wealthy.*

Gil walked over to her and said farewell like a recent acquaintance would. "Have fun skiing! I wish I was going with you." More quietly, he said, "Sorry for not giving you a heads-up on Jil's parents. I assumed the office . . ."

Betty put her coat on and checked for her hat in a pocket. She gave a weak smile and said, "No problem, you and Hanna have it under control." *It had to have been the adrenaline and me ovulating.—what the hell did I see in him to make me think I loved him?* she asked herself.

"I'll see you and Jil tonight, I'm sure." She waved over at Hanna and Jil and spoke up, "Bye, see you tonight at après. Text me where you land." She spun away from Gil before he could say anything else.

Gil gave a fake smile and watched Betty walk off, a little longer than he should have. Jil gave him a jealous look and he walked over to rejoin them.

"What were you talking about?" Jil asked.

"I probably shouldn't say anything." Gil said.

"About what?" Hanna asked.

"Well, our drinks are empty," he said as he drained his mimosa.

†

Betty spotted Karl in the foyer giving instructions to his junior concierge. There was always one on duty, twenty-four-seven. Karl usually had the early-morning to early-afternoon shift so he could ski later in the day. He nodded at her while he continued to bring his replacement up to speed. Today was Karl's day off, but he usually came in anyway to make sure the staff were on the ball. The Ritz-Carlton Vail was still brand-new, and the staff getting used to their positions. Some had come from other member hotels or time-share facilities in the Ritz organization, but the junior concierge was moving up from the Marriott organization next door. There were just some things that the Ritz-Carlton did differently than the Marriott, and the new man was having a hard time getting the hang of it. Karl took his role seriously, just as with any other mission he had done for Control, which is why he survived the Cold War and the intervening years with minimal damage to his body and soul. He wanted to call out to Betty that he would see her on the slopes, like friends would, but that was not the role he was playing, so the nod would have to do.

Betty decided to walk to the Arrabelle instead of riding in the Ritz-Carlton van. It was only a few blocks and it seemed like a good way to prep her legs for the slopes. One of the residents of the building, a man with dark hair, a dark tan, and two days of beard, called out to her. She had spoken briefly to him in the great hall the previous day. *King—his name was King*, Betty thought. *How could I forget a name like King Herr.* She considered waving at him and just continuing on, but he seemed certain to follow her anyway, so, playing the role of a trust funder, she let him catch up to her at the corner of the building.

"Hey, Betty, right?" he asked as he extended his ungloved hand, snowflakes landing on his bare skin and melting.

His hand was warm and firm. There was no softness to his grip. Betty pushed a little to see where his center of gravity was, something she would do with an opponent before a jujitsu match, if she could. "King?" she replied. He was wearing excellent-quality ski clothes, but in a shade of gray. His left knee had a slight tear, probably from being off course and catching a tree or a rock outcrop. He was the sort of trust funder who cared deeply about the quality and functionality of his gear but was not the least bit concerned with how he looked.

"Yes, hey, I'm off to the slopes too, mind if I walk with you?"

The Ritz-Carlton had an agreement with the Arrabelle to allow guests and residents to store their ski gear in lockers directly across from the Lionshead Village gondola. It was an expensive but worthwhile perk to keep your skis only feet from where you would put them on to start your day. "Not at all. What part of the mountain you hitting today?" she asked.

"I really hadn't made up my mind yet," King hedged. "You?"

"It's been a little while, so I thought I'd take it easy for an hour or so before hitting the harder trails," Betty said. She had not been skiing since the previous March, though she had been doing exercises designed to keep her knees in good shape for moguls. She would jump sideways from the ground onto a box or rock and then back down again on the other side. It forced her ligaments to grow stronger as she kept her balance, and it strengthened her calf muscles and quadriceps. "What about you, been on the slopes yet this season?"

"Me, oh, I've been moving around enough to ski straight through the year. Just up from Portillo and Cerro Catedral."

"Well, I'd ask you to hang with me, but sounds like I'd just slow you down." Betty could not decide if she wanted to hang out with King until meeting up with Karl. She would have to lose him to have any kind of meaningful conversation with her co-agent, but the idea of some real competition on the slopes was getting her thinking. *Maybe if I ski with King this morning, I'll be ready for Karl this afternoon. What the hell, why not.*

"Hey, I'm down with taking it easy this morning, but"—he looked Betty up and down—"based on your grip when we shook hands, I might be the one slowing you down after the first run or two."

Betty smiled at the handsome devil in front of her. "Bring it on!"

Sixty-Five

Power Powder

November 29, 2009 — Vail, Colorado

THE FIRST RUN DOWN THE MOUNTAIN was Simba, which provided an easy blue mixed with an optional short black diamond section. King stayed alongside or behind Betty, watching her style and skill. They slid to a stop just before the black diamond, where they could go right and stay on the easier terrain of the blue Simba.

"Looking mighty fine there, Miss Betty," King said.

"Just warming up." Betty unzipped her jacket slightly; she did not want to get too warm. Her spider-goat-silk bulletproof layer under her ski apparel had excellent wicking properties, but it was one layer too much for so early in the season.

"You ready for a little black?" King asked.

Betty answered by turning left and heading down, leaving him standing. "That is one mighty fine piece of divine," King said to no one in particular.

An hour later, when they reached the top of Game Creek Bowl, King spotted Karl first and skied over to him. After Betty pulled up, King proceeded to introduce them. "Betty, you know Karl, the concierge, don't you?"

"Why, yes I do—I didn't recognize you," Betty lied. Karl was six foot five and lanky, easy to spot.

Karl extended his hand, "Miss Thursten, a pleasure to see you on the slopes."

"Oh, don't be silly, call me Betty."

King gripped Karl's right bicep and declared, "Karl is one of the best skiers out here."

"You're the best one I've seen out here, or are there some pros on the slope today?" Karl asked. "What you might not know, Betty, is that King is about to go pro."

"Really? So you were just lagging to check me out?" she asked.

King smiled and looked back at Karl. "You want to hang with us?" He looked at Betty. "I shouldn't assume you want to hang with me, let alone Karl, but it would be a blast!"

"Sounds good to me—all warmed up, so let's go crazy!" Betty said.

They went right instead of left at the top of the lift and easily handled the four harder runs of Game Creek: Deuces Wild, Faro, Ouzo, and Ouzo Glade.

As they passed the Game Creek lodge on Ouzo Glade, King and Karl pulled up alongside Betty; she had stopped to admire the beauty of the club's buildings and their settings. "There's a big shindig there tonight. Crazy money," Karl said.

King looked at both of them. "You know the difference between crazy and eccentric?" he asked.

"No, what?" Karl asked.

Betty jumped in and gave the punch line before King could. "Money."

"Exactly," King said. "And for now, I am eccentric."

Betty smiled, thinking of her Black Card and her temporary yet extreme wealth. "Me too," Betty said.

Karl shook his head. "I guess that means I'm just plain crazy."

Betty gave him a one-armed hug. "That's why we love you."

"And because you take care of us," King said. "You're the best concierge in the valley."

Karl's dark tan from frequent skiing and being outdoors did not show it, but he blushed from their compliments. Being retired from fieldwork was turning out better than he had hoped, so far.

"Ready for the back bowls?" King asked.

"If I can keep up with you two," Betty said.

King nodded his head. "I have no doubt about your keeping up. I'm more worried you'll push me too hard and I'll do something stupid showing off." He pointed at his knee and the slight tear in his pants. "You don't want to know how I got that."

"Tell me after we get down, at après." Betty pointed to the back bowls. "Sun Down to China?" The snowfall had dwindled to a light dusting of medium-size flakes. The wind was mild, and the sun was peeking through the clouds. It was a perfect day for skiing.

Both men nodded in agreement.

The trio worked their way through multiple runs of each bowl, the lift lines were short and the snow below the fresh powder was expertly groomed. In a few hours, they had worked their way to the top of the Sun Up Bowl.

The sky was clear and astonishingly blue. The thinner air of the high altitude was catching up on Betty and she needed a break. "Two Elk Lodge for snacks?" she suggested.

King pulled his goggles off and squinted. He had a tan line from both his sunglasses and the goggles that gave him the look of a man addicted to skiing and the outdoors. He applied chapstick and rubbed some sunblock on his face. "I'm famished. I need more than a snack. What about you, Karl? I'm buying."

Karl could afford his own meals—his dual income from being a concierge and his salary from Control was a bit of a windfall for his retirement—but accepting a meal from one of his guests was a welcome tip. "You bet. I could go for a hamburger."

A few minutes later, as they sat in the huge building made of natural logs and timber, Betty thought of the history of the building. "You guys remember the original Two Elk burning down?" she asked.

"I knew the guy who did it," King said.

"Really?" Karl asked, not believing him.

"Yeah, crazy guy from Arizona. Part of ELF," King said.

"ELF?" Betty knew the story in general terms—it had been a hot topic of those who were anticipating the addition of the back bowls to the Vail stable of runs—but she did not know the finer details.

"Earth Liberation Front," Karl said. "What, it took the FBI six or seven years to find the guy, I think."

"Killed himself in jail," King said.

"Seriously?" Betty asked.

"Yep. Committed suicide with a plastic bag."

Betty was done with her pulled pork. The coleslaw and baked

beans sat untouched. "You ready to get back to skiing?" she asked Karl.

He nodded and finished the last bite of his Epic Burger. "You want my fries?"

King picked up Betty's trash after waiting for her to acknowledge she was done with a nod of her head. *That's gentlemanly of him*, she thought.

The group headed out.

Betty had felt King's presence behind her on every run. Any time she had suggested he go first, he would balk and say, "Ladies first." As they prepared to leave Two Elk Lodge with their stomachs comfortably filled, Betty insisted he go first for once. "This time I get to watch your technique," she insisted.

King smiled. "But can you keep up?" He launched down Dragon's Teeth and over the rock outcropping, crossed his skis in midair with his poles out, landed, and continued for a hundred meters before stopping to watch their jumps.

Betty looked at Karl, who shrugged his shoulders and followed. He disappeared from her view and then reappeared, cutting smoothly through the powder. Betty had jumped off Dragon's Teeth and many other drops in her youth while skiing with Jil, who would usually ski around the obstacles, too concerned about breaking a bone or damaging her looks. Betty gritted her teeth, launched, and did a backflip off the outcropping. *Shit!* she thought while in the air. Her landing was decent, but she had to recover from under rotating. The tips of her skis wanted to drive into the snow, but by pulling her knees up to speed her rotation, she barely recovered and did a squat landing, bounced off the snow, and straightened up. She pulled up to the two men smiling and applauding her.

"Pretty impressive," King said.

"I'm not doing that," Karl said.

"That's 'cause you're too lanky," Betty said.

Karl nodded in agreement. "Exactly—I'd need another ten feet of drop, at least, to make it around."

There were half a dozen more runs where King went first or last, but rarely so close to Betty, until they got to the middle of the China Bowl on Rasputin's Revenge. He flew past Karl and nearly ran Betty into the trees. He looked completely out of control.

“What the fuck, King?” Betty asked.

He pointed to the binding on his left ski as he sat in a pile of snow. “Give me a minute. I think I need to tighten this.” He reached into his backpack and pulled out a tool and made a slight adjustment. “Sorry about that, I was trying to save it and not blow out my knee.”

“You about blew me out,” Betty said.

Karl pulled up and asked what happened. “I couldn’t see much, King was throwing up a hell of a rooster tail,” he told Betty.

They gathered up and started down the last bit of the slope.

At the bottom of Rasputin’s Revenge, Betty checked her phone for the time and any messages. *I should get a selfie with King, I hate to think like this, but I need to send his photo in to have his background checked*, she thought. There was a series of text messages from Hanna and Jil, who had been drinking together since Betty left them at ten in the morning; it was now four. Several were selfies of them in front of B-list celebrities or well-known socialites. They had asked several times where she was and why wasn’t she with them. There was also a message from Tom indicating there was activity happening later that night at the Game Creek Club and that she should find a way to be there.

King pulled up to her. “Sorry about that,” he apologized again. “I should have just dropped instead.” He pulled his goggles off his face and propped them on top of his beanie.

Betty moved slightly and stretched her left arm with her phone out for taking a selfie. “Smile!”

The mountain was behind them; the snow looked incredible. She wished that the day of skiing could go on into the night. Even with the near collision and King’s ski-bum attitude, she was enjoying his company. The chairlift ride to the top was filled with laughter as they talked about the highlights of their day skiing.

Betty said to King, “You’re not all bad.” His rosy red cheeks, slightly hidden by his stubble, looked tempting.

He smiled and put his arms around the shoulders of both comrades. “A guy could get used to skiing with such fine company.” He pulled them both a little closer and turned to Karl. “Any chance you’ll follow me back to Chile next summer?”

They all laughed a little.

“Any five-star hotels at the slopes?” Karl asked

They worked their way back to Game Creek Bowl by reversing their route from China Bowl to Sun Up, then taking one last run down Wow, a black diamond, to get to the High Noon Express Lift.

"Wow, what a day!" King said. "Let's just take it easy on the way down, so no one gets hurt before we get drunk!"

"Oh, so now that you're tired, you don't want to race!" Betty took off fast, then started making lazy cuts back and forth.

King and Karl followed and let her lead them in. Without further incident, they found themselves at the Arrabelle to put their gear away before joining the others at Garfinkel's for après. Betty said goodbye to Karl, who was heading back with a group to the Ritz-Carlton. King excused himself and walked with Karl a short ways to have a private conversation with him. Betty did not wait for King, but headed on up to the deck of Garfinkel's, wondering what the two could be talking about.

Sixty-Six

Absolute

November 29, 2009 — Vail, Colorado

BETTY WOULD NOT LAST LONG at the après-ski. Hanna and Jil were beyond drunk. Gil was more lucid, but more intoxicated than he should have been per Control protocol. It was a disaster in the making.

"What?" Jil asked when Betty pointed out she had been drinking since the early morning.

"You're completely wasted."

"Well, you can't drink all day if you don't start in the morning," Jil said as she raised her French 76 in toast.

Hanna picked up her glass and toasted too. She was also inebriated. "You don't like us, Betty?"

"No, no, that's not the point."

"Well, what is your point?" Jil asked, whose voice was drunk loud.

"I guess my point is I am way behind you two." Betty looked at the drink in front of her. It did not look appetizing, and she had a lot of catching up to do if she was going to get into the mood her friends were in.

King entered Garfinkel's deck overlooking the gondola after talking with Karl for a few minutes. "Hey, everyone," he said, as if he were everyone's longtime friend.

Hanna smiled, thinking he had come to see her. She tried to make more room at her end of the bench, but Gil and Jil were not moving.

King ambled over to Betty's side of the table and gave her a high-five. "You guys should have seen her carve up the mountain."

Betty smiled. "I was just trying to stay ahead of you. You were holding back."

Jil knew Betty was an excellent skier from their time at Pepi's. There had also been rumors about King's abilities and the opportunities he had passed on over the years. "Are you going to finally go pro, King?"

King laughed, "I'm too old now. I think that ship has sailed."

Hanna knew of King's reputation as a skier who would rather be on the slopes than with a girlfriend. He might have been rich, but he was a ski bum at heart, focused on the sport and not the entourage of women like Hanna, who had tried to nurture him to respectability. "You going to be my date tonight?" Hanna asked.

"To what?" King asked.

Jil was suddenly aware that she did not know what time it was. She reached over with her right hand, her left holding her drink, and grasped Gil's thigh. "Lover boy, what time is it?" She had a watch, but did not want to put her drink down to check it.

Gil checked his Rolex, "It's almost five."

"Oh, shit. Betty, we have to go get ready. Big party tonight at Game Creek Club. We can't be in the big boys' room, but I'm having drinks for everyone at the bar. I have to be there, so you do too. We can catch up on things."

Betty smiled. She imagined this party continuing on for many more hours, but it was going to take something extra special to keep Hanna and Jil going, she surmised. "Sounds like a blast. Why not," she said.

Jil drained her drink and set the glass down heavy. "King, you coming too?" she asked.

"Why not!" he said as he looked at Betty.

Hanna saw his look and felt anger inside her. She had tried to seduce King several times in past years. Their circle of travel overlapped from time to time when he came north from the southern hemisphere. She knew his family was based out of Chile and associated with the wine country, but he was never willing to give up much in the way of details to her. "Great!" she said. Hanna leaned into Jil and whispered loud enough for everyone else to hear, "Let's go to the little girls' room. I need to freshen up my nose."

Jil smiled. A little coke would go a long way in getting her through the night. Since giving up cigarettes to make Gil happy, she had been fighting all of her cravings. Her heavier than normal use of alcohol was a symptom of her withdrawal. The thought of a line made her feel more confident about the rest of the night. Gil's minding her habits had kept her clean for several days. "Sounds like a good idea!" she whispered loudly back. The two women left the table and headed to the restrooms, but Jil turned back and said, "Meet us in the great room at six!" before she was yanked into Garfinkel's by Hanna.

Gil got up and headed the same direction. "I better keep an eye on them." He pointed one index finger at each of the two remaining friends. "See you at six?"

Betty smiled and said, "You got it," and she prepared to leave.

King called the waiter over and asked for the check.

"Oh, no, let me get it. I've known Jil since we were little, and she took care of a lot of things for me back then." Betty felt guilty, suddenly, for all of the times she had piggybacked on the Harpers, skiing, Europe, long weekends in New York shopping for Jil's pageants, and the miscellaneous things that just got taken care of so Betty could keep pace with their daughter. Now that she was rich—at least, as her cover—she needed to spend money like she had it to burn. She pulled out her Black Card to give to the waiter.

King gave a long whistle. "Damn, that's an expensive card." He put his wallet back. "I don't think I'm going to bother picking up your lunches anymore."

"That was nice of you to do, to include Karl and buy him lunch."

"He's been good to me. Well, I haven't asked for much, but when I have, damn, the guy just gets it done."

Betty assumed that Karl's military precision and longevity in the field were paying off in his ability to make things happen for the guests at the Ritz-Carlton. "What did he do for you?" Betty asked.

"The Arrabelle Club package for Ritz residence was closed. He arranged for it anyway. It sure is nice to have my skis right here at the gondola. That's what I was saying to him when I lagged behind."

"He certainly is one you can trust to get things done."

†

Two hours later, the group was due to gather, but Betty and King had arrived early and shared a drink at the bar while waiting for their friends. Their time talking together revealed to Betty his family's history in the wine business and his occasional work promoting their wines around the world, which gave him an excuse to indulge his habit of skiing. His Ritz-Carlton condo was his one lavish purchase, made possible by a small inheritance from his bachelor uncle who had died childless.

"I wanted to have something to hang on to, years from now after I've wasted my money skiing around the world. I can always sell it to cash out, but I'd like to retire here someday," he said.

"That is so weird, my uncle died too! But he left me a crazy amount of money."

"That explains the Black Card."

"Yeah, I shouldn't have it—my God, you wouldn't believe what I have to spend each month just to keep the damn thing."

"I know what it costs," he said. He nodded his head and had a thoughtful look. "Hanna tried to get me to settle down a few times. She's kind of pissed, I think, that I'm hanging with you instead of her."

"Were you a couple, before?"Betty asked.

"No—no, nothing like that, we just dated sometimes, when I was in the same hemisphere as her." He took a drink of his blended scotch. "She had a Black Card. In fact,"—King spread his arms wide—"she bought me this ski gear a couple of years ago."

Betty took a sip of her drink, a vodka tonic. "She was impressed that I had one. I didn't think she had one of her own, from what she said."

"Oh, she spent a lot of money on it—some to corral me—but she had to give it up, she told me, 'cause it was eating into her 'seed corn.'"

"Seed corn?" Betty asked

"She was spending more than she was getting from the income of her trust. Her parents sat her down and told her to be more responsible, that I was a bad influence."

"What happened then?"

"She got the dog." King rolled his eyes and took another sip.

"Good Lord." Betty looked over at the entry way of the great room where Gil, Jil, and Hanna were coming from, loud and boisterous. "Here comes the life of the party."

"Don't let her get me alone," he pleaded.

"OK, I'll do my best." Betty assured him.

After a quick cocktail hour together, the group headed out to the foyer. The Ritz-Carlton van would drive them to the gondola, which they would ride to the Eagle's Nest. From there they would ride in a snowcat to the restaurant. Betty looked at Jil's face. She could see a redness in her eyes and a little extra mucus trying to escape her nose. She handed her once-best friend a handkerchief. "Your eyes are a little red. Do you have any drops?" she asked.

"Oh, God, Hanna has the stuff," she whispered. "I mean, I've had some good stuff before, but she got this from one of the Colombian boys staying this week. So pure." She gave Betty the handkerchief back after blowing her nose.

"Keep it. You'll probably need it more than me tonight." She smiled as convincingly as she could.

Sixty-Seven

Vodka Like Water

November 29, 2009 — Vail, Colorado

AS THEY ENTERED THE LOUNGE of the Game Creek Club, Betty was pleasantly surprised to see Miller behind the bar serving. She looked away to avoid signaling that she knew him. She sidled up to the bar and ordered a vodka tonic with Grey Goose vodka. She took a sip of it and realized that Miller had used a vodka bottle filled with water to make her drink. She could drink like a fish all night and all she would have to do is slur her words a little more and become clumsy as the night wore on to mimic her friends. Gil ordered the same and received the same treatment.

"Put all of our drinks on my tab," Betty said as she passed Miller the Black Card. She noticed he was wearing a name tag. "Thanks, Devon." She had only ever known him as Miller. *Devon—that fits him nicely. I hope that is his real name*, she thought. "Jil, Hanna, King, get over here and tell Devon what you want. It's on me."

The other three had been engaged in serious discussions with the manager of Game Creek Lodge, Skipper-do had been discovered. Hanna had snuck Skipper-do in her purse. Non-service dogs were barred and the conversation was becoming heated. Skipper-do was not helping by barking at the manager, then jumping out of Hanna's purse and nipping at his ankles. Just as the situation was getting completely out of hand, an entourage of people arrived—including Marie, the woman from the most expensive house Betty had ever been in. Besides the bodyguards, there were three other men with her, one of whom had a cast on his foot and was using a cane. Jil broke away and mingled with a blonde haired, middle aged man who appeared from a private room to greet and direct the group.

Betty mentally reviewed her earlier briefing and thought, *Those three men with Marie must be Gustav, Pierre, and Charles. The man Jil is talking to must be Casper!*

Jil followed the group to a private room and emerged as Ernesto made his entrance with Max and Thor, which caused Betty to hide her face. Ernesto and Max were not a problem, but she half expected Thor to come over and challenge her to arm wrestling. She tried to hide behind King, who was curious what she was doing, but willing to play along.

"Who are you hiding from?"

"Oh, Lord, just an asshole who got abusive when I told him I wasn't interested," she said.

"I will protect you, my lady," King quipped.

"Oh, I can kick his ass—I did that time. I just don't want to deal with him again, we have Hanna causing a huge problem, she and Jil are high and tight, and I just want to have a relaxing drink."

King took Betty into his arms and kissed her, lightly, as if he wasn't really trying anything, but rather to shield her from Thor's view. At first she thought to drop him like a bag of potatoes to the floor, but she recognized he wasn't really trying to take advantage of her, just selling the pose. She decided to kiss back a little, and he gave a little bit more back. Meanwhile, Thor, Ernesto, and Max moved on to join Marie, Pierre, Gustav, and Charles in the other room. Jil floated between the Cabal and her friends, until she was drawn into the kerfuffle of Hanna and Skipper-do. Miller approached Betty and King and said, "I'm sorry to bother you, but it looks like your friend is about to be escorted out. Do you want me to close the tab?"

Betty looked over at Hanna. She did not want this to be a big deal and blow her opportunity to interact with the Cabal members. She sauntered over to the manager and asked, "Can I help solve this?" She picked up Skipper-do, who adored her, and calmed him down quickly. She looked at the manager's name tag and said, "Altti, I'm so sorry for this. Is there any way my friends and I can solve this without a big fuss? Whatever it costs, it isn't a problem."

Altti looked taken aback. Skipper-do was no longer barking, Hanna and Jil had stepped back from confronting him, and Betty stood before him wanting to set things right. "Well, I, ah—"

"This is normally a members-only establishment, correct?" she asked.

"Yes, we only allow the public here in the evening, as you know."

"Is the Chalet available tonight? I'm sure you would give a member the first option to book it. I'll be glad to buy a membership and pay for the accommodations at the Chalet as well. Skipper-do can relax there and not disturb your guests here."

"You would have to fill out an application, and I would need a check for fifty thousand dollars, plus the cost of the Chalet," Altti explained.

"Devon has my Black Card—could we put the charges on that? You can add whatever the extra fee you need to make this work." Betty felt giddy with power. She had been able to deescalate the incident quickly, and Tom was going to be buying her a membership to an elite club. The chance of him clawing that back after the mission was remote. She smiled at the manager, knowing she had won. "Could you bring me the form at the bar? I'm sure Devon has a pen I can use," Betty said sweetly.

Altti hemmed and hawed for a moment. "Yes, well, miss"—he pointed gently at Hanna—"would you please bring your . . . companion animal to the front desk so we can arrange accommodations for—him." Hanna took Skipper-do back from Betty and joined Altti in the walk to the front desk to arrange renting the Chalet. The group returned to the bar and Devon for fresh drinks.

Ten minutes later, Hanna returned to the group, sans Skipper-do, and gushed to Betty how much she appreciated her taking care of the manager, and by extension, the problem. "Oh, Betty, you have to let me put the drinks on my card."

Betty gave her a fake smile. "No, I don't." Her face grew serious. The power she now had among the group had grown logarithmically in the past twenty-four hours. She was realizing that with unlimited money, compared to how she normally lived, her place in the social strata floated to the top if she took care of those around her and refrained from asking for much in return. "Listen, Hanna." She pulled her friend aside from the rest. "What's the four-eleven on King?"

Hanna looked over at the man she thought she could tame but couldn't, the reason she had Skipper-do in the first place. "There is just something about him. He draws you in close. I would have trusted him with my life, even marry him, but—"

"But what?"

"There's a black hole in his heart. Something is missing or someone did something to him, I don't know. I thought I could heal it, but every time I got close, he'd pull away."

"An old girlfriend, maybe?"

"It could be, or it could be child abuse. He won't talk about his family."

"What does he talk about?" Betty asked.

"The snow. He's talked about all the words Inuit have for snow. If you let him, he'll talk about skiing for hours on end."

"And you don't ski, do you?"

"Oh, I did, I used to. He took the fun out of it for me. It was too intense, and for me dangerous."

"I see what you mean after being with him for the day." Betty considered the near accident on the back bowl. King had been staying behind her the entire day, never encroaching her space, but always being just near her. It was as if he were mimicking her technique move for move. *It doesn't make any sense*, she thought. *Or it doesn't if I'm thinking of him as the typical ski bum I knew back when Jil and I were coming here to ski in college.* Betty looked over at King, who smiled at her and raised his glass to her. *But what if I think of him as a spy, someone who works for the Cabal and is doing the same thing I'm doing, fitting in with the people next to my targets.* Betty smiled back at him and raised her nearly empty glass. She had not done enough hydrating after skiing all afternoon, so she was thankful for the extra water poured by Miller, but now she sort of wanted a stiff drink to wipe away her paranoia. *It can't be that. I'm just thinking too hard about it and trying to make sense of Hanna's interpretation of King.* She gave Hanna a hug and thanked her.

Hanna gave her a hug back, kissed Betty on the cheek, and said, "You be careful with him. He'll steal your heart. Let me know if you find mine."

As Betty and Hanna returned to the group, Dr. Eric Salizar and Boris, the one-armed man, entered the foyer of the club. They were greeted by Altti and escorted to the room with the Cabal members. As he walked past the bar, Eric stopped suddenly when he spotted Jil and Gil with their friends, started to smile, then saw Betty with them. Boris and Altti left Dr. Salizar at the door and walked around to the back area, out of sight.

Shit. His look isn't a good sign, Betty thought. The last time she saw Eric Salizar was in Denmark, just as the doctor was about to start a kidney transplant from Gil to Michel, his biological father. Gil had still been incapacitated by the anesthetic, so she'd forced Salizar to repair Karl's severed artery in his neck. Salizar knew who Betty was, as well as Gil. *There goes any shred of secrecy left—not that I really believed the Cabal wouldn't figure it out in due time.*

Charles called out to Salizar in a warm welcome from the doorway to the banquet room, "Good doctor! What a pleasure to see you."

Salizar pulled his gaze away from Betty and continued on to join his group.

Max exited the room ten minutes after Salizar had entered and came over to the bar to order a virgin cocktail for himself. He positioned himself between Betty and the wall, with Miller in front of him, so the conversation could be as private as possible. "You're blown. Slim's father wants you punished for his death."

"How lovely," Betty said. "Any idea how he plans to punish me? Write a hundred times on the blackboard, 'I will not kill Cabal children'?"

"Hah. Someone is already in place to do it. It's supposed to look like an accident, but you are to survive—either as a quadriplegic or with brain damage. He wants you to know why and by who. He wants you to suffer as long as he is suffering the loss of his son."

Betty forced herself to not look at King. *Is he the one? Is it to be a ski accident?* "Wow."

"Yeah. Be careful." Max took the drink from Miller and gave him a twenty. "Keep the change."

"Thank you, sir!" Miller replied with a smile on his face.

Max took a sip of drink and put it back down at the sound of shouts and thud coming from the Cabal's party. The door to the private lounge flung open and Boris rushed out and headed for the front exit and the snowcat.

Betty could see the hysterics through the open doorway. Marie was screaming, Pierre was hobbling toward a prostrate Gustav, and Charles was ordering a guard to capture Boris alive.

"Shit. Gustav's down," Max said as he bolted toward the chaos. Thor brushed past Max and went out the front door of the Club in pursuit of Boris.

Jil and Gil pulled away from Hanna and King and rushed past Betty—Jil toward the private room in the wake of Max, Gil following Thor into the blowing snow.

Betty fought her desire to follow Gil or Max and instead pretended to be distraught by the noise and commotion. The manager appeared and attempted to restore decorum by saying, "Please, remain calm, everything will be OK." He looked into the private lounge. When he looked back at the bar, his face was white as the linens on the tables.

Miller looked to Betty and said, "May I freshen up your drink for you?"

"Yes, please, make it a double." She watched Miller pour actual vodka into her glass instead of the water he had been using from a marked Grey Goose bottle. "Thank you. What's King doing?" she asked quietly.

"He's been watching you intently. Until the excitement, he was going on and on about skiing in Antarctica, but now he is trying to calm down Hanna."

She took her drink and rejoined the group. The bar was ell shaped, so they had not seen the commotion of the room from their angle. The conversation was now centered on the question of what actually was happening.

A woman was summoned from the dining room, who Betty assumed was a doctor by her stern yet calm demeanor. As the doctor entered the private room, Betty got a brief view of the action.

Hanna asked first, "Could you see what was going on, Betty?"

"Not really . . . I think someone fell or had a heart attack." Betty was sure Boris had targeted Gustav, but she had no way of knowing how the deed was done. *Don't need to tell them any more than necessary. Was it the same poison Yuri used on Eric's father?* she thought.

The group nodded their heads and leaned around the corner to see if there was any action remaining, but quickly returned to their previous conversation.

Hanna turned to King and suggested, "Finish your story."

"So that is how I finished my bucket list of skiing on every continent," finished King.

Betty smiled as if she had just missed something she wanted to hear. "You'll tell me that story later, right? I can't believe I just missed that one."

"Sure. I'd love to," King said.

The manager came over to the group and was perspiring, wiping his forehead with a handkerchief. "Please forgive me, one of our guests had an incident—nothing to worry about."

Hanna and King shrugged their shoulders and Betty just smiled.

The manager pressed on with procedural matters. "Miss Thursten, we are very pleased to have you as a member. Here is your packet with guest passes."

Betty took the packet and laid it on the bar. "Thank you, Altti. That is an unusual name—what does it mean?" she asked.

"Yes, I get asked that a bit. It is Finnish for Albert." His face turned serious. "I am so sorry, but the public hours are ending for the club. Would you like me to reserve the next snowcat for you?"

He's trying to rush us out the door, thought Betty. She did not look to her friends, but used her control of the group earned with her purchase of a membership to make a decision. "How long between trips to the gondola, Altti?" *I want a few minutes to poke around before we go.* "How about the one after that so we can collect Skipper-do and finish our drinks."

"It would be my pleasure, Miss Thursten." Altti took King and Hanna to retrieve Skipper-do while Betty excused herself to go to the restroom. As she passed the private room, she found Jil pacing back and forth, talking on her cellphone.

Casper stepped part way out of the private room and waved Jil in before Betty could talk to her. He gave Jil a stern look and closed the door to keep Betty out.

†

On the way down the mountain, Betty decided that if King was the person assigned to cripple her, he would do it on the mountain and not in town. She felt she could manage him even if he tried something. Betty whispered into his ear, letting her warm breath caress his neck, "Why don't you come up to my place and tell me about your trip to Antarctica."

"I would love to," he said, equally close to her neck. He pressed closer into her on the next lurch of the snowcat, but did not try anything bolder.

Betty considered holding his hand, but that would be more than she felt was appropriate, even though part of her wanted to be closer to the danger. The danger of casual sex or flirting with the man chosen to ruin her. Either one gave her a bit of a thrill. She let her hand brush his to see what he would do. He placed his on top of hers for a moment and squeezed gently but firmly for a moment. Betty let herself feel the thrill of pheromones; the possibilities were endless if she just let her mind go, but it drifted to the question, *What would Tom want me to do—and what would he think if I did something tonight?*

Sixty-Eight

Chap My Hide

November 29, 2009 — Ritz-Carlton, Vail, Colorado

HANNA WAS DISTRACTED BY ONE of her many moneyed friends that filled the Ritz bar area; another band was playing; and the pool was covered by a translucent, flashing, multicolored dance floor, leaving Betty and King to themselves.

"You want to hang out here, maybe dance a little," King asked.

Betty shook her head. Between running in the morning, skiing during the day, and hanging with her friends, she was exhausted. "Come up to my place and tell me the story about Antarctica. I have plenty to drink up there." It was part defensive; in her own space she would be able to monitor her drink more closely in case King or anyone tried to spike it. She also had her stash of weapons to turn to if she needed to defend herself—though, unless her opponent was a highly skilled martial artist, she did not need the guns. Her plan was to get him talking about Antarctica, then segue into his personal life, especially his parents. *Hanna had said he was closed off about those parts of himself. If I can get him to talk, then it was just Hanna he didn't want to tell, and maybe he isn't the one working for the Cabal.* Betty wanted to believe that she could meet someone intelligent, physically capable, romantic, and not attached to Control or the Cabal or anything that would prevent her from having a normal life. Or at least a life with a level of adventure that did not include gunplay or near-death experiences as part of her work.

King nodded his head. "I'd like that."

Betty's phone vibrated, signaling a message from Tom. She was expecting him to arrive in the morning, but to keep his distance until he was needed. She thought to look at the message since she had not heard from him or David about the selfie of King and her, which made her think that he must have checked out. *Probably just Tom reminding me of his arrival tomorrow. It's not like I'm going to be picking him up from the airport.* She dismissed the message without looking at the phone so it would not keep vibrating and took King's hand in hers for the walk to the elevator. *I might just be pretending, but I like the way this feels. There are so many conditions with Tom. So many things he hides from me.*

At the elevator, before they could board, Karl came from the concierge office with an envelope in his hand. "Miss Thursten, Betty."

"I didn't think you worked evenings," King said.

"I have to cover for Adam for a few hours, not a big deal." He turned to Betty and handed her an envelope with the Ritz-Carlton emblem on the flap and her name hand written on the front. "Here is that information you were asking for." It was sealed.

"Oh, thanks." Betty had no idea what it was, but obviously a message from Karl or perhaps Tom that needed to be hand-delivered instead of sent via encrypted message to her phone. *Why would they do it this way?* she wondered. *Everything is electronic now, no trace of paper—well, except for Tom Sr.'s missives, I suppose.* She put it into her bag without reading.

"If you get me an answer tonight about what you want, I can take care of it for you first thing in the morning," Karl assured her.

"Thanks." *He's trying to tell me something urgently, but I just don't know what it could be. I didn't ask for anything from him, but if he doesn't want to say it in person—maybe it has to do with King.*

The couple went up the elevator to the fourth floor. Betty opened the door to Günter's condo with her residence card and was surprised that the lights were already on. Sitting in the living room, flipping through real estate catalogs for the Vail area, was Tom Howell.

"Hey, cousin Betty! It's me, Tom." Tom greeted her as he turned to face her.

"Well, if the heavens aren't full of surprises!" she said. Betty moved through the room to Tom and gave him a fraternal hug and a kiss on the cheek. She whispered in his ear, "What the fuck are you doing here?"

"I might ask you the same question," Tom said.

They disengaged and turned to King. Betty made the introduction, "King, this is my cousin Tom, from my mother's side." *Which isn't too far from the truth*, she thought. Considering her Aunt Grace had a son with Tom's father, it was an accurate statement. *The best lie is one that leaves part of the truth out.*

King stepped up and shook Tom's hand. "It's a pleasure to meet you."

They shook hands for an extended time, each sizing up the other. Tom was testing King's core strength by moving his hand aggressively and judging how much his body moved versus just his arm. He realized it was a pointless exercise—King was a gifted athlete and daily skier, which required the same kind of core strength as special forces operator.

He probably thinks I'm family sizing him up, thought Tom. "It's a pleasure to meet you too." He let go and turned to Betty. "I hate to be a party pooper, but I have some important family news I need to share with you in private."

"I can tell you the story of Antarctica another time." King made half a step toward the entrance.

Betty knew Tom meant Control business, even if there truly was a strained family connection between them. "King, can you make yourself comfortable here?" she asked. Betty picked up the remote to the television and turned on a sports channel. *I'm making the assumption he is like other men, but he's smart enough to change the channel.*

Tom smiled at King, "It isn't going to take too long, it's just something that should stay among family."

"Thank you." King smiled and took the remote from Betty and sat down on the couch. The leather squeaked as he adjusted himself and leaned on a pillow.

Betty and Tom moved to the farthest bedroom of the condominium, toward the core of the building after Betty checked that the white-noise generator was turned on. The doors of the Ritz-Carlton had seals that dropped down when a door was closed to prevent noises from entering or exiting a room. With King listening to a television fifty feet away, the white-noise generator, and the door seal, she felt comfortable talking to Tom in hushed tones without fear of being overheard.

"What the hell are you doing here?" she asked.

Tom handed her a piece of paper that had been folded up in his pocket. It was printed on both sides and gave background information on the people she had seen at the Game Creek Club. The first and most prominent profile was Marie. "You were right, she's a real peach. A true-blue psychopath. Very rare in women, less than half a percent of the population. She has a trail of staff who have disappeared in the past, but no arrests or charges have ever been brought."

Betty thought about the staff changing the artwork when she visited the house on Beaver Dam Circle. They seemed efficient, but in absolute fear of their mistress. "I could see that happening."

"She recently had an entire village near Bern, Switzerland, torn down and moved half a mile."

"That couldn't have been cheap." Betty checked her phone; King was still waiting at the couch. "What about King—did anything come up on him?"

"Hmm. There were some incidents in the past two years that need more investigating, but he just appears to be a rich kid who hasn't grown up, skiing around the world, following the snow."

"What kind of incidents?" she asked.

"People skiing with him ran into trees or had bad falls off of outcroppings they were doing stunts from. He was the only witness, and there was no evidence of wrongdoing, so . . ." Tom let his thought drift off. It was not unusual for adventurous athletes to get injured or die.

He refocused and tapped his prosthetic leg. "You won't see me doing acrobatics, but I will be on the slopes this week."

"Really?" Betty said drolly.

"McFluffy made me a ski leg with built-in shock absorber," Tom said with a smile. He looked at her phone, which showed King still at the couch. He cleared his throat. "You should know that my father is dead. There wasn't an elaborate funeral and I appreciate your condolences."

"That ought to cover our long conversation in here." Betty gave Tom a fake hug, patting his back. "I'm so sorry for your loss."

"Yeah, I bet you are."

"So, what do we do about a girl like Marie?"

"I want you to go back into her place and find anything related to the Cabal's structure. You are authorized to kill anyone who gets in your way, but as per our standing policy, be sure there is nothing that traces back to us." Tom took the sheet of paper back from Betty.

She looked at her phone and saw that King had gotten up from the couch and moved to the wet bar to get a bottle of water from the glass-front refrigerator. He took a sip and sat back down, sinking into the cushions. "We better break up this funeral. He's getting restless. What about him?" she asked.

"Keep it business, please." Tom gave a curt smile.

"Someone is jealous," Betty teased.

"Maybe." Tom admitted. He felt a burn inside his gut that said he was more than jealous. He wanted to march King out of the condo and show Betty how he felt, but that would possibly unmask the reality of their mission in Vail.

"Well, why don't you come listen to his Antarctica story? You can chaperone us!" She smiled and tilted her head. *I should fuck King just to make Tom jealous.*

"Maybe one bedtime story, then I must be off." Tom motioned for them to leave the bedroom.

"Suit yourself." *I swear, if he really does try to chaperone me, I'll get in King's lap right in front of him.*

Sixty-Nine

Say Ah!

November 30, 2009 — Vail, Colorado

THE RUN TO BEAVER DAM Circle was more treacherous than the day before. Vail, Colorado, is blessed with over three hundred inches of snow annually, and today was one of those snow days. Vail Village and the company that owns most of the valley takes the job of maintenance seriously. Potholes are not allowed. Perfection is the goal, because when someone pays ten million dollars for a house, they expect the road to be clear, even if they are driving a hundred-thousand-dollar luxury four-wheel-drive SUV capable of climbing the mountain.

The walkway from the road to the house had been cleared at least once since the snow had started. Boris was nowhere to be seen; nor did Betty expect to see him after the events of the previous night at Game Creek.

When she grabbed the knocker, the door swung open on its own.

A Bavarian accented voice over the intercom said, "Come in, we've been expecting you."

Betty's breathing and heart rate increased slightly. There were no servants scurrying in the foyer of the first floor. All the artwork had been removed, save for the Picasso, which was smashed into shards. Jeremy was splayed on the floor, blood pooled under his head.

Betty turned back as the front door swung closed with a metal click, then the sound of a bolt being remotely triggered. *No servants, a dead Jeremy, a smashed multimillion-dollar Picasso, and the walls stripped of artwork*, thought Betty. Boris's warnings seemed all that much more ominous.

There was a circular stairway that wound counterclockwise up from the basement to the second floor. The basement level was built into the mountain, but appeared to be at least as large as the upper levels. The disembodied and ghostly voice came from multiple hidden speakers. "Come downstairs. Just follow the lights." LED lighting glowed warmly on the left side spiraling down, while the upward stairs remained dark.

Betty tentatively walked to the stairway and checked for any threat above before starting the circle down. The ceiling of the foyer was three stories—forty-five feet—high. Assuming the basement was also fifteen feet, Betty estimated where a point of attack might come from. She absentmindedly reached behind her back and felt naked without her SIG Sauer P229, but there was nowhere to hide it in this outfit, and besides, would a trust funder be out for a jog armed? *At least I'm bulletproof—assuming Tooker knows what he is doing.*

The lights continued to come on in front of her and started to extinguish behind her. As she landed on the floor below, the entire space lit up. There was a double door in front of her and an open hallway to the right and left. The lights above the massive carved wooden doors were off, and the hallway to the right was dark. She looked down the only lit path and saw no one. She looked back up the stairway and again, there was no one; she half expected the one-armed man to reappear. *Could he come in the house another way?* She listened for footsteps or doors, but there was not even the sound of a house breathing. She bent her knees as if she were going to retie her shoes. The floor, covered in massive chunks of slate, was radiating heat, which explained the lack of sound. *No ductwork or central air*, she noted. *Onward, ho.*

There were parallel doors along the hallway that were all closed. The door at the far end of the hallway was cracked open, but with the layout of the house, this seemed absurd until she realized this space was below the garage, which made the basement about ten thousand square feet by itself. *Where is all the staff to manage this place*, Betty wondered. The lights behind her had also gone out. A shaft of light shone down the staircase. Somehow it was concentrated, like in a cave, which did not seem possible even with the skylight at the top. *Must be some trick of architecture or artificial light source*, she thought.

The voice called out to her from behind the door, "This way, Betty." This time it was not from a speaker.

Betty pushed the door open. It was a large space set up as a gym. It was appointed with the finest professional equipment, from treadmills to ellipticals to stationary bikes. The middle of the floor was a large padded area that could be used for yoga or a more physical type of exercise like wrestling or even martial arts. From the weapons on the wall—swords, spears, halberds, and miscellaneous chain devices—she had no doubt that she was in an arena as much as a work out room. She stepped through and spotted two women dressed in white, heavy cotton garments, one with a brown belt and the other with a purple around the waist.

Both woman were the same height and size as Betty. The one in with the purple belt was poised as if waiting for an attack. Marie was the second woman and wore a brown belt and had her hands behind her back, as if ready to teach a class. "I've been waiting for you, Betty," Marie said.

"I just came to see if the Picasso was for sale, but now I'm not sure I want it," Betty said.

Marie laughed. She turned and walked away from the purple-belted woman and waved her hand. "Let's dispense with the pretense, shall we? You managed to buy some of the clothes I wanted from Gorsuch. I want them back."

"Seriously?" Betty gave a soft snort and shook her head. "You can have the clothes—they didn't look that great on me anyway." *I might as well play this out and see what Marie is willing to tell me. Always get your villain monologuing, I say.*

"Please, we have the same figure. I'm positive you look fantastic in them."

"Well, not for the office, anyway." Betty conceded.

"We know who you are, beyond the law office you rarely visit anymore." Marie tapped her palm with her phone, exhibiting impatience, but her stance indicated she was enjoying the banter. "You really should show up more often. People do talk."

"So, you know I'm a lawyer. Big deal. Why would I show up when I've inherited a fortune from my uncle?" Betty asked as she gently stretched her muscles in anticipation of a full-contact sparring match.

"Excellent cover, if your opponent doesn't have complete access to the banking system to see where the money trail leads." Marie gave a brief, broad smile, then arched her left eyebrow. "To Control."

"Interesting. To think I've always believed my uncle." Betty pretended to yawn and stretch. *Glad I'm warmed up from the run.* "If *I* didn't know, how is it that *you* know?"

"Your best friend gave you up, I'm afraid."

"I don't have a best friend."

"With friends like that, I can see why. Jil Harper works for us. Imagine our surprise when she hadn't told us about you before we asked, directly."

Marie pressed a button on her smartphone and the door behind Betty closed and latched by itself. She placed the phone on a pedestal behind her and picked up a gong mallet with a wool-covered head.

"Whatever. I'll drop your clothes off later today." Betty twisted her body as if to leave, but really just to stretch her core. *I'm not getting out of here without a fight, from the looks of things.* "Good to see you—unlock the door and I'll be on my way."

"If you defeat Duchess, you can keep them. If you lose, I get them."

"Duchess? You're kidding, right?" Betty asked.

Duchess bowed with her hands together.

"Actually, no." Marie moved over to a large bronze gong. "I know you are a brown belt in jujitsu. Think of this as Duchess's graduation. She wins, she graduates."

"As long as we are dispensing with pretense, Marie, what happens when I defeat her?" Betty asked.

"Dispensing with pretense, this will be to the death. Duchess dies if she loses."

Duchess made a rapid move toward Betty and began her attack.

"So now you know I'm an international lawyer specializing in immigration and a brown belt in jujitsu." Betty said as she rolled away from Duchess's sweeping leg kick.

"And to think we thought you were just a lethal killer working for the son of Tom Howell Sr., our American cousin." Marie said.

Betty was distracted enough by the information that she missed Duchess's telegraphing of her next kick, so it landed square on Betty's thigh.

"We also knew about you from Charles Jr., a man you knew as Slim."

Betty landed an elbow to Duchess's chest, knocking the wind

out of her. “Shame about him. I told him smoking kills.” Betty caught Duchess’s wrist and twisted it violently, but she did a backflip and used her weight to pull Betty closer, so Betty let go.

“You have been quite the pest lately. I can just imagine what trouble we would have had if José had lived to marry you.”

“Michel and Slim killed him.” Betty threw a particularly viscous kick to Duchess’s head as her opponent started to drop down for another leg sweep, a move that was becoming predictable.

“Well, yes, of course—only because you were outside the door beating it down and interrupted their . . . chat.”

Duchess parried Betty’s punch. “Fuck you!” Betty threw a knee into Duchess’s hip. “You can’t blame me for his death.”

“Boys will be boys. I’m afraid he wasn’t the suitable replacement for Ernesto that we had planned on.”

“So you ordered Slim to kill my fiancee?”

“No, of course not. That was Charles’s decision.” Marie was becoming disappointed in Duchess’s performance. “Duchess, you are dropping your guard. She leads with her left foot. Use the lotus combination I taught you.”

Betty had never heard of the lotus combination, obviously a code word for a technique the two had been working on. She became conscious of her left foot and her hesitation as she waited for this new method Duchess would use. “I’m going to kill you—and Charles.”

Duchess just stood, half crouched, waiting.

“Maybe I’ll burn his body like I did Slim’s,” Betty said.

“You’ll have to kill Duchess and then me to get to Charles, I’m afraid.”

“You ought to be.” Betty quipped.

Marie pressed a button on her phone and there was a metallic clicking sound. Duchess charged to the wall of weapons and removed a large knife, a tanto, almost a short sword. Marie pressed her phone again and a louder clicking sound emanated from all the weapons.

Betty rushed over and tried to grab a bo staff, but it was frozen to the metal hooks it was resting on. *These must all be magnetically locked. That bitch*, thought Betty. *Jujitsu, my ass.*

Duchess rushed Betty and thrust the blade at her. Betty was still wearing the spider-goat-silk gloves infused with carbon nano particles.

They were supposed to be nearly cut-proof. *I guess we're about to find out.* She grabbed the blade and pulled Duchess to her, close enough to land a left elbow to her head. The gloves mostly held, but there were slight cuts to the material, primarily to the interwoven Lycra. Duchess had enough of her senses left to twist and pull the blade, while Betty was wise enough to let go. She looked at her hand and saw no blood and she smiled.

Duchess looked surprised, by the ringing in her ears and by the lack of damage to Betty's hand. For the first time, Duchess looked unsure of herself, like it had dawned on her that she would lose—and die.

Marie looked frustrated and disappointed. "Kill her."

Duchess looked to her master and said, "I'm trying."

Betty tried not to laugh, but she involuntarily giggled.

Marie looked to Betty and pointed to Duchess. "Kill her."

Betty looked at Duchess and then Marie. "You're a psychopath."

Marie looked proud. "We're very rare, you know. Female psychopaths, that is."

"About to be even rarer."

Duchess thought of all the men who had abused her, and now the woman who she had come to trust. The one who had just told another to kill her. She tried to convince herself that Marie was just goading her on, but she knew better. She knew what to do. Duchess feinted like she would use her sweeping kick, but instead used the compression of her leg to leap up in an attempt to land a vicious kick to Betty's head.

Betty caught Duchess's leg and pulled it higher. Duchess lost her balance and threw out her exhausted arms to try to break her fall, but Betty twisted the foot to make Duchess fall on her back. Duchess tried to counter twist, causing a sickening sound in her knee. She landed hard on her ear and shoulder. There was another sickening sound from her neck. Duchess lay still on the ground, her neck bent awkwardly. Her chest did not move but her body twitched, nerves firing absent a working brain. Perhaps the final death throes of her cerebral cortex, or just the random firings of nerves unwilling to give up.

Marie smiled. "Rest yourself a moment, why don't you."

Betty landed on her knees next to Duchess and checked her pulse. There was none. She tried to control her breathing. "How kind of you." She pushed her knees and rolled back on her heels to stand up.

"Quite impressive, I must say," Marie said.

"But she was only a purple belt."

"Only because she hadn't had her advancement ceremony. She was no match for me personally, but she did cheat in your match." Marie unlocked the weapons using a voice command in Japanese as she walked over to remove a halberd, and with the similar words, locked them again. "You can use the knife, if you want, this time."

"Feeling threatened, are we?" Betty asked. "Is this still for the clothes or are the stakes higher?"

"Not really. You'll lose by my killing you."

"I thought we were sticking with jujitsu?"

"It would be silly of me to think you could be tricked twice. You are obviously better at hand-to-hand, but I doubt you've killed as many opponents as I have with a halberd."

"You're right. I normally use my gun. It saves time," answered Betty.

"Time is all I have, now, but if you are rested enough—" Marie struck a fighting pose.

"More than enough to kick your ass." Betty scooped up the knife and held it ready at her side but did not move forward.

Marie waited a few moments but became bored waiting for Betty to charge her. She started to shift her weight off her heels and onto her toes.

Betty saw the shift and adjusted her own stance slightly, more to antagonize Marie into attacking than to make any move of her own.

Marie could not stand the wait any longer and let her weight tip her off center and she started to move quickly at Betty, preparing to thrust the halberd at her heart. She was expecting Betty to parry the thrust with the knife, so she placed her point of attack low and to the left. Betty's parry would not be enough and the tip would pierce her chest wall and lacerate her heart and lungs.

Betty flipped the knife in her hand so she was holding the point, drew the knife up to throw it. Marie tried to pull up from her charge, not expecting this move, but it just caused her to be a still target.

Her mouth opened as she tried to speak, to say something that would change the outcome, but no words came to her.

Betty threw the knife. Marie tried to raise the halberd quickly enough to deflect it, but the knife was aimed higher than she could reach, at her open mouth. Her eyes grew large as her fate became obvious. She froze in midair, just like a boxer who missed with a hook, and her opponent had anticipated the off-balance fighter, poised to be knocked out. The knife entered Marie's open mouth and pierced the back of her throat, sliced her brain stem in two, and dropped her.

The smartphone was unlocked, the app for the doors and lights visible. Betty released the door of the gym and headed out. After searching the house for intel and finding nothing useful, she decided to head back to the Ritz-Carlton. Her thoughts turned to making sure she made a clean exit. *I didn't take my gloves off, so no fingerprints.* Betty considered the unique quality of the spider-goat-silk fabric. *They could identify that, but they'd never find a sample to compare against. I need to have Bud check the cameras, erase anything near Marie's.* She passed back under the gondola bridge and neared the Ritz-Carlton. The sound of the Gore Creek rapids soothed her mind. She slowed to a walk and closed her eyes briefly. *I love that sound.*

Her access card had been damaged in the battle. *I'll have to get a new one from Karl.* She walked around to the circular driveway and spotted Karl talking to the valet. Betty gave him a tilt of her head and continued on to his concierge station. He joined her and motioned for her to follow him into the small office just behind the desk where supplies and the digital recorder for the surveillance system were stored.

Karl looked at her closely. "Your face is puffing up. Looks like you're going to have a pretty good bruise around your left eye."

"That won't be my only bruise tomorrow." Betty's body ached. The thought of having a long soak in the jacuzzi tub in her master bath tugged at her to get moving. The sooner she iced the impact points and followed that up with an epsom salt soak, the sooner she would heal up. Skiing today was not a great idea, but she had to keep up appearances.

Betty described the scene at Marie's mansion. "Let me know when Boris shows back up. Between his sudden departure from Game Creek last night and both of us killing one of the Cabal members, I think we have a few things to discuss."

"You'll be the first to know." Karl handed Betty her new key card and checked the area outside the office for any busybodies. Sure enough, there was Hanna with Skipper-do, ringing the desk bell. "Oh, Christ."

"Don't worry about it. I'll tell her we were talking about the one-armed man."

"Right. Good luck."

The duo exited the closet-size office and Hanna gasped, then pulled Betty aside.

"Betty, what are you doing with him!"

"Are you off your meds? Come on, there's no way the concierge has it in for you and your dog."

Hanna pulled Betty farther from the desk to make sure Karl could not overhear them. "It was the chocolates, I'm sure of it now. I wish I hadn't thrown them out so I could have them tested." Hanna looked closer at Betty's face and noticed the swelling around her eye. "Betty! Did King do that to you?"

"What? No, no—" *Oh, shit, I wasn't ready for this.* "I slipped while running over by the village. Don't worry, I'll be fine."

"I didn't tell you before, but he has a temper. You need to be careful." Hanna looked like she had been holding a secret from Betty.

"Did he hit you?" Betty asked.

"Almost." Hanna looked down at her feet. "Well, he pulled back his hand as if he was going to slap me . . . but he stopped himself and stormed off instead."

"Don't worry, I can take care of myself." Betty took a deep breath. "Right now I need to get into a hot bath and put a bag of ice on my eye." She started to move away and break free of Hanna's grip. "Are you going to ski with us today? You can keep an eye out for anything unusual, in case King does try something."

"OK, I guess I can." Hanna brightened up a little. "Jil and Gil were talking about skiing today. We can all go together!"

"Great!" *Oh, shit. What have I done now. Ugh. I need that bath.* Betty headed to the elevator, thinking about the mob scene she would be facing on the mountain. *Safety in numbers, I guess, but right now, I need to find Tom and get Marie's house cleaned.* She stabbed the number six on the elevator dash. *Is Tom part of the Cabal?* Betty watched, without making a move to help, as the mirrored doors closed before a man could reach the elevator.

She could hear Karl calling out to him, "Mr. Stockpoint!"

The carriage lurched upward, and Betty shifted her balance to remain stable. *Is Control part of the Cabal?* Her image was duplicated many times in the facing mirrors of the carriage, each iteration a little less defined and a lower-caliber copy. "Is that me down the road?" she said out loud. Betty saw a tired thirty-five-year-old woman, with the start of a black eye. Alone, yet surrounded by the ghostly images of herself. *Do I really look this bad?* She reached out to the closest, most complete copy, touching her doppelgänger's face. She imagined all the people she had killed for Tom and Control replacing her duplicates. "What have I gotten myself into?"

Seventy

What It Is

November 30, 2009 — Ritz-Carlton, Vail, Colorado

AS THE ELEVATOR DOORS OPENED, Betty was startled to see Tom waiting for her. She shifted her weight back to standing instead of moving forward. She looked at the operating panel of the elevator and considered going back to Karl, or to any other floor of the Ritz. But then she would have to look at those damn faces in the mirror again.

Tom reached out and held the doors open to keep the elevator from departing. "Are you OK? Karl said you'd been in quite the battle."

Betty closed her eyes and thought of her options. *I could kill Tom now, but then I would never know the truth about him and his father. I could break his arm to get him to let go of the doors so I can leave. I could just beat the crap out of him until he talks.*

Tom knew he was likely the current focus of her anger by her lack of response. The elevator door tried to close again, but his arm stopped it. In an act of courage, he asked, "Betty?"

Betty clenched her eyes a little tighter. "I'm thinking." She tried to imagine what it was like in Georgetown, before Tom left. Before he lost his leg, before Tom Sr. had set his massive hooks into the man she loved. She opened her eyes. "You have some explaining to do." She brushed past Tom, and with gritted teeth, she did not throw her left elbow into his solar plexus.

Tom followed her to the condo and waited for Betty to open the door. "Whatever you—"

Betty spun and shoved her index finger within an inch of his chin. Tom did not flinch. "Shut up. Not until I've had a chance to clean up." They passed through the door and Betty headed to the refrigerator, grabbing a bottle of champagne and a flute from the cupboard. "Please ask Bud to erase, or whatever he does, any video tying me to Marie's house.

Tom nodded his head, thinking it best not to not even speak.

Betty took in a deep breath to calm herself. "Duchess broke her neck trying to squirm out of my grasp and Marie has a dagger lodged in the back of her throat." Describing the scene caused her to involuntarily visualized the carnage. "She killed her art guy, smashed his head in with a multimillion-dollar Picasso."

Betty continued, "I'm going to go soak in the tub and apply this champagne to my eye. If I need anything, I'll let you know. Be here when I'm done."

It was not a request as Tom heard it, so he just nodded again and waited a moment to see if she had anything else to add before he moved to the living room to make a conference call to Bud and David.

Betty entered the cavernous bathroom suite, placed the bottle and flute next to the handles, and started the Jacuzzi. She dumped a container of bath salts under the torrent of water and sat down on the tile edge of the tub. Betty picked the bottle back up and opened the Cristal 2006, gently rocking the cork out of the neck to keep the wine's effervescence from overflowing. The first glassful went down quickly, but it would hold her until she could strip and get into the water. She poured another so it would be ready as she slid into the calming bubbles. Feeling the water, she made a slight adjustment to the temperature, then stripped off her running gear and climbed in. The cool bottle felt wonderful on her face. Almost as good as the champagne applied to the inside.

†

After soaking for a half hour and dawdling another twenty minutes just to make Tom wait, Betty finally made her way to the living room via the kitchen. She threw away the nearly empty bottle—mostly to avoid the temptation of finishing it all—and grabbed an ice pack from the freezer to administer to her still tender eye. She was feeling relaxed enough, and kind enough, to ask Tom if he wanted anything, but stopped herself when she spotted his bottle of water on the table next to his chair.

Tom smiled as she came close. Betty was not trying to look sexy, but the mixture of the towel wrapped around her head and the short length of the robe spoke to the Tom Howell of Georgetown. He opened his mouth, then closed it, thinking better of speaking first.

"What's the word from the office?" Betty asked.

Tom smiled again, finally having permission to speak. "Bud is taking care of what he can and Grace is on her way to tidy up, assuming she can get there before anyone checks up on Marie. But from what you described, I doubt her staff are anxious to come back anytime soon, if they're alive."

"Can you imagine? Killing your top art guy over his choice of a Picasso and then destroying a priceless work of art."

Tom checked a note on his phone. "Jeremy Plithens was her fine arts director. He was in charge of procurement and safekeeping of her multibillion-dollar art collection."

"The walls were bare. What do you think they did with all that art? Not just the dozen in the foyer, but the hundreds of pieces on display throughout the house, let alone what might be in storage?"

"Three options come to mind. Either the staff have relocated it to a different mansion, which is why they are no longer on premise; or the staff have stolen the art and escaped with their lives; or there are more dead bodies in rooms you did not check, next to the artwork in storage."

"Which one do you think?" Betty asked.

"Well, she's a psychopath. *Lex parsimoniae*." Tom saw Betty begin to roll her eyes. "Occam's razor—among competing hypothesis, the least complex should be believed."

"So you think there are a whole lot more dead bodies in a room. Great. Maybe Bud should have kept the evidence to prove I wasn't there long enough to kill them and used self-defense to escape."

"Which is true." Tom smiled. Betty did not.

"Too late to start sucking up now, Tom." Betty looked back at the kitchen and mourned her decision to throw out the champagne. Then she remembered she was rich and there were more bottles. Betty got up and headed to get a fresh bottle and flute.

"There's something you should know . . ." Tom left the sentence dangling as Betty opened her second bottle of Cristal.

She cocked her head and made a face at him. "There's a shit ton of stuff you need to tell me, but I don't have that kind of time before I need to be on the slopes with my crew. Did I mention that King is probably working for the Cabal on orders to maneuver me into a tree to cause permanent brain damage? Not to kill me, but make my life a living hell for as long as I manage to cling to it?" Betty held up her hand holding the flute to stop Tom from replying. "Did I also mention that Marie asked me if I knew you and your father were members of the Cabal?"

Tom's mouth opened slightly, his right eyebrow went down and his left up as he tried to find the right words to respond.

"Shut the fuck up." Betty poured her champagne and drank a large draught of the flute. "How about the fact that you've been playing me for as long as I've known you. Everything you've done seems to be to motivate me to do your bidding."

"If that were true—"

Betty did not let him finish. "Shut the fuck up." It took a great bit of moral rectitude to keep from pounding Tom over the head with the bottle, which ultimately she managed because it would have wasted the champagne, bloodied the furniture, and add one more body to the count for the day. "Men! Why can't you just listen instead of always trying to fix it. You can't fix this. You're a lying bastard. Your father was a member of the Cabal, even if he turned away from them. At one time he was a fucking member! Which means his attempts at shutting down the Cabal were really about gaining control of everything, not protecting everyone. You sanctimonious bastards!"

Tom just shrugged and did not try to respond.

Betty took a deep breath. *Yoga breaths. Deep yoga breaths. I will not kill Tom. I will not kill Tom. Howell, yes, but not Tom.* "OK. Start explaining, and this better be good."

Tom took in his own deep breath. "I've told you everything I know about my father's creation of Control. As far as I know, he really did set it up with a financial windfall from Allen Dulles. I also have had time to look over the books. There was no great pile of money before Control, and all of what is now my wealth has been accounted for. The medical company, the patents, a massive pile of forged U.S. hundred-dollar bills, and a few metric tons of gold squirreled away allowed Father to make some savvy investments during the fifties and sixties in companies like IBM and others just as the New York Stock Exchange took off. Every penny he borrowed from Control went back into it, and he still had several billion dollars to give to me at the end." Tom considered what he had just said. "Of course, he was about as legitimate as all the other big investors. At least he paid back every dime he borrowed to start his fortune."

Betty did not want to stop his story but her own mouth opened a bit. "Why the fuck do you care how much I spend on the Black Card if you have that much money?"

"Most of Control's assets are tied up, and a lot of my money is invested in assets that are not liquid. I have to be careful with my cash flows, both at Control and personally, until I have enough time to unwind some of his investments. Having a cruise missile take out the mountain retreat cost me more than you could spend on that card in a year."

"Try me."

Tom smiled hard and started to point his finger at her but stopped. "Do you know how much it cost for us to fly back from Denmark on the G650?"

"No. Not really. I never knew how much it cost when Jil flew us around—I guess I never really wanted to know, since I couldn't pay for it anyway."

"Between the two planes, flight plans, insurance, maintenance contracts, pilots, security details, clearing the building at Århus, it cost one hundred and fifty thousand dollars. Hell, just trying to manage your rescue of Gil cost ten million dollars—not that I'm complaining. Gil is worth it."

"And I'm not?" Betty asked.

"Oh, you're worth it, but it all adds up. As Senator Dirksen of Illinois once said, 'A billion here, a billion there, pretty soon, you're talking real money.'"

Betty gave a weak laugh.

"So to answer your question, sort of, as far as I know, my father never was a member of the Cabal before or after starting Control. As I have mentioned to you before, I know he met with them from time to time to prevent the worst of the conflict, but I don't know if he met with the top people or their representatives. There just aren't any files on this. I'd ask Barnes if I could."

Betty thought back to the explosion of the Howell home on Observatory Hill. *What was it about those workers climbing onto the truck? I was right, but why?* "And now two homes blown up."

Tom took a deep breath and did not take her bait. "You killed Marie today, and Boris killed Gustav last night." Tom started making a list with his fingers.

"Wait, did that make the news?" Betty looked back at the kitchen where she had seen the *Vail Daily*.

Tom shook his head. "Not in the way you are thinking. It will be declared a heart attack and swept under the rug. There won't be any mention of Boris shooting Gustav in any news outlets." Tom took a sip of his water bottle. "Oh, and nice touch, buying a membership at Game Creek last night."

"So, you're monitoring the expenses, I take it." Betty fiercely glared back at Tom.

"A billion here and a billion there. It's all just pencil shavings, really, but we have to track it."

"Must be nice to be able to print your own money," Betty remarked.

"Hey, now, we haven't turned on the printing presses for years. Hell, I was a kid the last time they might have done that."

Betty squinted her eyes. "Are you sure? Aren't the Chinese still counterfeiting even the newest, latest hundred-dollar bills?"

"OK, OK, all I can tell you for sure is that as long as I have been in charge, we have not printed any bogus money. Truth be told, the medical side and McFluffy's patents are providing plenty of income to cover Control's expenses." Tom scratched his chin. "Come to think of it—" Tom grabbed his phone and connected to McFluffy via encrypted software.

"Aye, I'm a wee bit busy right now," the gruff old scientist said after answering the call.

"McFluffy, I have Betty here with me. What is the status of the cold-fusion project?" Tom looked at Betty to see if she acknowledged that he was keeping her in the loop.

"Oh, the lovely Betty! How are ya, sweet lass?"

Betty had grown to love the burr of a man for making her protective gear. "I'm fine, McFluffy. How are you?" She giggled a little thinking of him. *Or is it the champagne?*

"Tooker and I are about to save the world from carbon energy! I think we've just about proven our theory. You two will be the first to know in a moment or two if our latest test is a banger." There was some incoherent shouting—either because McFluffy was talking away from his microphone, or more likely, he was speaking in a local Scottish dialect to Tooker. "Oh, me lovelies. One kilojoule of energy per second!" There was some loud sounds coming from Tom's phone that sounded like a bagpipe.

"McFluffy has a flaming bagpipe. Did you ever see it back at Control?" Tom asked.

"Oh, my God, no!" Betty said.

"So, McFluffy, that's great, but we need to be producing a gigajoule, right?"

"Aye, this is the wee unit. The draft horse will be running tomorrow after a few tweaks."

"OK. OK. We'll check back tomorrow. Good work." Tom disconnected the encrypted link.

"Well, that was an exciting diversion." Betty poured herself a little bit more champagne to celebrate. "Now, tell me what that is really about."

"Our next big business is going to be energy. McFluffy and Tooker have taken the old cold-fusion technology that was a bust and boosted it with nanoparticles to make it more efficient. They can power a small town right now from their lab. The next step is generating enough electricity to run a good-size city."

"No way!" Betty raised her glass in a toast.

Tom raised his water bottle and took a sip. "Way. We crack this and I don't care how much you spend on the Black Card. Ever."

"Speaking of that, can Grace grab all the bags of Gorsuch clothes Marie had delivered?" Betty smiled sweetly. "They're my size and technically, I won them by killing her."

"Hmm. How about I just promise to let you buy as much as you want from Gorsuch. I'm a minority owner, anyway."

Betty shook her head in disbelief. "I don't know if it's the champagne or the fact that I killed two people this morning, but I really just want to take a nap now."

"Sure. Skiing with the gang after lunch?"

"That too. It's a tough life, being a trust funder." Betty said.

"Be careful. There are still two Cabal members left. Charles and Pierre. Not to mention Boris out there trying to kill them," Tom reminded

Betty.

"Yeah, what's up with him? He mentioned losing his arm for not killing a banker's daughter."

"All the money in the world doesn't mean you don't create enemies. The wealthy are targets just for being wealthy. One reason to keep a low profile or only doing your crazy partying in a place like the Ritz, where no one sees." Tom moved to the door. "Have a good nap. I'll check in with you after the slopes, OK?"

"What are you going to be doing?"

"I was afraid you'd ask. I'm meeting with the Cabal to talk about a truce. I don't want them to kill you to get to me."

"I guess it really is a bitch to be wealthy," Betty said.

"You have no idea." Tom smiled as he closed the door.

Betty checked her phone. Hanna, Jil, Gil, and King had been blowing up a message thread about going skiing and wondering where she was and why wasn't she answering. Hanna had told them that Betty had a swollen eye and an excuse about slipping while running. King had an alibi, which was true, but it bothered Betty that the group would even try to blame him. *Maybe I should invite him up, figure out if he's the type of guy to push me into a fir tree at fifty miles per hour—or if he's the kind of guy who would throw himself in the way.*

Betty typed up a message to lure King to her bed for questioning, but knocked over her champagne flute before pressing send. "Maybe I should just take a nap." She deleted that message, then responded to the group that she would meet up with them at two p.m. at the top of China Bowl.

Her pillow felt expensive, and it was. Her bed felt soft yet firm, and it was. The duvet was the perfect color and pattern. "It's good to be rich," she slurred before passing out from the exhaustion of doing battle, a warm bath, and a bottle or two of fine champagne.

Seventy-One

Room for Sugar?

November 30, 2009 — Ritz-Carlton, Vail, Colorado

BETTY BOLTED UPRIGHT. *That sounded like a chair being moved in the kitchen.* Normally, she would not have been able to hear such a sound thanks to the advanced soundproofing of the Ritz-Carlton. In the blur of the champagne and her fatigue, she had left the bedroom door open. She looked at the alarm clock by her bed. It showed one p.m., which meant she had been asleep for three hours. "Who's out there?" Betty said as she climbed out of bed. "Tom?" She grabbed her spider-goat-silk spy suit and hurriedly put it on. "Karl?" She fumbled with the zipper—her motor skills had not quite recovered from the liquor and the sleep. "Is that you, Gil?" *Did I order room service? I think I smell coffee.* She yawned and stretched. *Shit, this isn't a hotel, no room service.* The slightest sound of clothing rustling could be heard. *Wait, I did hear something.* She paused and listened closely for any stray bit of sound. The sound of someone clearing their throat drifted to her ears. *Son of a bitch.* Betty pulled her pistol from the concealed holster tucked inside her jeans laying on the chair and checked that a round was chambered, then ejected the magazine and made sure it was fully loaded before quietly reinserting it. The metallic click was audible, but just barely. Betty led with the muzzle of her pistol and peeked around the door for the intruder.

Sitting at the kitchen breakfast bar, blowing on a lidless paper cup of coffee, was Boris, the one-armed man. "Good morning, Miss Betty. I bring you coffee." He pulled a second cup of coffee from a cardboard carrier and slid it toward Betty, who was carefully approaching with her pistol aimed at his forehead.

"Why are you in my kitchen?" Betty asked.

"You maybe have wrong idea." Boris held up his left hand. "I come to you because want same thing."

Betty was within ten feet of Boris now. She did not want to give up her advantage, even if the coffee smelled delicious. "How could we possibly have the same interest?" she asked.

"I kill Gustav, you kill Marie." Boris slowly reached for his coffee, making sure Betty was OK with him taking a sip. "Coffee is from downstairs. Very good." He nodded toward her cup before taking a sip of his. "Hot." Boris moved her coffee as close to her as he could without getting out of his chair.

He wouldn't have laced it with anything—hell, he could have gotten me in my sleep. The smell of the coffee was enticing. *What the hell, I definitely need it.* Betty let go of the SIG Sauer with her left hand, which had been helping to keep her aim steady on Boris's forehead, stepped forward one pace, and picked up the coffee. She sipped it and said, "Hot. But perfect. Thank you."

Boris smiled and nodded slightly. "See, we want same thing. Coffee, kill Cabal." Boris showed his hand to Betty then opened his jacket to show a folded piece of paper in the inner pocket. "OK to get out? No shoot me, please."

Betty nodded quickly, put her coffee back down, and held her pistol steady with both hands. "Go ahead, but I'll shoot you if you try anything."

Boris scrunched his chin and nodded, then slowly reached into his pocket and removed the paper. He unfolded it and placed it where Betty's coffee cup had been before. It was an enlarged photo of two men: Jil's boss and the one with crutches from Game Creek.

"I've seen both before. The night you killed Gustav," Betty said.

"Yes, I make big mistake. Pistol instead of grenade." Boris tilted his head and made a face. "Now I not get close." Boris tapped Casper in the photo with his left index finger. "You kill this man or . . ."

"Or what?" Betty asked.

"You get me in, I kill, then help kill Charles." Boris nodded as if he was agreeing with Betty.

"Why do I want to kill Charles, or for that matter, who is this guy?" Betty asked, not wanting to tip off that she knew who Casper was.

Boris leaned back slightly and raised what was left of his

amputated arm. "He Casper, my old boss. He took my arm." Boris lowered his shortened appendage and leaned in closer to Betty. "Charles wants you dead."

"I would think he wants you dead too—for Gustav," Betty said.

Boris nodded his head as if agreeing again. "Da, me dead, you maybe just mostly dead."

"So I've heard." Betty picked up her coffee and took another sip. It was just about the right temperature to take a bigger drink, which she needed, post-champagne. "What did you hear—about why he wants me dead, or brain dead?"

"You piss him off." Boris laughed.

"People piss me off all the time and I don't kill them," Betty said as she thought about Tom in particular.

"You piss him off good. Kill his son, Slim."

Betty had to smile at the thought of pissing off a member of the Cabal. Knowing now that Slim was Charles's son, she recognized why her life was in danger. *But there seems to be more to this puzzle.* Slim had been the one, with Michel, to kill José. *Michel is Belarusian, like Yuri.* "You're Belarusian, aren't you?"

"*Da*," Boris said.

"You know Yuri and Michel?" Betty asked.

"*Da*. We all work together, back in Cold War." Boris agreed.

"Michel killed my fiancé and then kidnapped my partner," Betty said.

Boris scrunched his chin and agreed again with her. "*Da*. Michel needs new kidney, one from Yuri failing. Yuri gone." Boris took a drink of his coffee. "Charles order José work. Slim not good at . . . how you say . . . interrogation." Boris sipped his coffee again. "What Michel do when boss's son fucks up?" he asked.

"So, what do you want from me?" Betty asked.

"You help me get past your friends upstairs, I kill Casper, then I help you kill Charles."

"You said that already." *He's either persistent or we have a language problem.* "Besides, why would I need your help killing Charles?

"Do you know where he is?"

Betty was reluctant to admit that she did not know where Charles was. "No, not right now, but I'm sure my people will let me know."

"Your boss meet him now."

"What?"

"See, they not want you kill him or you there now, right?"

Betty was flabbergasted. "Wha—" She wanted to throw her coffee in Tom's face, but he was not there to receive it. "He promised me!"

"You bring me to penthouse upstairs, distract friends, I kill Casper."

Betty was trying to take a deep yoga breath to calm herself down. She pointed her pistol at Boris's forehead and said, "Then what?"

"I take you to boss and Charles."

"Why don't you take me there now—what do I care if Casper dies?"

"Casper kill Harpers. Marry daughter," Boris said.

"That's not true, Jil . . . oh, you mean Ruth." Betty bit her lip.

"Casper kidnap daughter, Ruth, hold hostage, make father do things."

"How do you know so much?" Betty asked.

"I took Harper's finger he not do what told. I kidnap daughter for Casper." Boris shrugged and pointed at himself. "Friend of family?"

"Hah, some friend." Betty glared at Boris for a moment. Neither spoke. "Maybe I'll kill you, go find Casper and make him take me to Charles."

"Maybe you do. He not know what I know." Boris smiled. "I die today—or maybe tomorrow. Someone kill Casper. You kill me. No one kill Charles."

"You seem confident you know where my boss and Charles are."

"I plant bug on Charles while guarding him. No one find it yet." Boris smiled again. "Casper took arm. Your boss shoot me twice." Boris used his left hand to point to each shoulder. "Your boss cost me finger, girlfriend, America, and old job."

"So, you want him dead," Betty asked.

"Meh," Boris shrugged his shoulders. "He die, I not mind, but Casper"—Boris raised his stump again—"Casper take arm, kill family, piss on grave of mother."

"Yeah, sometimes I want to kill my boss too," Betty admitted. Betty dropped her guard just a little. "OK, what's the plan?"

"You go first, check out situation, send message if OK. I come in, kill Casper, run away. No one know you help."

"What, text you that it's all clear?"

Boris nodded.

"Give me your number," Betty said.

"Two zero two, five five five, seven five three two." Boris raised an eyebrow. "You need me write down?"

Betty's phone was back in her bedroom hooked up to the charger. *I shouldn't give Boris my number.* "When I text you, the number you'll see isn't my number."

"Can text you back, right?" Boris asked.

"Of course. The system automatically routes your text to my phone. You can even call me back, but don't."

"Right." Boris nodded.

"So, you'll be waiting . . . where?"

"Stairs."

Betty thought about it for a moment. "Right, no one's going to climb six floors, are they?"

"No," agreed Boris. "You got number?" he said as he pointed to his head.

"Two zero two, five five five, seven five three two," replied Betty.

"You pretty good."

"About one hour?" She asked.

Boris nodded.

"Now, get out of my condo before I change my mind about killing you," Betty said, waving Boris on with her pistol.

After Boris left, Betty texted Gil through the Control system so that Gil and Jil wouldn't receive messages from her at the same time.

Op Infil Pent Boris. Preserve for intel.

Then she texted Jil, knowing that Gil would get her to the penthouse if they were not there now, or she would have to maneuver them, if not.

Important, can we talk?

Betty finished getting dressed while she waited for Gil's response, with a hand towel over her phone just in case Bud was watching. *I actually have choices to make, don't I!* Betty rummaged through her new clothes purchases for what to wear on the slopes. Her dirty-clothes pile was growing, something she would have never allowed to happen back home. But then, having so many options had created a new problem. She looked at her new outfit in the full-length mirror and admired how well the clothing fit and the quality of the finish. "Maybe money can buy happiness?"

She checked her phone and still no answer from Gil. *I need to talk to Tom. Why hasn't he checked in with me?* Betty typed a quick "Hey" to her boss and thought, *Wait, I am his girlfriend again, right? I know I'm in an active mission and playing a role, but ultimately, we're dating, so why don't I have anonymous flowers, or a small token of his love that only I would know came from him?* She pondered that while waiting for his response.

Nothing. Betty checked her makeup and hair while waiting for replies. *I should take advantage of a spa day while I'm here. I wonder if I can get Jil to go with me. I know Hanna would gladly go along. I need to be careful—am I trying to get back the friend I used to know and love, or am I on a mission? Damn it, they seem to be impossibly intertwined.* She checked her phone again. Nothing. She checked to make sure her phone was working, that she had a signal. *The Ritz-Carlton probably has at least one repeater tower to strengthen the signal in the building. Can't have trust funders unconnected.*

Betty tried calling Karl's cellphone. It seemed like it answered, but no one was speaking. It didn't go to voice mail. *What the hell is going on?* Betty tried calling Bud. *He'll pick up on the first ring!* she thought. But he did not, so she checked her encrypted email account. Nothing. "Well, son of a bitch!" she blurted out. Betty decided to use her phone's web browser to surf the Internet. *Well, at least that works. I guess I can look up a spa to make an appointment.* She found the number for a RockResorts Spa at the Arrabelle and called. No answer. Betty threw her phone at the couch in the living room, where it got lodged between the pillows. "Fucking technology!" The condo had a traditional land line. She looked at it and glared. "Bud, you're on my shit list! If you're listening in, my phone isn't working and I hate you for it." Betty moved to the land line and dialed the spa, set up an appointment for an hour later, then called Boris's number.

"*Da*."

"Meet me upstairs in five minutes. I don't have time to fuck around on this."

"*Da*."

"I'll get you in, but you better damn well get me Charles."

"*Da*. Five minutes. Stairwell."

Betty hung up and noticed the red message light blinking. She started to read the instructions on how to listen to her voice mail, but looked at her watch and realized there wasn't time. *I will listen to whatever bullshit message is waiting for me later. Things to do.* She gathered her gear and, out of routine, checked that her SIG Sauer P229 was loaded. She was out the door and closing it when she heard the land line ringing. *Fuck it. Probably Karl calling me back. I'll see him when I get downstairs.*

Seventy-Two

Control

November 30, 2009 — Ritz-Carlton, Vail, Colorado

"CHARLES," TOM SAID, TRYING to draw the man away from the window.

"A moment." Charles was surveying the mountain slopes where thousands of the most beautiful and rich people were playing in the snow. People who he could control for the love of wealth. Bankers who would do as he wished lest they be ruined. Artists and actors whose product depended on his beneficence. Industrialists could be brought to their knees in a moment of panic over his decisions. Charles could even control the weather, to a limited degree, through pollution, cloud seeding, and resource management, such as surface water retention. He controlled the activity on the mountain indirectly, that was true; but if he chose to destroy any of the little figures sluicing down the trails, their replacement would be under his thumb in due time. Charles took a deep breath and let out, "Ahh," as he exhaled. "All as it should be." He turned and joined Tom and Ernesto at the table large enough to seat twenty. Their guardians lurked outside the doors. This was one meeting that could not be overheard, even by the most loyal protector. Besides, each man was equally important and would have no inducement to want the other dead. Game theory. If they worked together, they would amplify their growth. If they worked against one another, they would devalue all they controlled. There was no way to win if they did not align their objectives. Charles withdrew two identical sheets of paper, folded in half, from the inside pocket of his sport coat and smoothed them out before sliding one to Tom and the other to Ernesto.

"What is this?" Tom asked.

Ernesto held up his hand, put on his reading glasses, and scanned the page before whipping the spectacles off the bridge of his nose and waving them at Charles. "These are not trades you've placed through me," he said.

Charles steepled his fingers with his elbows on the arms of his chair and leaned back slightly, a power move intended to show his superiority. "You will notice that these synthetic derivatives are strategically placed throughout the world, interlocking all of the largest banks together."

"Yes, and if they are triggered, it will cause a liquidity crisis like none we've seen before," declared Ernesto.

Tom had been trained by Ernesto in the art of reading these kinds of trades for exactly this moment. *Charles will be assuming I have no real clue what these trades signify*, he thought. "What is the triggering event?"

"My death, without a successor named by me." Charles smiled as he rested his chin in the opening of the steeple of his fingers. "In the unlikely event that I should be killed, these transactions will be triggered and the world will come crashing down."

"A deadman's switch," Tom stated. "Why would you even considering setting up such a dangerous weapon? This is more destructive than all of the Cold War arsenal of the world powers at their peak."

"I foresaw the deaths of Marie and Gustav. I am surprised Pierre is still alive, considering the self-destructive course he has taken. It is no small thing to know you are considered expendable."

Ernesto had put his glasses back on and studied the derivative trades more closely. The interlocking nature of the transactions assured a snowballing effect of destruction from one bank to the next, but each transaction had a negating match to stop the crisis as long as the first trade was never triggered. "You've created control rods, like a nuclear power station. I must say, Charles, you've been paying far more attention these past few years than I thought you were."

"It's beautiful, isn't it?" Charles asked Ernesto.

"I'm afraid it is," he agreed. "Beautiful in its symmetry and perfect in its destruction if activated." Ernesto's lips had been moving as he added up the value of the trades. "One quadrillion U.S. dollars in value, roughly." He tossed the sheet away lightly.

Tom took in a deep breath. "What do you want?" he asked.

Charles smiled broadly. "Complete control."

"Of what?" Tom asked.

"Of everything," he said.

†

Betty bounded up the stairs two at a time, counting silently as she went. The rhythm of her legs in sync with the rhythm of her mind. Boris was waiting for her at the sixth-floor landing, inside the stairwell. She stopped at the fifth-floor landing and said quietly, "I'm coming up," to make sure Boris knew it was her. She listened for a moment and heard over her heartbeat the slight rustle of clothing and a minute scrape of a boot on carpet, the sound of Boris returning to the door in preparation for the next phase. As she stepped onto the next tread, it occurred to her that she was always subconsciously counting things. Steps, the number of people in a room, leaving a room, or coming into a room. She counted place settings, cars in a parking lot, anything that would indicate the number of people either at a location or anticipated to participate in some fashion. *There are eleven steps between landings, two landings per level, twenty-two steps between floors.* Memories of Beth teaching her to count everything around her flooded Betty's mind. She vaguely remembered being asked how many cars were in a parking lot, the number of diners in a restaurant, or even how many railcars made up a train zipping past. At some point, Beth stopped asking or rewarding Betty for being right, but there were other memories from her high school days, like when Beth asked casually if anyone knew how many members there were in the opposing team's band. *And I always knew the answer!* Betty stopped on a stair. *And I was proud of myself for knowing, basking in the knowledge that she was pleased with me, even if she didn't say it out loud.*

Boris stepped forward and looked down the stairs at Betty standing midflight. "What you doing there?" he whispered.

Betty thought it was just her mind focusing on the memories, but now she heard something from the bottom of the stairs. "Someone is coming," she whispered back. *One, two, three, four, step, step, one, two, three, four, step, step*, she counted silently. "He's taking three stairs at a time," she whispered into Boris's ear as she joined him at the top. The climber was halfway up the stairs now.

"How you know three?"

Betty smiled, pleased with herself, "The fourth step is quicker, only two treads, because each section is an odd number of stairs."

"Must be very tall," Boris whispered.

Karl! Betty thought.

There was a slight noise coming from the sixth-floor hallway, beyond the door they were about to cross through, as a small herd of people passed by. Boris braced himself. He looked at Betty quickly to see if she was prepared. He was not going to wait; he feared that the intruder from below would keep him from his mission. Before she could stop him, Boris burst through the stairwell door and began firing at the group.

"What the fuck?" Betty hissed at the vacuum left by his sudden departure. She darted to the railing and looked down. Two floors below was Karl looking up. She returned to the door and peered around the corner. *Boris has fired three rounds from his .45. I heard return fire—9mm. Six rounds, maybe.* She saw two guards who had put themselves between the targets and Boris. One man was on the ground clutching his chest. The elevator doors had just opened to reveal Richard Stockpoint with a couple of prospective buyers for the last remaining sixth-floor condominium, both appeared to be Colombian to Betty. The governor of New York was pressing the elevator button and waving Stockpoint and company back into the car. The prone man rolled his head to the left, revealing that it was Senator Bolden with a gaping chest wound. *The man protected by the bodyguards must be Casper. If I don't do something now, Boris is going to die and I won't know where the meeting is taking place. Fuck!* She put her gun back into the holster wedged between the small of her back and her jeans.

Betty raced across the hallway toward the elevators with her hands up, acting as if she were terrified, drawing the attention of the guards, who were confused by her direct approach. It was just enough of a distraction for Boris to have the upper hand on them, shooting two more rounds into each as they wavered over target selection. The guards had been correct to consider her a threat; they just were not prepared for her to come in unarmed. Betty pushed the governor deep within the elevator car and pushed the fourth-floor button while drawing her pistol from its holster. She purposely shot over Boris's head and into the ceiling. *I need them to believe I came to protect them.*

The elevator doors closed, and mercifully, the car moved

gracefully downward, gently landing at the fourth floor.

"Governor, come with me," she ordered, pulling the politician's hand with her free left as she marched him to her condo. He complied, trained by experience to follow the lead of his security detail.

Richard Stockpoint removed the handkerchief from his breast pocket and wiped his brow. "This is not the Ritz-Carlton way!" he exclaimed to his customers as the doors closed.

†

Tom looked past Charles, to the window and the mountains beyond. "Control. Yes. Ultimately, that is what we all seek. Control over our own destinies, other people, our finances—what have you."

Charles snorted. "What do you know of control?"

Tom forced his attention back on the bridge of Charles's nose. The one he wanted to smash with his fist, but through self-control, did not. "True control is self-control. Not reacting to the words or deeds of those around you, staying true to your cause or convictions." Tom looked over at Ernesto. "Please explain to Charles how we now control everything that he owns."

Charles snorted louder this time. "What kind of charade is this?"

Ernesto cleared his throat, then slid a small stack of papers toward Charles. "If you look through these, you will find that I am the hidden counterparty to most of the synthetic CDOs you've created. As you look through the listings, you will see that I have countered your positions and even have some of them circling back to your other positions." Ernesto glanced over at Tom and then back at Charles. "In essence, you have only succeeded in surrounding yourself with dominoes that will topple into a mess at your feet without disturbing the rest of the global markets, at least not significantly."

"How did you—" Charles started to speak several times and then did not finish as he flipped through each page, comparing the numbers and counterparties until the bare-naked truth was self-evident. All his capital was trapped in transactions he could not unwind without destroying the value of all. "Pyrrhic."

Tom smiled slightly, just enough to let Charles know that he was fully complicit in Ernesto's actions. "Yes, Pyrrhic, indeed. Your biggest concern now will be Pierre. He has the only liquid investments left, that you know of." Tom looked to Ernesto and signaled for him to explain with a tip of a finger.

"Pierre is unstable, as you know, and recently changed much of his portfolio to oil-related stocks, perhaps in an attempt to corner the market and control the price." Ernesto slid another packet of papers to Charles. "As you can see here, he is locked up rather tightly with the House of Saud and the Middle East in general, Brazil, Venezuela, and Mexico." Ernesto looked at Tom. "I'll never really understand his position on Mexico, very foolish."

Tom slid a one-page press release explaining the newly developed cold-fusion technology of McFluffy and Tooker. "There is a company that has finally cracked the cold fusion puzzle. This press release is heading out into the world. The value of Pierre's petroleum bets is going to tank by tonight."

"That is a fraud!" shouted Charles.

"I'm afraid this is the real deal," Tom said. "Anyone betting on fossil fuels before this, well, they are going to have to reevaluate their positions in the morning after the demonstration of the refrigerator-size unit that can power an entire town at one tenth the cost. Electric cars will replace gasoline, and your group's investments are either tied up or worthless by the end of tomorrow."

The trio turned and looked as Pierre clambered through the door, clumsily striking his crutch on any object near his path. He was unsteady from the large dose of morphine he had taken to numb the pain of his foot.

"Where the hell have you been?" demanded Charles.

Pierre's eyes grew more alert, but his speech was slurred and slow. "I was tied up. It's time for our treatments."

Charles slammed his fist on the table and stood up. He reached behind his back and drew out a pistol, aimed at Pierre's head, and pulled the trigger.

Tom rolled out of his chair and pulled Ernesto to the floor before rising to confront Charles with his own P229 drawn and aimed.

Charles ejected the magazine and loaded round, then put his pistol down on the table and sat down. He removed a handkerchief from his breast pocket and wiped his face. "I will be leaving in an hour to return home. Please take the time to enjoy Dr. Salizar's treatments, if you like;

he insisted on prepayment." Charles looked at Tom with one eyebrow cocked. "Can you imagine?" Charles gathered the paperwork, leaving the pistol on the table, and walked out of the meeting.

†

Betty surveyed her condo quickly, checking rooms for any threats before depositing the governor in the living room with the TV remote. "Stay here. Whatever you do, don't talk to your people."

"I don't understand what's happened. Where are 'my people,' if you aren't one of them, and why are you protecting me? You *are* protecting me, right?"

"Well, first off, I'm a native New Yorker—Rochester, so I'm just looking after my own. I was in the wrong place at the right time."

"You certainly were, I don't know where you came from, but when the bullets started flying, there you were, my guardian angel."

"Yes, well, this guardian angel needs to get back to find out what really happened up there. So just stay here, don't call anyone, don't do anything, don't answer the door until we know if you were the target. OK?" *Jesus, I know you weren't the target, but what the hell are you doing without your detail?* thought Betty.

"Please find out if Senator Bolden is OK." The governor handed Betty his card with a phone number handwritten on it. "That's my cell number. Call me when you know something."

"I'll let you know what I find out." *Like why are you getting free plastic surgery from the Cabal via Salizar?*

Betty disengaged from the governor and sped out the door, down the hallway to the stairwell. She took the stairs two at a time, skipping across the landings, and barely caught herself at the door to the sixth floor, forcing herself to check her weapon and carefully survey the corridor before exiting. On the floor, moaning, was one of the guards. The other was at the elevator, facedown with a large pool of blood soaking into the carpet. Karl was propped up against the wall with Senator Bolden cradled in his arms.

Karl's eyes were barely open. His own pool of blood spread ominously around him, blending with the senator's own. His words slurred, Karl said, "He's dead."

Betty pulled Bolden from Karl's arms and checked him for

wounds. The blood draining from the senator's chest, the lack of a pulse, and the foamy red speckling his purple lips told Betty that it was too late to get him to a hospital. "Give me your arm!" Betty lifted Karl's arm over her shoulder and tried to get him to stand. He didn't resist, but he wasn't helping.

"Don't." He coughed violently, spraying blood on the carpet. "I'm done."

Betty slumped to the floor with Karl. His six-foot-five frame and two-hundred-thirty pounds were more than she could handle without his help or something like a tarp or wheeled chair. She looked at the doors in the hallway and thought of her own condo. There was an office-type chair at the business desk. *My key card is good on any door. One of these condos has to have a chair like that!* Betty rushed to the first door, knocking three quick raps before inserting her key card and pushing the door open. "Hello?" she said as she rushed to the part of the condo that logically would have the chair she needed. Nothing. She opened a bedroom door and found a room converted to an office—there was the chair. Rushing back to the scene of the gun battle with the chair in tow, she found Karl, on his belly but ten feet from where she had left him, passed out. *Or dead*, she thought. She lifted his jacket and pulled out his shirt to check for an exit wound only to realize that he had been shot in the back. The entry wound was a perfect hole, leaking blood. She rolled him over and checked for an exit wound, ripping the buttons off as she tugged his fine Egyptian cotton shirt apart. "No exit wound. You still have a pulse. You're going to live, damn you!" She slapped him hard on the cheek. "Wake up! I need you to get in this chair."

With a rattling cough and spit blood on the carpet, Karl rolled onto his knees. Betty grabbed his armpits and helped him to his feet. Karl collapsed into the office chair. She hit the elevator button and tapped her foot as they waited for the car to arrive. *I need to get an ambulance here, but I don't have my phone*, she thought. "Karl, give me your phone!"

He swatted for his phone in the breast pocket of his dress coat, but his motor skills had deteriorated from the loss of blood and the resulting low oxygen in his brain.

Betty pulled the jacket open to get the phone before his blood-streaked hands soiled it. The screen was cracked and black. It had stopped a round and died a brutal death in saving Karl's life—if she could get an ambulance rolling. *No time to go back into the condo and call, the elevator is here. I'll use the phone in the lobby at his desk.* Betty pushed Karl into the car and pressed the button marked L for lobby. The ride from the sixth floor to the ground would take fifteen seconds, but it seemed like an eternity. She said a short prayer, *Please, no one hit a button on our way down.*

The lobby was empty. The guests who were going skiing had already left and the alcoholics had not yet arrived downstairs. No sign of Jil, Gil, King, or Hanna. She rolled Karl to the concierge desk and grabbed the phone, dialing 911, and when a woman answered, she quickly gave the operator instructions. After hanging up, she grabbed Karl's cheeks and told him, "Hold on! I have to go catch the guy who did this to you." She paused to look at the security cameras, quickly figuring out how to change the view. She checked the different zones for Boris or the security guard who had bailed on the senator. She didn't see anything but knew where she needed to go next. She kissed Karl's forehead, said "Hold on" one more time, and darted for the stairs. The four flights up was not enough to wind her, but her breathing was fast as she burst onto the floor. *No one in the hallway. Where is everyone?* Usually she would be passing someone somewhere in the building. To be completely alone now seemed eerie. She ran to her door and called out as she entered, "I'm back," to make sure she did not draw any fire, but the governor was gone. "What the hell?" she asked. "Where the fuck is everyone?" Betty raced from room to room, checking for the governor, her pistol drawn. As she returned to the kitchen, she heard a banging noise coming from the front area of the condo. "The loft!" she said. Betty had forgotten about the hidden loft area, designed for visitors, the kids, or a security detail, depending on what kind of household you were operating. She dashed up the staircase and pulled open the door to the bathroom. Inside was the governor of New York bound with cable ties, one around his ankles and two used as handcuffs. He had been trying to use his feet to open the door. Betty pulled a knife from her pocket and freed him.

"Thank you," he said as Betty put her knife away. "Will you tell me your name, now?" he asked.

"You can call me Betty. It's my name." Betty gave him a hand up. "What am I supposed to call you—Governor?"

"That is my title, but, please, call me George."

"OK, George, who tied you up?"

"A one-armed man came in and threatened to kill me and my wife if I didn't tell him where Casper ran off to."

"The ghost disappeared, eh?"

"What—oh, hah!" George grinned, getting the joke. "Yes, he ran when Bolden went down and left me behind to be saved by you." He rubbed his wrists where the plastic had been chafing his flesh. "Bastard probably headed for the airport and bugged out." George looked up at Betty. "We need to find my wife!"

"Where did you leave her?" Betty led the way back down the stairs, pistol at the ready.

"Sharon was at the Salizar clinic in the penthouse, getting treatments."

"Well, you better stay with me this time. He'll probably come back for you." As she came around the corner to the main area of the condominium, she said, "Too late." Boris was standing mostly behind a woman who Betty recognized as George's wife, the first lady of New York. Blood was streaked from the corners of her mouth down to her chin. Her sleeve had been used to wipe most of the blood off, leaving a ghastly stain on her white puffy shirt. Boris had blood dripping from what was left of his right ear, running down his jacket, and was making a mess on the floor of the kitchen.

"Put gun away," Boris said.

"Now why would I need to do that, Boris."

"Put gun away or I kill her."

"Well, you could do that. George here might not like it, and I'm sure that Sharon doesn't want that to happen." Betty stepped closer to Boris, closing the gap to twenty feet. "I thought you gave up your arm over women and children being killed."

"Gave up arm for little girl. No problem killing bitch who bites." He moved directly behind his hostage. Without having a spare arm to restrain her, he was at a distinct disadvantage.

"You are quite the mess, and you're ruining my floor." Betty waited for Boris to duck behind Sharon. She was taller, due in part to her three-inch heels, but Boris was below average height and Sharon was above. When he was momentarily hidden, Betty mouthed the word *Drop* and nodded her head sharply down for just a moment. She took a proper shooting stance and aimed for where Boris's head would be when the first lady took the hint and dropped to the floor.

"You shoot, you kill her, not me," Boris said.

"That would be a bitch, wouldn't it." Betty said as she mouthed Now and nodded her head again.

Sharon elbowed Boris hard in the ribs with her right arm and dropped to the floor toward her left at the same time.

Boris gave a cough as he tried to control himself. It was too late.

Betty wanted to only wound Boris. He knew where Tom and Charles were having their meeting. She wanted to preserve him to get the information out of him, but she had been trained, since childhood, to shoot at the center of mass. Not a head shot, which was less likely to be successful, but at the heart of the victim, the lung area. Her bullets were a special design with a hardened outer coating that would pierce Boris's leather jacket, shirt, and sternum before turning into a whirling dervish of destruction, destroying soft tissue in his chest cavity. The tiny encased-lead projectile would leave a sonic wave of destruction that could kill a man, if placed correctly, as assuredly as breaking his neck. Her training dictated a center of mass shot; her reflexes moved her aim to the head when she spotted the damage to his coat from the earlier firefight. Boris's jacket was bulletproof. He dropped like a sack of potatoes off a farm truck."Fuck me," Betty said. *What am I going to do now?*

"Oh, my God!" screamed Sharon.

"Holy shit," George said. He rushed over to his wife and helped her up and over to the living room couch.

Betty considered stopping them—the blood would be everywhere—but thought, *What the hell, this isn't my place and I doubt I'll be here tomorrow.*

Seventy-Three

Control Absolute

November 30, 2009 — Ritz-Carlton, Vail, Colorado

"WELL." TOM BROKE THE SILENCE in the room. Pierre's dead body continued to drain blood onto the cream-colored wool carpet. It was an attractive color combination, if you could look past the body and the blood.

Gideon looked inside the room after Charles's exit to see if anything was needed, and he decided there clearly was. He used his cellphone to contact Grace and informed her there was yet another body to dispose of and a room to clean. After sizing up the mess and making eye contact with Tom, he went back outside the room to stand guard.

"Do you think the family will want the body back? Or can we just cremate it and move on?" Tom asked.

Ernesto looked at the body of a man he had known for, what, forty years? He had watched Pierre mature from an impetuous young man into a controlling, conniving sadist. He did not have any compassion for the loss of the man, but he did worry about ripples the death would have in the financial world. Control of the markets was Ernesto's goal. Pierre's trades and positions would have to be unwound and the estate settled to the heirs. He was not certain of what the will would stipulate, and that bothered him more than the crimson stain surrounding the crown of the dead man's head. Ernesto cocked his head to the right, looking at the death scene slightly askance. The blood looked similar to a halo, a devil's halo. "Cremate the body; they can have the ashes. He was little loved, at least of late." Ernesto pulled a trifold stack of papers from the inner pocket of his jacket. "You are now the wealthiest man in the world. As we agreed, I am the caretaker of that fortune until I die or choose to relinquish control. You will receive, at minimum, five hundred billion U.S. dollars to spend as you choose each year, or the remainder will be reinvested into the capital. If you need additional sums, it will be granted as long as it won't materially alter the stability of the markets." Ernesto placed the papers in front of Tom. "Sign here," he said, pointing to a signature line.

"Somehow, I doubt I could ever spend that much money in a year," Tom said as he scribbled his name.

"You'd be surprised at how quickly you will find ways for it to melt away. An island here, hobbies, gambling . . . There are many ways for fortunes to slip away." Ernesto handed Tom the duplicate sheaf of papers. "There are many household staff, gardeners, maintenance workers, and overhead costs that are deducted before you get your share of the yearly income. This is a list of all the properties you now own and can visit on a whim. The staff will keep everything running in your absence. Twenty-four-hour notice of your arrival is appreciated by the staff, but not necessary." He flipped the stack to the last page. "I highly recommend you take Betty to this island nation." He removed two pamphlets from his inner pocket where the papers had been. "These are your passports. They show that you are the sovereign of that nation and have diplomatic immunity wherever you go."

"That is rather handy." Tom looked at the documents. One was his and the other was Betty's. It listed her as a minister without portfolio. *She might like that*, he thought.

"You are now part of an elite cabal that is much smaller today than it was a week ago."

"Yes. Just how many are there of 'us,'" Tom asked.

Ernesto looked up at the ceiling with one eye closed as he made mental calculations. "There are, currently, fifty-nine people who control half the wealth of the world."

"Where do I fit on that list?"

Ernesto smiled and made a slight snort. "You alone are equal to the other fifty-eight. I am not on that list—I now control the greatest fortune ever assembled, but I do not own it, nor would I ever want to."

"A monk to the end, eh?"

"The Jesuits taught me well and impressed upon me that wealth would never make me happy. I learned on my own that controlling wealth does." Ernesto plopped down in his chair. He really would have rather left the room to get away from the blood and mess of Pierre, but in the end, he was an employee and too tired from the stress of perfecting a trap for Charles and company to rush off. "Is it true, the cold fusion? Is the end of carbon based energy really here? Or do I need to rework our investments?"

"I asked McFluffy to make it as real as possible for the press and markets. I did not expect him to succeed. I suppose I better find out," Tom said.

"In case it is true or if it is false?"

"Yes, either is rather important, I suppose." Tom thought about his wealth and the implications if McFluffy and Tooker's experiments were valid. "If—and this is a big if—the cold-fusion apparatus is a success and can be scaled to supply metropolitan populations . . ." Tom waved his hand as if willing the future of the world to appear.

Ernesto thought a moment. "If it scales and is a magnitude cheaper to run. But you have a monopoly, you charge less than the other suppliers but only enough to put them out of business . . ." Ernesto let the thought trail off, just as Tom had done.

"What if we just charged the usual ten percent profit after expenses?" Tom asked.

"Market chaos at first, but to our advantage, knowing what the new price structure would be." Ernesto did some calculations in his head. "You would still be the wealthiest person on the planet, but you would have half the wealth to yourself within ten years, instead of the twenty-five percent you have now."

"What if I shared it with my staff and close friends, so that there was a new group of fifty-eight or so."

"You would be more likely to survive. Concentrated wealth has a history of bringing an early death to the holder."

"Then that is what we will do with the cold fusion, if it is real. Please set up the corporation and distribute stock to the appropriate people," Tom ordered.

"It shall be done, but you will have the voting stock." Ernesto made a note, written in Latin, on a strip of paper and put it and the pen back in his pocket. "If this project fails, they will at least have a memento to keep, I suppose."

Tom looked surprised. "I never noticed that you write your notes in Latin before. Clever, really."

"Ah, yes, very few people can write or read it these days." Ernesto smiled. "A lingering benefit of my rather rigid and rigorous Jesuit education." Ernesto pulled the strip of paper and the pen back out. "Shall we call the company Helios, after the Greek Titan?"

"And make the symbol resemble a sunflower," added Tom, nodding his head. He looked at his watch. It was nearly two. "Oh, shit, I need to find Betty and explain a few things."

"Right. I will be heading to the airport, unless you need me for anything." Ernesto got up to leave.

"You're taking Max and Thor with you, I presume?"

"Yes. You should start taking your security more seriously. You'll need an advance team, and perhaps several more guards to be with you at all times," advised Ernesto.

"Anonymity will be my cloak of invisibility. No one is to know what I am worth. With you controlling it, you are the one we need to protect," Tom said.

"You'll change your mind when you have children."

"I suppose you're right. Well, safe travels, Ernesto. *Bona fortuna!*"

"*Bona fortuna.*" Ernesto left Tom with Pierre's corpse.

Grace entered immediately, pushing a cart with supplies, and surveyed the damage. "I need to get someone else to help. There are three other corpses on the sixth floor that need to be dealt with."

"Good Lord, what did I miss?" Tom asked. "Are they in the open?"

"I moved the bodies to a vacated condominium and changed the lock code." Grace surveyed the pooling blood. "Senator Bolden is dead, along with two of the Cabal bodyguards. I'm told the governor of New York was rescued by Betty. Karl is on his way to the hospital. It doesn't look good."

Tom nodded. "I'll check with the hospital on Karl. Can Bolden go with the rest?" "We can't just make a senator's body disappear," Grace said.

"Right. Where was he shot? What are our options?" Tom asked.

"Sucking chest wound, so a skiing accident—say an impaling, but we only have a little time to get his clothing changed. Otherwise we could restage the shooting and claim he saved someone's life. We'll need his blood type or there won't be enough blood at the new scene." Grace looked down at the bloodstained carpet. "Rather beautiful, actually." Grace looked quickly over at Tom before returning her gaze to Pierre's corpse. "The colors," she said as she tilted her head and smiled, admiring the death scene. She had developed a paradoxical love/hate relationship with her job. She hated messes, but if time was not a factor, she would linger, staring at death, contemplating the perfections and weaknesses of the human body. Knowing how hard it was to make blood disappear, especially from carpet fibers, tended to push her out of her dream state and back on task. Grace snapped on a pair of gloves and began her task.

Tom noticed her pause before working, the wry grin, the almost-loving look on Grace's face before she started. *I'm glad she's on my side.* "As always, I defer to your wisdom on how to clean this all up. I don't know what we would do without you, Grace."

"You'd be ankle deep in blood by now." Grace dropped a blood-soaked, formerly white towel into a heavy-duty black plastic bag and placed a second towel down to soak up the blood. "Would you be a dear and get Miller up to help. I'm just a little swamped trying to keep up with your friends."

Tom reached for his cell phone, which had been silenced and in his pocket, out of sight and out of mind for several hours. There were twenty-two messages waiting for him. He flipped through the ones that could wait, saw Betty had tried to call and decided she was the more important, but he still called Miller first, to get him moving. *I can't put off calling her back—it won't help.* He tapped the call icon and waited for her to answer. His call went to voice mail, so he hung up and tried again. Voice mail again. He did not leave a message, and proceeded to return calls and messages in the order of importance. "She's probably in one of her moods."

Grace looked up from zipping Pierre's body bag closed. "Who is?"

"Oh, sorry, Betty isn't answering her phone. I see from Bud's message he had an update for our phones and hers got stuck in a loop of some kind. I'm sure she is managing just fine without it, but she'll be annoyed that she couldn't reach us." Tom looked out the window at the falling snow. "She'll either be on the slopes with her friends and Gil or back at the condo. I'll go check on her." Tom left Grace to tidy up the room. As he left the suite and joined Gideon, he said, "I don't suppose you want to let me go on my own right now, hm?"

Gideon laughed out loud, but quickly sucked in his breathe and said, "No."

"Well, let's go track Betty down, then."

"Great, but you remember Thor?" Gideon directed Tom's attention to Ernesto's former security agent.

"It's a pleasure serving you, Mr. Howell," Thor said.

"I—" Tom stopped and pulled Gideon close and whispered, "I thought Thor was going with Ernesto. What's going on?"

"He's been vetted and incentivized. You need the best protection money can buy, and you can afford it," explained Gideon.

"What, was there an envelope?" Tom shook his head slightly and sighed. "Jesus, Betty took him."

"And she took down Slim, who was six foot nine. You can't afford her on your security detail. Too many complications."

"Obviously." Tom closed his eyes and breathed in deeply. "What about Miller?"

"He's better suited for operations." Gideon nodded his head slightly and said, "Thor is the right man for this job."

"OK. I trust you. So I'll trust Thor."

"Thank you," Gideon said as he clamped his left hand on Tom's right bicep. "For saying you trust my opinion and respect my decision."

Tom thought to himself, Does he know we're brothers? Should I tell him even though I was ordered not to? "Right, don't let it go to your head." Tom slapped Gideon on the right shoulder and said in full voice, "Let's go find Betty." Tom turned to Thor and said, "Welcome to the team. I'm glad you're on our side."

Thor nodded and moved to clear the exit and make sure the hallway was safe. Thor was the sort of person who loved to follow winners. Tom had won the battle against the Cabal, the mark of a leader. Thor's employment as a security agent for Ernesto had come through Pierre; he had joined for the money, not out of loyalty to either Pierre or Ernesto. Thor stood a little taller, or perhaps his spine was just a little straighter, as he risked his life for Tom Howell.

Thor arrived at Betty's door first and used his key card, conveniently coded to open any door in the Ritz-Carlton, and pushed the door open. He stopped in the threshold and signaled to Gideon one down and two visible, no guns, using his left hand behind his back. He did not draw his weapon and moved forward after he had visually cleared the area.

Tom entered ahead of Gideon. He stopped at the edge of Boris's death scene, inches from the blood pool, and squatted down. He rubbed his eyes and face with his right hand and stood up. "Gideon, call Grace and let her know." He looked over to Thor, who was talking with the governor and his wife. Gideon was on the phone to Grace and keeping guard by the door. Tom walked to the living room and looked around. He spotted Betty's cellphone on the coffee table and picked it up. On the screen was the message "Reboot your phone." He walked over to talk to the governor and pulled him aside. "What went on here?"

The governor knew who Tom Howell was from his brief conversation with Thor and longer ones with Betty. "We found that phone in the couch cushions. She saved my wife's life by killing . . ." he glanced over at Boris's prostrate body, his head turned toward them, dead eyes unfocused and a single entry wound in the bridge of his forehead. "She pulled me out of the gunfight and brought me here to be safe. Boris then went to the Salazar penthouse and took my wife hostage when he couldn't find Casper." The governor took a deep breath and sighed. "Did Senator Bolden make it?"

Tom frowned. "No, he didn't. But we are going to need your help in—staging this in the best interest of all parties. My staff are working to frame this as heroic as possible, Bolden saving your life and such. Are you willing to go along—for the greater good?"

"No mention of . . . his mistress?"

"There is no mistress to mention in this story. It wouldn't help the narrative, would it?" Tom said.

"OK. Whatever you think is best. After we announce his death"—George involuntarily looked over at Boris, the murderer of Bolden—"I'll have to appoint a replacement until there can be a special election next November."

"Hopefully, I can help you with that selection," Tom said with a wink.

The governor hemmed and hawed for a moment. "Well, one must be very careful about how one goes about selecting a replacement."

Tom smiled. "As the former governor of a midwest state might advise from his jail cell."

"Yes, quite."

"My organization is about to make a major energy technology announcement. Senator Bolden's former aid, Jil Harper, would be able to easily step into the senator's role for the next year. I'm positive that she would be the kind of senator we could work with to make the Empire State our new headquarters for the most significant advancement in clean energy in the history of mankind."

"Well, that is quite the endorsement of Ms. Harper." The governor looked over at the corpse of Boris, then his wife, Thor, and finally Gideon. "Shall we continue this conversation in a calmer, happier location? Or rather, I should say, if we need to talk further, it should be somewhere else at a later date."

"I'm confident that I don't need to say anything further, and I will be pleased with whoever you decide to select."

Their conversation was interrupted by Miller and Grace entering to handle Boris's body. Gideon nodded to Tom that it was time for everyone to leave.

"Governor, perhaps you and your wife could join me for lunch?"

He looked over at his wife, who was flirting with Thor, and said, "Yes, I think that would be a great idea."

†

Betty was reaching for her gear in the Arrabelle locker facility when King called out to her, "About time you hit the slopes today."

"Oh, hi, King." She started bagging up her skis and gear.

"Seriously, you're taking off without going one more time?"

"I'm kind of not feeling it right now. In fact, I plan on flying out later today. Thinking about somewhere warmer."

"All the more reason you need to make a few more runs before you go, to feel the glow on the beach." King reached to help. "But if you're dead set on leaving early, who am I to stop you." He moved close and looked into her eyes. Few women had ever resisted his powers of persuasion.

Betty could smell his sweat from skiing all morning; the scent of his pheromones and testosterone stirred her libido. *He's dangerous. He might be the one hired to kill me. Karl is in good hands now, probably in the hospital complaining about the food. Gil and Jil are out on the slopes—I might get to say goodbye. Fuck it, why not? I might even . . .* Betty took one more deep smell of King. "Why not. Something to think about on the beach." Betty grabbed King's crotch, clasping his cock, then, sliding her hand down to his balls. "Maybe if you're good, I'll give you something to remember me by, after we come off the slopes."

†

"What do you mean you've lost all connectivity to the surveillance equipment?" David asked.

"I don't know . . . I . . . look, something is eating up all my bandwidth, I'm calling you on my cell instead of through the network. I need to shut everything down and pick this apart. I'm transferring the system to your account and taking mine offline." Bud was getting nervous. He had lost more control over his systems than he was letting on. "I gotta go—I'll keep you . . ." The connection was lost before Bud could finish his sentence.

David let out a long breath of air. "What the fuck just happened?" He logged in to the system and took control of the surveillance panel. The first view was a group of people leaving Grace and Miller with a dead body. Switching through the other views, he was slightly disappointed to see nothing as exciting. David toggled through the activities log and saw the entries indicating Bud losing then regaining control of his account. "What a cock-up." He sent a message to Tom that said, "Shutting off ears, closing eyes. Deaf and dumb here." David then turned off and effectively deactivated the surveillance system Bud had created for the mission.

Seventy-Four

Absolutely

November 30, 2009 — Vail, Colorado

BETTY AND KING RODE THE GONDOLA up the mountain and caught the Game Creek lift to the ridge line. Betty did not see Jil and Gil leaving the Wildwood restaurant because King moved her along before Betty could spot them.

"What gives? I thought you only liked the back bowls," Betty said as they pulled up at the top of Kangaroo Cornice.

"I want to see you go down Pepi's Face, show me what you learned from the man himself," King said. "Let's go down Challenge and work our way to the NASTAR, then Mudslide to Pepi's. If you're still feeling like leaving, I'll head to the back bowls. Otherwise, we can make a day of it."

Seems somewhat logical and thoughtful, on a certain level, thought Betty. "All right, Mr. Showboat. Lead the way."

"Ladies first," King said as he bowed slightly.

"Whatever." Betty leaned forward and pushed off with her poles. King stayed close to her, never allowing any large gap between them. This pushed her harder, making the desire to take each turn sharper, cutting harder into the groomed snow to get farther ahead, but King kept close no matter what she tried. At Mid-Vail, they stopped. Betty's heart was racing from the adrenaline surge.

"Damn, girl, you trying to lose me?" King said.

"Lose you, hell, you're practically in my boots," Betty said as she used her breathing techniques to slow her heart rate and regain center.

"I'll be in the trees if I don't follow your line!"

"I'll be in the trees if you push me any harder," Betty answered.

"Well, I'm not trying to push you, but if you need me to go first . . ."

King is trying to goad me on. What do I do? If he is trying to kill or maim me, it's going to be on Mudslide. I need to get him ahead of me by then. Or I need to change the route. "Maybe you need to go first just so you can take it easy is what I think you mean," she said, but thought, *Two can play the game.* Betty pushed off onto Lion's Way, a slow green run that led to the short black diamond run, Cady's Cafe. This time, King hung back a little farther, almost as if he was pouting over being called out for following her so close, but as soon as she turned hard left onto Cady's Cafe, King was following her close again, skis clattering as he made hard turns to catch up. He backed off immediately as they entered Gitalong Road, another green, easy run that tied the more difficult runs together. Betty took a small jump as she passed the Pumphouse double-black diamond run, the route she would rather take, and continued on to the top of the NASTAR course, where she pulled up.

"What's the matter?" King asked.

"Let's make a bet." Betty pointed her ski pole toward Mudslide.

"OK, what's the wager?" King asked.

"Whoever loses has to do what the other one wants," she said. "First one to the bottom wins."

"Gondola?" King tilted his head quickly toward the bottom of the mountain. "First one to the gondola entrance wins?"

"Yep."

"Doesn't seem like a fair bet."

Betty cocked her head. "How do you figure?"

"I've already won and know what I'm going to make you do," King boasted.

"Oh, really, now?" Betty asked.

"I know exactly the line you're going to take down Mudslide, based on your skiing. You don't have a chance."

"Well, hot shot, I guess you better put your money where your mouth is." She pushed off and took a slight head start. *If I get him ahead of me, he can't fuck with me.* Her skis were perfectly waxed, with keen edges. *I'll take him again on Pepi's Face for the win.*

King cut through the NASTAR course, causing the staff to yell at him, and he passed Betty at the entrance to Mudslide. She stayed close to him, never allowing him to have much of an advantage. They were about to leave the aspen stand when King pulled up short, directly in Betty's path.

She could suddenly see her mistake. He had goaded her. She had goaded back. She wanted to fuck him to push Tom to declare his love. She had seen King as a tool, even while knowing he might be the one tasked with smashing her head into a tree to mete the revenge for Slim's death. It was all crystal clear in the moment she had, but the clarity meant nothing, because she had already planted her weight on the edges of her skis. She was committed in her trajectory. King had won. Just past him was a large aspen. Large enough to absorb all the energy of her forward motion. This made her think of Newton's first law of motion: an object at rest remains at rest or a body in motion remains in motion unless acted upon by a net force. At best, she could hope for a broken clavicle. If his aim was on, her face would be a bloody pulp. Even if her head missed the trunk, she would be incapacitated long enough for King to slam her head against the tree enough times to destroy her frontal lobe. If she survived—a fate worse than death—she would spend the rest of her life in a nursing home, unable to ever talk properly again, but cognizant enough to know that she was in a prison managed by underpaid staff, eating institutional food, and her greatest joy would be television, the shows that popped back and forth quick enough to hold her attention without straining her intellect.

Betty had amazing reflexes, but not good enough stop the train wreck that her life was about to become. It was in that moment of feeling her skis grabbing the snow under the fresh powder while visualizing her predicament that she caught motion to her right—a skier moving faster than her was on track to hit King. The skier had taken a direct line, no cutting, no slowing of forward momentum, and was moving thirty feet per second faster than Betty. In the amount of time Betty could normally react, in just over a sixth of a second, the blur was already reaching King and making contact.

Betty's vision was obscured by the snow thrown up by her skis and the crash of the two bodies. She skidded to a full stop, which threw up more snow, and tried to turn around to figure out who had just saved her from King and whether either of them had survived the crash. This reminded Betty of Newton's third law—when one body exerts a force on a second body—like a pool table, the cue ball had hit the eight ball. She recognized the crumpled and stationary cue ball from the colorful gear, it was Jil; the eight ball, King, was now moving with the energy and direction of the cue ball, tumbling down the slope until righting himself. Betty hopped side to side as she climbed back up the slope to where her former best friend was sprawled out on the snow, which was turning red with blood. As Betty reached Jil, Gil came to a full stop next to them.

"What the fuck, Gil!" Betty said.

"We saw you and King take off up at Wildwood." Gil answered. "We've been trying to find you, where's your phone?"

"Jesus, she's bleeding like crazy!" Betty looked down slope and saw King shake his head as if to clear it, look at her, then turn and head down the slope, getting away.

"Her femoral artery is severed." Gil had his hand inserted inside Jil's ski pants through a slit cut by King's ski. The razor-sharp edge had slashed the cloth and severed the major artery running on the inside of her leg. "I've got this. Go get the bastard!" Gil yelled.

Betty righted herself and headed downhill to catch King, but he had enough of a head start to lose her in the crowd and go down one of three routes to the bottom. Her only chances were to catch up to him now or find him in the village after. *How can I possibly catch him? He's a better skier and weighs more than me*, she thought. "What choice do I have?" She tucked herself as tight as possible and imagined being a giant slalom skier. King quickly disappeared around the bend from Mudslide to Mill Creek Road, an easy Green route to the final run of their race. *I doubt he'll stick to the planned route. He could get to Giant Steps before me and disappear completely.*

As Betty entered Mill Creek Road, she scanned ahead to see if King was visible. *His gray ski outfit should stand out, ironically, among all the bright fashion plates, Betty thought. Too many people!* She had to weave between the casual skiers, the ones who felt they needed a break after each black run, and narrowly missed a string of friends blocking her path. Just as she came to the junction of Frontside Chutes, she spotted him. *He's skipping Giant Steps. Fuck! I can't catch up!*

King turned hard down Head First, and Betty lost sight of him. She slowed her pace. *No way to catch him—better to make it down without running into someone. I'll find him in the village or at the lockers.* As she turned down Head First herself, she was startled to find Gideon standing guard over Tom as he checked on a skier who had gone into the trees.

"Hey, Betty!" Gideon said.

She pulled up to him and pulled down her neck warmer to let some of the heat escape. "Did you see—" Betty let the words drift off. Gideon was pointing to the gray form impaled by a broken branch of a fir tree. "What the fuck?"

"Karma—ain't it a bitch?" Gideon asked.

Seventy-Five

Après-Ski

November 30, 2009 — Ritz-Carlton, Vail, Colorado

THE MOOD IN BETTY'S BORROWED condo was a mixture of elation, anger, and gloom brought on by so many deaths. Gideon ended his call and rejoined the group.

"Karl is in critical condition. We won't know until tomorrow if he'll pull through," Gideon reported.

"I should be there with him," Betty said.

Tom shook his head. "There's nothing you can do."

Betty glared at him. "I can hold his hand and give him encouragement."

"Hanna is there, she's holding his hand." Gideon walked to the kitchen to get a water bottle from the refrigerator. "Can I get anything for anyone?"

Betty stood up and shook her head with her eyes closed. "What? Hanna? She accused Karl of trying to kill Skipper-do." Betty rubbed her face and flipped her hair.

Tom leaned back in the sofa, stretched his neck to look back at Gideon, and asked, "She doesn't have that dog in there, does she?"

Gideon smiled. "I didn't ask."

Grace entered and, out of habit, opened the door with a handkerchief to keep from leaving any prints. "That's the last of it. Or do you have more work for me?" she asked.

Tom stood up and walked to the kitchen to join Gideon and Grace. "Thank you, Grace. Impeccable work as always. And the senator?"

"It should be in the news reports tonight. Miller and the governor are working with the police to explain what happened." Grace smiled and gave a slight laugh and a sigh. "Well, I have a plane to catch if that is all."

"I only have one thing. Miller—did he work out?"

"Oh, yes, fine young man. He can work with me anytime. Such a boy scout," she said with a smirk.

Betty looked around the refrigerator door with one eye cocked. "I can only imagine." She pulled out a bottle of champagne and asked Grace, "Can you join me in a drink before you go?"

"Why, yes. I think I have time," she said as she joined Betty at the counter. "I should tell you, before you rightfully ask, your parents are fine, your—Beth is recovering . . . I'm afraid I might have been a little hard on her."

Betty grimaced as she pried the cork gently from the bottle. "A little hard on her?"

Grace pulled two crystal flutes from the glass front cabinet and placed them on the counter, closed her eyes, and inhaled deeply. "I'm afraid my sister allowed some terrible things to happen when we were younger. We—I explained to her how hurtful it had been to me. Do you really want me to tell you?"

Betty poured the champagne into both glasses and thought for a moment. "If she's going to recover and you two have settled your differences, well, I suppose that is all between you. Isn't it?" She picked up her glass and made a toast: "To better family relations."

"Why, yes, to better family relations." Grace drained her champagne, put the glass down, and said, "I really must be going." She gave Betty a quick hug and a peck on the cheek. "Thank you, dear."

"Safe travels," Betty replied as she tried to hold her glass steady with right hand while giving back the quick hug with her left.

After Grace had gone, Tom pulled Betty to the grand view of the mountains and whispered into her ear, "Let's get out of here, tomorrow."

"And go where?" Betty asked. "To some getaway hideout to plan our next grand adventure?"

"Yes and no, but it is one hell of a getaway hideout," Tom flashed their passports with a gold-embossed logo and the name Santo Tomás de Aquino. "It's off the coast of Brazil between Sao Paulo and Rio."

"What the fuck?"

"I inherited it from my father, but I plan to sell it after our visit. If you want to go, that is."

Betty snatched the document from Tom and checked her photo out. She shook her head with her eyes closed, took in a deep breath, and thrust the document into Tom's chest. "If—and this is a big if—if we are left alone for a month with no contact with the office, I'll consider it."

"You understand that Gideon will be there and I'll need to spend at least an hour a day working on unwinding my father's investments."

"Will he still be cooking? 'Cause I could stand another one of his mixed-blessings omelets." *Oh, Jesus, what am I getting myself into. Why can't I just walk away from him?*

"I'm sure he'd love to cook for you more than for me."

Betty glared at Tom. "Just so we're clear, no missions, no bullshit, no setting me up for doing your dirty work."

"Got it." Tom looked over at Gideon and winked without Betty seeing the signal. Gideon turned away and busied himself.

"I'm going to kick your ass if you're lying."

"I'd expect no less." Tom pulled Betty close and buried his nose in her softly scented hair. "Who knows, maybe this is the end and we can move on."

Betty nuzzled Tom's neck and snuggled into his shoulder. "If I could just have that one thing."

December 14, 2009 — Ritz-Carlton, Vail, Colorado

Two weeks later, the door to the fourth-floor condo swung open. Günter stood in the entryway and admired his home. "*Gut wieder Zuhause zu sein!*" He walked in, anticipating shaving his three-month growth of beard. Karl had arranged for him to be part of a team studying the pygmy sperm whale, so he had only been on dry land for a week. He crouched down and looked toward the front room. A sunbeam splashed on the carpet. There was a trail of discolored spots leading to the couch. As he moved to stand directly above them, they disappeared into the texture of the carpet. "*Was ist los hier?*"

Günter's face turned severe as he turned and marched back into the kitchen to check the refrigerator. He was going to complain about the staff obviously having a party in his condo while he was away, but he needed to survey all of the damage before making his report. He had purposely stocked it with Cristal, but from the 2006 vintage, a less desirable year. In it's place was a dozen bottles of the most prized, nearly perfect vintage, 2002. He smiled and thought of Karl's promise of a surprise upon his return from the Antarctic. Any thought of carpet replacement vanished. "*Gut. Sehr gut!*"

December 14, 2009 — Ritz-Carlton, Vail, Colorado

Hanna wrangled Karl's wheelchair into her condo and parked him next to the couch. "You OK or do I need to help you move over?"

Karl smiled and moved over on his own power. "Come here!" he called, and Skipper-do jumped into his lap for some chin scratching. He reached for the remote and turned on the sixty-inch TV. CNN's anchors greeted him with a summary of the day's news while Hanna went to the kitchen to prepare—or rather, to order—some snacks.

"And on a happy note, recently appointed New York Senator Jillian Harper has announced her engagement to Gilbert Richardson . . ."

Acknowledgments

Any inaccuracies are mine, they are intentional—for the sake of the story. This volume would not have been possible without the talents of Johanna Rosenbohm, editor extraordinaire. Thank her if a fourth volume is written. She left an opening for Betty to return.

The Staff of Gorsuch Vail provided assistance in providing finer detail to the Black Card shopping scenes. Special thanks to Scott Mohr. The Staff at Axel's of Vail were equally helpful and responsive to my queries. If you are looking for something a little less ostentatious for your stay in Vail, I highly recommend Antlers. David Alt provided excellent information regarding the Game Creek Lodge of Vail Resorts.

Robert Wennerholm caught an error regarding my portrayal of Gil's Glock in Power, which has been fixed in the second edition. I spent a few hours with him in the twilight of his life. Had he told me he was dying, I would have suggested he find a better way of using his precious time. That he chose to spend some of it with me, I am grateful.

There were many small gestures and kindnesses extended to me while I wrote The Betty Chronicles, Volumes I-III. I wish I could name them all here.

Finally, I would like to thank @DuchessGoldblat for her uplifting tweets and imagination. It is that sort of Walter Mitty thinking that started this trilogy.